The King of Nightmare

The King of Nightmare

A. Rogers

Published by Demented Tours, LLC
demented-tours.com

The King of Nightmare

Published in the United States of America.

Demented Tours, LLC
1657 E. Stone Drive
Ste B #139
Kingsport, TN 37660

Hardcover ISBN: 978-1-7358702-0-5
Paperback ISBN: 978-1-7358702-2-9
ePub ISBN: 978-1-7358702-1-2

1 2 3 4 5 6 7 8 9 10

Cover artwork created by Fesbra · www.fesbra.com
Cover layout by Demented Tours, LLC
Book design by Maureen Cutajar

To all those with stories you think you cannot tell...
please, go tell them.

Chapter One

Jason gazed at the water and wished the waves would tell him where to go. He'd like to go home, but he didn't have one. He'd grown up in the Appalachian Mountains, but he'd shaken off their old magic clutches and had moved away to all points westward, northward, and any-ward that got him someplace new to see. It'd been great until his band, Judith's Hell, fractured, and Jason's heart got crushed by a skinny girl with a glass soul. Jason hadn't seen his heart or the girl since, and he drew designs in the sand with one fingertip, thinking of how cool it'd be for his heart to show up among the seashells and the debris. It'd be shriveled and wasted in a bottle with a wax-sealed cap, and the note would read: "Couldn't make it work. Return to sender, postage paid upon delivery." As Lord only knew, Judith didn't give away anything for free.

The sun was rising, orange and blinding, and it promised to be another hatefully hot day. The breeze rustling the sticks of grass jutting out of the dunes along the shore of the Taylor Point

Sound was barely enough to chill the drops of humidity clinging to Jason's bare arms and shins. Gulls and grackles called overhead. Voices drifted on the wind. Pavement met beach met water in quick succession on this south-eastern coast, and Jason had parked his van in the free public lot next to a community pier. The wooden pier marched out into the water like a soldier on a drowning mission, and Jason watched a man with a cane hobble his way toward the bench at the end. The man carried a sack, alcohol or bird food, and the way the light hit the water and seemed to wake up in the warmth of the rays made Jason lonelier by the moment. He missed so many things.

For the last few months, he'd been lucky to have dimes enough to rub together for bread. Listening to his belly grumble, Jason stretched his legs and took an apple out of the recyclable shopping bag sitting next to him. With the band, he'd eaten like a king. Over the years rambling around on his own, he'd become the pauper at Save-a-Lots and fresh markets that sometimes didn't notice or care when food fell into the hands of the hungry guy with the crooked smile and colorful tattoos. He and Judith used to sleep on silken sheets in penthouse suites. Now, he chased weather to stay warm since his portable roof didn't offer much more than shelter from the rain, sleet, or snow. He could dumpster dive and sneak a wallet out of the most coveted of pockets, but he hated that part. He liked to earn his keep, and he knew what a body had to do sometimes to do the earning, and it wasn't ever easy. He didn't like to take things that weren't his, but he had and would again if his luck didn't change.

The wind blew, but it smelled of fish, not fortune. The Granny Smith was overripe, but the salt breeze added to the flavor. He bit, chewed, and didn't hear the brat until it was too late. A kid, a boy in a plastic skull mask, flew out of nowhere. Jason had just enough time to think, *But it's not Halloween*, before the kid snatched Jason's bag and darted away to the angry cry of disrupted seagulls.

"Hey!" Jason called, choking on a bit of apple. He tore after the thief. The boy seemed to float across the sand, and Jason, though plenty swift, couldn't make up lost ground. Jason yelled all manner of obscenities and threats while he had the wind to do it, huffing and puffing and zagging to follow the kid up the steps and across the pavement. The concrete singed Jason's feet, and Jason cussed anew. He hoped to hell nobody wanted his ratty sneakers.

"Stop that kid!" Jason wheezed to a fisherman chewing the cud, but the wrinkles on his tanned, leathery face just shifted into a mask of amusement, and Jason chased the thief across an unlined street and down a sidewalk in front of shut down shops and tourist traps. The snotwad zipped a sharp left down an alleyway, and Jason followed, but when Jason made the corner, the kid was gone.

"Son of a..." Jason snarled, jogging between the brick wall of a diner and a glass wall of a laundromat. There was a narrow passage hidden behind a dumpster, there was a parking lot behind both buildings, and Jason checked both, but it was no use. The bottom feeder was gone, and so was the bag and the last of Jason's food.

Jason made fists, was reminded of his half-eaten apple, and he tore a hunk out of the Smith's hide. He stalked back to the street, across it, and toward the steps leading to the beach. "Thanks for nothin', man," Jason growled at the fisherman. Wordlessly, he chewed and spat and passed Jason, headed for the diner. He smelled like fish guts and cheap tobacco, and Jason's stomach churned. His sneakers were where he'd left them, and he picked them up, dusting off the sand. He slipped on the shoes, climbed a dune, ignoring the sign asking him not to, and made it to his van.

When luck was bad, it was bad all over, and there was nothing he could do while that wind blew. Jason banged the Honda's hood, taking his frustration out on the old girl, and he yelled like a crazy person, but all he did was hurt his hand and scare off some birds. He thought about Victor "The Rage" Swinson, who had, coincidentally enough, often played onstage while wearing a range of skull masks, not unlike the boy's.

But Rage had worn no mask while hanging from a gashed neck nearly severed by guitar strings and nylon rope, and with that image once again fresh in his mind, Jason turned and sat hard on the gravel in front of the bumper. Jason clutched his head, willing the pictures to go away, please, oh please. Jason mouthed the words and was interrupted by somebody clearing a throat nearby.

Looking up to find the fisherman who'd gone to the diner, Jason tensed and scowled. "What do you want?"

The fisherman tipped his head toward the shops, still chewing... chewing... His pale eyes were colorless like the fish he caught, his white hair was all wisps, his overalls were sagging, and his boots were covered in an inch of sandy mud.

Gooseflesh broke out over Jason's arms, maybe in warning, maybe as a call to pay attention to this man, this moment, this decision. Jason could hear Papa Jack say, "Son, somebody done kissed your tombstone. Done a little soft-shoe, whistled a little tune." Papa Jack would have laughed, and he'd have cuffed Jason's head. Would have told Jason he was a stupid one, all right, seeing ghosts in little boys' masks and sensing meaning where there was nothing at all.

"What?" Jason asked the fisherman. "The hell? What?"

The fisherman spat a steaming wad. "She's waitin'."

"Who is?" Jason asked, but the fisherman stared, shuffle-turned, and walked away, vanishing from line of sight down the steps toward the pier.

Hair still prickling, Jason scooted and peered around the Honda's tire. The only building that looked lively was the diner. A woman was opening the vinyl blinds to let in the morning light. The sign on the front door hung slanted and said, OPEN. Jason curled into a ball, knees to chest, and took a bite of the apple, thoughtful. There probably wasn't a "she" to be waiting on anybody, much less Jason. The fisherman probably had a screw loose. Or maybe the guy was sending Jason toward the sherriff or the thieving brat's mother or... A thousand and one possibilities, and no way of knowing without the doing.

Whatever was inside the diner was probably nothing that would work out in Jason's favor. He'd likely cross the street, open the door, and get chased off for smelling like an open sewer and being an outsider. A fisherman's word would not gain him entry into the land of the clean and gainfully employed.

Still, anything had to be better than crouching here all day, angry at the kid, feeling sorry for himself, and trying not to think of Rage or Judith or Papa Jack. At least if he did get into the diner, he could enjoy the AC for the ten seconds it took for management to realize he couldn't pay a bill.

With a glance at the spot where the fisherman had stood, Jason got up. He stuck a hand in his pocket, squeezing the Honda's key where it was latched to one of the hooks he'd sewn in all the pockets of his shorts and pants. Nobody was stealing Jason's key to home without taking a hunk of him with it. He finished his apple, gnawing on the core, and tossed it into a trash can that sat on the sidewalk next to a street light. A banner flapped above Jason's head, announcing a festival that was two weeks past, and he yanked on the metal door handle, making the diner's chimes ring.

Sixties music played, the tune upbeat, but still about misery, and Jason heard the hiss of frying food coming from the kitchen. It smelled too good, and Jason hugged his belly over his t-shirt. A waitress clinked a coffee cup onto the counter in front of a man in a suit. She smiled at Jason. "Hey, hon. Take you a seat, and I'll be right with you."

"Thanks," Jason muttered, rubbing his arms and glancing around for a booth in a corner next to a window. He liked seeing everything at once, including the ways out.

"Yoohoo!"

Jason stopped on his way to a red, padded booth. He spotted a round, soft woman somewhere between fifty and seventy, who was waving a checkered napkin at him. She grinned when they locked eyes, and hers sparkled like Judith's used to, right before taking stage. They were blue eyes, crystal blue, like the sea outside that had given this stretch of coast its name.

"Yoohoo," she called again, still waving. "Young man? Over here."

The lady was old, the accent was Southern, and the smile was kind, but Jason approached the woman at her table with wary caution. Jason had started his roaming life believing himself invincible. That had all changed one night at a shelter in a big city up north. Jason wasn't even too sure which city it had been, now. They were all a blur of concrete and strips of sky. But Jason had been asleep on a cot, and he'd heard a noise. When he'd looked, he'd seen a kid, scrawny and blond, quietly suffocating an old man. Jason had wanted to call out, to say or do something, but he'd been frozen in place, horrified. The man quit twitching, the kid stole the man's shoes and tote bag, and the kid had slipped out of the place, silent.

Earlier that same night at dinner, Jason had sat next to the tiny murderer, breaking bread and comparing notes about losing parents and gaining guardians. The kid had claimed to have been there with a woman and two other kids, and he'd gone so far as to point them out. Jason had bought the entire story, the kid had sold it so well, and Jason was no baby duckling, wet behind the ears.

He hadn't felt so experienced staring at the old man's corpse. The kid had been a quarter the man's size, but younger and more determined. Jason had caught himself wondering why he hadn't thought of murder as a way out, and when killing people started to make too much of the wrong kind of sense, Jason had moved on from the big cities and into smaller towns. Plenty of bad happened in places of smaller population, but it had the decency to happen less often and away from public view. Or just away from Jason's point of view.

The lesson with the shelter kid had cemented the idea that evil wears the same clothing as the rest of humanity, and though Jason was pretty sure he could outmatch and outrun the woman with the checkered napkin, he didn't want to get caught at a table with a Bible thumper or with a crazy woman who claimed Jason looked just like her poor dead baby son.

"There you are," the woman said when Jason was within arm's reach. "Goodness, you're a tall one."

"Yes, ma'am," Jason said. "Have been most of my life."

"What are you, six-three?"

"Six-four, ma'am."

"Gracious." Her grin never wavered. "Forgive me; I'm being rude. Won't you have a seat?" When Jason hesitated, the woman continued: "It's only that Vern came in here, told me you are the unfortunate soul to be the latest victim of petty theft in our fair town."

"Vern?"

"Gentleman with the fishing pole," the woman clarified.

"Oh," Jason said, mostly because he didn't know what else to say. He couldn't imagine the creepy guy speaking so many words all strung together.

The waitress came over with a platter heavy with food on her shoulder. "Here we go, Miss Teedee." The waitress started piling plates onto the table. "That was a number six special with extra butter, an omelet—"

"Oh, Gracie, I forgot to tell you," Miss Teedee said in distress that seemed strained to Jason. "It'll just be me today."

Gracie's thin, hand-drawn eyebrows went up to meet her bleached hairline. "Thought you said you was expecting company?"

"I did, and I was, but you know how it goes." Miss Teedee sighed.

"Well, hon, the food's made and here..." Gracie was working very hard not to look at Jason, and Jason smelled a plot under the sweet, sweet aroma of fresh biscuits, eggs, and bacon, but he was having a hard time caring. His guts were twisting in ecstasy this close to protein.

"Well, fiddlesticks." Miss Teedee drummed her fingertips on the tabletop. "I don't suppose you might be hungry?" she said archly to Jason. "Help me out so as this food won't go to waste? Gracie's husband's in the kitchen, and one cook about another, he makes a mighty fine meal."

"I could eat," Jason said as calmly and politely as he could. "But I can't pay."

"Oh, posh." Miss Teedee gestured for Jason to sit down, and this time, Jason did as suggested. "You'd be doing me a pair of favors. Now eat up."

Jason managed to get the silverware out of the paper napkin and use it instead of his bare hands, and he dug into the eggs first, shoveling them into his mouth with a strip of bacon. He bit back a moan, closing his eyes to savor, and the eggs were gone before Gracie managed to finish refilling Miss Teedee's glass of water and pouring Jason some of his own over ice.

"Gracie, honey, could you bring us some extra everything?" Miss Teedee said quietly.

"Sure." Gracie's glance at Jason was long and piteous, but Jason didn't mind so much. He was used to it, for one, and he was too busy trying to remember the last time he'd had real butter for the other.

"Vern said Toby had stolen food from the hungry." Miss Teedee clucked her tongue. "I swear, that child."

Jason glanced at Miss Teedee, gulping down his glass of water. "Vern didn't seem the talkative sort."

"Did you two meet?" Miss Teedee asked.

"We crossed ways," Jason replied with care.

"Oh, well, he's just picky about who he says what to. He talks to me." Miss Teedee smiled. "Lots of folks do, and I'm grateful. Helps me with the lonely."

Jason slowed, a pang of pain in his chest. He tried to blame the grease, but he knew it was more likely because of all he'd lost.

"My Charlie passed years ago, now," Miss Teedee continued. "We didn't find our way around to having children, so it's just been me." She brightened. "But then I found people, and they found me, and it's been better."

"Are you from here, then?" Jason asked, unsure if he should be having this conversation at all, but he could feel eyes on him, Miss Teedee's the sharpest of all, and her voice was pretty. Soothing-like. Sweet and gentle. Jason tried not to let it make him more nervous.

"No, I hail originally from Richmond, Virginia. You ever been up that way?"

"Once or twice," Jason hedged. He bit his tongue to keep from saying more, and he stuffed his mouth full of biscuit. It melted on impact, and Jason slathered more butter on the next one.

"I thought I detected a note of Southern in your voice and your manners." Miss Teedee seemed pleased. "You grow up around here, somewhere?"

"No, ma'am."

"Oh?" she pressed, and Jason fidgeted. "Ah, well. I see."

Now she looked disappointed, and Jason swallowed a mouthful of his free bread. "I'm from Tennessee," he said.

Her smile returned. "Oh, well, that's lovely. I've a sister in Nashville, though we don't talk much anymore, but when we did, she told me all the time how pretty a place it was, Tennessee. Are you from Nashville, by chance?"

"No. I grew up in Clarketown. It's near Roan Mountain, on the Tennessee side of the North Carolina border."

Miss Teedee sipped tea from a coffee mug, and Jason stared at the teabag tag. It was De-Stress tea, the morning blend – the same stuff Judith used to drink. "Why, I think I know exactly where that is. I spent a spell in Mountain City."

Jason nodded. "I know it, yeah."

"Well, isn't that something? What do your people do in Clarketown?"

Jason finished off his water. "I don't have people like you mean. The man who raised me was a forest ranger."

Miss Teedee pushed her water closer to Jason's hand. "You lose your family?"

Jason snorted. "Yeah, misplaced them somewhere." Miss Teedee's eyebrows went up, and Jason mumbled, "Sorry."

"It's all right. It's a poor turn of phrase."

"I guess."

"And I'm forgetting myself." She held out her hand. "I'm Tallulah Darlene Brown, as you heard, but everyone calls me Miss Teedee."

"Jason," he said, squeezing her fingers. "Jason Hart."

"Oh, Hart! Is that your adopted peoples' name?"

Jason put down his fork and wiped his palms on his shorts. "Ma'am, I don't mean to be rude, and I'm grateful for the meal, 'cause I don't know when I last had one or when I will again, but what do you want?"

Miss Teedee looked steadily at Jason. "Well, now, you're right. I've not been completely honest with you, and that's wrong of me, and I apologize, but what I have to say may seem strange. And though you don't look like a man intimidated by much of anything, I wanted to get to know some about you, first."

"And then what?" Jason asked.

"What do you mean?"

"If you got to know something about me and didn't like it, then what?"

Miss Teedee's eyes sparkled. "I guess you'd have gotten a meal, and I wouldn't have had to be strange, today."

"Lady, no offense, but I think you probably can't help yourself but to be strange most days."

Miss Teedee laughed, rich and real, and she patted Jason's hand over the skull tattooed between his thumb and forefinger. "I think I like you."

"Been a while since anybody did," Jason said and made himself shut up. He reminded himself that danger didn't always need to have a gun pointed at your head. Sometimes, it was anything that made you feel like you could relax, even for two seconds.

Gracie came by with more to eat, and she refilled glasses. As she walked away, she patted Miss Teedee on the shoulder. "You remember how I said you eating the food would be paying me two favors?" Miss Teedee asked Jason.

"Yeah. Yes."

"Well, one of those favors has to do with penance, and the other has to do with signs."

"Signs," Jason deadpanned.

"You don't believe in them?"

"I don't know, ma'am. I guess it depends."

"Ah, well. Hear me out. The boy who stole from you is Tobias Creed. His parents have a house a few blocks thataway." Miss Teedee waved to the north. "Good people, his parents. Gave Toby everything, provided for him, take him to Bay Beach Baptist every Sunday and then again on Wednesday for church dinner, but Toby's an odd one. Doesn't say much. Watches people. You know the type... What do they call it these days? Autism?"

"I guess," Jason agreed, keeping an eye on the doorway. He was starting to wonder if he was in his van, sound asleep, and this was all a weird dream.

"Anyhoo, the boy steals. Takes things, all kinds of things, but he doesn't do it very often, and when he does it, I've noticed that there's a reason."

"Other than him being a thieving brat?" Jason asked.

"Other than that, yes." Miss Teedee smiled. "A few years ago, a traveler came through town. We get all sorts of visitors. The water, you know, it brings them. And the best place to stay in town is the Taylor Point House, right on the Taylor Point Sound. It's an Inn, and I work there."

"As a cook?" Jason asked, remembering how Miss Teedee had recommended the diner's food.

"Yes," Miss Teedee said, pleased. "So this traveler, he arrives at Taylor Point saying he'd been robbed by a kid just that morning at the visitor center. Strange thing, though, was that the kid had stolen his pen, right out of his hand. Can you imagine? Signing the guest book, writing in where you're from, and this little boy snatches the ballpoint and runs out the back door."

"I can imagine," Jason said dully.

"Yes, well, I'm getting to that. The traveler, he was telling us the story mostly as a joke. Toby was a little thing, then, barely seven, and the traveler went on to his room, chuckling about the incident. Later that night, at dinner, though, we were gathered in the dining room, enjoying a nice meal. And another guest, a woman, she started to choke on her steak. But she was quiet about it. Most people choking, you'd see them. They'd flail, or they'd wave, but not this poor thing. She was dying right next to us in front of our very eyes, and none of us were the wiser until the traveler leapt out of his seat and thumped the woman on the back. He pulled her out of the chair, wrapped her up in his arms, and in the next second, a chunk of meat went flying across the room to hit the window. I still remember the way it slithered down to the sill. Such a small thing, and so deadly."

The chimes on the diner's door rang, and a man came inside, and on his arm was a woman, Jason thought, but for a moment, the glint of sun off metal and glass was blinding. He blinked, seeing stars, and then had to stop himself from gaping. The girl – she was much younger than the man, at least – was stunning: long, sleek, white-blonde hair that looked every bit of natural or so well maintained, it wouldn't matter; curves and long lines in all the right places, like she walked out of an artist's sketchbook; flawless skin with the hint of peaches in her creamy cheeks; and enormous blue eyes which would have been bewitching if they hadn't broadcast a kind of desperate sadness in the second they met Jason's gaze.

"Ah," Miss Teedee said, her tone heavy with knowing. "That's Madeline and her current beau of the moment. Poor girl."

"Why poor?" Jason asked, trying and failing to wrench his eyes away from the girl as she slid into the booth where he'd originally intended to sit.

"Well..." Miss Teedee paused as if deliberating. "She's just so lost."

The girl smiled at the man before picking up a menu and hiding behind it. The spell broke, and Jason shook his head. "Sorry," Jason said. "So, what happened next? After the man saved the choking woman?"

"The woman said thank you, cried a little, and excused herself. She checked out the next day. The traveler stayed the week, and I've never seen him since. But!" Miss Teedee leaned forward. "A few months later, I was in the drug store, picking up my medication. I have trouble sleeping. And there was Toby with his mama. He was reading a comic book like so many boys do, and I waved at him. He's a good boy, despite it all, and I like to think we understand each other. He grins at me and then rushes past to the counter. He steals the clipboard where you sign for your pills right out from under Randy Monroe's nose — he's our pharmacist — and Toby starts for the door. Toby's mama caught him, of course. That woman's gained a second sight where her son's concerned, and she gave the clipboard back. Toby kept giggling at Randy, though, and I remembered the whole thing, wondering if something was going to happen. I do enjoy a good mystery."

"I can see that, ma'am."

"Oh, and I'm carrying on, but the point is, the very next day, our hotel manager, Monica, she tells this crazy story of Randy rescuing a puppy out of a tree."

"A dog?" Jason asked. "In a tree? I thought that was a cat thing."

"That's what Darryl said. He owns the Taylor Point House, the sweet man. And Monica says it's true. Some nasty boys had put this poor puppy into a tree and left it there. The puppy belonged to Randy's neighbor's little girl, and he got there in time to get the pup down and to chase after the boys who did the deed. Now, Randy's never struck me as a particularly spry man, but he climbed a tree and ran six blocks without consequence. The boys got grounded, from what I heard, and should have gotten worse than that, but all was well again."

Jason chewed the last piece of bacon. "So, what you're saying is that this kid steals shit — sorry, stuff — from people who...matter somehow?"

"I believe so, yes. There are other stories I could tell, but you seem to have gotten the gist."

Jason shook his head. "Lady, I don't matter to anybody. And what I do definitely doesn't matter."

"Not even to the man who raised you?"

Jason stiffened. "He's dead."

"Oh, I'm sorry." Miss Teedee reached for Jason's hand again, but he tucked it into his lap before she could. "Do you have anyone else?"

"No." Jason heaved a sigh. "Sorry to break your pattern, but..." He shrugged.

"Well, I don't know that you have broken it, just yet."

"I swear to you, I'm just a guy passing through."

"On your way to where?"

"Anyplace I can find work, I guess."

"What can you do?"

"Anything I need to do."

"Hm." Miss Teedee's eyes narrowed, thoughtful, and she finished her tea. "What if I told you I knew of a job to be had around here?"

"I'd tell you the chances of them hiring me were slim to nil," Jason said before he could stop himself.

"Now, why do you say that?"

"Told you. I'm not worth anything to anybody. I'm just somebody's bad idea."

Miss Teedee frowned. "Well, I disagree. You've been worth company to me, already, and you've given Vern something to think about while he casts his lines all morning."

Jason had a lot to say about both of those things, but he kept his peace, afraid of the avalanche that would follow a crack in his control.

"Do you want to work?" Miss Teedee asked.

Jason rubbed the condensation off his glass until it squeaked. His other hand was a trembling fist resting on his thigh. "I do. Yes, ma'am."

Miss Teedee studied Jason for a long, tense moment. "My late husband liked to gamble. Not much, not Vegas, just over to the Cherokee Reservation from time to time with some bonus money when work was generous. I never much liked betting, but what if I was to bet you that they would hire you?"

"What are the stakes?" Jason asked, amused, but with sincere interest prickling.

"If I'm right, you buy me lunch when paychecks start to roll in."

"And if I'm right?"

"Then I'll buy you food and enough gas to get you to the next town."

Jason ran a hand through his hair. He couldn't believe this woman, this place, or this day, but he liked being fed and full. If he could get some cash, then he might be able to enjoy the sensation on a more regular basis. And if the job was a complete waste, which it had to be, the gas money would come in handy. Jason had two gallons of fuel in containers in the back of his van, so the money could get him farther away from here.

It didn't pay to look too eager. "You just want to see if Toby's stealing thing was right about me."

Miss Teedee giggled. "I'm an old woman, sugar. I've got to have something to occupy my time. Make my own fun."

"What do I have to do to see somebody about this job?"

"Do you have transportation?"

"I got a van."

"Well, then you just give me a lift, and I'll show you right where to go."

"You want me to meet somebody now?" Jason asked, distressed.

Miss Teedee's eyes went round with sincerity and concern. "I thought we might, yes?"

"I've not had a shower in the last seventy-two hours, and not had clean clothes for a lot longer."

"Oh, don't you worry about that. You're a little fuzzy, smell a little worn out and a little like the seashore, but that's the worst of it." The sparkle came back to her gaze. "You out of excuses yet?"

The edges of Jason's mouth twitched toward a smile despite himself. "Almost. You said that the ways I was helping you out had to do with signs and penance."

Miss Teedee studied her hands on the table. "I did, yes."

"Penance for what?"

"We all have something that we're paying for, don't we?" Miss Teedee asked. "Some wrong we've committed, or some slight."

"What could you have possibly done wrong?" Jason blurted.

Miss Teedee laughed. "Oh, you're a sweet one, all right." She tilted her head. "And I think you're someone who'll understand when I say that it's hard to know all of a person."

Rage's body surrounded by a lake of blood rose again in Jason's mind. "Yeah. I hear that."

"Mmhm. You didn't know me when I was ten, twenty... forty... sixty." Miss Teedee chuckled. "All you know is the person at the moment. And this version isn't the same as the one from yesterday. If I'm doing it right, the version of me that wakes up tomorrow will be better than the one you're talking to today. Everything and everybody changes."

"Every seven years," Jason cut in, hurriedly explaining. "I read somewhere... It takes seven years for all your cells to regenerate. Organs, skin... everything."

"You know, I think I've read that, too."

"I like to read," Jason mumbled.

"Me, too. And what I can tell you that you need to know about me and penance, is that helping you in any small way also helps me."

Jason was nodding before he knew it, before it was a conscious choice, and he wiped his mouth with the back of his hand. "Okay," he said.

"Good." Miss Teedee leaned forward. "Now, what do you say we get some homemade key lime pie to go?"

Jason bent toward Miss Teedee, her conspirator's whisper as contagious as her grin. "I say I love pie."

"Well, all right then," Miss Teedee pronounced. "Let's get ourselves some, and then get ourselves gone."

Chapter Two

Andrew heard footsteps and heavy breathing echoing up the brick walls defining the space between the old furniture store and the old clothing store. Now all they sold were dust and moths, but the shops' bike rack, which was bolted into the alleyway concrete, was perfect for his scooter. He locked it up, patted the seat, and spun with his arms thrown wide. Toby screeched to a halt not a foot away, his mouth smeared with fruit juice and his blue eyes big with surprise.

"Hi," said Andrew.

Toby sped around Andrew and laughed when Andrew caught his arm. "That's not yours!" Andrew said, loudly, because he knew the bag of food wasn't Toby's the way he could tell when someone wore borrowed clothes or drove a new car.

"So?" Toby struggled. "I had to take it, okay?"

"Why?"

"'Cause the dream told me to."

"Mama says don't listen to dreams."

"Maybe you should, anyway."

Andrew brushed his chest and knocked away an invisible dart that had hit truth. He'd had a dream just last night, of being small and trapped in a garden filled with strings, mirrors, and chimes. He kept trying to dig, but the earth wouldn't move for him; the worms wouldn't help him, the grass was stubborn, and the soil stank of rot. And that was why, at first light, he'd been up and out and away – just to prove he could have an effect on his world and move within it.

Toby knew he'd struck a nerve, and Andrew knew Toby knew; they were a closed circle of knowledge. "That isn't yours, either," Toby said, jerking his chin at Andrew's scooter.

"It is, too, mine."

"Bull."

"I found it and made it work."

"You shouldn't have it. And I know what they'll do if they find out you've got it."

The dream filled his mind, and fear colored him gray and red, and he let Toby go. Toby skittered away, dug into the stolen sack, and tossed Andrew a half-eaten candy bar. He grinned a grin that would match a man three times his years, and then he was gone, racing down the sidewalk and cutting across lawns toward home.

Andrew didn't like chocolate, but he liked littering even less, so he tucked the candy into the scooter's side compartment. He'd throw it away later. From the other side satchel, he removed a stuffed Crown Royal pouch that he'd need for this morning's rounds, and, after he'd locked the bike's compartments once again, he headed toward Castle Street. He tugged the bill of his baseball cap low over his forehead and eyes. He wore his sneaky clothes, the ones that didn't have patterns or colors so they would be noticed less, and even though he was sweating under it, he wore the windbreaker jacket that had once been deemed "An old man's coat" by the very man on whom Andrew was going to go spy.

Well, spy might be too harsh a word. Andrew hoped it was, anyway. More like, look in on or check up on or drop by to see, except Andrew couldn't let the man see him, or the game would be over.

But after the dream, Andrew had to do something to prove that he could, so he'd thought it'd been a sign to go on his rounds. Now, though, he worried a little that the thing he should have done was hang on to Toby, but he'd let Toby go. Though Toby shouldn't be stealing. Especially not food. Andrew's stomach growled in sympathy, and he hoped that the person missing the food wasn't starving. That would be just awful, and Andrew paused, listening to see whether he should abandon his plans and go hunt down Toby and then locate the hungry victim.

A breeze rustled the trees (*gordonia lasianthus* and two *acer rubrums)* at the corner of Castle and Perry, and the wind told Andrew not to worry. The bereft guy was going somewhere, and he would get fed. Another rustle that carried the fragrance of Mrs. Waxford's Southern Magnolia's (*magnolia grandiflora),* and Andrew was informed that he might meet Toby's victim, later, and make a new friend. Andrew loved friends. He had so few of them.

Andrew sighed in relief and patted a crabapple (*malus angustifolia)* in thanks, just before he zigged off the sidewalk and across the yard of a vacant duplex. Nobody had lived in that one since the woman had turned the barrel of a gun on herself and gone *splat* across the walls. The insides had been scrubbed clean, but everyone who went in there could still imagine the stains, so it had stood solitary and lonely for over a year. Andrew felt terrible about that because the wooden plank siding and support struts were lonely, so he paused on his way to his real destination so that he could kneel in the garden patch on the eastern side of the empty house.

"Hi, hi," he whispered to the dry mulch and the weeds. "Sorry, sorry," he said to the plants as he uprooted them and put their dying bodies around the single beauty berry bush struggling to survive. "Feed each other," he instructed, and he dug a shallow hole with his fingers. Andrew had good hands for digging, or so *he* of the most-important *he's* had said, once, after dinner. Happiness helped things grow, and Andrew hummed with the nice memory while undoing the drawstrings on the Crown Royal bag. Inside was a packet of wildflower seeds that would grow practically anywhere and in any circumstance, particularly when Andrew put them in the ground. He poured a few of the seeds into the hole, buried them, and repeated the process in a circle next to the beauty berry. When the wildflowers were all sleeping under their dirt blanket, Andrew fished around in the bag until he found a cocktail umbrella. It was cheerful, pink and orange and yellow, and he buried it in the center of the wildflower ring at the base of the bush. "Friends by the end of summer, and every summer after that," he said to the beauty berry. And, he thought to himself, maybe now that the umbrella lived in this garden, people would see the hope planted here instead of the blood on the walls, inside.

"Okay." Andrew brushed his hands on his jeans, closed up the bag, and caressed one of the bush's leaves. "See you next week." The beauty berry was tired, so much flowering to do, but she liked Andrew, and the wind helped her wave goodbye.

Andrew wiped his forehead and was singing *Honky Tonk Woman* by the all-knowing Stones under his breath when he reached the fence. He looked left, right, and up, and when he didn't see anyone or anything, he hoisted himself over the property divider. The duplex on this side of the fence was occupied, but the woman worked nights making men (and sometimes women, or so the snapdragons gossiped) happy, and the man worked security at the mall. One was asleep, and the other already gone as Andrew tiptoed across their lawn. Or skulked. Maybe he skulked. That's what Mama was apt to say he was doing if she ever found out.

But she wouldn't. Andrew wouldn't tell her, and nobody knew about Andrew's early morning rounds except Toby, who had so many secrets that he needed Andrew to carry some of them around. It was fair trade. People looked at Toby and saw a boy, but Andrew didn't see *only* a boy. He saw Toby in the middle of bone-white web strings that stretched to connect all across the town. Curiosity led the boy to places to pick up items that needed to be carried elsewhere. It was tough work, especially when you had to be two things at once. And maybe two places at once, now that Andrew thought about it. Both here for the deliveries and *there*, wherever *there* was, to get the instructions. For a second, Andrew thought he saw a dividing line across the lawn. It was a big, dark shadow and on this side was *here* and on the other side was *there*. Andrew blinked hard at the line, and then it was gone.

Even though Andrew sighed in relief, he was no stranger to the idea of being two things at once (or two places at once). He was his Mama's son, who listened and obeyed, but he was also a gardener. And a man, he supposed, though he was that all the time, even though sometimes he felt like a woman or a kid and sometimes he felt like a redwood tree. Mama tried hard to understand and to remember everything about everybody, and she didn't like anything to be more than one thing at a time. She said that standing still and knowing what was real was hard enough without making something be more than it needed to be. So, a song was a song, a tree was a tree, and a boy was a boy.

Until he was a man, and then he wasn't to be trusted, unless that man happened to be her son, but only if her son was being good. Just like she trusted Darryl, but only if Darryl wasn't drinking. If Andrew wasn't good or if Darryl drank, then they'd be something other than her son or her long-time boyfriend. Two things at once. That was no good.

So Good Andrew and Sober Darryl were the only exceptions to Mama's rules. Otherwise, it was, *Keep to yourself and like people all you want, Andrew, but don't rely on anyone but family, and for God's sake, Andrew, don't tell anyone the stuff that goes on in your head.*

Because people would think Andrew was nuts, and they had every right to think that because Andrew was nuts. And leaves. And dirt. And wind and rain and, at the moment, a big man trying to be as small as possible, so he could sneak past the row of pine trees (slash and longleaf, both, because they'd found ground to sprout), take the four huge steps across open lawn, and duck behind the overgrown boxwood. The hedge grew in an L-shape starting at the back of another dark brown duplex, numbers 611 and 612, and Andrew crawled from the rear of the property to the western side. There was a hole in the hedge, there, just large enough for Andrew, though he needed to bring his sheers some night, again, and recut it. And trim the tops of the hedges, too, while he was at it, though he couldn't do as good a job as he wanted because somebody would likely notice if the wild growth morphed into neat lines and tidy corners. The woman in 611 loved vodka and the Home Shopping Network and rarely ever ventured outside, and *the man* – the oh-so-important man – in 612 didn't think he could take the time to make anything grow. Not friendships, not relationships, and certainly not plants. The man was wrong about his supposed (and, Andrew supposed, quite literal) black fingers, but there was no explaining to people what they weren't ready to understand.

Andrew had learned that life lesson long before the ones Mama had taught him could sink in. He'd been on the playground when he was five years old, and he'd cried and cried when Marcus Soliderworthy had pulled the heads off the dandelions. Flowers were far closer to life's cycles than humans, so they tended to understand when they had to die young, but those dandelions had been babies plucked before their prime, and Marcus had just been *mean.* He'd cussed at Andrew, too, called him a *damned crybaby*, and Andrew had screamed and screamed that he wasn't a crybaby, he was a *sequoia sempervirens,* and he was angry.

And then Andrew'd hit Marcus until his nose went *blat*, and Andrew had never gone back to that school and its dead baby dandelions again.

Andrew pressed himself against the side of Number 612. A colossal oak trunk stood between him and the front lawn, and more oak cousins blocked the line of sight from the street. The garden patch on this side of the duplex was huge. The couple who had lived there before had loved shrubs and the smell of mulch. But then they'd moved out, and *he* had moved in, and the garden had started to go wild. Mostly, Andrew still let it, but he added some order into the chaos. Two years ago, Andrew had planted blazing stars in big bunches, and now their purple flowers were getting ready to pop. It was a tad early, but this summer had been wet and warm and steady. Today, Andrew would add more wildflowers to the mix so that *he* would have butterflies. Andrew knew *he* liked having pretty things around.

And speaking of, a ladybug landed on Andrew's shoulder as he started to dig shallow beds for the seeds. "Hi, hi," he whispered, and he whistle-warbled in answer to the doves, but under his breath, because it wasn't until the alarm started to beep inside Number 612 that its occupant was even close to awake.

Andrew counted to five, held his breath, and slowly rose to peer into the window. The Nurse Man, Tio, of the literal black thumbs and strange-pretty eyes, sat on the far side of the bed with his back to Andrew. Knowing it was rude to stare at someone when they were naked (unless, maybe, if that person invited you to look, which Tio hadn't, but maybe someday), Andrew focused on the peacock robe that Tio took off a hook on the back of the bedroom door. It flowed like silk around him, and Andrew ducked to the seeds again when Tio left the bedroom, heading for the shower. Andrew knew every minute of Tio's morning routine, and sometimes that made him feel like a cheat, sometimes a pervert, and sometimes just sad, but Andrew kept coming to see Tio. If nothing else, the flowers needed him.

The wildlings were planted by the time Tio was done with the shower and shuffling into the kitchen for coffee that would get made and be put in a tall, rainbow thermos. Andrew stayed low, and he plucked a pink flamingo out of his Crown Royal bag. Tio was like the strange bird: vibrant and impossible, graceless out of its environment but perfect in it, and Andrew buried the plastic bird in the graveyard next to its kin. He was patting soil and putting happiness into it (because wouldn't it be so cool if, perhaps, one day a flamingo tree erupted? Who knew what so many pieces of buried flamboyance could do?), when he heard a car stop on the street, followed soon by the strike of heels on the decaying front walk. Andrew hit the dirt, asking it to hide him, and he felt the inching of branches, twigs, mulch, and vines snaking across his prone body while someone *knock-knock-knocked* on Tio's door.

Straining, Andrew listened as Tio answered—

"What do you—oh. It's you. What the hell are you doing here?"

—and heard when Tio got angry—

"—paid you early last month. Give me a few more days. I've got to eat, you know."

—but no matter what he did, Andrew couldn't hear the other man's voice. The low drone, yes, but not the words themselves, though when Tio slammed the door and the visitor stalked away and slammed the car door, Andrew's guts tied themselves into a big, fat knot. Because Tio didn't tell the *knock-knock* visitor that though the Taylor Point House paid him well and regularly, it wasn't his only aspiration. He had a room, a small room but with good light, full of canvas and paint and oils and metal tins of chemicals that singed nostrils and made eyes water. The caring in his hands handled brushes and people with equal attention; they created so many kinds of beauty.

But the shows to display the beauty were few and far between, and the cost of keeping hope and art alive was high. Andrew knew this because he'd been with Tio at least one morning out of seven for the last three years. Ever since Andrew had found the yellow scooter abandoned in the woods on the edge of the Taylor Point House property, left for junk, most likely, and ever since he'd cobbled together parts and made them work and started stealing gasoline from the stash he kept on hand for the lawnmower, he'd skulked, and he'd spied, and he'd planted. At that moment, covered in ground growth and one or two friendly centipedes moseying about their days, Andrew was grateful for every time he'd been able to visit, no matter how few and far between, because he was there now when Tio needed him.

Tio left for work right on the tick of a quarter to seven, and instead of watching him leave, as usual, Andrew snuck around to the back door. The key was in a planter of fake mums on the tiny square of a porch, and the screen door hinges needed oiling. Andrew would bring the WD-40 next time, he promised himself, and he crept into the darkened kitchen. He was so scared to touch anything because these were Tio's things in Tio's sanctuary, but Andrew took deep, deep breaths and inched to the counter next to the sink. Behind the coffee pot were a series of four white urns. Andrew pulled the third-largest from its spot, and it ground against the Formica with a noise that sped up Andrew's pulse, no matter how deep a breath he took.

Again and again, he checked out the window and listened for the locks on the front door, but Tio didn't come back, having forgotten his wallet or a scarf. So nobody but the ladybug still on Andrew's shoulder saw Andrew lift the urn's lid, carefully avoid the mousetrap at the bottom of the jar, and remove the bundle of cash Tio stored within. It wasn't the only stash Tio had, but it was the one stored closest to an exit.

Guilt made Andrew seem to weigh a hundred pounds more than he did, and though he wasn't quite sure why he felt that way, he pulled out his wallet, determined. He was paid for his work at the Taylor Point House, and he cashed the checks like always, but he never, ever spent it all. When the money got too thick for Andrew to sit comfortably, he gave it to his mama, who took it to the bank, but Andrew hadn't done that in a while. Andrew counted out a couple of hundreds, changed his mind, and went to the twenties. A few of those and a few tens and a couple fives would be easier to explain away than a few big, fat hundreds. And, besides, Andrew got paid again soon, and next visit, he could add more. Tio would never know, and that was best. Tio didn't like taking anything from anybody, even when it was a gift. Tio was very much like a rabbit that way, and Andrew giggled at the idea of Tio with bunny ears.

When the kitchen was in order, Andrew left, returning the key to its spot. He put the ladybug on a blazing star leaf, thanked her (and it was a *her*, because she was more brown than red, though the hims of the ladybugs were used to being mistaken for women and didn't take offense, and Andrew liked that about them), and made his dash back to the hedge.

Andrew felt better than good about helping Tio, who gave so much and asked for so little in return. People had to take care of one another, after all, especially when one person felt like Andrew did about Tio. The Nurse Man made sunrises prettier and gave direction to all points of Andrew's compass. All the roads leading to home would be brighter because Tio would be at work today, and because later, Tio would be confused but grateful, and that would be because of Andrew, even if Tio didn't know and never would.

Andrew sang the Stones' *Happy* on his way back to the alleyway. It was a nice day.

Chapter Three

Though the speed limit was thirty-five, the car in front of the van hadn't broken twenty for the last three blocks. Jason gripped the steering wheel like a lifeline, listening to Miss Teedee speak of each passing house and its occupants with enough detail to make Jason wonder how anyone sneezed without getting noticed in this town, much less committed a crime or cheated on a spouse.

"And there's Ken Pucket's little house. Isn't it just darling?"

Jason glanced at yet another small, one-level white shack subject to constant sea breezes. Still, most of the homes were more than Jason had ever had. He'd grown up in a trailer and spent years in hotels. All the places he'd laid his head had wheels or deals. "Yeah," Jason said. "I guess."

"You'll want to turn just up ahead."

Jason took a right, following his passenger's directions, and he swallowed a lump of fear. For most of their drive, he'd been increasingly more terrified, not of the impending job interview he'd likely fail, but of the faint glimmers of hope beginning to stir in his chest. He wanted to bury that emotion as deeply as he could; tuck it under his liver or hide it in his bowels so he could shit it out later. He couldn't start to think any part of this crazy plan would work out. The second he did, it'd be destined to crash around his feet.

"Now, this part of town's a nice mixture of old and new," Miss Teedee narrated, her black, leather purse on her lap and her ankles neatly crossed. "Since we're insulated by the Sound, here, lots of new neighborhoods have been going up, brick houses and all. But a lot of these homes and buildings have been around since the town was first founded in the early 1800s, including the Taylor Point House."

Jason crept by manicured trees and lawns, and he watched the homes go from one level to multi-story to sprawling manors for the elite. After another Teedee-guided turn, the houses vanished from the roadside altogether, retreating behind woods to the center of their allotted acreage.

"The Taylor family made this town," Miss Teedee said. "It was meant to be a port city, big enough to compete with the big boys up the way, but it never quite had the clout. The town was dying when Leonard Taylor proposed the town be marketed as a summer getaway for the wealthy and as a tourist attraction for everybody else. Little boats would take people out on the Sound, go out on fishing expeditions, and the town built parks and had fairs, and..." Miss Teedee shrugged. "Soon enough, tourism became the biggest industry."

"Cool," Jason muttered.

"Not a town history buff, are you?" Miss Teedee asked archly.

"Don't really think I'll be around long enough to put any of it to use, ma'am," Jason said.

"Mmm. We'll see. Up there's the B&B. That wooden sign? That's us. Turn this side of it."

The trees and shrubs were dense enough that Jason might have missed the turn if Miss Teedee hadn't pointed it out. The bright white sign declared the Taylor Point House in scrawling golden script, and a manicured landscape divider separated the sides of the street.

"That's the Fisherman's Shack Museum," Miss Teedee said, pointing to a two-story brick building with a tidy little parking lot on their right. "Has the history of the Sound, the Taylors, the town, and sells little trinkets, you know."

Jason hummed with feigned interest. The woods crept up to the sides of the road, the trees making a tunnel over the road that spanned a few hundred yards, and when it opened up, Jason got his first look at the main building.

The Taylor Point House looked like a dollhouse had mated with City Hall. A wide porch sporting a row of rocking chairs encircled the house on two sides, and white columns marched along the painted railings. Two bay windows were stacked three-stories high, one in the front and one on the right side, and the house itself was made of old red brick and pale lavender shingles. A weather vane perched on top of a tower that Jason could see at the rear of the house, and all the windows were shaded on the inside by lace curtains.

"There are seven bedroom suites and common rooms on the main floor." Miss Teedee practically oozed pride, and she watched Jason closely enough to make him sweat. "Andrew, that's Monica's boy, maintains the rose garden and the hiking trails on our land that link up to the ones owned by the park. We've got a dock, boat access, and four buildings to manage on the property."

"Nice?" Jason said, and it came out with a question mark.

Miss Teedee beamed. "It is, isn't it? Just lovely." She sighed and gazed adoringly at the massive, double front doors. "Home away from home."

"So, what's the job, exactly?" Jason asked. "Working with this Andrew kid or what?" Jason wasn't about to turn his nose up at any kind of work, manual labor or not. Getting to be outside all day wouldn't be the worst thing in the world.

Miss Teedee's grin turned mischievous. "Come on inside and find out."

"You're really not going to tell me anything first, are you?"

"Nope. You can just leave your van parked right here for now." Miss Teedee hopped out of the van with a spring in her step, and Jason killed the Honda's engine. He ran his hands through his hair, trying to smooth it, and he wiped his palms on his shorts. Wishing he had a breath mint or something, he climbed out, and he reminded himself not to slink. His shoes were thin enough that he felt every pebble on the black tar pavement. He squared his shoulders and climbed up the wooden stairs behind Miss Teedee, and their footsteps echoed across the porch boards. Insects hissed and scratched in the trees, and birds called warnings from their hidden perches. Jason tried to see everything at once without actually turning his head, and he hastened to grab the gothic, metal door handle, letting Miss Teedee into the building before himself.

"Such nice manners," Miss Teedee complimented.

Jason followed her inside and got slapped in the face by climate control. He shivered, the cool air drying the sweat on his skin too fast. He stood in a foyer full of antique-looking furniture, old paintings, and ticking clocks – a lot of ticking clocks. The walls had dark red and green striped wallpaper with gold edges, and a chandelier with fake candle tapers hung from the high ceiling. To the left was a pair of pocket doors spread open to reveal a library, the shelves stuffed to the brims with novels. Big, fluffy chairs sat interspersed about the room on rugs covering the hardwood, and dust motes danced in the hazy light filtering in from the broad front windows. A tiny woman with gray hair and wearing a green shawl sat ensconced in cushions, reading glasses perched on the end of her nose and a book on her lap. She turned a page while Jason watched.

"Darryl should be around here, somewhere," Miss Teedee said. "Probably in the office." She patted Jason's arm. "Wait here."

"Sure," Jason said amiably, smelling lemon cleaner and the faint hint of coffee. Miss Teedee disappeared into the room on

Jason's right, its door a normal swinging one. Through the gap, he could see a window and a desk and leather chairs. While he stood waiting, footsteps thumped overhead, and he heard the whir of a vacuum cleaner. When he swallowed, he realized his heart was thudding in his chest. Not faster than normal, just harder, and he thought the place seemed simultaneously familiar and utterly foreign. Like maybe he'd lived here in another life or something, but in this one, he was going to get thrown out on his ass at any moment.

"Fiddlesticks," Miss Teedee said, returning to the foyer with her hands on her hips. "I bet he's in the kitchen. Come on."

Jason rubbed his arms and followed Miss Teedee through a doorway across from the entry. "Whoa," he said, stumbling at the unexpected sight of a room covered top to bottom, side to side in shiny, dark wood, perfectly camouflaging the curving staircase rising to the second floor.

"The Center Hall," Miss Teedee said over one shoulder. "Oak paneling, most of it carved by hand and put in place with much care. Amazing, isn't it?"

"Something," Jason agreed, flinching at the sound of even more ticking clocks – what was it with these people and time? He shied away from the chairs and tables and hanging decorations, terrified to touch anything.

The far end of the Center Hall opened onto a dining room with a table that could seat at least twenty. A curved wall of windows made up the rear of the dining room, and through it, Jason could see the railings of the back porch, swaying trees, and the water. He didn't get much time to stare, though. They made a sharp turn into a claustrophobic hallway on the left. It was papered in more red and green, like the front room, and Miss Teedee pushed open a swinging door, holding it for Jason.

"There you are!" Miss Teedee exclaimed, and Jason came up short behind her. The kitchen was full of sparkling white cabinets and cream tile and marble countertops. It gleamed, whereas the rest of the house so far sort of loomed. Jason smelled fresh bread and the sea, the latter spilling in through an open pair of doors leading into a glassed-in room off the far end of the kitchen. Men and women sat at wicker tables, watching the water and sipping drinks out of glass flutes and white mugs.

In the center of the kitchen was an island covered in platters of food and silver pitchers, each with a little placard in front of them declaring what they were or what they held. A broad, heavyset man in his sixties or so, with deeply tanned skin and close-cut white hair, sat on a stool with a newspaper in hand and a pastry on a plate. "Woman, you ever going to learn what 'day off' means?" the man asked, smiling at Miss Teedee.

"Likely not," Miss Teedee answered. "Darryl Taylor? I'd like you to meet Jason Hart."

Darryl's eyes were light brown and inquisitive, and he nodded at Jason. "Pleased to make your acquaintance."

Jason kicked himself into gear and walked around the island to offer his hand to Darryl, who took it with a firm, dry grip. "Nice to meet you, sir," Jason said.

"Jason and I had a lovely breakfast," Miss Teedee said, turning to bend and put her purse in a low cabinet near a fridge that was one of the biggest Jason had ever seen. "He's new in town and looking for work—"

"Teedee," Darryl said, holding up a hand and already shaking his head.

"—and so I thought I'd bring him by so you two could get to know each other, and then you could introduce him to Monica."

Darryl groaned, a strange, uninhibited sound to be coming from a fully grown man. "Teedee, why are you putting me in the middle of this? You know that woman wins blue ribbons in stubborn year after year."

Miss Teedee stood up straighter and crossed her arms over her chest. "Darryl, I say this in love, respect, and sincere honesty." Miss Teedee's mouth shrunk in seriousness. "Grow some gumption and speak frankly to your woman."

"I've tried," Darryl protested, gesticulating.

"She's tired. She needs help. She cannot do all this on her own. There is too much, and that boy of hers is utterly useless indoors."

"I've told her!"

Miss Teedee didn't seem to hear Darryl. "Do you know he broke my good vase? The Lenox one that Charlie bought me?" Miss Teedee scoffed and screwed her face up into an expression of pure displeasure.

"Teedee..." Darryl tried one more time, but Teedee snatched up an apron off a hook on the side of the island.

"Go on, now, shoo. Speak of manly things and explain yourselves to each other. Be honest, and Jason, just be yourself. I'll watch the guests 'til you're done and Monica comes down for her third cup of coffee, and then we'll see what's what."

Darryl muttered under his breath and snatched more pastries, piling them on his plate until Miss Teedee lightly smacked his hand. "Come on, kid," Darryl said to Jason. "One thing I've learned is that when the women conspire 'round here, there's no use in fighting their plans."

"There is no conspiring, only common sense," Miss Teedee said, and she poured and handed Jason a glass of juice. She winked at him. "There you go. Make sure Darryl shares. He's got the high blood sugars." Miss Teedee raised her voice, calling after Darryl, who had already disappeared out the door into the hallway. "And can't be eating like he was thirty, anymore!"

Despite being entirely out of the loop, Jason was amused, and his nerves were calmer on the return trip through the hall, dining room, central hall, and finally into the office where Miss Teedee had first looked for Darryl. Like the kitchen, the office was a brighter place, with wave-patterned blue paper, wide white trim, and worn furniture that appeared to be at least from this century.

"Sorry about the mess," Darryl said, weaving around boxes full of gears and metal bits and bulbs. "Keep meaning to finish these projects and never quite get there, you know?"

"I think so, sir," Jason said, not sure if he did at all, but dying of curiosity over what all the machine parts might make. Jason peered around, hesitating while Darryl settled his bulk in a squeaky chair behind the desk.

"Darryl, son, call me Darryl. And sit." Darryl pointed, and Jason sat, obedient.

Munching on a gooey bit of dough, Darryl scooted a coaster and the plate of pastries closer to Jason. "Can I ask you something personal?" Darryl asked.

Jason froze in the act of reaching for food. "Uh, yes?"

Darryl chewed and swallowed. "You aware that you have metal in your face?"

Jason blinked. "Ah, yes, yes, I am."

"And not just in the ears, there, but seems to be something in the nose and in the lip."

"That's... that's where I remember it being."

"You do it on purpose?"

"I did," Jason answered, and for the life of him, he couldn't tell if Darryl was teasing.

"Why?" Darryl asked.

Jason considered his words before he spoke. "Well, it seemed like a good idea at the time, and now I'm sort of attached to the way it looks and feels, so..."

"It's all healed and everything, right?"

"Oh, yeah, yes. For a long time, now, si—Darryl."

"Well, okay, then. I guess if they aren't going to erupt in blood or something."

Jason opened his mouth to try and comment on that visual, but Darryl carried on before Jason got the chance. "What did you do before you got here?"

"A lot of things." Jason drank juice and carefully set his glass down on the coaster. "I've picked fruit in orchards, done engine repair, mowed lawns, washed windows and cars, and I was a DJ for a while at this club, but it went under." Jason wiped his mouth so he wouldn't keep babbling. He was pretty sure this was the interview, but it was more conversation than inquisition, and Jason wasn't used to that.

"You like music?" Darryl asked.

"Yeah." Jason hesitated for two seconds and thought, screw it. The man wanted the full work history? Then Jason would give the guy the complete download. "I was a roadie tech for a band called Judith's Hell for seven years. Heavy lifting, light set up, tuning, sound equipment, the works."

"How'd you get into that?" Darryl asked, swiveling slowly back and forth in the chair with his hands folded on his belly.

"Kid I knew in school—Vic, but we called him Rage."

"Because he liked to fight?"

Jason smiled. "No, because he didn't. Never got mad at all about anything."

"I see," Darryl said, poker face impenetrable.

"Uh, yeah. He played bass for the band, and he told me they'd gotten a deal and were going on a road tour. I dropped out of school and went with them."

Darryl chuckled. "Bet the parents loved that."

"I didn't have parents." Jason's knee bounced, and he put a hand on it to stop it. "Or, well, I guess I did, but they left me. A man found me and raised me."

"Huh. What was he called?"

"Papa Jack."

"Huh," Darryl said. "He a good man?"

Jason shrugged. "People thought so. He was a forest ranger and a volunteer firefighter. He tried to teach me things. Used his fists a little more than I liked. Didn't—well." Jason forced a tight smile, kicking himself for his mouth getting away from him.

"Didn't what?" Darryl asked.

"Papa Jack thought I was dumb."

"Well, are you?"

"What, dumb?" Jason asked.

"Yeah."

"I don't think so. No genius, but I'm..." Jason didn't think he'd ever had to answer such a question. "I'm not dumb, no. I notice things other people don't, and Papa Jack didn't like that. But I could connect 'em, the things I'd see. I used to help Judith fill in the holes in the music that way, sometimes. She'd come to me with some song, and I could hear what was missing. Sometimes, I mean."

Darryl grunted. "But you don't have much education?"

"No, sir." Jason braced. "I did bad in school. Couldn't read good. But Judith, she taught me, and I've been at it ever since. And I learned a lot with the band, about equipment and machines and how to fix a bus so it can roll on to the next repair station. And I'm not afraid to learn or of work."

"What happened to the band?" Darryl asked.

"They broke up," Jason said, proud when he didn't choke on the words.

"When?"

"Two years ago."

"Oh, so all those odd jobs..."

Jason nodded. "Have been since then, yes."

"Mm." The chair complained as Darryl reclined, hands moving behind his head. He was staring so intently at a spot on the ceiling that Jason almost looked to see if there was something up there he should be noticing.

"What do you think your worst trait is?" Darryl suddenly asked.

"Worst...?"

"In a job situation, kid. What's the worst of it?"

"Papa Jack said I talk too much and tell people stuff I shouldn't," Jason said.

"Sounds like that's because he didn't know what to make of what you did say. Anyhow, I didn't ask what somebody else thought of you. What do you think your worst is?"

There was a dark place in the corner of Jason's mind reserved for memories of when he was a kid. He could still feel Papa Jack's fist slugging him that last time. A hundred times before, it'd been an open-handed slap. A sort of, *Get it right, boy,* kind of thing. But that last time, it'd been a solid hit that had sent Jason staggering backward. He'd told Papa Jack he was going. Papa Jack hadn't liked that one bit. Said it was some thanks from the boy he'd taken in and raised and clothed and cared for when nobody else would. Jason had fired something back, and Papa Jack had raised his fist again.

And that time, Jason had fought back. Threw fists until Papa Jack had gone still beneath him.

"*I'm gone, you son of a bitch,*" Jason had said.

He had left with his bag over one shoulder. Rage had been at the end of the drive, waiting.

"Temper," Jason said. He cleared his throat. "It takes a long time to get me angry, but when I do, I just..." Jason closed his eyes briefly. "I don't think. I do. And it can get ugly."

Darryl's sharp gaze made Jason squirm. "The law ever been involved?"

"No, sir."

"Darryl."

"No, Darryl, sir. Never."

"Mm."

"I've been working on it."

Darryl stared through Jason. Finally, he grunted, as though coming to a decision. "If a bill of sale is two dollars and sixteen cents, and somebody gives you a fifty, what's the change?" he asked.

Jason did the math. "Forty-seven... eighty-five? No... four. Forty-seven dollars and eighty-four cents."

Darryl nodded. "Do you know what a Dyson is?"

"A vacuum cleaner?" Jason replied.

Another single nod. "Favorite Rolling Stones song?" Darryl asked.

"Old or new school?" Jason countered.

"Both."

"'*Time is on My Side*' and '*Laugh, I Nearly Died.*'"

Darryl flashed a grin, and like a bolt of lightning, it was gone a second after it appeared. "You have any problem taking orders?"

"Not if I'm okay with what they're making me do."

"You got any issue with gay people?"

"No," Jason said, tumbling into his answer before he could wonder if it was a trick question.

Darryl barreled forward. "How about crazy people?" Darryl asked.

"What kind of crazy?" Jason blurted, and when Darryl's eyebrows went up, Jason clarified: "I mean, we talking come after me with a chainsaw kind of crazy or muttering to yourself crazy or just, like kind of depressed and weird about it crazy?"

Darryl considered. "More the last two."

"Then, no." Jason shrugged. "As long as the crazy isn't coming after me, I'm cool."

Darryl laughed, a big and heartfelt belly roar. "Son, I think you'll fit in just fine."

Jason's heart fluttered in his chest. "That's, I mean, great, but, can you tell me what the job actually—"

Miss Teedee chose that moment to knock and stick her head into the room. "Monica's here. You all caught up?"

"We are," Darryl replied, lurching forward in his chair. "I suppose you want me present for this?"

"It'd help." Miss Teedee grinned.

"I doubt that," Darryl grumbled, but he got to his feet and jerked his chin at Jason. "Come on. Time for round three."

Resigned to his fate, Jason didn't ask questions, choosing to rise and follow Miss Teedee and Darryl to the kitchen. They entered single-file and took positions next to the island, Jason shuffling in last with his hands in his pockets.

"Monica?" Miss Teedee said to the petite, dark-haired woman refilling a thermos. "I'd like you to meet someone."

The woman spun fast enough that Jason worried about whiplash. She was older than Jason, though younger than Darryl. She had golden skin and dark eyes, a wide, full mouth, and a seriously nice rack that went with even nicer curves farther south.

"Hi," Jason said, forcing himself to meet her eyes and not stare at anything below her chin. "I'm—"

Monica capped and slammed the thermos on the counter. She glared at the three of them. "What are you up to, Teedee?"

"Finding you help," Miss Teedee said, sweetly.

"I told you I can handle it. I always have." Monica practically vibrated, and Jason couldn't tell if that was anger or caffeine.

"You did," Miss Teedee agreed. "But I thought you may need some assistance. So hard to find people, sometimes, and—"

"And you just thought you'd stick your nose in my business." Monica violently screwed the lid on her thermos.

"I don't understand why you're so adverse to the idea of help," Miss Teedee said.

"Maybe because most of the 'help' around here is more likely to fall out of a window than to clean it."

Jason chuckled, and Monica, Miss Teedee, and Darryl all looked his way. "You got something to laugh about?" Monica growled.

"Sorry," Jason said. "Thought it was funny."

Monica cocked a hip and an eyebrow. "You think falling out of windows is funny?"

Jason knew that tone. The challenging undercurrents were intimately familiar. It didn't pay to give them an inch; they'd take the rest of the mile out of one's hide. "It was the time I did it."

"You've fallen out a window?"

"It was more a jump, really."

"You've *jumped* out a window?"

"Well, yeah," Jason said, remembering a particular Halloween night and a haunted house gone awry when fans had found out that Judith's Hell was in the building. "But don't worry, I wasn't trying to clean it at the time."

"What were you trying to do?"

"Get away from the guy with the chainsaw."

Monica blinked, Miss Teedee cleared her throat, and Darryl gave Jason another one of those lightning grins.

"It was a Halloween costume. He was trying to get an autograph," Jason started to explain.

"Who are you?" Monica asked.

"Jason Hart." He held out his hand. "Apparently here to interview for a cleaning job."

"Apparently?" Monica repeated, not doing Jason the honor of a handshake.

"Until you said something about windows, ma'am, I wasn't sure what the job was."

"You were here and you didn't know—" Monica spun on her heel. "Teedee?"

"Toby stole food from him on the beach this morning," Miss Teedee said.

Monica fell against the counter and crossed herself. "You know I don't believe any of that signs and portents horse crap."

"Of course not," Miss Teedee said.

"All coincidence," Monica insisted.

"I respect your opinion," Miss Teedee answered with wide-eyed innocence. "But it happened, and you know my affection for that boy, and Jason, here, needs a job—"

"And a shower," Monica interjected. "He smells like a dead sea rat."

"It's been worse," Jason muttered, flush warming his cheeks.

"Don't push it," Monica replied, but Jason detected just a hint of amusement, despite Monica's perma-scowl. If the woman had a sense of hidden humor, then she was nothing like Judith. The hope woke up again, and Jason struggled to gulp it down.

Miss Teedee watched them with her eagle eyes. "—and you've been so tired, lately—"

"According to you," Monica said.

"—so I thought I'd bring him here, and we'd see." Miss Teedee smiled.

Monica swung her head toward Darryl. "And I suppose you're on board with this?" she accused.

Darryl seemed to shrink beneath her stare. "He's a good kid," Darryl said. "Honest to the core, can make change, knows which end of the vacuum sucks, and clearly isn't intimated by any of us."

"Have you introduced him to everyone?" Monica asked, with not so subtle emphasis.

"No," Darryl admitted.

"Then how do you know if he's unaffected?"

"I guess I don't," Darryl said.

"Exactly. You don't know anything about him. You'd let some random man walk in and take up residence beneath our roof with free reign to our valuables, but that's just fine, isn't it? Because you'll leave it to me to watch him, introduce him, show him the ropes, and it all just adds to the list of what I have to get done around here."

"Monica, we're trying to help you," Miss Teedee said.

"Mmhm. Right off a cliff." Monica slurped her coffee. "You Southern?" she asked the mug.

"Yes, ma'am," Jason replied.

"Where do you live?"

"I have a van," Jason answered.

"You live in your car?" Monica's dark eyes flew all over Jason. He felt strip-searched.

"Yeah," he said.

"You can't do that."

A hundred remarks from the penitent to the wise-ass crossed Jason's mind. "What would you suggest?"

"Well, you certainly can't stay in the rooms."

"I wasn't asking—"

"They're for paying customers, only."

Jason wondered if Monica knew how to speak without shouting. "I understand."

"And the family quarters are all full." Monica huffed. "What are we supposed to do? Put you up in a hotel? Find you an apartment? Am I the only one who remembers we actually have a budget?" She whirled to Darryl and Miss Teedee, who idly leaned on the island. "Oh, I know what you're thinking, and that means I'm what, supposed to work him and stable him?"

"I like carrots," Jason said when nobody else dared to answer.

"What?" Monica snapped.

"Carrots. You said... And horses, you know. They like..." Monica gave Jason the Are You Nuts once-over. "Nevermind," Jason finished.

Monica squinted at Jason. "I don't like this."

"I see that, ma'am."

"And I'm not sure I like you."

"Is that required?" Jason asked.

"Yes," Monica said.

"Then, do I get the chance to win you over?"

If Monica was a cat, her tail would be twitching and her ears back. "Fine. You'll get an hourly wage. I'll decide what it will be after seeing you work. If guests tip you, it's yours, but I don't want to hear you asking for it. You'll clean, you'll do windows and toilets and anything else I tell you to do. No questions, no smart-mouthing, no whining. There are twenty-five rooms in this house, excluding hallways and family quarters. It is our responsibility to make sure all of them are spotless. There is also the museum and outbuildings. You will work them, clean them, repaint them, or stand on top of them like a lightning rod if I say you should. We work six days a week. We take meals here. I don't tolerate gossiping, laziness, or tardiness. All that clear?"

It was clear and it was wonderful. "Yes, ma'am."

Monica stabbed a finger into Jason's breastbone, and she glared up at him. "If you break any one of my rules or give me one ounce of trouble, I will fire you so fast they'll have to reattach your head to your body, you hear me?"

"Yes, ma'am," Jason said, meekly with a straight face. He didn't say what else he was thinking: if she'd shown him how to do that in advance, he could have used the skill two years ago to save Rage.

Monica wrinkled her nose. "And you'll bathe. Regularly."

"Just point me at a hose or something, and I will."

Monica sighed, communed with the ceiling in what appeared to be a silent prayer, and began to stalk out of the room. "You can use Andrew's shower after your first shift. And he's got a couch. You will sleep on it. I won't have vagrants on the property." She shoved open the door into the hallway. She threw one last lingering glare at Miss Teedee and Darryl, started to leave, and stopped. "Well?" she demanded of Jason. "Are you coming?"

"Yes, ma'am," Jason said, jogging to catch up to his new boss.

Chapter Four

The lilac lace curtains dropped into place over the window panes, and Helen petted the pattern with her fingertips. She'd made these, long ago, when she'd been better with her hands and with numbers and concentration. Once, she'd been good at knitting, at baking, at smiling and laughing and twirling on the dance floor. Her daddy had thrown that sweet sixteen for her in the sweltering heat of July, and that neighbor boy, the one who drowned two years later, he'd danced with her, dipped her low and held her close, and Helen had thought that happiness was made from the sweat of youth and the swell of summer and the hope of a life just begun. She'd believed that, written it in her journal with the pink hearts on the cover, and thought one day she'd be a poet. She'd tucked her dreams away under her pillow that night, giddy because she'd confessed, dear diary, that she had wanted the dead boy to kiss her, though, at the time, he'd been very much alive.

She'd been so good at the normal things. The girl giggles, the human hopes, Oh, Dear Diary, I want to teach children and paint pictures. Then she'd found a crack between worlds – several of them. One in her room and one at the edge of their property and one in the water. She'd picked at the edges of those cracks. She'd pointed them out to the people in her life even though everyone told her the cracks weren't there. She'd stared at them solitary, contemplating spelunking in that darkness. And that darkness beyond the veil, well...

It had liked her. It had spoken to her. It had shared pieces of its history. It'd warned her of the chaos to follow; of how when you could hear the darkness and shouldn't be able to, the chaos knew. So now it was all work-work-work, sleep-sleep-sleep, swallow-swallow-swallow little pills, all in the name of managing the un-normal.

Footsteps thudded up the wooden steps leading to her front door. She lived in an apartment above an old garage that had once been an even older stable. Horses had lived down below, and where she now stood, in her bare feet and pale cream cotton pajamas, haystacks had sat, waiting to be pitched to hungry mouths. Or spread under heavy hooves. Or rolled in by horny teenagers. Little dead boys and girls, all rotten teeth and faded curls.

The secret knock came, rap-a-tat-tatta-tat, and Helen dashed to the locks. She undid the deadbolt, the push lock, and she stroked the worn place where once had been a chain. She couldn't have chains anymore. What if she caught fire? What if she went tumbling down? Daddy worried. Daddy cared. And so, Daddy said no chains, and he sent her Mercutio.

"Afternoon tea, pretty lady!" Mercutio said, his voice a rich boom. "We're going all high society today." He shouldered aside the door and waltzed in with a serving tray. It was the one with the rose vines and the baby cherubs.

"Is it green?" Helen asked, fisting her shirt into knots. She didn't drink black tea or eat dark food. The darkness beyond the veil was everywhere, and it would climb into her if it could. It meant she could hear it better, but it also meant at some point it would leave, and the chaos would scream through her.

"It is," Mercutio said, standing tall in his jeans and his purple shirt and his scarf that made no sense. It was hot, today, not cold, but Mercutio had rainbows around his neck, the knot to one side of his chin. When he smiled — and his smile was big and bold and white-white against his beautifully dark skin — the knot moved, and the rainbows were just part of him.

"Sugar?" Helen stepped closer to the low table and the tray.

"Who do you think you're talking to?" Mercutio took the top off the sugar pot and showed that it was full.

"Thank you," Helen murmured.

Mercutio waved a hand and swept up the dishes from her breakfast that morning. "You skinny thing. You need the calories. You eat, and it all just dissolves." Mercutio sighed on his way to the little kitchen tucked into the next room. "Some of us ain't so lucky. I've got candy that I ate when I was thirteen hanging around on my hips." He paused and picked up one foot, wiggling his toes in his flip-flops. "And I think that apple pie is still lingering down there somewhere. Oh, well." He ducked through the crystal bead curtain. "It was tasty, I swear."

"You're beautiful, Tio," Helen whispered.

"You say something, sweetness?" Mercutio called.

Helen didn't answer, snatching up her teacup and tiptoeing to the curtains. She heard water run, dishes clink, and without looking, she knew precisely when Mercutio stuck his head around the doorjamb. He always heard when she didn't say something for too long, and he always saw her, except when he couldn't see anything because the chaos around her was too thick. "What's outside today?" he asked.

"The garden," Helen answered, and from her ex-horse house, she could see the roses and the hedges and the beds of lilies and daisies and hundreds of other blooms. Butterflies circled and landed on the wheelbarrow near the coil of a garden hose. Even the trees had flowers, the pair of massive magnolias in full glory.

The landscaping swept around the porch, marched out from under the shade of ash and willow and black gum, and they made whirls and pathways behind the house and all the way down to the sidewalk next to the water. There was a white-painted swing and a bridge over a tiny, human-made creek. One entire section of the garden was all purple with bursts of magenta, and that was Helen's favorite. When there was enough light in her to walk beyond her safe walls, she would go there, first. She'd shove her toes in the mulch and smile when she got splinters. She'd swing until the darkness drove her inside.

"Andrew out doing his thing?" Mercutio asked from the kitchen.

Monica's son was pacing along the edges of the landscaping, a jet pack on his back and a cutting blade on a long arm in his hands. "Yes," Helen answered, listening to the growl of the weedeater.

"He's like family, huh?" Mercutio asked absently, putting a plate away in the cabinet next to the short, squat fridge.

"We're connected but not related," Helen said, forgetting for a moment what Mercutio knew.

"Mmhm," Mercutio agreed. "Monica and Andrew have been around for years enough that it's hard to see life without them."

Helen glanced over her shoulder at the bows and arrows the cupids aimed at unmarked hearts on the tea tray. She thought they'd had this conversation before. She wondered if they had it every day, and Mercutio was simply too kind to say anything.

Mercutio's head appeared around the doorway again. "Well? Go on. What else is out there?"

"I can see the water." Helen rested her head on the cool glass. Longing for her mother choked her. She swallowed a gulp of air, blew it out, and fogged the glass. "I've seen fishing boats and a houseboat and a barge, so far."

"You see any pirate ships?"

Helen yanked herself away from the window to frown at Mercutio. Hot tea splashed on her hand. It hurt. "Of course not," she said, licking up the drops.

"Dang." Mercutio grinned at her, and his feet did a dance step, one behind the other — *quick-quick*. "I'd love to tango myself up with some pirates."

Helen saw Mercutio in rags and belted-on swords swabbing decks, climbing rigging, and strutting around with a knife between his teeth. "Do you want to dance with them, fight with them, or love with them?" she asked.

Mercutio's laugh rang silver. "All of the above, sweet lady. Oh – *all* – of the above."

"Huh." Helen wandered to the window on the other side of the door. The curtains over it were blue, and she'd made them, too, but not with knitting needles. These she had done with a bucket and dye that had turned her as blue as the night sky for a week after she was through. "I've never thought about pirates."

"You too busy thinking more important things." Mercutio finished in the kitchen and came into the living room. He started sorting through magazines and catalogs that were stacked on the table in the corner. "You done with these?"

Helen shrugged. The magazines didn't matter, but the rest did. Mercutio was right. Pirates had no place in her head, because her head was full of the knowledge the darkness gave her. She'd understand everything so clearly – her part, their part, the other worlds and what they needed and what had happened – but then the chaos would come for her. She'd lay down and pull the covers over her head and spend days feeling too small to matter.

Head beginning to ache, Helen rubbed her face. When she opened her eyes, Mercutio had taken up position at the other window. He had a *Vogue* under one muscled arm. "Now, I know you see everything out these windows, miss pretty, so you tell me," Mercutio's so-black-they-were-blue eyes flicked to Helen and then out the window. "You see anyone new?"

"I do. I have." Helen nodded.

"Mmhm, me, too. What's your take on the new guy?"

Helen swung her gaze to the main house. Her view was of the north and east sides of the Taylor Point House, and she could watch all three floors. The ground floor patio tables were unoccupied. They were white and heavy and uncomfortable for sitting. The second floor portico rocking chairs moved with the breeze, like they were occupied by spirits happy to have the place to themselves. The drapes on the second and third floor hallway windows were drawn open, and all day long, since the mysterious minivan had arrived, Helen had watched an unfamiliar boy pass back and forth.

"He's not a guest," Helen said. She knew all the regulars and the passersby, and she knew the differences between the two. The regulars had routines, and they were quiet people, keeping their business to themselves. Right now, the Snapdragon Suite was occupied by Ms. Adlewilde, who liked the library most of the time, except when she'd escape to the porch for a single, daily cigarette. She'd smoke it slowly, legs crossed at the knees and eyes closed. She only took supper with the rest of the house on Sundays, though she and Miss Teedee liked to chat over breakfast. Miss Teedee didn't mind Ms. Adlewilde's habit of adding champagne from a flask to her orange juice. And Ms. Adlewilde didn't mind the way Miss Teedee would rather ask questions than answer them.

Mr. Kirkland was in the Magnolia Room, and he liked the chess tables on the porch outside the rear parlor. He'd play both sides of the board, making a move, sitting a while, getting up, and doing the same thing in the opposite chair. He wore hats and suits, would only pet small dogs, and he couldn't abide children. He would leave when they came around, though he would have dinner with the rest of the house almost every night, screaming toddlers or no. He never came down for breakfast, though. Helen wasn't sure Mr. Kirkland ever saw the day before the far side of noon.

"I didn't think he was staying here," Mercutio said. "I think he's Monica's new help. Strange choice, if you ask me; think he was a member of the wandering homeless."

But Helen hadn't asked, and she couldn't say what she knew to be true: that the choice hadn't been Monica's or Andrew's or Miss Teedee's or even Daddy's, really. The choice had been made by gods of other worlds. Or maybe the Universal God, the one that put people and places together for purpose. Whoever had done it, this was a sign. It was *the* sign – the one the darkness sang to her about in a child's sing-song rhyme, spoken in a language she shouldn't know but understood:

When seven come together
They can heal the seven, worlds apart
Before darkness falls forever, they must
Find and reclaim the heart.

A simple little poem, but it stayed with Helen when so many other facts and faces didn't. "I've seen him cleaning," Helen said, out of breath from the importance of it all and shaking too much to drink her tea. "And taking out the trash. But before that, he followed Monica around."

Mercutio snorted. "Getting the grand tour, I'm sure. Lord, I wouldn't want to work for Miss Martyr. Maybe somebody should warn him to get out before he gets gotten."

"No!" Helen yelled, and her teacup hit the rug, bounced, and slung tea on the front door. "Oh," she gasped, hands over her heart and feet trying to take her anywhere but there.

"It's okay, sweetness." Mercutio snatched a towel out of his pocket and bent to mop up the mess. "You'd drunk most of it bone dry, and the cup didn't come to any harm."

"He can't leave," Helen said. No sooner had the words escaped than Mercutio's expression went soft and hard at the same time. Mercutio wasn't cruel or impatient, and he seemed genuinely to like Helen, unlike so many others who couldn't cope with her darkness.

But Mercutio was a man divided. He was a nurse. People were well or unwell. The sky was up, and the earth was down. One world, one reality, and nothing in the way between.

However, Mercutio was also an artist. He drew things in the sketch pad he thought he kept hidden that Helen recognized. The darkness had shown her similar things – creatures, worlds, that magenta light. And when he'd had a bit to drink – which was so rare to be almost never – and when Helen grew brave enough to ask about his drawings, about what he'd seen in his dreams, for a little while, it was as though he believed Helen. Believed her when she spoke of other worlds and the need to save them.

It never lasted. And Helen understood why. It drove her mad to hold two realities at the same time. It cost her so much, and it took more each day. Mercutio couldn't afford to lose himself like that. He had to carry on and fulfill his purpose, even when the rest of them were incapacitated.

"Now, why's that, honeybunch?" Mercutio asked, pretending to believe every word out of Helen's mouth while Helen pretended not to notice he pretended. "Why does he have to stay?"

Helen chewed on her lip. She'd been waiting an eternity for the sign; she'd been waiting for so long, she'd begun to worry she couldn't tell a sign from a lamp. It had been long enough that she'd begun to wonder if everyone was right, and she was, in fact, crazy. Maybe the darkness hadn't spoken at all. Maybe she'd made it all up. And the worst part was when she started to believe that she was as insane as everyone said, she couldn't hear the darkness anymore, and that, of course, was what the chaos was waiting for. And then she'd despair and wake up to fog outside and inside, and she'd scream until Tio came, with that hard-soft look in his starry eyes. He'd put ice in her veins that froze her in place. Helen would close her eyes.

Sleeping, sleeping, sleeping... swallowing, swallowing, swallowing...

"I need to tell him a story," Helen mumbled, but she didn't know which one. Across the lawn, the new boy stood in the Hydrangea Room's bay window. The panes framed him, and though Helen could see little more than his shape, Helen knew who he was. And he would listen to the story she chose – to all her stories that weren't stories at all. He would believe her. He *had* to.

Mercutio appeared at Helen's elbow holding a pill bottle and some water in a pink glass. "Good enough reason by me. Your stories are beautiful, sweetness. Which one you going to tell him? The tale of the hippo? Or the one about the little girl who is also a star?"

Helen got sucked into a painted memory of herself, much younger, in an apartment much neater and wider and brighter. She was sitting at a desk with a pen in her hand, and her clothes weren't pajamas or hospital gowns. There was a pear in a bowl with teeth marks and a hunk missing, and Helen could taste the fruit. It'd been sweet and sour. "What... what did I do?" Helen muttered, stepping out of the painting and putting it where it belonged: behind her. "What do you mean, hippos and stars?"

Mercutio set down the medicine and water and swept out of the room and through the hanging lace that lead into Helen's bedroom. He came out holding two flat, hardback books, their covers satin-shiny. "See?" He held up one, and it had a picture of a little hippo with a red bow. He held up another a girl that seemed to glow from within. "You wrote these. They're children's books, and they're adorable."

"No." Helen touched the glossy cover and pushed the deer book toward Mercutio's chest.

"Sure you did, and they most definitely are cute. Especially the little star girl. What's her name, again?"

For an instant, Helen couldn't say the girl's name because the girl had two names, and she couldn't remember which one was real. A lump rose in Helen's throat, the responsibility of what she was supposed to do far too big for her narrow shoulders, and when she glanced at the hotel, the boy in the windows had vanished.

Sometimes she wanted the fog to find her. Let its teeth sink in and make all the responsibility – the knowledge – go away. "I... I don't..."

"No worries, doll," Mercutio soothed. "We'll read the book later, and you'll remember." He tucked the books under his arm along with the magazine. He unscrewed the top of Helen's pill bottle and spilled one yellow mystery into his palm.

Helen frowned. "Have we... have we done this before?"

Mercutio's eyebrows went up. "Mid-day pills? Honey, this little ritual is our thing. Meds every day keep the monsters at bay, remember?"

"No, not that."

"Well, what, then?"

"This conversation." Helen snatched the medicine and swallowed it without water in frustration. The pills didn't do anything. Made her tired, maybe, or made it harder to keep the worlds' boundaries straight, but that was it. Everyone thought the chaos had to do with chemicals in her head or events in her childhood or tragedies in the more recent past. When she'd tried to tell the people she loved and the professionals the loved ones trusted that the imbalance came from another world and that she straddled the line between this reality and that one, the family and doctors and the medical students and the head-shrinkers had collectively stepped away from Helen, opting to medicate her more and listen to her less. "Have we spoken about the little star girl before?"

"We talk about a lot of things more than once, pretty."

Mercutio was considerate and cautious, and that made Helen angry. It made her think he was afraid, or, worse yet, tired of her. She grabbed him by the rainbow tail. "Tell me of when we first spoke of her. Of it. The book."

After studying Helen for a long, silent moment, Mercutio sighed and patted Helen's clenched fist where it dangled from his scarf. "Okay, but you get upset, and it's another pill and quiet time, understood?"

Helen nodded, letting go of Mercutio. She crossed her arms and tried to listen so hard that she wondered if she could transform into a full-bodied ear.

Mercutio leaned against the wall next to the lilac lace. "One of the first little chats we had after the how-do-you-do was over was about other worlds and creatures. You'd written one book, already – the one about the hippo that had adventures."

"Before Mother," Helen whispered. A shiver of grief slithered through her insides.

"That's right," Mercutio agreed, tenderly. "But when we met, you went on and on about a little girl who was a star who was lost and needed to make her way back to the sky. You were trying to write her story, and to help, we painted some pictures for the book. It would have been... Well, I was with Rob, then. He joined us once or twice, though I told him to stay away from me at work." Mercutio huffed. " I kicked his butt to the curb soon after, and aren't we all glad that little narcissist is gone?"

"Yes," Helen whispered.

"Amen," Mercutio said. "Anyway, you remember painting?"

Helen squinted into the part of the past labeled "Two Point Five Years Ago When Tio Was with the Man of Many Faces." It was blurry with chaos and the medication to stunt it. She looked and looked, but she didn't see a sign of herself with brush in hand and canvas before her.

Helen shook her head. "No."

"You did," Mercutio insisted brightly. "And we even put enough of them together that you had your book. They changed some things, hired in other talent to smooth the edges, but... You did it, pretty!"

"I did," Helen said, but she didn't remember.

"Mmhm. Now, not all of the pictures... Well. Not all of them could go into the book for the little ones. Some of them were too dark. The girl star and graves and a swirling darkness chasing her heels." Mercutio clucked his tongue. "Daddy Darryl didn't know what to think."

"I didn't mean to upset anyone," Helen said.

"Of course you didn't, pretty lady. But not all specimens of humanity are down with the eccentric among us." He paused, and his tone grew distant, as though it was going for a walk way ahead on the path. "He kept saying some of it looked like his nightmares."

"Nightmares?" Helen said sharply. "Daddy said he had nightmares?"

"Sure, honey. We all have 'em."

"You have nightmares?" Helen asked.

"Oh yes, sweetness, but don't you worry none. My bad dreams are just a big ol' jar of nothing. It's kind of comforting, in its own way."

Helen could see the king of nightmares in her mind, and she could see the swirling darkness.

"Nothing," Helen whispered, a plan taking shape.

"What's going on with you?" Mercutio asked.

And when the darkness had form, that form was, "Nothing," she said again.

"Okay, sugar pie." Mercutio crossed his arms and smiled like he was teasing. "Then where you going?"

Helen looked up and saw she stood under the arch of her bedroom doorway. Strands of lace tickled her face. "I'm going..." Helen turned and flew to the standing wardrobe in the far corner. "...to get ready for dinner."

"Come again?" Mercutio walked into the bedroom and flopped on the bed, one knee bent and the other foot on the floor.

"I want to tell a story at dinner."

Mercutio narrowed his eyes. "The star girl?"

"A little about stars, but also about... nothing." Helen flung clothing that reeked of cedar and time aside, searching for an outfit that would make her look normal.

"This about the new boy?"

"Yes," Helen said impatiently, yanking out a long, white dress.

"You want to tell a story to Monica's new help?"

"Yes." Helen hooked the hanger over the door of the wardrobe, eyeing it critically. She'd want to look her age, which was confusing, as she was older than she remembered being. Over the hill, but not yet through the woods.

"Why you want to do this, pretty lady?"

Helen heard the undertone of suspicious concern, and she knew she had to tread carefully. One misstep and she'd be drugged and under covers through dinner with her portion of food sitting on a serving tray at her bedside and Mercutio sitting in the wicker chair next to the bed reading a book. Mercutio cared, but that caring could be implacable. "Because..." Helen slowly turned around, hands clasped in front of her so she wouldn't shake, and she firmly planted her feet on the rug so she wouldn't sway to the sound of a world only she seemed to hear. "Because you're right," Helen admitted. "The stories are good, and I can't write them anymore. We both know that. But I could tell them. I *do* tell them. Even when I don't remember it, even when I paint it instead of speak it. So maybe, if I meet this boy and choose a story that he would like, then... he could find a home with us."

"A home," Mercutio repeated.

"You said he didn't have one."

"Mm," Mercutio hummed, agreeing. "And if he doesn't stay?"

Helen made her face form a smile that she desperately wanted to feel and not to fake. "Then we'll know he couldn't handle our crazy."

Mercutio laughed and sighed at her, but Helen could tell her plan had worked for the time being. His expression was all affection. "I can't pretend it all makes sense to me, but here's what I do think: you ain't been down to dinner in weeks, your storyness. So I say, let's get you done up right and then let's get you to the supper table. I think your daddy and Monica and Mister Andrew would be delighted to see you."

"Can you make this dress smell less like death?" Helen asked.

"Oh, but yes." Mercutio swept himself up and off the bed, and he unhooked and swung the dress around himself. "I am a magician with a steam iron and rose water, and we've got a few hours to perform our magic tricks."

"Thank you, Mercutio." Helen clasped her hands over her heart. "Thank you."

Chapter Five

Jason yanked the soiled duster cloth off the end of his cheerfully yellow cleaning wand. He tucked the cloth and the dust bunnies into the trash bin of the rolling cart parked outside the Lily Suite, and he grabbed the bottle of glass cleaner and a rag. He was on his last room, and it was a good thing, too. Jason was dead on his feet.

The hotel had three floors, and Jason had seen them all today on Monica's whirlwind, order-barking tour. The lowest level opened at the back onto the grounds and the garden, and Monica, Andrew, and Darryl had their bedrooms on that floor. There was also a media room and a game room for guests. The rooms on that floor were named after people. The Bridget Game Room was named after Bridget Taylor, who was somebody's grandmother, and the McKinnley Tavern Room was named after a family cousin by marriage. Jason was expected to clean and care for the guest's spaces, as well as the storage room and the office on that floor.

The first floor turned out to be the easiest. When they went up the round staircase to the main floor, he'd wished he had a pen and paper to make notes of everywhere else he was supposed to memorize and manage. There were two parlors, front and rear, the kitchen, the central hall, the receiving room, the library... Jason lost track of the official names. He focused, instead, on carrying the cleaning gear Monica kept throwing at him. There was no elevator, so Monica kept cleaning carts on all three floors, and the things were accidents waiting to happen. The wheels would fall off at odd moments, and they squeaked if not oiled daily. Darryl, both owner and general handyman, was supposed to take care of loose screws, but Monica made it clear that anything involving cleaning or coordinating staff and grounds was more her territory than Darryl's. The boxes of machine parts in his office turned out to be clocks in the process of being rebuilt, or so Monica said in passing, and everywhere they went, Jason could see Darryl's hobby on display. Jason stopped trying to count the number of timepieces when he hit triple-digits, and he made note to get headphones or earplugs as soon as possible, or the ticking was going to drive him batty.

The third floor was where all the bedrooms were, and Jason had listened to the litany of instruction involving linens, curtains, windows, toilets, and bathtubs, and mainly what he had taken away from his crash course training session was clean everything until it begged for mercy and maybe, if Jason was lucky, Monica would be satisfied.

"I'll be taking half of the rooms, you the other," Monica had said, tour complete and empty thermos in hand. "Now, you see that building?" Monica had asked, pointing a blunt nail out the window above the cushioned seat in the Rose room.

There was a two-story garage-type structure surrounded by crape myrtle and sitting northeast of the Taylor Point House. "Yes, ma'am?" Jason had said.

"It's off-limits. You don't have to clean it, do anything with it, or even pretend it's there. We clear?"

Jason had remembered her rule on questions, so he had bit his tongue on asking if that was the tower where they locked away the maiden fair. "Er, yes?"

"Good." Monica had shoved a mop bucket at Jason. "Get to work."

After spending half an hour getting lost and finding the third-floor cart, Jason had gone about his business, pretending he belonged in the hotel in his ratty clothes and yellow gloves. He didn't see a single soul the entire time he trundled from room to room, meticulously dusting knickknacks and vacuuming old rugs. The air conditioning was sweet on his skin, and the cleaner Monica liked smelled of citrus. It was surreal, being worried about food and sitting on a beach one hour and three hours later having a full belly and diving head-first into a jetted tub with a scrubbing sponge, but Jason had done harder, stranger jobs on short notice, for sure. Scoring drugs for the band, selling catheter kits for men in that god-awful telemarketing job, and smuggling goods into Canada were all notches on Jason's resume that he didn't like to mention unless pressed. And none of his work experience had fed him half as well.

Some hours later, when the last of the cleaning streaks came off the mirror with one final swipe of the rag, Jason jumped when a sharp knock rapped on the open hotel room's door. "You in here?" Monica called.

"Yes, ma'am."

Jason stood at attention until Monica appeared, her hair piled on top of her head with a bunch of metal clips. She held out a bottle of water, and Jason took it. "Thanks," he said, cracking the cap and drinking.

Monica surveyed the room and ran a finger along the edge of a TV stand. "Did you get the baseboards?"

"Yes."

"Toilets?"

"I have visited every toilet today, ma'am."

Monica gave him a look. "Did you eat lunch?"

Jason hesitated. When he'd gotten hungry around one, he'd snuck downstairs into the kitchen to find the food put away, the guests gone, and nobody around. As quietly as he could, Jason had opened the fridge, taken a few pastries from under wrappings, and scarfed them, guiltily eyeballing the door the entire time. "I did, but I wasn't sure if I should..."

"Should what?"

"Pay?"

Monica put her hands on her hips. "What, do you think we'll beat you for feeding yourself?"

No, Jason thought. Throw him out, call him a thief, or make him feel like a beggar, maybe, but not beat him. "Worse things have happened," he said.

"Well, not around here." Monica crumpled her empty plastic bottle and dug into her pocket. She pulled out a wad of cash tied in half by a rubber band. She stuffed the money into Jason's outstretched hand.

"What's this?" Jason asked quietly, fear and disappointment surging through him and making him queasy.

"It's your wages."

Jason took stock of the money's heft. "Are you paying me off?"

Monica stared at Jason. "It's complicated around here."

"It seems pretty nice?"

"More complicated than it seems, then."

"I think that's how it usually goes, ma'am." Sweat trickled from his armpit to his side, and he repressed a shiver.

"We're got plenty of problems and troubles."

"I understand," Jason said. "You want me to go?"

"Do you want to stay?" Monica countered.

"I'd like to."

"Why?"

Jason hesitated, and Monica scowled. "Because," Jason said hastily. "I've... I like the..." He sighed. He knew to this family, he was a drifter off the beach, no more reliable than any other visitor passing through. But he liked it here, in this house of moderate insanity, and he was tired and weary and sweating. "I've not had people for a really long time," Jason said softly. "It was nice, today. Feeling like I had people. Folks who gave a shit, who made me not want to fuck it all up. I tried today, and I'm not sure when the last time I fucking..." Jason realized he was cussing at the last second. "Sorry."

Monica's eyes were bright in her otherwise expressionless face. "That money's for the week. You leave without warning, don't ever come back."

"Yes, ma'am," Jason said humbly, wanting to crumple to the tile and sit for a while.

"Fine." Monica screwed herself taller and more rigid. "I'm going to take you to meet Andrew. You will not give him one iota of trouble."

"No, ma'am."

Monica nodded, evidently satisfied, but she didn't immediately stalk off and expect Jason to traipse along behind. "Andrew's different, but he's my boy."

Judith had been different, too, and Rage not exactly normal. Jason could cope. "Okay."

Together, they rolled the cart down the hallway, past the central staircase, and into a closet where the cart lived. Monica showed him how to lock all the wheels, and Jason gathered up the trash bags.

"Take it down the rear staircase to the ground floor and over to the dumpsters. I'll meet you."

"Okay," Jason agreed. He opened the wrong door on the first try to find the back hallway, but he got it right on the second attempt. Even though the wallpaper and decorations in the hotel were strange and stranger, he was grateful that they were all so different. It made it harder to lose his way.

Outside, the air was still muggy, and late afternoon clouds were rolling in. Jason trotted down the steps off the side porch and crossed the path to the parking lot and boat access. The big green dumpster was mostly empty, and the bags rang the metal sides when Jason tossed them through the sliding door. He shoved it shut when he was done, wiping his hands on his shorts and jogging around a bay window to the ground-floor entrance. A stained-glass pane sparkled when he swung the door open, and the washing machines hummed in the laundry room to his left. He passed a hallway leading to an emergency exit, and he shivered. It was cool and grey inside the house, and quiet like an attentive mother rocking her children through their naptime.

Monica stood at the base of the main stairwell. "Dinner is at seven every night," she said, leading Jason to yet another door and opening it for him. "It's for guests and staff, and to join the guests in the dining room, you'd best be clean and well dressed."

They stood in a narrow, dark hallway lit only by a door at the other end, which was wide open and swinging on silent hinges in the faint outdoor breeze. Jason spotted shoes lined up in a tidy line along the wall, and there was a row of hooks holding up coats and hats. "I don't have a lot of good clothes."

Monica's lips twitched like she fought a smile. "I figured. You can get some later in town, but if you can't dress the part or get your job done and get cleaned up in time, you can eat in the kitchen. Miss Teedee does most of the cooking, though Jennifer's lending more of a hand, now. That's the waitress. Sweet thing but dumb. She's just part-time. All Miss Teedee really does is meddle, cook and bake and start all over again, so you can help her out, especially on nights when the Solarium is open to the public."

"Okay." Jason glanced at the single shut door off the hallway. "Is this..."

Monica glared at the start of a question, and she knocked smartly on the door. "Honey?" she called sweetly. "It's me. I've got someone for you to meet."

After a few seconds of utter silence, music split the air with a deafening screech. It cut off so abruptly that Jason didn't have time to name the tune, and the bedroom door opened in the next instant.

Jason's first impression was that if he ever wanted to build major muscle, screw the gym and hand Jason the hedge trimmers.

Andrew was big. Only a little shorter than Jason, wide, built, and, currently at least, bare-chested and breathing heavily. A pair of headphones rested around his corded neck. He had on jeans, but the button fly was mostly undone, revealing a pair of white briefs beneath.

"Hi, Mama," Andrew said, completely unflustered and utterly focused on Monica. Andrew had a voice to match his size, deep and drawling, and he was older than Jason thought a son of Monica's would be. Andrew was at least Jason's age. He had lighter skin than his mother, though it was darkened almost maroon in a mean outdoorsman's tan. His hair was a shock of brown on top of a square head, and it matched all the rest of the hair Jason could see. Jason studied the wall's paper pattern with intense scrutiny.

"Andrew, get your clothes on," Monica said dully.

"Oh." Andrew looked down like he hadn't been aware his body was there until that second. "Oh," he said again, shut the door, and reappeared a few seconds later with fastened jeans and while pulling on a t-shirt.

"Better," Monica said.

"Hi," Andrew repeated to Monica, tugging the shirt into place.

"Were you dancing?"

"Yeah." Andrew smiled.

Monica returned the smile like she couldn't help herself. "Thought so." She put a hand on Jason's arm, and the hair stood on end at the touch. "This is Jason Hart. He needs to use your shower to get clean, and he'll be sleeping on your couch at night."

As Jason wondered at Monica's careful specifics, Andrew turned to Jason for the first time. Andrew's eyes were brown, and there seemed to be somebody home in there. "Okay," Andrew said.

"Good boy," Monica said. She let go of Jason. "Come on up to dinner when you're done getting clean, all right?"

"Okay, Mama."

"Don't be late." And with that, Monica whirled and was gone, leaving Jason in the hallway with Andrew staring at him.

"Hey," Jason said.

"Hi," Andrew replied.

Jason gestured beyond Andrew. "Is the shower in there somewhere?"

"Oh." Andrew seemed sheepish, and he stood aside. "Oh. Yeah."

"Okay then," Jason mumbled, nodding at Andrew as Jason stepped past him into the room. It was to be Jason's room, too, he guessed, and it wasn't a bad one. It was at least eighteen feet on the longest side. There was a bricked-up fireplace with a mantel covered in toy cars, photographs, pink flamingo figurines, and one Batman action figure still in the box. There was an unmade bed in the far right corner, and it was covered in record albums. A stereo system and speakers that were anything but modern, but that could probably blow roofs off buildings, took up most of the wall across from the door.

"Nice place," Jason said politely.

"Thanks," Andrew replied.

Jason wandered to the couch, which was a long, squat, plaid thing against the left wall, and it was clear of clutter except for, and Jason had to blink to make sure he wasn't seeing things, a yellow rubber ducky perched on the central cushion.

"That's Ralph," Andrew said.

"Who is?"

Andrew walked over and scooped up the duck. "Ralph," he said, gesturing to the toy. "We were dancing."

"Uh-huh."

"You dance?" Andrew asked, petting the duck's head with a thumb.

"Not so much," Jason said, praying that Andrew wasn't about to make the duck "talk" or anything like that. He eased away from Andrew toward what he thought was the bathroom. "Is there a towel or something I could use?"

"Oh." Andrew considered. "Oh, yeah. In there." He pointed toward the door at Jason's back.

"Thanks." Jason ducked into the bathroom and locked himself in it. The room was small, with a window above the tub-shower combo, black shower curtain, pedestal sink, and toilet. There were shelves hung at weird intervals on the walls, and they had everything on them from toothpaste to flamingoes to a picture of Keith Richards.

"Sure," Jason muttered to himself. "Why not?"

Blowing a sigh, Jason stripped and stepped over the lip of the shower. The tile was black with white grout, and the floor around the shower was sealed concrete covered in a black rug. The water came on in a shock of arctic ice, and Jason cussed. He should have known better, and he squeezed himself into the furthest nook until steam started to roll. The temperature seemed to have only those two settings: frigid or boiling. Jason made do, helping himself to shampoo and body wash. He had his own stuff, but his bag was in the van, and he hadn't thought about grabbing it before meeting Monica. Jason hadn't exactly walked through the front door thinking he'd be moving in, but he hadn't lasted this long as a modern nomad by turning away decent gigs when he found them. Or when they found him, as it were. Sleeping on that couch was going to be a damned sight better than on the thin, foam egg crate thing he had in his van. The idea of shutting his eyes in an air-conditioned room while resting on cushions was almost enough to make Jason drool on himself. And this water, though temperamental, was clean and clear and got hot when he cranked the knob in that direction. There was a real roof over his head and more food and steady cash flow in his future. What was a roommate with a duck fetish stacked up against all that?

When Jason shut off the water, he heard the rumble coming through the wall. Jason toweled himself dry and regretted his lack of clean shorts. Clean anything, really. So much for dinner with the rest of the house, tonight. He'd eat in the kitchen and help Miss Teedee, and that wouldn't be so bad.

Jason put his jeans back on, wincing at the smell of his shirt, and he stepped out of the bathroom to find Andrew was in nothing but his undershorts, shaking his ass to music being piped in from the stereo to his headphones. His eyes were closed, his body doing that loose-but-controlled thing that people who knew how to move often had, and he spun, stepped in rhythm, and mouthed lyrics that only he could hear. Jason thought he should be uncomfortable, but he couldn't quit watching. Andrew had an innocence to him that made Jason want to hang around, not run for the hills. Jason didn't know much about dance. His experience was limited to hitting up the occasional club or catching the odd dancing reality TV show that Judith had watched in their hotel rooms. From what little Jason did know, though, he thought Andrew might be pretty good. He seemed completely in his element, lost to the beat that was vibrating the sheetrock.

A twirl, a backward sliding step, and Andrew opened his eyes and grinned at Jason. "Hey!" Andrew yelled breathlessly.

Jason waved, not bothering to bellow, and Andrew frowned at him. "You need to borrow something?" Andrew called.

Jason held up his hands, indicating that he'd be fine, but Andrew was already stalking toward the narrow door near the bed. The cord on the headphones stretched, and Jason lunged and held the plug in place so it wouldn't get yanked out of the jack. Andrew's headphones came flying off when he reached the closet door, and he spun around, staring down at them where they landed on the floor. "Oh," he said, and he laughed, big and goofy. "Oh. Whoops."

"Little rough on the equipment, man," Jason said.

"Yeah. It is," Andrew agreed.

"How are you not deaf?" Jason asked.

"I am," Andrew said, staring at Jason.

"You... huh?"

"A little." Andrew shrugged. "Mama says it's hearing loss. I've had it all my life. So I hear people better when I can see their mouths." Andrew opened the closet and started digging through a rack of shirts that was bowing under the weight.

"I really don't need anything," Jason said, putting the headphones on top of the record player cover and hitting the red master power switch. "I've got stuff in my—"

"Here." Andrew tossed Jason a brown shirt covered in comma-shaped paisley.

"I don't—" Jason began, but he had to catch the pants that followed. "There's no way I could wear these, man."

"Why?" Andrew asked, throwing more clothes onto his bed. A shirt and jeans for himself, Jason assumed.

"I don't think we're the same size," Jason said patiently.

"Oh." Andrew grinned. "Oh. You're skinny, but those are from when I was a kid. They'll fit."

Jason inspected the soft clothing in his arms. It was supple and a few grades up from the Wal- Mart brand. "You still have shit you had when—"

"Don't swear." Andrew's mouth set in a thunderous thin line, and he froze in place like he'd stumbled upon a dead body.

"Sorry."

Andrew eyed Jason warily and circled the room in a wide arch, heading for the bathroom. "I've been tall since I was twelve."

Jason stepped out of Andrew's way. "Yeah, don't meet too many guys who are up here with me."

Andrew cocked his head. "I'm not up anywhere with you. I'm over here with me."

"Yeah, I... I know. I just meant... tall, man. I meant tall."

"Oh." Andrew's frown faded. "Oh! Yeah. That's why those'll fit."

"Well, I'll give them a try, I guess. Thanks."

Andrew's shoulders sank. "Good. I like that shirt. It has flowers. You like flowers, right?"

"Sure." Jason would have liked devils roasting puppies on pitchforks if it got Andrew into the bathroom and Jason out of this conversation.

"I knew you were cool." The smile came back. "I'm going to take a shower, and then we'll go to dinner, like Mama said, okay?"

"Sounds like a plan."

"Okay." Andrew nodded, and when he'd disappeared, Jason breathed a sigh of relief. He tore off his dirty shirt and shorts and slipped into the long-sleeved shirt. It hung down far enough, which was awesome because usually shirts hit him wrong, and it wasn't too big for him. The pants, which weren't jeans, exactly, but something more like linen, were the same. A little loose, maybe, but with the shirttails over the waist, nobody would be able to tell.

"Huh," Jason muttered to himself. Fed, sheltered, worked, and clothed all in the same day. That settled it, then, Jason thought. Any second now, he'd wake up in a hospital bed with an ugly old nurse telling him that everybody was dead, but he was going to keep on living whether he liked it or not.

Jason wadded his clothes up and dropped them in front of the couch. In the bathroom, the shower ran, and Andrew was singing. He danced much better than he sang, and Jason winced through broken notes and bad pitch, taking a slower tour of the room. The guy definitely had a thing for flamingoes. And Batman wasn't the only superhero on-premises. Jason found an open plastic bin full of X Men and Transformers. He put a Bumblebee back together again and idly dusted a bookshelf with his palm. Most of the novels were missing covers and shelved upside down, but Jason recognized *Curious George* and *Alice in Wonderland,* among other children's classics.

Band posters covered the walls, all of them in black frames. Rolling Stones, Pink Floyd, Led Zeppelin, Aerosmith; it was only rock and roll, but Andrew definitely liked it. When Jason got to the bed, he slid his fingers across record album covers. Most of them were old 'Stones records. Jason sat down and gently shuffled the albums into a pile. Motown, eighties hairband, Slayer, Guns 'n Roses...

"Jesus," Jason whispered. Judith would have died right there at the sight of these. She had a nice collection of vinyl, herself, but these were priceless.

"They were Papa's," Andrew said.

Jason jumped, so engrossed with flipping through LPs that he'd not heard the water stop or Andrew emerge. "These were your dad's?" Jason asked.

"Yeah." Andrew hitched the towel higher around his waist and rubbed a smaller towel against his head, drying his hair. "They're all I have of his. He's dead."

"Sorry," Jason said.

"I didn't kill him," Andrew said with a shrug.

A shiver raced along Jason's spine. "Did somebody else? Kill him?"

"Some*thing* else," Andrew said, voice muffled. "He got hit by a train."

"You're kidding me?"

Andrew came out from under the towel. "Why would I?"

"God, that's awful. I'm sorry."

"Don't apologize to me. I didn't get hit. Apologize to him when you see him."

Jason's fingers flexed on the stack of records. "I thought you said he was dead?"

"He is."

"Then how would I see him?"

Andrew paused near the bed, contemplative. "I don't know. So if you do, tell me. Papa would be in the wrong place, and that would be bad." Andrew dropped the towel, reaching for his jeans.

"Jesus, man, cut that out," Jason complained, getting up to give Andrew all the space he needed for his naked junk.

"What?"

"Ground rules, okay?" Jason said, loudly so Andrew would be sure to hear. "No walking around bare-butt naked."

"Oh."

Jason waited for it and mouthed the second, "Oh!" along with Andrew.

"Sorry," Andrew said. "I've never had a roommate before."

"It's all right," Jason called. "Now you know."

"Anything else I should know?" Andrew asked.

Jason turned around with his eyes shut. "Let's start with the no nudity rule and see where we go from there."

"Sure." Andrew paused. "Should I dance in clothes, too?"

"Yes. Definitely."

"Okay," Andrew said cheerfully. "You can look, now."

Jason opened his eyes and confirmed Andrew was in jeans and shirt. Jason walked over to the bed to put the albums back where they had been. "Your dad liked music, huh?"

"Mama says he played with the Rolling Stones."

"No fuc—freaking way!"

Andrew crossed his arms and scuffed his shoe. "It could have happened. It's what she says. He came through town on break from the band. They made love like people who care about each other do. He left her the records but had to leave us."

"And you buy that?" Jason asked before he remembered who he was talking to.

"What do you mean?" Andrew asked.

"You believe her?"

"It's my mama," Andrew said, but he chewed his lip.

"But...?" Jason prompted.

Andrew looked left and right and stepped so close to Jason that if Jason hadn't seen Andrew coming and didn't think Andrew acted like someone who could hurt anybody on purpose, it would have made him seriously nervous. "Ever since I grew up, I've thought maybe Papa was just a huge jerk who didn't love Mama the way he should have loved her. And the records weren't his, but Mama's, all along, or maybe somebody else's, but I listen to the band every day when I work just in case there's something of my Papa in the music that I need to hear."

Jason rocked his weight onto his heels, giving himself some breathing room without flinching away from Andrew. "I didn't know my father, either."

Andrew's eyes shone. "You didn't?"

"No, not my real one, and it's good, you know? That you've got the music he liked. Or that somebody liked. It's a place to start and not a bad dead end if that's all it ever is."

Andrew's expression grew curious. "Do you like music?"

"Yeah. I toured with a band."

"Which one?"

"Judith's Hell."

"Are they a rock band?" Andrew asked, his sober expression kind of adorable in that kid brother sort of way.

"Metal," Jason said.

"Do they have records?"

"They have CDs."

"I can play those, too!" Andrew grinned. "I like you."

The swift, easy affection tried to knock Jason off his feet. "Thanks, man. You, too." Jason made a show of stepping toward the door. "Shouldn't we get up to dinner?"

Andrew turned to the clock on the wall with the oversized Roman numerals. "We should," he agreed. "I'm hungry."

"Me, too." Jason slipped into his shoes, and Andrew hopped on alternating feet, putting on a pair of loafers with no laces. When they walked out the room, Andrew locked both the door into the bedroom and the door at the end of the hallway heading outside. It reminded Jason of the way he triple-checked the Odyssey's power locks before even thinking about shutting his eyes at night, and it made a knot of worry inside Jason start to unwind.

On their way up the curving staircase, Andrew babbled about bands and songs and Miss Teedee's lemon bars. Andrew seemed to love all of them equally, which made Jason's stomach rumble in anticipation. The thing was getting greedy with all this consistency, and the scents of fresh food that struck him when they reached the main level central hall were intoxicating. The tables in the hall had been covered with creamy cloths that matched the maroon-and-ivory wallpaper in the dining room, and they were laden with coffee and tea and cups. The glass-paned doors leading into the dining room were open, and the brass chandelier flickered above the enormous table. Each place had been set with linen napkins in shiny metal holders, goblets and glasses, and china in alternating complicated and simple patterns, the colors, again, were red and tan. It was all so coordinated that Jason hesitated, not wanting to get too close and disturb the picture.

"Oh, oh!" Andrew said, stepping directly next to Jason, and Jason managed not to flinch this time.

"See, people can gather to drink stuff in the hall?" Andrew explained. "And then we all get plates and serve ourselves in the kitchen. Sometimes Miss Teedee will get all fancy-schmancy and serve us instead, but most times, we buffet like Buffet. Just remember to unfold your napkin on your lap and to say our version of Grace before you eat the first bite," Andrew cautioned grimly.

"No problem," Jason said. "Maybe I should go help with the setup."

"Nope," Andrew said, and he grabbed Jason by the wrist and started dragging Jason toward the base of the main stairwell. A well-dressed, white-haired man wearing a suit and using a cane to steady himself stepped off the final riser. "Mister Kirkland!" Andrew called, tugging Jason along. "Have you met Jason Hart?"

"I do not believe I've had the pleasure," said Kirkland, smiling beneath his mustache at Jason.

"Nice to meet you," Jason mumbled, shaking Kirkland's hand.

"Mom hired him," Andrew said proudly.

"Is that so?"

"It is so." Andrew grinned. "He likes music."

Kirkland gave Jason a long, lingering look that seemed to be adding Jason up to the sum of all his parts. "Good to have you on board, then," he said and began making his way toward the dining room.

"Mister Kirkland's nice. Stays here during the summers. He fought in a war, and he collects old photographs of men on beaches."

"He... what?" Jason asked.

"He has dozens of them," Andrew said seriously. "He says he's looking for a particular one, but he won't say which one. Oh, and he digs hats."

"That's—" Jason began, but a hand clapped onto his shoulder and squeezed. Jason whirled in shock, and Darryl dropped his arm and peered up at Jason.

"How'd the first day go, son?" Darryl asked.

"Good," Jason nearly gasped. "Fine."

"Nice to hear it."

"Hi, Darryl," Andrew said.

Darryl hugged Andrew, pounding the bigger, younger man on the back like Andrew was choking on something, but Andrew just laughed, goofy grin in place.

"Let's go claim us some seats, boys, what do you say?"

Andrew looped an arm across Darryl's shoulders as they walked toward the head of the table with Jason following behind them. "Did you know Jason likes music?" Andrew asked excitedly.

"No!" Darryl said with a wink at Jason. "Do tell?"

Content to let Andrew fill Darryl in on any details, Jason ducked through a swinging door near the big bay window at the far end of the dining room. He stepped through a pantry as big as any kitchen he'd ever seen, with deep shelves climbing high up the twelve-foot walls and stacked to the gills with food and supplies. Another swinging door led him directly into Miss Teedee's domain. Miss Teedee was bent over at the fridge, her generous backside bobbing as she reached for trays. A tiny, pretty, auburn-haired girl with bangs that fell into her eyes stood next to Miss Teedee, and she froze at the sight of Jason.

"Honey, take this," Miss Teedee said, rising and handing over a dish to the girl, who squeaked in Jason's direction and made Miss Teedee turn to look.

"Oh, well, hey there, handsome." Miss Teedee wiped her hands on her apron, and the girl darted to the counter, set down the food, and dashed out the door into the Solarium. The glassed-in porch was packed with people sipping wine and drinks and eating finger foods off of tiny white plates. Beyond the Solarium, the tables on the porch were crowded, too, and Jason could hear music coming from hidden speakers, and the faint drone of conversation and humanity mixed in with it.

Miss Teedee sighed and nodded after the scurrying girl. "That'd be Jennifer. She's shy all on her own, but that boyfriend of hers makes her even shyer, if you get my drift."

Jason suspected he knew too well. "What can I do?" he asked.

"Not a thing except go claim a seat, grab a plate, and get on in here to help yourself." Miss Teedee ripped off the apron and hung it on its hook.

Jason glanced back the way he'd come, not exactly eager to return to the roomful of friendly strangers, and Miss Teedee walked around the island and gave Jason's elbow a nudge. "Go on now," she said quietly. "They're no firing squad, and you're no prisoner. Darryl, Monica, and Andrew will do all the talking, I promise." She clucked her tongue. "And it's good to see Andrew's already taking a shine to you."

"Huh?" Jason asked, allowing Miss Teedee to push and encourage Jason into the pantry and toward the dining room door.

"I remember Andrew wearing those clothes when he was thirteen and scrawny and well into his, 'the seventies rocked' stage. That boy, I swear. He never wears anything out or throws anything away. It's a marvel."

"Pretty sure it's hoarding," Jason mumbled, but by then he was awash with Darryl's booming voice. He and Andrew were arguing over the best Police album, while Kirkland looked upon them, mustache twitching in amusement, and Monica stood behind Darryl's chair, one hand on her hip and the other on Darryl's shoulder.

"No!" Andrew wailed, hands in his hair. "Greatest Hits compilations can't be better than the original releases. They don't count!"

"Why not?" Darryl asked, clearly teasing and laughing when Andrew gaped at him.

"Darryl," Miss Teedee admonished. "Stop haranguing the boy."

"Time to eat?" Darryl asked, utterly unapologetic.

"It is."

"Perfect!" Darryl picked up his plate, and Andrew did the same, still bemoaning Darryl's album choice. Jason shoved himself against the wall as Darryl, Monica, Andrew, Kirkland, and Miss Teedee filed by him, all carrying their china dishware like the plates were nothing more important than plastic. Jason gingerly picked up a heavy dish, trudged out of the room, down the hall, and into the kitchen through the main door instead of the one leading through the pantry. Jason brought up the end of the food line, and the smells made his stomach growl in anticipation.

Jennifer bustled from the kitchen to the Solarium, carrying pewter pitchers and wine bottles. Miss Teedee carried a slice of cheesecake on a plate onto the porch, embracing a frail woman with silver hair that fell to her waist. Darryl and Andrew kept up their debate on music, Kirkland filled his plate high with mashed potatoes and green peas and nothing else, and Jason followed Andrew's lead, taking pretty much one of everything. Mashed potatoes swimming under pats of melting butter, chicken breasts, wings, and legs fried golden brown, steaming beans, fried okra, corn on the cob, peas, rolls, cornbread muffins, at least two casseroles that Jason couldn't identify, but did want to try, and that wasn't counting the desserts, which were on a different counter and tidily displayed on silver serving ware. There were even placards indicating that some of the food was allergy-sufferer friendly, gluten-free, or dairy-free.

Humbled by the spread, Jason followed Andrew and Darryl through the line and back into the dining room, intrigued by how everyone treated the Taylor Point House like an extension of home. After everyone except Miss Teedee was seated at the long table, Darryl boomed, "If you will join hands for Grace?" Andrew took Jason's hand, and Jason bowed his head.

"We are grateful for the food and the kinship," Darryl intoned. "We are grateful for the health we have, the blessings bestowed, and the kindnesses shown. When we walk, may we each walk in love. To any and all the benevolent listening, we say amen."

Jason mouthed his amen, and he picked up his fork. Evening guests milled about the central hall, sipping out of teacups and chatting in groups. A few women sat at the far end of the dining table, and a pair of twin blonde girls ran loops through the dining room, pantry, kitchen, central hall, and around again. Nobody seemed concerned about formality or particularly worried about who had paid for what or if anyone would take more than they should. It was more party than business. There were plenty of handshakes, hugs, and friendly hellos to go around, and the only words spoken in a tone even approaching chastising were when Monica reminded Andrew to put the napkin in his lap and to hold the fork properly and not like a shovel.

Jason had never seen anything like dinner at the Taylor Point House. He'd been to parties, gigs, orgies, press events, and drug fests. He'd eaten, drank, smoked, and slept with strangers he'd treated like friends for an hour or for a night, but never with this much hospitality. Growing up, he'd gone to church with Papa Jack every Sunday, and he'd been to a couple family reunions with his adopted father, but those were stiff and cold affairs. You were more likely to get frostbite from the disapproval than you were to get embarrassed by a kiss on the cheek.

Jason inhaled half his food before he forced himself to slow down. Nobody was going to take it away from him if or when they noticed him eating and enjoying it. He was not a stray dog who slept in its food bowl to protect what it had missed the most. When Jason drank his glass of water dry, Andrew slid a new one over. Jason joined the applause that broke out when Miss Teedee came through the pantry door. She laughed a golden trill, and Andrew hopped up to hold her chair. She swept into it like a queen, and she tugged Andrew's head down to kiss his hair before he went back to his seat.

Some piece of Jason wondered if it was all an elaborate show. Nothing could be this easy, no group this accepting, no gifts this freely shared. Where was the catch? It couldn't be that he had to earn his keep. The job was too easy, and this was too magnificent. Was this his hell, being thrown into a house where he wouldn't want for the best in life, only to have it ripped out of his hands when he got comfortable? He poked at his food, his thoughts growing bleak, and he was so lost in the shadows of the fear sprouting from the roots of his hopes that he didn't notice right away when the chatter began to die and the clatter of plates and forks began to still.

"Oh," Andrew said softly to Jason's right. Jason frowned at Andrew's shocked face, and he followed Andrew's stare. "Oh!" Andrew said again, though hushed.

Framed by the warm wood tones of the central hall, a man and a woman approached the dining room. The woman wore a white gown, lace over a sheath underneath, and her long black hair that tumbled in tight curls over her shoulders was shot through with gray. She was pale and slim and pretty, if a little on the frail side. She had a small chest and narrow hips, but her eyes were huge and deep as the dead of night, luminous even at this distance. Her mouth was drawn and tight, and she had a panic grip on her companion's arm, hers linked through his. He was wearing a royal purple suit jacket over a paler lavender shirt with a narrow black tie and shiny black slacks. He had a rainbow silk scarf looped around his waist, and dangling from one earlobe was a long, black feather. Give the man a top hat and cane, and he'd be a shoo-in for a circus ringmaster.

"Hello, house peoples," the man called, oblivious to the way everyone watched them like one or both were about to draw weapons and launch into a killing spree. "How are you all this fine evening?" He grinned like he had a secret.

"Helen," Miss Teedee said affectionately, and she was the first to rise and go greet the pair. She kissed Helen's cheeks. "So good to see you, sweetheart."

"Thanks," Helen mouthed more than said, and she tentatively smiled at Darryl. "Hi, Daddy."

Darryl had tears in his eyes. "Hi, honey. You want to join us for dinner?"

Helen shook her head, but Miss Teedee harrumphed. "Pish posh. I'll get you some cake."

"Mostly, I wanted to meet..." Helen lifted one thin, shaking arm and pointed right at Jason. "You," she said.

The hair on Jason's body wasn't standing on end; now, it was dancing in waves. Rippling electricity bolted through Jason, and his shoulders rocked in an involuntary shiver. The heavy, solid weight of importance bore down on him, and he could not, for the love of riches or peace, tear his eyes away from Helen's. Her gaze was so urgent, it sucked Jason inside, like a whirlpool drawing a victim toward the central current of doom. He wanted to say something, be polite, and do the right thing that would make people stop staring at him because they all were, but his lips and tongue and throat were numb.

"Oh, oh," whispered Andrew, and he squeezed Jason's forearm.

"That's just Jason," Monica interjected, and the weird spell cast by Helen's eyes lessened, but it did not go away. "He's cleaning rooms, here, for a while," Monica continued.

"I met him in town," Miss Teedee said, returning with Helen's cheesecake and another plate with a small slice for the man with Helen.

"Thank you, Miss Teedee, you doll." Helen's companion hugged Miss Teedee.

"Mercutio, you sweet talker. What have you two been up to, showing up here in the finery?"

"Well, what's dinner without a little class?" Mercutio answered, playfully swishing the scarf around his middle. "The lovely lady wanted to come down and see y'all, meet the new member of the indentured servitude family, and maybe... even..." Mercutio gave a meaningful glance at Helen, and though Helen didn't meet it, she screwed herself upright and set her stance, as though preparing for battle.

"I want to tell everyone a story," Helen said in a crystal chime voice. Every time she spoke, Jason got dizzy.

"I don't think that's a good—" Monica began.

"Why not?" Miss Teedee challenged.

"Yes," Darryl said. He wiped a tear off his cheek and stood up. "You absolutely can tell us a story. How large an audience would you like, my love?"

Helen let go of Mercutio. "As many who want to be here."

"Darryl," Monica said.

"Andrew," Darryl said, ignoring Andrew's mother. "Go spread the word that our premier author in residence had decided to grace us with a story. We've not had a tale at dinner in years. It's a rare thing. Tell them that and tell them to get in here if they want to hear it."

"Okay." Andrew shot out of his chair and dashed through the swinging door toward the kitchen.

"You'll be the biggest hit of the night, beautiful," Mercutio said to Helen with a sideways squeeze.

Helen didn't answer, smiling at the table and tracing patterns on it with her fingertips. Jason wanted to hold her hand, and he didn't understand where the need was coming from, only that it existed. He stayed planted in his chair, taking a long gulp of cool water. Darryl went to his daughter, speaking quietly to her, and guests began to traipse from the Solarium to fill the room, and their excited chatter came with them.

"Ms. Adlewilde," Kirkland said, standing when the woman Jason had seen earlier in the library came into the room.

"I was having tea and heard there was to be storytelling?" Ms. Adlewilde asked, setting down her teacup and adjusting her long, purple skirt.

"So it would seem," Kirkland said, and Monica appeared between their chairs, whispering to Ms. Adlewilde. After a moment, Ms. Adlewilde cocked an eyebrow at Kirkland, who shrugged. "Should be different, regardless," Kirkland said.

"I think so," Ms. Adlewilde agreed.

Andrew appeared, breathless, "I've told everybody," he said, plopping into his chair next to Jason.

"Good job," Darryl said. Mercutio moved the empty chairs away from the far end of the table, clearing Helen a place to stand and relaxing into a dining chair against the wall. The cluster of women who had been at the far end of the table now sat along the wall opposite Mercutio. Miss Teedee brought Helen a glass of water and took her place next to Mercutio, who rolled his eyes and feigned exaggerated delight over the cheesecake. Miss Teedee giggled, Monica sat in her seat next to Darryl with a stiff spine, and everyone else sat in hushed silence. All they needed was a storm to roll in, the room to flicker and dim, and the atmosphere would be set.

Instead, it was twilight beyond the bay windows, and the blonde twins shrieked and chased each other up the central hall's stairs. Jason trembled like he'd had a shot of espresso, and he clasped his hands in his lap so they wouldn't accidentally send silverware clanking across his plate. There was no way to leave without drawing attention to himself, and Jason didn't want to offend Helen by running from the room. She was delicate like a trembling blossom in a downpour, and so Jason stayed, and when their eyes met, he didn't look away.

"Hello. I'm Helen," she said.

At the head of the table, Darryl leaned forward, elbows pushing his plate out of the way. Helen spared him a glance and tried to give him a smile, but it didn't quite make it to full form. "It's been many years since I spoke of the things I know to be true, but tonight, I was feeling well and thought I should come tell you a particular story. It's one that you need to know. It doesn't have a happy ending. It doesn't have a clear beginning. It simply is."

In the silence surrounding Helen's deep sigh, clocks ticked – *click, click, click* – but their sounds were gradually submerged beneath the rising, hypnotic intonation of Helen's voice. "It is common knowledge to some that there are worlds next to ours. Invisible places, ghostly people, all with different hours to tell their time and different rules by which they abide. If you do not know it, then you've felt it. When something you just set down goes missing, when you don't quite see something out of the corner of your eye, when the prickles start on the back of your neck and slither down your spine to your toes, then you know. They're right there. Beside you, walking through you, whispering to you, the people in these other worlds.

"And in the center of all the worlds is one that links all other worlds. That world has many names in every language, but I know it as Via'rra—"

"Sorry, sweetie – the world's called 'via,' what?" Ms. Adlewilde asked.

"Rah. Via'rra. In a language older than ours, it means 'By the paths of gods.'"

"Ooh, how lovely," Ms. Adlewilde said.

"Via'rra spins in the middle of all other worlds, and there are gateways from this world, and in all worlds, Via'rra. These gateways are sometimes doors, sometimes dreams, sometimes unexplained whispers that come to us when we're alone, and it's quiet, and the day is fading into the night. Via'rra is the place that artists paint when we can give no explanation for what their brushes make come to life. It's the land that writers visit, and later, they cannot tell us where they get their ideas. It is where inspiration lives, where memory is stored, where truth is the law, and such a land can only exist because it is balanced."

Helen held out one hand, palm down and fingers together and straight. "The most powerful creatures who rule this world can come to ours, or to any of their choosing, when Via'rra is steady, and all the pathways are aligned." She spread her fingers. "They come to learn, to spread knowledge, to fulfill their unique purposes, and to keep the pathways open. The creatures of Via'rra who have such power call themselves the Walkers of the Veil – it's their word for the doorways between all worlds and Via'rra.

"How the Walkers came to be is a collection of stories unto themselves, but the first one came into being by the hands of The

Seven Sisters. They're stars and they stand for the best virtues of any land, and they called forth the first Walker who, in turn, called forth Via'rra. This creator of Via'rra was the Walker most often seen when the Walkers crossed Veils to and fro with ease and frequency. She was a muse, a goddess, a battlefield legend, and a fairytale used to keep children in their beds in the hopes that their dreams would let them meet her." Helen smiled and dropped her arm. No one moved, no one spoke or coughed. Next to Jason, Andrew was transfixed, mouth agape and eyes wide. Jason didn't even want to breathe heavily, lest Helen lose her nerve or vanish in thin smoke.

"Lady Creation, or the Lady to her friends, is strong as the pillars of time. When she walks, the very air is charged with her power. You would know her from afar by her magenta light and by her laugh: a cackling howl that split the early silence of Via'rra. And you would know her up close by her white, glittering skin and her great comb of hair, which is the color of every shade of red, magenta, and gold. You would know her by her armor and her tail and her too-wide mouth with its too many teeth. But she would know you on sight because of all her *eyes*.

"The Lady has hundreds of eyes, all sizes and shapes and species. When they are shut, they are thin slivers like new moons, and when they are open, they are covered in an impenetrable film. And where we would think normal eyes would be, there are two black pits that sometimes open to show the jewels of Via'rra: the many-faceted, diamond rainbow eyes of Lady Creation."

"Sounds like a foxy minx to me," Mercutio said, startling them all into chuckles and smiles.

"She is!" Helen agreed. "Very foxy, very sly, and not only a great warrior, but a great gardener."

"I like a well-rounded woman," Kirkland interjected, and Ms. Adlewilde lightly smacked his arm.

"And she would like you," Helen said, which gave the room pause. "She would!" Helen insisted. "But her garden is no ordinary garden. It is where she grows all living things and creatures, great or small. The Lady, herself, is both male and female, and the seeds she plants are labored by the land. They sprout into men, women, beasts, and flowers, and she sends them out into Via'rra, infusing it with life. It is said she grew the whole world this way, high up in her House of Five Bridges, which floats in the cosmos, in the abyss of space and outside the realm of time, itself.

"And it is said that in the beginning of all things, which was also the end of the last known reality, the Lady's power came from the destruction of a former existence. It was granted to her by the Seven Sisters, who knew she would need much to make and keep Via'rra turning. But such a source is not infinite. So she sought out a companion with the power to consume that which must fall and then feed her the energy that destruction provides."

Helen's lips twitched. "Reduce, reuse, recycle?"

Helen got her laughter from the room and her breath at the same time. "Her most constant companion is known as Lord Nothing. He may have been a man from our world or another land much like it. A great king who roamed and ruled, for surely, that is what he made himself to be on Via'rra. It is thought he had magical power all of his own before he and the Lady found one another, and that power lead him to the Lady. Then Lord Nothing and Lady Creation were lovers most dear, and she eventually brought him to Via'rra from wherever he once lived.

"But when he stepped foot onto the Lady's land, Lord Nothing grimaced and fell to the ground. Fortunately, the Lady understood, and she spake it be that Via'rra would be cast into shadowy Twilight. The sun exploded into a thousand fragments, making a sky of pale sun-stars, and the land was shaded in Forever Purple Twilight.

"When that was done, Lord Nothing rose, and he and his Lady stood in the fields in the center of Lord Nothing's new universe, and he called his Lady by her true name, and he asked, 'Where shall I stay? With you, my love? Please say with you.'

"'In my land, you are always welcome and may always be,' the Lady answered. 'But do you not want a kingdom of your own?'

"'I do,' Lord Nothing replied. 'But I cannot make with my hands, for my gifts are in the unmaking. My power is in the shadows, not the light, and my task is to consume that which must be unmade, so I might bring you its essence for remaking.'

"'And this you swear you will always do?' the Lady asked, but needlessly, for she already knew his reply.

"'I will, I will, I will,' the Lord Nothing swore thrice, and Via'rra trembled, for now, it had its Maker and its Unmaker, combined.

"'Then, my love, I shall give you a home of your own,' the Lady said to her other half. 'Tell me what you desire, and it will be yours.'

"And so for seven days and nights, Lord Nothing spoke his wishes, and he and the Lady made love and drank of fine wine and partook of rich food. In the dead of night on the last day, the Lady took Lord Nothing to her garden. In the middle of a field was a bubble no taller than the Lady stood. The bubble was full of winter amidst all of Lady Creation's growing spring. For all of Via'rra is temperate, which is the best climate in which the Walkers and the creatures who live there thrive.

"'And this I give unto you,' the Lady said to Lord Nothing. She sent the bubble down to Via'rra, and Lord Nothing and the Lady followed its fall. The bubble burst and became reality, and the land began to change. The Lady made a mountain range on the edge of the world, and, surrounded by mountain peaks that pierced the sky, a fortress sprang, bigger than any ever known. The back walls dangled over ledges that dropped away to the end of existence, and winter blew into the mountains, settling to stay. Mist and clouds, fog and sleet and snow, and it seemed barren to Lord Nothing upon first glance, and he grieved, for he loved the Lady's springtime. Then it is said that the Lady laughed.

"'What is amusing?' Lord Nothing asked.

"'Everything, My Lord, but just now, I laugh because I love defying Nature. It thinks it wins and outlasts all, but it forgets that I made it and its ways.'

"And so, while Lord Nothing watched, black roses on thick, shiny vines, and pure white orchids with rich, dark leaves, sprang from the frosty ground and grew in the acres around Lord Nothing's Fortress. 'A bit of me, my love, to remember when we are apart,' the Lady said, and Lord Nothing kissed her in gratitude and in love. 'You will need attendants to make the flowers grow, and guardians to mind the pass,' Lady Creation warned, and before their kisses turned into full desire, she placed a kernel of creation into his palm. 'Eat this and make of your own will, servants and warriors and riches for yourself and for them all. So long as you fulfill your duties, so shall I sustain your kingdom.'

"Lord Nothing ate the kernel, and its energy made Lord Nothing's Shadow Guardians and field tenders and household servants. It made furniture of the most lavish wealth, and rooms in which Lord Nothing could study, could read, could paint, could rest. And when he was apart from the Lady, he wrote her letters, sent to her by phoenixes. And when they were together, they roamed the wintry fields, snow falling in the Lady's long hair and onto the train of Lord Nothing's fur cloaks. They were happy for a time."

When Helen stopped speaking, Jason realized that he and the rest of the Taylor Point Household were no longer in the safe and sane four walls of the dining room. They were seated at a great oak table in the middle of a meadow in a strange, purple land, beneath a canopy of unknown glittering and falling stars. Around them the field was edged with massive trees never seen on Earth, and in the distance rose peaks of mountains, snow-capped and looming, clouds making the bulk of them invisible.

"What happened?" Jason asked, as the air crackled with tiny sparks of magenta lightning.

"Yeah," Andrew said. "Are they still together? Or did Lord Nothing like painting more than he liked his Lady?"

Helen frowned and sighed. "They are not together. In fact, they've been torn apart, but it wasn't because of their love or due to the lack thereof." Helen's shoulders slumped and she bowed her head. "A great plague came to Via'rra."

Around the oak table, the land began to rot, morphing into piles of stinking char. "It eats the land as we speak," Helen said in a dull voice. "Consuming it in flames and ash, and that is why this story had to be told tonight. That is why you had to hear." Helen beseeched Jason with her gaze. "I don't know the source of the chaos that befell Lord Nothing or Lady Creation or any of the other Walkers, and all of them are in danger. And if they die or vanish, if their world is not put to rights and the balance restored, then our world – and all the others – will topple. At first it will be the end of beauty, of stories and songs and art. Then it will be the end of sanity, for without the means to create and the purge of energy that goes with creating, human minds will crack under pressure. But then it will be as though the center of the wheel of all of creation dissolves. The cogs will not turn. The roads will not connect. We and every other world connected by Via'rra will careen off into space and time without purpose, and that will be the end. Of everything."

Jason saw the trees burning, the stars winking out, and chunks of the universe breaking off and colliding with great destruction. No one else was talking or asking the questions Jason knew had to be asked, so he wet his lips with a patchy-dry tongue. "How do we help them? The Walkers and their world?"

Helen sadly shook her head, and Jason nodded, understanding that she didn't know. When he blinked, he sat in dim gray pre-dawn with Darryl and Monica and Mercutio, Andrew, Miss Teedee, Kirkland, Ms. Adlewilde, and all the rest of the people whom Jason couldn't name, and the longer he sat, the more the dining room came into focus. Clocks ticked, the twins giggled, doors opened and slammed shut, and a collective sigh of relief blew out the last flickers of the illusion. One glance at the rest of the room told Jason that he wasn't the only one who had seen Helen's infected world, and Jason touched a drop of condensation on his water glass, rubbing it between thumb and forefinger and telling himself that this was real, not the other place.

"That's it?" Monica asked. "The end?"

"That's not it," Helen said. "But as I said, no happy ending. Not yet."

"Well, it's an awesome story, pretty lady. Wasn't it?" Mercutio warned the room with a distinctive arch of an eyebrow, and at once, applause erupted.

Helen bowed. "I'd hoped you would understand, so..." She sought out Jason once again. "Thank you."

Jason's vision tunneled. Any energy he had drained out his ears and all he wanted was to go to sleep.

"You okay?" Andrew asked, and he was too close and personal. Jason could smell his breath and hear the moisture of a coming cough.

"Yeah," Jason said, leaning away from Andrew, as he cleared his throat. And Jason was all right, but he was also exhausted and full up on the new, the unusual, and the weird. Despite not knowing Helen or anyone here, he felt, strangely, as though he did. Helen's world was... familiar as much as it was bizarre. The sensation of knowing and not knowing at the same time made Jason's entire body itch like one big mosquito welt. "Think I'm going to head to the van, get my stuff, and turn in early."

Andrew bit his lip, and he looked at Jason, then Helen, and then Jason. "You should probably tell Helen you liked her story. She said she wanted to meet you, and she's real sensitive."

"I think what we did sort of counts as meeting," Jason said, though he wasn't sure why he said that or what he meant. Not precisely. "You tell her for me, okay?"

"What should I say?"

Jason wasn't sure. Should he tell Helen that he saw the world? That the pictures she created with words were so vivid that they would haunt his dreams? For a few moments, he hadn't been Jason at all, but someone else who mattered but who had a dark purpose. A bloody purpose. He knew that wasn't true, in the here and now, but he couldn't quite shake the images of blood pooling on the ground and of the longing in his heart that always seemed to ache. “Tell her I’ll remember her story,” Jason said at last because that much at least was entirely accurate.

“Okay.” Andrew dug into his pocket and handed Jason a key. Jason stood and took his plate and dirty fork and knife into the kitchen. Jennifer watched him from a corner and said that he should just leave his dirty dinnerware on the counter. Jason didn’t argue, already sleepwalking.

Somehow he made it past the people and through the halls, rooms, and doors to the outside. He smelled honeysuckle and damp grass, and when he got into his van, he shocked himself by having no urge to drive off or run away. It should be all he wanted to do – flee from this odd bunch of people.

But it didn’t feel right, the idea of being anywhere but there. He wanted to park the van in the lot near the lapping water, so he did. He wanted to gather up as much of his stuff as he could carry with weary arms, and he went through with that plan. He navigated locks and more doors, which never seemed to end around here, and he dropped his bag and sacks at the head of the plaid couch. It was cooler downstairs, almost chilly, and Jason sent up silent thanks. He took off his shoes and slacks and shirt, folded the borrowed clothes and laid them on Andrew’s bed, and Jason crawled onto the sofa in his boxer shorts. The folded blanket was soft fleece, and Jason shoved his pillow, mushed over time to conform perfectly to his shape, under his head. He was out almost immediately, but before he belly-flopped into unconsciousness, he saw a flash of black eyes ringed with red and long, black-wrapped, boney limbs reaching… reaching…

For him.

Chapter Six

Far below the blasted wastelands of what was left of Via'rra, the King of Nightmare slumbered on his throne and dreamt of a white house tipped with spires next to a river with a garden the Lady would love.

"*We burn... WE BURN!*" chanted unseen voices, and Nightmare strained toward something – someone, a vague shape – just beyond his grasp. He reached, arms aching, and at last, he woke when he tumbled to the cavern's floor. He blinked in the low glow emitted from the blue and green phosphorescence sparkling from the walls and high ceiling and stared at his hands. The dull, gray bone was visible in places not wrapped with the shiny, black-brown sinew that passed for his skin, his muscle, his tendon and veins and lifeblood. Ash and rot filled his nose, though from an unknown source. He could not remember how it had come to pass that he was in this chamber, and not his quarters or among his 'mares: feasting, fighting, fucking. Celebrating the life and bodies he gave to all fallen paradigms that landed in his kingdom, his Undermaze.

Pained, and unused to the sensation, he rocked back on his heels and touched the edges of his fractured ribs. They gaped open with ragged edges, leaving his midsection vulnerable, a worry if there had been a power in the Undermaze that could destroy him. His chest was hollow save for a dull, green glow. He reached inside himself and touched a bit of green ooze smeared on his sinew and bones – the healing salve, so rare, now. It'd been coated along what was left of his chest and torso, and it must have been done some time ago, as it was nearly as dried and desiccated as he. Touching a shattered edge of rib with one finger, he struggled to remember if he had always appeared a cracked-open king, or if this breaking was new.

A hollow sound, pestle-on-stone, echoed in the room. Beneath his hands, the packed dirt glittered and trembled. Soon, dozens upon dozens of bone faces broke the surface of the floor, the walls, the ceiling. Tiny red pinpricks of light grew larger, bolder, until the bone faces glowed with sentience.

"The King... the King awakens..." Voices began to chant, low and dull and grinding, until the room sounded with the thunder of an enormous Bone Ghost emerging from above. Gems and bits of glittering Shadowrock tumbled to the floor as so much dust. This Ghost's head was ringed with bony appendages like spider legs, and it resembled a shield, its forehead twice as wide as its chin. Its face was long and angular, and the single eye socket, jagged husk where once may have been a nose, and protruding, upper and lower jaws lined with vicious fangs were aligned down the center of the lower half of the skull.

The King of Nightmare did not remember all, but he remembered this Ghost: "Adimoas the Wise," Nightmare said in greeting. In his life Topside, before falling victim to inevitable change, Adimoas had been a very great idea. The kind of idea that altered the pathways of lives, and, Nightmare assumed, likely did, judging by the strength and perseverance Adimoas had exhibited in his time as a wandering Nightmare in his King's land. Adimoas had gone to the Feed willingly, and now, the spirit of one of the greatest, oldest ideas was the closest thing Nightmare had to a friend and advisor. He had retained the faculties of his Undermaze form, which few Bone Ghosts ever did.

The eye socket came to life, glowing red. "Mal'uud 'au Keen, My Liege Lord and Sire, the King of Nightmare, Lord of the Undermaze, I bid you a welcome return from the land of dreams."

Slowly, some of what was true began to return to Nightmare. "I have slumbered too long."

"And yet you are awakened, now; perhaps because energies and forces gather in this realm and beyond. And you were allotted time enough to rest and recover some of yourself," Adimoas intoned.

"This," Nightmare said, gesturing to his chest. "What caused this?"

Adimoas grew mournful. "There was an explosion, Sire. A crack in our foundation and the world. We lost half the 'Maze and too many Ghosts and 'mares to number. The catastrophe was too great. We do not know what occurred."

Nightmare remembered. There'd been an incredible war brewing among factions of 'mares – a pure delight for the bloodthirsty. The cause of the war need not matter – if there had been a cause at all. Oftentimes, wars were just games arranged to count the passage of eternity. And as always, Nightmare had been there, cheering on the armies and sending the true dead to the Feed, and then...

"Darkness," Nightmare muttered. He winced, and without his asking, the floor roiled. A Ghost shaped like a small, sea creature flowed through the earth as though it were water to where Nightmare knelt. It offered up a small jar of salve in its pinchers. Long ago, the earth of the Undermaze had positively oozed the healing salve. Chambers had been built to collect it. Many a twisted dream or ghoulish thought had used the salve on their temporary Undermaze bodies to recover from battle wounds, construction injury, or self-inflicted trauma. Some had used it simply to remember enough of their purpose to serve Nightmare and his realm. The embodied Fallen had a tenuous grip on sanity, though it was a grip that could nevertheless last centuries. The stronger Fallen remembered longer what they were and who they served and what Nightmare did and why. The rules of the land were simple: maintain the Undermaze, obey the King of Nightmare, and when they were but shadows of their former selves, go to the Feed and the walls, for Via'rra was a world supported by the Ghosts of what once was.

"What of Topside?" Nightmare asked as he dipped his fingers into the salve and began coating himself in a thin layer, only using as much as was necessary.

"The land above the Undermaze lives and dies in terminal war," Adimoas answered. "The smoke and the screams touch the sky and clutter the cosmos beyond."

Nightmare paused. "The Horrors?" he asked, remembering and wishing he did not.

"Yes, My Liege."

"And we as yet do not know what unleashed them?"

"We do not."

Nightmare dipped his head, and the Ghosts rustled to him, nudging him in comfort. He petted his children. "Do we know of the others, my Brethren?"

"You are the only Walker of the Veils who still has dominion over their kingdom. All others are fractured."

Nightmare leaned hard against the base of his throne. "Meaning I am likely then the only one who can still Walk the Worlds?"

"Yes, My Lord."

Nightmare recalled when Veils to the millions of worlds that spun adjacent to Via'rra were as common as the trees had been Topside. Going to and from had cost energy, it was true, but replenishment was easy to find. The Feed had perpetually grinded. The salve had poured. Now resources and means had all dwindled, faded, gone missing. The balance above had been upset, and if the other Walkers had not found a way to stabilize it, yet, then he didn't have much hope of their finding a way soon. He did not want to think upon the days ahead when his realm grew smaller and smaller, and his 'mares grew scarcer, and his citizens turned to so much malnourishing grit.

"I have not the strength to Walk," Nightmare confessed. He felt the weakness in himself and knew that opening a portal to another realm would be no easy task. Possibly it would be one that unmade him, which meant that the other worlds languished. He could not go and harvest dead ideas and remove them to his Undermaze. This meant the other Walkers could not accomplish their tasks, either, leaving the universes in their multitudes unbalanced.

These may well be the ending days before the long, cold darkness returned.

"And it is strength you shall need, My Liege, for though the news brought to me through the bone webs is dire, there is a glimmer of possibility."

"Speak it quickly."

"I have learned where the Storyteller now dwells."

Nightmare's head snapped backward, all his focus on the Ghost on the ceiling. "Speak on!"

"Though the Walkers were once thunderous gods, they have been silent to my seeking. Until today. The Storyteller invoked your true name and made himself known to me."

All Walkers had titles and also names, which could be invoked to call power and, in this case, minion attention. "Why now?"

"I could not speak on it, Sire, but one assumes it is knowledge upon which the Storyteller acts. Knowledge he perhaps went to gain and returned, so armed, to us here."

"'When the Storyteller Walks, it is through Time as well as Veil,'" Nightmare quoted in a whisper. "If he went to the future or the past and gleamed some reason for this unbalanced blight upon our world..."

"Then perhaps he has come to us with words meant to reach your ears."

"Which means I must go to him." Nightmare rose, swayed on his feet, and steadied himself on his throne.

"My Liege, I fear going Topside will prove more dangerous and taxing than Walking."

"I know this to be true," Nightmare agreed, and he began to pace. "But I cannot be a blind king. I cannot turn my back on the droves that have died and that continue to die eternal as the Undermaze shrinks. I can hear them, Adimoas, the 'mares trapped in fallen chambers, cut off by avalanches and beyond our skills to recover. I can feel the absence of the Walker's power, once a great river, a gossamer thread, that connected and synced us all, now cut. I can feel my very power draining from these limbs, and I fear to fade, for without me, there is nothing to stand between the Undermaze and—"

"Speak not his name, My Liege," Adimoas moaned above the combined, grinding and wailing of the Ghosts. "Please, I beg you."

Nightmare clacked his jaws together and ground his teeth. "The Walkers are the gods of this world, Adimoas, each with their own dominion, should they still have skill to execute it. And so I fear to falter, for should I, we may all fall prey to the great unmaking."

"It is energy you need, then," Adimoas said.

"I do, but we are so few, and to traverse Topside..."

"Sire, you may not yet need to embark upon a long journey overland."

Nightmare frowned. "How can this be? With so many of my halls destroyed, that leaves me little flexibility where I can emerge Topside."

"Yes, Sire, but you see, I have determined where Storyteller is. He has made his position most clear, and what's more, I do not believe he will or can move."

"Why is that?"

A pause: "He is surrounded by the Horrors."

Had Nightmare entrails, they would have twisted. "And he holds them at bay?"

"It seems he has this ability, yes, if but for a time."

"If ever there were something to fear more than the one whose name you do not wish me to speak."

"Agreed, Sire."

Nightmare stood taller. "I will still need energy, reserves of it, for if Storyteller is surrounded, then I may have need to fight."

"It is as you say, My Liege."

Nightmare paced to the carved Shadowrock in which his throne was situated. He touched the stone and wanted to weep for the power that once used to hum, an electric current, and that now was barely a weak pulse. "Do any Builders yet survive?" Nightmare asked.

"Aye, my Liege."

"And what of the Warriors?"

"Many, Sire. They are difficult to kill."

"As I made them to be," Nightmare said with no small amount of pride. "The location of the Storyteller – what chamber is closest?"

Adimoas's red eye faded a moment as he considered and sought the answer. It returned to brightness in short order. "The Scrying Cavern, My Liege."

"Good. A fortified place. Send a summons to the Builders, the Warriors, any 'mares in the area with bravery still left in their flesh. Tell them to come and meet with me."

"Yes, My Liege."

"And send your Ghosts to every Healing Chamber still standing. Wring the salve from the walls and from any container. Gather it and bring it to the Scrying Cavern as well."

Adimoas sank into the ceiling in a slide that loosed pebbles and sand to the ground. The other Ghosts vanished in a wave, making the room seem alive and mobile until they were gone. Nightmare bent and gathered the small pot of green soothing salve and tucked it away inside his chest before stalking to the arched gateway to the throne room.

Nightmare set his pace short of a run, caressing the Ghosts that emerged seeking contact as he raced by. He wove through his kingdom, taking corners left and right and steadily descending. Through narrow passages and grand, wide chambers he strode, deeper and deeper into the bowels of the Undermaze, until the glowing stones had all but winked out of existence. The red rings around the black pupils of his eyes offered sight even in pitch darkness, and the rings showed him the path ahead. He also spied rooms with debris stacked to prevent entrance, no doubt home to 'mares trying to avoid him, thinking he searched to find 'mares for the Feed. Once, they had less to fear, longer to spend in their flesh. Once upon a time, hundreds of new forms were born into this land every day. It would have taken many, many Via'rra turns to roam all the tunnels and rooms, and that was only if nothing new was being built.

But now, for as many rooms as were left, there were more cave-ins and dead ends that showed where there was nothing left but rubble. A pain slithered through Nightmare's hollowed insides. He quelled it and used its echoes to put determination in his steps.

At the end of a long, narrow, low passage was a hole half Nightmare's height. Nightmare had to duck and crawl. He came out on the other side in a domed room tall enough that ten of Nightmare's considerable height could have stood and four times that many could have laid across it. The cavern sides were smooth and black, sediment in the dirt twinkling like lost fragments of the Topside cosmos. There was a pit in the center of the cavern, a deep, dark pit, that some thought went on forever, down and down and down again. The Ghosts and 'mares feared this place, for they believed that in ages past, the Scrying Pit was the doorway through which other Walkers could enter the Undermaze. And there was one Walker in particular that no Bone Ghost nor 'mare, nor even the King of Nightmare, himself, wanted to allow admittance to the kingdom.

Nightmare circled the Scrying Pit. The cavern was utterly silent for countless moments. Time was tricky for Nightmare; an hour or a day or a year could all feel the same. Time was a Topside concern; a demi-god worshiped more in other realms than this one. Time was Storyteller's burden, truly, and Nightmare was happy to let Storyteller pay that toll.

Coming to a halt on the southernmost side of the Pit, Nightmare gazed into its depths. A memory pulled at him, distant and unclear. He thought that even before the explosion – the catastrophe that had harmed his form and taken 'maze and 'mares – power had been waning. A strange thing, as Nightmare was usually so unaffected by anything outside the Undermaze, and the 'maze was sound and solid. And he had known something was amiss because he'd come to this very cavern attempting to know more, and the visions that once danced and swirled as he gazed into the darkness were gone.

Testing the knowledge of memory, Nightmare sought out the blackest recesses in the Pit, willing it to share its secrets once again, of the future, of the present, of anything at all. Nightmare craved answers to questions he couldn't even remember, and he despaired when only blackness and silence answered him.

Nightmare rested, and eventually, a rumble awakened him to full consciousness, and he watched the hole leading into the chamber begin to crumble. Wider and wider, as though someone chipped away dirt and rock and gems with a chisel, the opening expanded, and Nightmare waited, eagerness kindling in his dried veins.

When the hole was twice Nightmare's height and width, the blackness beyond the entrance shifted and showed itself to be not darkness at all, but a living creature. Nightmare's face split into a wide grin.

Errvyn the Roamer, one of the oldest Warriors, shoved his wide shoulders through the opening. He had four arms and six legs and two heads. More limbs made for easier killing, and two minds allowed one to plan and one to act. What each 'mare had been Topside was usually known only to Nightmare, and Errvyn had been someone's purpose, and once fulfilled, Errvyn had fallen. To Nightmare's realm, Errvyn had come, and he had taken form and had begun his second life.

A life that had recently, Nightmare saw, taken a toll. Errvyn wore a coat, of sorts, made from the hides of those he'd killed. Bits of Bone Ghost skulls were tied on strings and draped around his necks and wrapped around all his upper arms. He'd lost two of his legs, the stumps oozing green pus. Tusks erupted from Errvyn's faces and he, like so many 'mares, had no eyes, but he had two mouths on each face. One head was missing most of its scalp, and brains pulsated in the cracked skull. Errvyn carried a weapon staff that was also a walking stick and a digging spade, and he bowed before clearing away from the hole to make room for the rest of the 'mares.

In came Merdoth the Bloodied, taller than Nightmare but wisp-thin. Open wounds bled on her top half, and the blood, pus, and fluids dripped across her purple-gray flesh to feed the open, lapping mouths that dotted her pelvis, legs, and feet. Two great swords crossed in straps over her back, showing her strength could not be underestimated. Merdoth had actual eyes, though now two of them were blind and one put out of her skull. She was nude, her breasts swaying and bleeding from twin gashes. She was missing one of her hands, but she'd sewn someone else's to the stump. Merdoth had been someone's vengeance.

Twinpierce came next, their short, stout bodies attached at the trunk. They moved with innate stealth, no eyes or mouths to be seen. The hilts of dozens of knives protruded from their green skin – not wounds, but simply sheathed in their forms. They had six hands between them, and plenty of dexterity and life still left. They had once been secrets, never shared, and likely they died with their bearer, having poisoned the soul to their last breath.

Prince Variegas entered, his servant 'mares in tow, attached by ropes to hooks on his belt. He'd lost two of his minor 'mares, Nightmare noted, and their bloodied, torn collars were around Variegas's neck in honor. His purple robe was stained and tattered, and his long head had sprouted more vines since last Nightmare had seen him. The vines wrapped around his body, providing a kind of armor. His two obscenely luscious mouths pulled back into gaping grins as he took his place near the wall. A ruler's vision, Prince Variegas had been in his intangible life before falling to the Undermaze still full of the need for a court and ostentation.

The last to enter was Kuribit, who scampered away from the Warriors to stand by himself. Slight of build with greasy, yellow hair and light, tan skin, he carried a bag over one shoulder that he touched as though it comforted him. No doubt the bag contained some of the tools he needed to do the magic of building. He crouched and toyed with his toes, picking off the nails and chewing them absently, his face turned toward the gathering of Warriors. Nightmare could smell his fear all the way across the cavern and the Scrying Pit. Kuribit had been an anxiety in the time before he fell; anxieties tended to be some of the greatest builders in the Undermaze. They knew how to expand their territory better than even some of the Warriors.

"My Warriors and Builder," Nightmare intoned, sweeping around the Pit to draw closer to the gathering. None of them would go near the Pit willingly. "My gratitude for answering my summons."

"His Majesty calls, and all loyal will answer," Errvyn boomed in a voice like gravel tumbling into a bucket. "Now tell us why we are in this forsaken place."

Variegas made a rude sound. "We give little care to the time and location and would know more of what befalls us."

"Yes," Merdoth agreed. "The land above turns to so much excrement, my King. It oozes ever closer to our home, and meanwhile, we die in droves. That pustule," she gestured to Kuribit, "is the only builder left standing. And we are but a few of the Warriors remaining. Most of the other 'mares pull out their teeth and pluck out their eyes as the chaos of life's end consumes them."

Nightmare bowed his head. Slowly, he told them of his waning power, what little he understood of the catastrophe that had rocked their world, and that the Horrors raged above, their cause and origin unknown. They were silent for a moment when Nightmare was done.

"Is it the Shadow that does this?" Merdoth asked, voice soft with fear.

"That is not his name, only his location," Variegas said with haughty pride.

"For all our sakes, no one invoke the Destroyer of Worlds when we're so near the black pit and so close to real death," Errvyn warned. He turned to Nightmare. "The Horrors, do they do the work of the Destroyer?"

A prickle of pain tugged at Nightmare, and he curled his fist inside his chest. He should know this, and yet, he did not. "I cannot say. But there is one who might know – the Storyteller. The other Walkers are out of our reach, but he announced himself to Adimoas the Wise."

"Topside," Errvyn said with a curl of his lips.

"Yes," Nightmare agreed. "I will need a doorway, a chamber, a stairwell, and a gate." He turned to Kuribit, who flinched and clearly wished Nightmare had forgotten that he was even there. "Can you manage those things?"

"Maybe, possibly, probably," Kuribit muttered to his feet. "But I am so weak, so tired, my King, and I smell.... we all smell... the *green*."

Nightmare calculated in his mind how much salve he hoped the Bone Ghosts could find to bring, how much he thought he'd need, but Twinpierce threw a blade that missed Kuribit's head by a hair's breadth. The stink of Kuribit's waste quickly filled the air.

Undaunted, Twinpierce stepped forward and pointed all hands, each with blades, to Nightmare.

"Yes," Merdoth agreed, though with obvious reluctance. "All the green should go to the King. He ails, and should he fall..." She didn't need to finish the sentence. The rest of the 'mares visibly shuddered or gagged.

"But," Kuribit whined. "I am weak. I see the visions. I fight not to rend my own flesh. A door and a chamber, maybe, but stairs and a gate..."

"What if we came to your aid?" Errvyn asked.

Kuribit squeaked. Variegas cursed in the language of Fear, sending shivers up all their spines. "Warriors do not *help* the builders." He spat.

Twinpierce and Merdoth were immediately on Variegas. A struggle ensued, and weapons clashed. Variegas squalled in pain and rage. "Enough!" he called. "I submit."

"We help builders when the world is about to be unmade, you useless bit of rot," Errvyn droned.

"Even if we did, what of it?" Variegas replied. "He builds, a gate is made, and then what? We send our King to the Storyteller to learn of Horrors and unmaking? What if there is more to be done? What if he must Walk or fight? The build will not be enough."

Merdoth shouted down insults, and Twinpierce positioned himself between her and Variegas, else more violence erupt, and at last, Nightmare could take no more. He called power and stamped his foot.

The cavern boomed, all sound and air sucked out at once. When it returned, the 'mares gasped and bowed their heads. "In existence, who do you serve?" Nightmare bellowed.

"We live at the pleasure of our King," the 'mares said in unison.

Nightmare acknowledged them with a nod. "Variegas speaks no truth that I have not foreseen. Which is why our gathering is not only to discuss a build."

"A sacrifice," Errvyn said, without emotion.

"Yes," Nightmare said. "You will round up 'mares for the Feed."

"How many?" Merdoth asked.

Nightmare closed and then opened his eyes. "As many as you can find."

The room grew somber. "It will still not be enough," Variegas said.

"It will not," Errvyn said. "Which is why we will draw straws and join our lesser 'mares."

Variegas screeched protest, but Merdoth spoke above the din. "Why straws?"

"We can't all go to the Feed," Errvyn said. "We need to help the builder and collect the 'mares."

"So, what number of us go to our death?" Merdoth asked.

Ervvyn spoke to Nightmare, not Merdoth. "Your Majesty, I believe we can spare two."

"Then take these wretches," Variegas cried, shoving his servants forward with violence that put them on their knees. "Three of them should equal at least most of me."

Anger welled in Nightmare, rich and lush. He narrowed his eyes. "You would send your servants to avoid your fate at the Feed?"

Variegas opened his mouths to answer, attempting to appear calm, but he failed to regain his threads of control on his wavering sanity. He shrieked in fear and turned to run, his servants struggling to stand and not weigh him down. Merdoth and Twinpierce took steps in advance, weapons drawn, but Nightmare was faster.

He was always faster.

Nightmare sent power through the Undermaze. He rushed at Variegas and shoved him and his servants against the cavern's wall. Bone Ghosts erupted from it, their talons sharpened to razor's edges. They pierced Variegas and his servants with a hundred points and then neatly tore them asunder. Variegas's dreadful screams abruptly ended, and the sharp scent of death and the quiet sound of dripping filled the cavern.

"Guess that's one less for the lots," Errvyn said calmly.

Dulled anguish filled Nightmare, and he knelt next to a piece of Variegas's skull. He remembered when Prince Variegas had filled halls with tales that raised raucous laughter. He remembered when they were legion, not numbering so few, so desperate. "Draw your lots," Nightmare said dully. "Call for Yaferjull and his cart and take these 'mares to the feed."

"No lots," Merdoth said, voice quavering only slightly in her resolve. "I'll go. I've always wanted to know what shape I'll be in your walls, Your Majesty."

Before Nightmare could sanctify the oath, however, Twinpierce came forward. They knelt in front of Nightmare. They gestured to themselves, and Nightmare understood with an ache in his bones. One of Twinpierce's hands offered up a blade.

The other hands swiftly drew knives and sawed off their own heads. It took devotion, strength...

...and it took time.

"They were two," Nightmare said, at last, and over Twinpiece's fallen bodies. "More fuel for the Feed."

"I will gather more 'mares," Merdoth murmured.

"And we will build," Errvyn said, shoving Kuribit with one foot.

"So it begins," Nightmare agreed, and he turned to work side by side with his warrior and builder in the hopes such acts would not be among their last.

Chapter Seven

Madeline stood wearing nothing but a blue silk robe at the open terrace doors of the penthouse suite that her lover rented for her by the month. The long-occupancy hotel was by the water, and with her eyes closed, Madeline could hear the song of the ocean, louder and clearer, now, in the dead of night. She'd always lived near the water – went mad if she couldn't hear it.

Because its constant drone was *his* song. The song of her *Blue.*

Mouth parched and lips dry, Madeline didn't know how long she'd been standing there, her toes with their perfectly pedicured nails digging into the plush nap of the bedroom's carpeting. A weight in her hand told her she held a cup filled with coffee. With effort, she put it to her lips. It tasted like stale motor oil siphoned through cow dung. Too strong, too bitter, and a day old. At least a day – maybe more.

How long had she been here?

Shifting, she shivered, cold, and her shoulders complained, as did her back and legs and sex. She longed to lay down and fall into a bottomless pit of dreamless sleep, but someone was in the bed. Someone who had been in her sometime recently. Someone who would demand things of her, of her body, if she roused him. So she would not.

Plus, Madeline knew the sleep would not be dreamless. It so rarely was, and lately, it was so much worse. In the dreams, she stood on the edge of a bottomless pit. She'd crouch down, crying in fear or sadness or both, and she'd strain to hear it – a soft singing. A lullaby or a lover's tune. It was a man's voice, lost and alone, and she'd try to scream that she was there. She could hear him, but when she spoke, darkness stole her voice. Water began to fill the cavern, pouring up from the pit. Soon the water tried to take her breath, her heartbeat, her life.

And the darkness tried to steal anything left.

Move. You have to move.

Madeline unrooted herself from her spot near the terrace and padded silently across the room. The scent of roses stuffed her nose, and she gagged. The flowers were everywhere: on the tables, the bedside nightstands, next to the bedroom's TV and into the next room, on every surface. Dozens and dozens of red, pink, orange, lavender blooms, and Madeline quieted the desire to knock a vase to the floor just to watch it break and step on the glass, make the blood flow. She wanted this just to have him come running, pick her up and take her away from the damage, ask if she was hurt, and dote over her wound.

This one would bandage her, comfort her, and worship her body again and again until she begged him to stop. The other one would hit her – flat of his palm, no mark left behind – and call her useless and bend her over something, rutting while she cried. And the third one – the boy who didn't know he was supposed to pay her, to buy her pretty, expensive things and keep her in a cage – he would hold her hand. Wouldn't do anything else until Madeline lost all patience, gave in to her need to feel something to feel alive, and she'd do a mixture of the things done unto her to him.

And those were just the ones she could manage. There were more – at the bar, at the restaurant, at the art gallery, at the benefit. Eyes always on her, appraising and desiring and longing to possess. To own.

"*Such a lucky girl!*" the women would proclaim, malice lacing their words like sweet poison. And all Madeline could do was smile and nod and know that she wasn't lucky.

She was empty. And she was sorry – so very, constantly sorry. She was sorry for the way everyone seemed to think beauty and sex were cause and effect and somehow always related to real affection. She was sorry for the way people fell in love with her because she was sorry for the way she didn't love them back. She was sorry for never feeling connected to her body unless there was someone on top of it or driving into it with their own. She was sorry for the way she drank and snorted lines of powder and swallowed rainbow pills even though the numbness they gave her only lasted for a little while. Never long enough.

There weren't enough rooms of flowers or admirers or lovers or diamonds to make her feel full. Because they were not her *Blue*. The one she heard from the bottom of the pit. The one she sometimes felt entwined around her, warm at first, but then not. Cold. With scales. And then the eyes would find her, not human, and she'd scream and scream while her dream body gave in to whatever the creature wanted. It was like the dream version knew who he was and what he was to her, but it still added up to *monster.*

And she wanted that monster with everything she had, and so what did that make her?

"Freak," she whispered, shocked to hear her voice in the darkened living room. She put the cup next to an overflowing vase. The flowers, they had a reason to be there. An apology? No, not this one. He never had anything to be sorry about. So then, what? Asking to do something she normally didn't do? Maybe. Madeline frowned. She flipped open a white card.

Happy birthday, beautiful.

Oh yes. Her birthday. Which wasn't her birthday at all. It was just the day she'd walked out of the woods.

A flicker of motion out of the corner of her eye caught her attention, and she jerked her head toward the glass windows lining the back wall. Through the windows was the marina, glowing gently in the dark, and also in them was a ghostly reflection of the room.

And a shape made of darkness that coalesced into a man. A tall man with horns and gleaming eyes. Who stood behind her.

Right behind her.

Madeline whirled with enough force that she twisted and fell onto the floor, a scream trapped in her throat. Of course there was nothing. But she swore she saw more shadows move – a shift, just out of sight – and she scrambled onto her feet. She sped to the bedroom and had to force herself not to slam the door. At least in this room there was company – a small comfort. He was the kind one, the gentle one, the one who'd leave rose petals in a drawn bath and kiss her neck in public.

Panting, Madeline turned and leaned against the bedroom door. Cold to the bone, she wrapped and fastened the robe, arms crossed over her chest. Maybe she could lay down – just for a while. She didn't need to sleep. And if she felt like sleep was coming, she could wake the bed's companion in the way he so dearly loved. Then sleep wouldn't come for some time.

Madeline carefully climbed into bed and tucked herself in. Shivering, she rolled over, thinking to cuddle close to him, but next to her was something else.

Madeline's hand tangled in hair – thick, black hair, coarse and inhuman. It crowned a face with a flattened nose, gray skin, and eyes that were obscured by bangs. A girl? A woman? Madeline blinked over and over and over, trying to make it go away.

Another blink and the thing in the bed was looking at her.

Another blink and the thing's mouth opened. Slowly. With a creak like a door hinge that needed oil.

Worms instead of a tongue and teeth. Worms that scrambled

across the creature's chin, reaching and reaching and spilling out laughter.

Horrible, hideous, high-pitched laughter that bordered on screams.

Madeline didn't know if she made a sound, because all she heard was the cackling. She flailed out of bed, rounded it. The creature's head turned to follow her, and it was rising, it was getting up – oh God, oh God – and Madeline made it to the bathroom. She may well have slammed this door, but she didn't hear it. Her ears popped painfully, like she was underwater, and her skin felt numb. She threw the lock with fingers she didn't really feel. She backed away.

And saw more shadows in the bathroom mirror. Looming.

She crawled into the shower stall, closing the door behind her. She curled into the corner, knees to her chest, and she couldn't *hear* anything. She couldn't *feel* her body on the cold tile or her back against the glass wall or her head as she hit it, over and over, trying to make it stop. Make it stop. *MAKE IT STOP.*

Warm arms and a warm body, and Madeline fought like a wildcat until she realized it was just him. His usual head was back, short hair and normal mouth, lips, tongue, teeth. He was speaking, but Madeline just heard a hum like feedback. It didn't matter. She understood he wanted her to stand, so she did. She went to the bedroom. She sat on the bed. She drank the whiskey when he handed it to her.

Slowly, as her hearing came back, she nodded when he asked if it was a nightmare. His sister had night terrors. He cared for her. How sweet.

She laid back on the bed while he worked between her legs, the solution to every problem for this man and most men like him. She faked things he wanted her to feel, and finally when he was asleep again, and she was next to him, not asleep, she tried not to cry.

The nightmares were worse. What the hell was happening to her?

Madeline squeezed her eyes shut and didn't fall asleep.

Chapter Eight

Nightmare, Kuribit, and Errvyn stood in a small, newly-hewn, square room adjacent to the Scrying Cavern. Once enticed with a tiny drop of salve, which Nightmare spared despite Errvyn's protests and grumblings, Kuribit set himself to the task with adept efficiency. He summoned thousands of tiny 'mares with a horn that blew notes so sour that it made Nightmare's sinew crawl. But the 'mares came, scrambling through crevices and the new doorway and hauling stones, gems, and baked bricks of Undermaze grit on their backs. They cut the stones with their teeth. They chewed and swallowed bits of dirt, earth, grit, and shat out solid material that Kuribit took and began to use as foundation for the stairs. The Bone Ghosts, catching onto the game, began to appear in the walls and from the floor, shaking more vigorously than necessary to dislodge chunks of dirt and stone. The tiny 'mares seemed delighted at this.

At regular intervals, Kuribit vomited into a bucket. He mixed the sticky filth he spewed with a paste of the dead, and the mixture served as a way to set the stones and bricks. Soon, the stairwell began to rise. Errvyn and Nightmare helped haul raw materials for the building 'mares and held pieces in place to make the work go faster. Kuribit never quit flinching when either of them came too close, but he carried on despite the shaking in his hands.

But the building was fraught with the need to hurry, made all the more urgent by the wails and screams echoing throughout the Undermaze as Merdoth did her work. Nightmare was pained with every 'mare the fell, and Merdoth excelled at her task.

"Tell me of life as a Ghost, Your Majesty," Errvyn said when the stairs were half done.

"My Ghosts are the veins and arteries of this world," Nightmare said, grateful for the distraction. "Their bones and essence become part of this kingdom, the home in which they once walked, built, and lived in 'mare flesh, which they always desired but were never granted Topside. The Ghosts truss the world above and give shelter to their brethren below. Without their presence in the walls, they decay and fall. In the early days, it was a hard lesson learned."

"What do you mean, 'learned?'"

"Though I do not remember being made, I do remember coming into existence. I remember standing next to the Lady, and I remember her saying I would have a home and a kingdom and a people to rule. The original Undermaze was composed of Shadowrock, and it was the throne room, the Scrying Cave, and the Feed room. At first, I was alone, and then, slowly, my citizens began to arrive."

"Ideas needed to die, even in the beginning of everything, eh?" Errvyn grunted and cursed at a minor 'mare that bit him as it tried to eat more raw material and make more bricks.

"Ideas, concepts, intangibles," Nightmare said. "Ours is a land where the darkest concepts, the vilest and reprehensible and destructive ideologies, can find some measure of peace and purpose beyond pure destruction and chaos. The Lady knew a repository for such things would be needed. And she also gave us a purpose as well – for it is we that support the world."

"Poetic," Errvyn said. "But I was aiming less for poetry and more for reality. Ghosts cannot fuck or feast in the walls, can they?"

"No such desires exist for Ghosts, insofar as I know."

"But they can fight?"

"Oh, yes." Nightmare glanced through the doorway at the pile of flesh and bone and blood of the fallen 'mares, waiting for Yaferjull's cart and the Feed. "Ghosts fight."

Errvyn grunted as though this satisfied his curiosity. They built and built, and Merdoth eventually returned, bloodied and somber in pyrrhic triumph. She wordlessly fell to the task of assisting, and soon, the stairs were complete. Nightmare and his kin stepped away, gazing above them and waiting. Kuribit climbed to the topmost stair and began to carve a large square in the dirt overhead while the minor 'mares below gnawed a stone into the shape Kuribit cut. When it was done, they carried it up to him, the room alive with the noise of hundreds of skittering feet. Kuribit took and heaved the doorway with a mighty grunt, shoving it into its nook. He then cut his arm and began to draw sigils in blood that would set the slab in place. It was the first part of the spell that would turn the stone into a gate that would allow Nightmare to go Topside. The symbols pulsed to half-life, shining silver on the black-gray rock, and the room trembled. The quake sent the minor 'mares running away from the steps and toward the solidity of the remaining walls, and terrified whimpers filled the air.

"Kuribit, is it done?" Nightmare asked.

"I have but to speak the final words, your Majesty, and the portal will be finished."

"Then do as you've been bid," Nightmare commanded.

Kuribit trembled. "You're going to kill me once I do, aren't you?"

"There is power in Builders, sometimes unmatched even by Warriors," Nightmare said by way of answer. Around them, flickering red pinpricks came to life, the Ghosts on watch. Errvyn braced, and Merdoth relaxed her stance into one of readiness.

Kuribit said nothing for a long moment. Then he hissed syllables of a spell, invoking a builder's magic, and he splayed his hand on the stone above his head. The sigil came to life, and Kuribit did not move away from the gateway. "I could go Topside," he said, tone tinged with hysteria. "What's to stop me?"

Fingers of sadness scratched at Nightmare. "No 'mare can walk above once he has been below. You would revert to your original state. You would become the idea or the dream or whatever intangible you once were but are no longer. You are irrelevant above the Undermaze. No one wants you; no one can use or have you; no one believes in you or loves you. Kuribit the Builder, you fell. You collapsed. Once important, you are now obsolete and forgotten. If you went Topside, you would wane, you would wither, and you would be torn asunder by the ideas and dreams and creations that currently rule the Topside world."

Kuribit still did not move away from the portal, and Nightmare was loathe for it to be opened before he was ready to cross it, and a Builder could throw the gate open as well as he. Nightmare raised his voice to a booming thunder. "Those ideologies would not be kind, as I can be. They would not give mercy, as I can give you. The ruling paradigm would chew you slowly, savor you, study you and see if any part of you had any merit left. It would torture you, and if it liked anything of you, it would steal that piece, keep you and it imprisoned, voiceless and helpless, until it, too, finally fell into my domain. And you'd be a part of a better idea than you ever were. And you would be its slave." Nightmare paused for a watery breath. Though they were twisted beyond compare, often foolish and occasionally traitorous, Nightmare loved his children. "Only in the Undermaze do you have meaning and can you have life. Even your death, here, is your own, and in it, you find purpose. You are mine, banished unto me, and I will keep you. Forever. It is my promise to you."

Kuribit held to the portal for long moments more before finally, he wept, bitter and fearful. Nightmare looked to Merdoth, who climbed the stairs and dragged Kuribit down them until he knelt in front of his King.

"What if you have needs to build?" Kuribit cried in one last protest.

"Then I will use your power to Walk and claim an idea to be a new Builder."

"But Kuribit did as asked! I built, and now I—"

With speed and control, Nightmare reached down and twisted Kuribit's head off his body, setting the pieces down gently on the floor when it was done.

"Merciful," Errvyn judged.

Nightmare rose to his full height. "And how would you wish your death to be?"

"A fight," Errvyn said.

"A Warrior's pleasure before the end," Merdoth agreed.

"So may it be," Nightmare allowed, and he turned to give honor to the last fight between two of his greatest Warriors. They did not make it last for delay or theater; in a mere seven moves, they ran the other through with their weapons.

And in quick succession, Nightmare was more alone in his land than he ever wished to be.

"Yaferjull!" Nightmare called, knowing the 'mare lurked in fear. In short order, a thin, pale blue creature dragging a cart behind him entered the room. In Topside life, Yaferjull the Wordless had been a silent, blind suspicion, for in his Undermaze existence, he was gaunt, stick-limbed, long-faced, and never-spoken. Rows upon rows of eyes marched down the flat surface of his head, all of them the milky white of the sightless. Two nostrils dotted his chin, and he sometimes gurgled from the puncture in his frail throat that served as his mouth. He had the odd sprig of black hair dotting his body, coming out of his skull, on the backs of his elbows, the sides of his legs. He paused in the doorway between the Scrying Cave and the new room.

"You've nothing to fear of me, as yet," Nightmare said, and Yaferjull rushed forward to kiss Nightmare's feet before turning to his cart and the bodies in the rooms. He had three fingers on each hand, all of them six-joints long, and he deftly began to dismember the 'mares, tossing the pieces into his cart. Adimoas and other Ghosts soon emerged, assisting.

Though he wanted to linger, to pause for a moment of grief for so much lost so quickly, Nightmare did not. He swept out of the room. He closed his eyes, listening for the thrum of the Feed like he imagined other creatures listened to their mother's heartbeat in the womb. Always there, always comforting, always calling, the Feed was at the center of the Undermaze. It was behind the simplest door at the end of the longest, darkest hallway. Nightmare didn't know if he'd taken the shortest path to reach the Feed's catacomb, only that despite feeling as though he'd walked for miles, he entered the Feed's room before Yaferjull or the cart had arrived.

Nightmare left the door open, but as soon as his feet touched the floor of the Feed's room, it shut quietly behind him. The door, the sloping floor, the domed ceiling, and the walls of the Feed's room were entirely composed of Shadowrock. Only a single overhead circle in the exact middle of the ceiling directly over the Feed, itself, was Undermaze dirt, and the dirt was solid as though sculpted with meticulous hands. Written into the dirt were words in a language even older than Fear, and Nightmare no longer knew what the inscription said, only that it stored the magic that allowed the essence of the creatures being put to the Feed to meld with the Undermaze. Legend said the spell was carved there by the Master of Shadows: Lord Nothing, himself. Shadowrock was Lord Nothing's element, and since this room was made of it, Nightmare believed the legend could be true. Sometimes, Nightmare thought he could remember standing in the Feed's room and watching Lord Nothing stand flat-footed while embedding a spell writ in burning Shadow smoke on the ceiling.

Falling into a crouch, Nightmare gingerly placed his fingertips on the shiny rock below his feet. The rock itself was clear on the surface, like glass. Nightmare could see himself in its reflection. But it was obscured in places by a density of crystals that grew beneath the smooth surface. The crystals in Shadowrock tended to be black and deepest, darkest, richest red, giving Shadowrock its dark color.

But the most fascinating quality of the rock was its silver. Gleaming strands of silver-white glitter danced deep inside the rock, swirling around the crystals like mini galaxies and shining like stars. When someone touched the rock, the silver responded. It broke its pattern and sped to the point of contact, erupting in bursts of silver-white. The clarity of the paler colors was dulled by the depth of them beneath the surface and by the dark crystals, but when Nightmare finished petting the rock and playing with the swirls, they followed his feet across the room. Clouds of silver storms lit his path, glowing like dissolving footstones.

Nightmare paused next to the depression in the floor where the Feed stood, and he stared at the rock around him, at the dimmed starlight exploding beneath him. He seemed to recall, in the haze of stories that could be oral tradition spoken by those people tricked by recollection, that the Shadowrock was Lord Nothing's element because it was the product of the Lord and Lady's energies. Lord Nothing could not create, but the Lady could, and when she gave unto her lover the power to make what he willed, Shadowrock was born. The crystals were the Lady's fire and darker nature. The smooth surface was akin to Nothing's wintery existence. The silver was threads of the cosmos that were Nothing's eyes.

If that was the case, then it was possible that everywhere the Shadowrock existed, so too did Lord Nothing. And that could mean that every time Nightmare stepped foot in the Feed's room, the Master of Shadows knew of Nightmare's comings and goings. Not even the King of Nightmare, himself, could hide from the darkness.

The door opened, and Yaferjull pushed the cart of dismembered 'mares into the room. His sightless eyes whirled in their sockets.

"Bring them here," Nightmare said, though Yaferjull had done this often enough to know the routine. The cart squeaked, and Nightmare descended the steep, sloping sides of the concave depression, at the bottom of which was the Feed itself.

For a machine so feared, it was surprisingly simple. A rough-edged, rounded Shadowrock platform about a hands-width in height rested at the lowest point of the basin. Above it, the two columns of the Feed arched to a peak, the walls of the arch about twice the platform in width. At the bottom right side, a coiling shell grew out of the arch, and it twisted, turned, and grew larger and wider and up the side of the arch, over its top, and halfway down the other side. The shell opened into a wide funnel, the opening pointed at the ground. Another shell funnel branched off the main shell and opened at the peak of the arch, aimed at the ceiling. That funnel was the same circumference as the sculpted ceiling patch of Undermaze dirt.

The Feed only responded when Nightmare stood within it; any other who climbed onto the platform disintegrated into dust. Many 'mares took this as proof that Nightmare had created the Feed, despite the legends. Nightmare didn't discourage this, though he knew it wasn't true. The reality was simpler and personal: the Feed was a sentient creature and it just didn't like anyone other than Nightmare.

Yaferjull positioned the cart beneath the south-pointing funnel of the Feed and scrambled away as fast as he could. He cowered near the door, one hand wrapped about the handle as though ready to run at any moment. Meanwhile, Nightmare climbed onto the platform. There was no tingle, no recognition, but Nightmare petted the arch in friendly greeting, anyway. He stood beneath the apex, hands slack by his sides, and he watched the funnel that loomed above the cart.

For a long time, nothing happened. Perhaps the Feed had to rouse and smell its food, and when it finally did, a thin, rope-like appendage snaked out of the funnel and hooked around its edge. It slid along the lip, knocking against it as though reminding itself of the funnel's shape. Soon, more appendages followed, all black and dark grey, all thin and whippy, and all gingerly seeking through the air and along the sides of the cart.

When one of the tentacles brushed the pile of 'mare meat, however, it recoiled, and all the other appendages flew to the one that had found dinner. There was a thick, wet sound, as though something unstuck itself from a damp surface, and the bulk of the Feed lowered partway out of the funnel. It was a round, bulbous mass with hundreds of the appendages jutting out of its body. The Feed and all its arms settled atop the 'mares, and Nightmare heard the slurps and sucks of the Feed beginning to eat.

Nightmare turned his attention to the insides of the arch, which began to writhe as though the sides hadn't been one smooth construction at all, but instead been made of millions of inky baby snakes. Without warning, the snakes began shooting out from the arch to latch onto Nightmare's body. It was not particularly gentle, but it didn't necessarily hurt.

At least, not until the snakes began to worm their way into Nightmares bones, sinew, and insides. That was a strange mixture of pleasure and pain, of suffocation and freedom, and Nightmare relaxed into the strangleholds, allowing the snakes to crawl into his mouth, his skull, his empty chest cavity, his sex, and the corners of his eyes. A lull overcame him, rendering him oddly calm and complacent, and Nightmare went limp in the Feed's hold. He fought the urge to shut his eyes, though, wanting to see... waiting to see...

As the Feed consumed more of the 'mares, the shell and the arch began to glow orange-red-gold. The shell began to pulsate with light, as though it grew a temporary heart, and soon the entire structure and the snakes began to thrum in time. As the transformation took the 'mares and turned their bodies into energy, the energy inflamed the Feed's arch, sped through the arch's snake-like tendons attached and buried in Nightmare's body, and the energy began to enter Nightmare. All Nightmare could do was moan in pure bliss. There was no fight, here, only hunger and satiation. Nightmare stared at the beautiful red-gold arch until it nearly blinded him and finally, he had to shut his eyes. He dangled in the squirming snake web, and he ate and ate and ate the fuel the Feed took, changed, and fed to the only creature the Feed deigned to give such favor.

Chapter Nine

Jason picked up the freshly-vacuumed bathroom rug in front of the sink in the Snapdragon Suite and shook it. Ms. Adlewilde shed hair in such quantities that it was a wonder she wasn't bald, and hair stuck to the bathroom grout was one of Monica's pet peeves. So was dust of any variety, spots on mirrors, dirt on top of baseboards or light switch covers, and clocks that did not tell the correct time. Jason was considering making a list of Monica's irritations and putting them in alphabetical order. Maybe framing them, wrapping the picture, and presenting it on Christmas morning. After vacuuming up all the pine needles from under the tree, of course.

In just a few short days, Jason had worked out a routine that, at least so far, had all his rooms done in plenty of time. Monica might be meticulous about her standards, but she didn't care what Jason did to meet them or how fast he did it. Yesterday, he'd been finished by three, and he'd gone into town to buy some clothes. He'd found Goodwill easily enough, as he was unwilling to drop a huge amount of cash on a wardrobe, but he'd come away with some button-downs, some slacks that mostly fit, and a new pair of jeans without rips. He'd gone to Kmart for shoes, and he'd gotten back to the hotel in time to put his purchases away and take a nap before dinner.

When Andrew had come in from the garden, Jason had leaned in the doorway and pumped the guy for more information about Jason's new home, however temporary it might turn out to be. Helen lived in the apartment over the garage, just like Jason had suspected. Mercutio was her nurse and companion, of sorts, and he'd been with the family for seven years and eight months, according to Andrew's offhand, but oddly precise, calculations. Helen was crazy, but what sort of crazy or precisely how afflicted with said crazy she was, Andrew wasn't sure.

"She used to teach, and she used to write books, but then one day she stopped, and ever since, she's been the lady over the old stable," Andrew had said on Jason's second night while shucking clothing on his way to the shower.

Jason followed Andrew to the doorway. "Did she fall? Have an accident or something?"

Andrew shook his head. "No, I don't think so. I would remember that."

"Huh."

"Uhm, I'm going to take off my underwear?" Andrew had made it a question, and Jason had booked it out of the room and onto the porch to get some fresh air. The evenings were less humid, and the rocking chairs were comfortable. Jason was determined to enjoy every small moment. He wanted to make each of them last.

There'd been no sign of Helen at dinner on the second night or the third. After helping to set up the tea and coffee stations, Jason had opted to stay in the kitchen for the rest of the dinner hour. He'd supposedly been helping Jennifer and Miss Teedee, but Jennifer never spoke a word to Jason, and Miss Teedee flowed from one task to the next and fed Jason bites of dessert in between. So mostly Jason sat on a stool, ate, and watched, and it was easier than being in the big dining room with the guests and family.

Jason hadn't known how tired he was until he had a comfortable, safe place to rest his head. He slept like the dead, though he often woke up feeling like he'd been dreaming something important but couldn't remember it. Andrew was a quiet sleeper and a better roommate than any member of Judith's Hell had ever been. Monica watched Jason like a hawk, and he knew she did, but she didn't have any unkind words to say about the job he was doing or the way he was acting. Jason wanted to keep circumstances at that level of peaceful, so he scrubbed the bejesus out of the Snapdragon soaking tub, working up a sweat and sneezing when the cleaning powder got up his nose.

With Ms. Adlewilde's rooms done, Jason only had the hallways to do. There was a new guest in the Iris room, but the Do Not Disturb sign was dangling off the doorknob, so nothing to do there. He put the supplies back onto the rolling cart and stretched. His stomach rumbled, and when he checked one of the three clocks on the wall, he saw it was a little past one. No wonder he was starving. He pushed the cart out of the way, banging his knee in the process and cussing. He'd forgotten to oil the beast that morning, and Monica was right; you noticed when you didn't lube the sucker up before using it.

Hunched over to rub at the forming bruise, Jason hobbled around the corner toward the central stairwell, and when he stood up, he nearly ran into Helen, who was wrapped around the banister railing. One of her legs was between the posts, and she was hugging the decorative top of the rail with both arms. She wore baggy jeans, a loose white shirt with shimmery buttons, and her hair was a tumbling mess of black curls framing her too-pale face and throat. She looked more like a fourteen-year-old than what Jason guessed was about a forty-year-old.

Helen glanced twice down the stairs while chewing on her knuckles. "Hi," she said at last, eyes coming to rest on Jason.

"Hey." Jason swallowed. He didn't know if it was the clothes or the shyness, but Helen seemed fragile. He had to fight the urge to go to her and take her hand or hug her. "Haven't seen you since dinner the other night."

"No, you haven't."

"... Right." Jason never was good at small talk. "So, what's up?"

"Did you like my story?" Helen clung to the railing as though it was the only thing keeping her standing.

"I did," Jason said. Since hearing it, haunting visions of a massive mountain of a dark man and a tiny elf of a woman-man-beast had filled his head at night when he shut his eyes. He doodled their portraits on napkins while he ate Miss Teedee's homemade tarts and key lime pie. There was a stuffed raccoon in the library, and the taxidermist had chosen to leave the creature's mouth slightly open. Jason thought it was supposed to be a smile, but the rows of pointy teeth made Jason shudder every time he passed. It reminded him of a too-wide, thin pair of lips spreading in delight before a meal.

"You left right after I was done," Helen said.

"I know. I'm sorry. I was exhausted. I've been really tired lately."

"I understand." Helen nodded. "I've been tired for a long time, too. It's tiring."

"What is?"

Helen almost smiled, and instead of answering, she asked, "What did you do before coming here?"

Images flash-flickered through Jason's mind: lights, stages, tour buses, cheap vans, bad hotels, bottles of whiskey, Rage's smile. Judith's bare breasts and her sighing between Jason and Rage. Judith's smile – the one that made her look like she wanted to eat you alive. Blood. "I was a musician. Well. I was in a band. *With* a band." Jason huffed at himself. "I didn't play music, exactly, more like I was a roadie and..." He couldn't bring himself to say he'd been in one of the most intense relationships he'd ever experienced or heard of with the two main band members. "That kind of thing, you know?" he added lamely.

"I think so," Helen said.

"Ah, yeah. I guess it's a bit odd for around here."

Helen laughed, then, startlingly full and carefree. "You'd be surprised at what passes for 'odd' here, I think."

"Oh yeah?" Jason felt a grin threaten to take over his face. "What did you do, then? Or do you do?"

Helen glanced down the stairwell again. "I was a teacher."

"Of what?"

"Children." A smirk played with her mouth, and Jason wanted to touch it with his fingertips to see if it was real. "Some of them had very unusual stories. Odd ones."

"The kids did?" Jason asked, more just to keep her talking. Her voice was low and husky.

"Mmhm. There was one girl in particular. Blonde. Beautiful. And so sad. She walked out of the woods one day." Helen looked as though she was about to say more and stopped herself.

"She was abandoned?" Jason asked. "Where were her parents?"

"No one knows. She was adopted. Such a beautiful girl. No memory of what came before her walking out of the woods, and she was about six when she arrived, so there should have been. I've been thinking a lot about that little girl."

An old ache stirred in Jason's chest, oozing downward until his feet felt made of lead. Miss Teedee must have told them his story, or what he'd told of it. "Why, 'cause it reminds you of me?"

Helen tipped her head to one side. "Why? Were you lost, too?"

"Maybe," Jason said. "I didn't fit in with the people who raised me. I didn't fit in with the band. Not really. I guess I'm still looking for my people."

Helen studied him until Jason wanted to squirm. "Now that you've found us, are you going to leave?"

"Leave?"

"The hotel."

"What, like, now? Or for good?" Jason quelled a spike of anxiety.

Helen twisted slightly as though she was listening to someone standing on her left, but her eyes stayed on Jason. "Either," she said.

"I was going to go get some lunch," Jason said. "I was just going to the kitchen. I still need to do the hallways. And I have to be around tonight. I told Andrew I'd show him how to play Blackjack."

A smile danced across Helen's lips. She pushed away from the railing, her hands in a fidgety knot in front of her breasts. "Are you afraid of me?"

"No," Jason sputtered. His heart began to hammer harder with every step she took toward him, her big, almost black eyes wide and open and gazing up at him, but Jason didn't think fear had anything to do with his reaction. Other than maybe fear of what her father would say or do to him if Darryl found out how much Jason wanted to take Helen's hand, go somewhere private, and listen to her tell her stories until he fell into a deep, deep sleep. "Why should—No. I'm not afraid of you."

The smile flickered again, like a spark trying to catch. "Are you afraid of this place?"

"The house?" Jason asked.

"Yes."

Unease crawled through him, but it wasn't because he feared the house. More like he feared the shadows that chased him. "No."

"Good."

"Miss Pretty?" Mercutio called from one floor down. "Where'd you get off to?"

"I have to go," Helen said in a fast murmur before fleeing down the stairs with a flick of dark curls. She left behind the scent of books and rosewater – musty and yet sweet.

"The hell?" Jason whispered to no one but himself.

A sense of disquiet followed him through lunch and the rest of his chores. After another dinner spent in the kitchen, he and Andrew sat in the dining room and played cards. The game quickly devolved into a game of "Go Fish," and honestly, it was more Jason's speed, too, at that moment.

When Andrew announced, "I'm going to get pie and go watch the Home and Garden Channel," Jason was relieved and declined the offer to join.

He needed out – needed to scratch an itch that ran away and hid from his touch. He left by the front door and walked around the veranda to the wide, rear steps. He kept checking the wallet that hung from hooks he sewed into all his pants, just to see if it was there. He didn't trust pockets, and he didn't trust people, but all his money was accounted for. And when he pulled out his keys, they were all there, too. He played with them, absently, as he made his way to the far corner of the parking lot – the spot near the utility shed near the dock. It was marked "Employees Only," and Jason still felt a pang of pride that Monica had told him he could park in that space after ordering him to take "that heap of metal and rust and get it out of the guests' sight."

As twilight settled cozily over the water, Jason opened the van's door and dug in the center console. Soon enough, he found a lighter and two cigarettes in a crumpled pack. He highly doubted Monica would approve – nor Miss Teedee, honestly. He smiled to himself as he set one cigarette between his lips. He locked up the van and walked toward the water and onto the dock. It ran along the Soundwater's edge, and Jason followed the path west, toward a signpost straight out of Alice in Wonderland. Arrows went in all directions: RESTROOMS, DOCK, BAIT & TACKLE, TAYLOR POINT HOUSE, GARDEN PATH, TOWNSENDE TRAIL & SOUNDSIDE PARK. Jason picked the GARDEN PATH, which let him meander along cobblestone pathways through Andrew's labors of love. The garden wall on the far western edge of the property marked the line between the Taylor Point House land and the forest beyond it. The forest was part of a state park, full of hiking trails, and if he'd chosen TOWNSENDE TRAIL instead, it would have taken him across a white bridge and into a carefully manicured park with playgrounds and picnic areas. Or so Miss Teedee had explained in painstaking detail while rolling dough for biscuits one morning.

Parks and playgrounds weren't his thing, but this garden was. Jason knew exactly nothing about flowers, shrubs, or trees, but he recognized beauty when he walked through it. Night-blooming flowers scented the air, along with dozens of rosebushes and other flowers. Manicured trees formed a protective bow across much of the pathway, their limbs gently rustling in the late evening air. Deep green vines crept over trellises shaped to look like enormous animals, and twinkle lights flickered, hidden in the foliage so well, they could have almost been fireflies. A small creek ran through the flora features – occasionally even crossing the path and inspiring the need for a footbridge. Andrew had shaped the creek to babble along quietly, and it'd pool here and there in ponds with fish and frogs. Jason passed a small blue and gold sign that directed him to a Meditation Garden, which he decided not to explore. Ahead was a large fountain, its current gushing loudly in the quiet, and the fountain's lights slowly changed colors, illuminating a crossroads in the trail. Above him was a domed, wooden structure with open latticework, and trees and plants twisted around it. Vines dangled and swayed overhead. There were four benches next to each of the cardinal point directions. Jason could see that the northern one took him out of the garden. From here, he could see the old stable with Helen's apartment above it. West would take him through more garden but back to the house, planting him near the back porch. East went toward the meditation garden, Jason supposed, and that side was the darkest. He sat on the fountain's edge, lighting up his second and last cig.

"Rage, you would've loved this shit, man," Jason whispered. He bent forward, elbows on his knees, and he stared at the stone beneath his feet, remembering their last gig – his view from the edge of the outdoor stage. It'd started to rain during the last two songs of the set, just a light mist, and Judith's hair had gleamed like onyx as she'd danced and stormed and sang her guts out. The bass had pounded like it was the heartbeat of the sold-out crowd – frenetic and constant and consuming. They'd screamed lyrics. They'd screamed her name. They'd—

"Jason."

He focused his eyes and realized the light from the fountain had gone dark.

"Jason."

The whisper was watery and soft, and he shivered, but not from cold.

"Ja-son!"

This was a hiss, and Jason turned to look into the water. Its surface rippled with the churn of the fountain's flow, but the creature beneath the water was clear. Its head was misshapen, and one eye was lost to the wreckage. The other was closed, squeezed tight, and embedded in skin that looked vaguely like tree bark. Jason had been to Hawaii once with the band, and he remembered Banyan trees – their ropey trunks and roots sprawling everywhere. The thing's flesh looked a bit like that. While Jason watched, the creature's lower jaw trembled. Its sadness, its loss and loneliness and fear, were palpable. Jason leaned closer, stricken and horrified. When a tear crawled down the thing's face, one escaped Jason's eye, too.

"*Jaaaaaay-sssssson*," came the voice again – not the creature. Worms began to fill the fountain: thick, pink, bloated worms. He heard a beat – a heartbeat, loud and steadily getting faster. He thought of the logo for Judith's Hell: an anatomical heart speared through with steel rods. The worms pulsed to the heartbeat, grew bigger and thicker to its rhythm, until one lashed up and caressed Jason's hand on the fountain's edge. It was feverish and slimy, and Jason was frozen. He was stuck. He was too close to the water. They were going to grab and drown him. He wasn't sure he minded.

"*Jason*," the voice in the fountain said, "*Don't worry, darling. I'm coming. We'll be together...*" The worms touched his face, pressing like kisses. "*Soon.*"

At the last possible second, Jason jerked backward, fumbling and falling on his ass. He scrambled to his feet and ran-staggered away, catching himself on the bench at the northern path. The heartbeat grew louder, louder, louder, and he sank into a crouch, covering his ears. After a moment, when nothing happened, he dared to look.

All he saw was the fountain. The lights were blue, green, lilac, and normal. There was nothing in the water. Nothing was coming for him.

Just a nightmare.

Or maybe a warning.

Chapter Ten

When Nightmare came to consciousness, he was sprawled on the Feed's platform. Above him, the open archway was quiet and still. The Feed's chamber glowed faintly silver, the light thrown from the threads of stars lurking in the Shadowrock, and Nightmare pushed himself into a crouch. He could hear the faint whispers of his Bone Ghosts beyond the Feed Room's door, the whimpering of his servant, Yaferjull, and, most incredibly, the tick-surge of energy coursing through his form. Nightmare looked at his hands. The shining sinew was thicker, closer to the midnight skin he usually wore, rather than mere connective tissue. He patted himself from face to chest to thighs, discovering that every inch of him pulsed as though he had a heart, not an empty cavern, and when he slipped a hand within his cracked breast, the stored energy from the Feed whirled green and yellow around his fingers, licking and kissing them.

Nightmare shivered. He did not know if it would be enough energy to do what must be done, but he was more alive than he could remember, and it was glorious. He rose, and he could smell the remnants of the decay that had once filled the cart next to the Feed. The cart was empty, but the stain remained. He thought he could hear the Feed in slumber, a high whine of an inhale followed by a low wet exhale. The rhythm was that of sleep and recovery. Nightmare stepped off the platform, and the Shadowrock burst into colors and danced.

Yaferjull hovered next to the door. "You are dismissed, loyal one," Nightmare said as he approached his servant, and Yaferjull fled, vanishing in the hallways beyond the Feed Room. Nightmare stepped out of the Shadowrock room, too, and he touched the walls next to the silently shutting door, caressing the Bone Ghosts who rose to greet him. They murmured and purred like kittens, and Nightmare took his time retracing his steps.

"Majesty... Majesty... he walks... Walker... Walker..."

Nightmare kissed many of his loyal citizens, and when he entered the room where the staircase to Topside had been built, Admioas emerged from the walls.

"My Liege," Adimoas greeted him. "You seem much revived."

"My thanks to you, the Ghosts, and the 'mares, may they be remembered." Nightmare kissed the hollow of Adimoas' nose.

"All hail the King of Nightmare," Adimoas said reverently. "Praise him. Keep him safe. Keep him strong."

Nightmare reluctantly stepped away, studying the stairwell. "Keep my peace while I am Topside, Adimoas."

"You bring us life, my king, and we all, each loyal servant, will await your return."

Still, Nightmare hesitated. "Should I not return, and should the quakes worsen, and these Horrors draw near..."

"We will retreat to the Feed Room, My Lord. Its walls are impenetrable."

"Yes. And guard the Scrying Cavern, too. We know not where those depths lead, but it may be an escape, or it may be a place of weakness."

"Yes, Your Majesty."

Nightmare bowed in respect. "Thank you, friend."

The stone stairs were cool beneath Nightmare's bare feet. He ascended slowly, and he knelt on the topmost slab when he reached it. Bone Ghosts began to emerge from the walls on all sides, hundreds and hundreds of them, every one of them chanting a low prayer in the old Fear tongue. Adimoas lead them, his voice the loudest and the surest.

Surrounded by the cadence of the spoken words asking for hope and strength and for the Feed blood to flow, Nightmare began to draw the sigils that would open the gate. He etched them with a steady claw, the edge of it cutting into the rock as though he sliced skin. Going Topside required many of the same sigils as creating a Veil between worlds. Topside was, Nightmare supposed, a different world than the Undermaze. Different rules governed it, different beings ruled it. Going Topside was always risky and exhausting, but now, with the Horrors raging and the war taking casualties, it bordered on suicidal. Nightmare steadied himself, resolved in his lack of choices but hopeful that he had at least this one to make.

Nightmare took his time carving the ancient symbols used by Walkers. When the marks were finished, Nightmare brought the same claw to his long, coiled black tongue, and he cut himself, letting saliva and blood flow. Two life liquids per one sigil, that was the rule, and he touched each symbol in turn. When he was done, there was a hiss, like a spark igniting a blaze, and the magic sprung to life. The signs burst into brilliant red, and the edges of the stone darkened. Nightmare put both hands on the gate and pushed, and the rock gave way with a crumbling groan.

Nightmare rose, shoving the gate up and out of the way. He winced. The lavender-blue Twilight of Topside was a hundred times brighter than the caves of the Undermaze. Below Nightmare, the Bone Ghosts' prayers grew to a deafening volume that faded to nothing as Nightmare hooked his hands on the edge of the Topside World and hauled himself into it. He moved fast and forced his eyes open as he crouched beside the gaping hole between the Undermaze and

Topside, claws at the ready. When no immediate threat showed itself, Nightmare dragged the stone into place, sealing off the Undermaze.

He was in a building, a wooden structure made of Topside tree logs and mud that enclosed Nightmare on all sides. It was always cooler Topside than it was in the Undermaze, and it took time for Nightmare to adjust to the changes in climate. The Undermaze was humid and hot, heated by its fiery energy core. The same energy flowed up and out to Topside, feeding rivulets that flowed to the Ring: a magenta-flame, molten circlet that wrapped around the edges of Via'rra. The Lady controlled the Ring, fed it, and used it, and it was said a miniature one encircled her House of Five Bridges, high above in the swirling space that hovered over Via'rra's lands.

Nightmare didn't think he'd ever seen the Lady's Home, nor met the Lady. And wasn't that peculiar? Surely he had. But if he had, surely he'd remember?

This place seemed familiar, or, at least, not threatening, but he just couldn't remember if he'd been there or had met Storyteller, and, more importantly, he couldn't remember if it was important that he'd lost those memories.

Nightmare slunk and put his back to one of the walls. The roof over his head was flat and tall enough that he could stand beneath it, though, for the time being, Nightmare stayed hunkered low. A stove sat in a corner, no fire within, and iron pots and pans sat on top of it. Next to the stove was a simple bed on a wooden frame. A table stood beside it, and books were stacked high on its surface. On top of the books were a knife and a piece of wood, half of which had been shaped into a bird, mid-flight. The other half was still rough, only vaguely carved. There was a rug on the floor, braided in brown, green, and yellow, and more rugs on the walls. The windows had shutters that were closed and latched on the inside, and fingers of light shone through the crevices and sliver-sized flaws in the wood.

On the other side of the single room was a rocking chair, more stacks of books, and shelves full of carved treasures, handmade pots with lids, dried herbs, and all manner of other, personal effects. This place had to be the Storyteller's Cabin. He remembered stories of its simplicity, or maybe those were memories. Nightmare couldn't be sure. Slowly, he rose to his full height, listening.

The quiet was disconcerting. Storyteller's Cabin was in the Endless Forest. Some parts of that Forest were darker and more dangerous than others, but Storyteller's portion was a safe haven, full of bright light and lime-green shade. Here and now, however, Nightmare heard no birds, no animals, and no signs of life. Nightmare strained to hear anything at all, his claws digging into the wood at his back with the effort of concentration, and he snarled in prelude to attack when the cabin's door opened.

"Peace, brother," the old man said, shutting the door behind him. "It's only me."

Upon seeing him, Nightmare recalled that Storyteller could appear young or old, depending on where he was in time. Storyteller's version of time was tricky for Nightmare to grasp; essentially, all points in all universes were the same, and Storyteller existed in every universe simultaneously. Some worlds, notably Earth and the humans on it, had a nickname for Storyteller; Father Time. But the only reason Storyteller told time was to remember all the stories of all the ages.

Nightmare found comfort that his memory wasn't entirely gone.

Today Storyteller looked like a wizened old man. Wrinkles folded the skin of his face and neck, and it all crinkled kindly when he smiled. His eyes were purple, a rich color that mimicked the Twilight around them, and they were set deep into sturdy bone structure. His nose was bulbous and reddened, his shoulders wide and strong, though his back was humped with age. He wore a long, brown leather duster with a hood, a red and green shirt, brown pants, and brown shoes. His hair was curly, light grey streaked with darker grey, and so was the healthy, bushy beard that brushed his chest. He petted it, the beard, and keenly gazed at Nightmare.

"You're looking a little thin," Storyteller said.

Nightmare glanced at himself and back at Storyteller. He wasn't sure what to say to that, as he simply was himself, but Storyteller chuckled. "You kids. No sense of humor."

"Kid?" Nightmare repeated. "I am no child, Storyteller."

"Oh, let's not rest on our Walker titles. Call me Daanske," Storyteller said, smiling when Nightmare sucked air as the power of a Veil Walker's true name trembled in the air between them. "It's my name, and we are friends."

"Da-an-skay," Nightmare sounded the syllables, tasting them to rediscover their familiarity. "Very well. Let me be Mal'uud 'au Keen, then, to you.."

Storyteller smiled. "I was there when your true name was given to you."

A chill came over Nightmare, and the comfort he temporarily had found was now dust in the wind. He thought he might be afraid. He didn't recall when he'd taken his name, or if or when someone had, as Storyteller said, given it to him. He should remember that, thought it would be a significant moment, possibly one to cherish, and he shuddered again. "This talk of names is not why I am here, Daanske."

"You don't remember, do you?" Storyteller asked.

The question would have irritated Nightmare, but the tone Storyteller used was calm and reasonable. "No," Nightmare admitted. "I do not."

Storyteller nodded, approached, and patted Nightmare on the shoulder. It was disconcerting, the ease with which Storyteller handled him. "It's all right, son," Storyteller said.

"I am not your son," Nightmare said.

"No." Storyteller went over to a window and picked up a crowbar, beginning to pry the nails loose. He smiled at a bent nail. "One day you might find yourself sitting around with nothing better to do than to think on things long gone. And you may ask yourself, what had to come first? The idea for the universe, or the person to have the idea?"

"I do not know this riddle," Nightmare said.

"Well, think about it." Storyteller pulled out nails longer than Nightmare's fingers and then went back to prying.

Nightmare made an exasperated sound. "I do not know. I suppose the person or creature to have the idea."

Storyteller paused. "Huh," he said with a shrug. More nails popped to skitter across the floor.

"Is that not the answer?" Nightmare asked.

"Eh, well, the story of creation is the greatest one ever known, and I'm sort of inclined to believe that stories exist out there with different details and their tails all unraveled until someone picks up the threads and starts to weave them into whatever form the story must take so everyone who needs to understand it can."

"Are you telling me that stories are sentient?"

The board came off the window, Twilight spilled into the cabin, and Storyteller leaned heavily against the wall. "I'm telling you that I didn't make you, but the question of who did and in what order is still up for debate. I'm also telling you I'm feeling my age these days, and I was working up to saying that I don't remember like I used to, either, especially not with Zee out of commission."

Nightmare's spine locked in place, absolutely rigid. He could barely speak, and when he did, he stammered. "Y-you invoke him?

Storyteller chuckled. "The shadow critter doesn't bother me." His eyes grew darker. "I know what makes the Shadows. Zee's a good one to look after them."

Nightmare put a hand inside his chest to feel the energy there. It comforted him and reminded him of who he was and why he was here. "You say the Shadow Lord is weakened? How did that come to be?"

Storyteller nodded to the window. "Look."

Nightmare stepped to the window and rested his hands on the ledge and the other shutter. The window was next to the door, which opened onto a wide-planked porch. Heavy metal pots sat in the corners and were full of tools. There were more chairs outside, all rocking in a soundless wind. A gust rattled the chimes hanging from the roof's edge, and their music tinkled and crawled down Nightmare's backbone. Beyond the porch was a footpath leading to a creek bed that snaked around Storyteller's cabin in a horseshoe shape. It was completely dry, now. Judging by the cut of the banks, though, it had once been a wide, steady flow. The ground around the path was green, rich moss, sporting tiny white and yellow flowers. Several old trees dotted the clearing where the cabin sat, and they, too, were green and robust.

Surrounding the clearing, however, was a white, swirling fog. It crackled with sickly pink-and-cream bursts of light, and, when Nightmare peered closer, he saw thousands of mouths emerging, silently screaming, and then disappearing within the smoke.

"What is it?" Nightmare asked.

"The Horrors." Storyteller's voice was not, as Nightmare would have expected, tinged with disgust, hatred, or fear. Instead, he sounded calm and resolute, perhaps a bit sad.

"What stops them from advancing?"

"Oh, I can still weave a good spoken spell when the urge is upon me. What I've said will keep the mess of them quiet and keep them at bay long enough for us to talk and to do what needs doing."

"Quiet," Nightmare mused, staring at where the clearing's ground touched the fog. It was churning, as though someone dug through the earth so fast it was a blur of movement, flinging mud and greenery.

"Yeah, they can make an awful racket. Screeching, day and night." Storyteller cocked his head. "Though, it's not as bad as the noise their creator makes."

Nightmare whirled on Storyteller. "You know what makes this abomination?"

"How do you know it's an abomination?"

"What else could it be?"

Storyteller's eyes glittered lavender-cornflower-white. "How do you know it isn't something with great purpose?"

Nightmare considered. "I confess, I do not much care if it is or is not meant to exist. It's killed many of mine. The Horrors, they are what cause the tremors that collapse my caverns, is it not?"

"Maybe," Storyteller conceded. "Some of that might be the fighting."

"Who fights?"

"Most of Via'rra, actually, though it's a battle they cannot win."

A brittle piece inside Nightmare threatened to snap. "I have taken great risk and suffered greater loss of some of my strongest and bravest to answer your summons." As he spoke, Nightmare advanced upon Storyteller, who didn't retreat, choosing instead to regard Nightmare with a faintly curious expression. "You speak to me in riddles. Do you mean to say that this battle – the Horrors, this curse upon our land – is the end of all? Is there no hope? Then why call unto me? Why make yourself known? Why not leave me to my subjects so I could die with my children?"

Storyteller sighed. "Do you know what you and the Shadow Lord have in common?"

Nightmare thought of the Feed, of consumption, of terror. "I—"

"You can both be awful demanding. Why don't you sit down and just listen a spell?"

Quite suddenly, Nightmare was across the room and in the rocking chair, his weight tipping it almost to toppling. Nightmare quickly righted himself, too shocked to be irritated. Storyteller went onto the front porch, and he dragged another chair inside. He put it opposite Nightmare and eased himself into it.

"First of all, Mal – do you mind if I call you Mal?"

Nightmare tried to answer, but it was as though his lips were glued together. He felt his face for the culprit, but it was only his face and nothing more.

"Mal it is, then." Storyteller leaned to one side and picked up his carving off his bedside table. He pulled out a knife, flicked it open, and began to rock. "You'll find things tend to obey me when

I use certain tones. Don't worry; it doesn't last for any great length of time, these days. I'm too tired. I'm sorry about using the forceful route, but I know you a little better than you know yourself. And I'm familiar with the youthful drive for action and answers, even if the better idea is to wait for the right questions to come along.

"And before you tell me you're not a child, or, well, try to, anyway." Storyteller whittled his wood and smirked at Nightmare. "I'm going to tell you that compared to me, you're an infant. I'm old, son. Real, real old. You remember much about the way I work?"

Nightmare's understanding of Storyteller was clearly and rather critically limited. He shook his head.

"Mm. Well. It's not all that important, but here's what is: time is a loop. The snake eats its tail, and Mal, I'm close to the tail end, at the moment. I've not done more, here and now, because I've been there and then trying to make sure everything is in place for our last shot at fixing this mess. It took some time, and as our bad luck would have it," Storyteller laughed quietly under his breath, "the longer it takes, the less in each of our right minds and memories we are. Like you, I have a hard time recalling things. Used to be, I could see Zee, and it got better, but..."

Nightmare couldn't imagine paying a social visit to Lord Nothing, and he grew more fascinated with each passing second. There were keys to understanding, here, and he had to collect them.

"Anyway, there's not merely one me. There's a lot of me, in a lot of different times, and in a lot of different places. I used to be connected to all of them. I could run the time loop and stop and go at any point, but the power gets less and less as the Horrors burn the world. Because that's what they're doing — burning and destroying. I suspect that as soon as this plan of mine is put into motion, what we've been through up to now will look like a siesta." Storyteller laughed, rich and full. "Oh, I know, I know. You fail to see the humor. But we're on our last strike, last legs, and last shreds of sanity. And we're operating with sacks over our heads. It's so impossible, it's funny. And you have to laugh, or you'll spend all your time weeping."

"That I can understand," Nightmare said, surprised when his voice worked.

"Told you I didn't have a lot of oomph anymore." Storyteller shrugged and brushed wood shavings off his knee. "I've got enough energy for what comes next, and that's it."

"And what is it that comes next?"

Storyteller's knife paused mid-cut. "I need to tell you the story of Light and Water."

"They're Walkers," Nightmare said. He suddenly knew it to be true, and he shuddered to think that he had almost forgotten their titles.

"They are," Storyteller agreed. "Well. They were."

"Tell me," Nightmare said. "Please."

"Of course, Your Majesty." Storyteller rested in his chair and rocked it as he spoke. "Do you remember stars?"

"From Topside? Less so, but the Blue World – Earth – they have many, and I always liked them. They're the ghosts of planets and entities far, far away."

"Do you find yourself thinking of Earth more often than not? Maybe it's seeming a little more real than this one?"

"Yes." The confession was not pleasant. "Why is that?"

"It's a simpler world. Doesn't have the permanence problem this place does. Or, for that matter, the infestation of gods."

Nightmare laughed, and he touched his throat to be sure it was him making the sound. It was. "True, I suppose, yes."

Storyteller's eyes danced with brief mirth. "There may be other reasons, too, but first, the stars. Our stars are pieces of our shattered sun, which the Lady broke so her boyfriend doesn't get fried every time he leaves the house. They are close to our land, our stars, and offer light and warmth that keep us temperate. Most of those star bits still have their firepower, excuse the pun."

"Excused," Nightmare conceded with mock grace.

"Mmhm." Storyteller hummed in amusement. "The sun stars are also camouflage for the real stars that aren't only stars."

"Light?" Nightmare asked.

Storyteller tapped his nose. "Light is the name given to the constellation of seven stars which can only be seen in Via'rra's sky. These seven stars form a ring like a crown above our land, and they aren't distant space entities at all. They are the Universe's greatest and all-enduring ideals. Clockwise from the North are Love, Gratitude, Understanding, Curiosity, Forgiveness, Kindness, and Hope. Altogether, the group of stars form Light. The Lady and her Lord closely and ferociously protect Light. Do you know why? Do you remember Light's purpose?"

Nightmare's skull ached when he tried to recall it. "No."

"Mm. Well, then first, a history lesson." Storyteller turned the carving in his strong hands. "Long, long ago, when the worlds were fewer, the Lady, in her infinite, if occasionally incomprehensible wisdom, created the Veils. It's said that she did this so that when creatures traveled to or through Via'rra, they could glimpse Light. Everything in our universe operates on balance, Mal. You know this to be true in your own kingdom, so I know you can understand it is true in every kingdom. Light must be used and kept in balance to create and maintain balance."

"How?" Nightmare asked.

"Via'rra is the center of all worlds. All worlds have access to Via'rra and, thus, to Light. In the connection – or when creatures traveled through our land – they take a bit of Light to their own world. Those worlds balance themselves accordingly, taking neither too much nor too little Light from this world. And so everything spins.

"Now, in order for everything out there in the worlds beyond the Veils to spin in check, Light's got to do her own spinning right here in Via'rra. It's like a clock. You know clocks and their cogs, yes?"

"Not really."

Storyteller chuckled. "Nevermind, then. Suffice to say, Light has her own kind of orbit, much like so many worlds have around a sun. Light has her orbit with Via'rra. Once in a very particular cycle, one part of Light falls from the sky to Via'rra. While the Light Sister is here, we know her as a Walker, and her name is her virtue: Gratitude, Love, etc. Do you follow?"

"I do," Nightmare confirmed.

"Anyway, a piece of Light comes down here, and for a time, she gives courage and inspiration, and all the good, warm, cuddly crap creatures below the heavens need. She is also to shine upon things which are useful so that big bad Nothing won't eat 'em. So long as Light spins in her cycle here in Via'rra, she is the balance for the Lord and Lady. Lord cannot eat, and therefore, Lady cannot remake that which Light deems worthy." Storyteller made a deep cut in his block of wood. "It's a lot of responsibility for one pair of slim shoulders."

"Especially for someone like Light. When she first arrives, she's stable and confident and knows her purpose. Unfortunately, as she stays on the ground – which is not her true home – she will fade. Her inner light will dim, and she will eventually grow weary. She will shine less and less, become more and more despondent, unstable, even reckless, and eventually, the very darkness she tries to govern will overcome her."

"You mean..."

Storyteller nodded. "Lord Nothing consumes Light at the end of her days on Via'rra. He carefully gives her energy to the Lady, who remakes the formerly missing sister star of Light. Another star of that constellation then falls to the earth, and the process begins again. Much like I dance around the wheel of time, Light goes around the wheel of her seven parts. In this way, Via'rra is equally graced with all parts of Light, and we can share all parts of Light with the other worlds in equal, balanced measure. Everything, as I'm sure you're beginning to see, is hinged upon her. Like I said: it's a lot for one entity. Especially if that entity is forevermore only one-seventh of herself while she's doing all she must do. And the most fragile one – but also, I must say the most powerful – is Hope. She was the virtue who most recently graced our land. Hope is a force of nature, an unstoppable beast, at least early on and when she is with others." He smiled ruefully. "You see, the most troublesome and the most fantastic thing about Hope is that she is strongest when *had.*"

"Had?"

"Yes. And the more who are connected to her, the greater she is, for a time. But there is a tipping point. There comes a moment when she is spread too thin, and that is when she begins to fade. Unfortunately, it is also when those who have her – who are connected to her – will cling the most.

"She will lose herself in others, and as she grows more and more lost, she longs for her missing pieces more and more – for her full self. For the sisters she eventually forgets she even has." Storyteller paused and sighed as if pained. "The story goes that she was perched on a big hunk of sun one day, weeping because she was lonely. She wiped away a crystal tear and spotted something down below her on Via'rra's surface. Now, she'd likely seen it a hundred times before, but on this particular day for whatever particular reason, she saw it, was fascinated by it, and she went to investigate it. What she saw supposedly reminded her of her own crystal tears. It was a glimmer: a white sheen sparkling back at her. Maybe she thought she'd found the world's biggest mirror, but when she touched the ground, she found the Sea.

"It's huge, this sea, and likely to Hope, it was as though she'd discovered it for the first time, not the millionth. The Sea's edges touch the Lady's magenta power Ring. The Sea is so powerful and vast that it flows to the very edges of the world, erupts into mountain-tall plumes of rainbow mist where the water and the Ring kiss, and it spills off the lip of the world.

"Hope was helplessly transfixed, so she did what any young, curious critter would do: she grew closer, waiting to see if it was going to love her or bite her. When her toes touched the sand and the foam touched her feet, Water solidified into his Walker shape and came to greet her.

"Now, I know you don't remember when Water was around,

and even if you did, he's a confusing sort. He's both liquid and solid, he's either-or at will, and in both states, he's very much awake and aware. When solid, he has a form that he uses to swim, and that form has a tail long enough to wrap the world. Water also has a form he uses to walk on land, and that form tends to be of the two-armed, two-legged, and one-headed variety. And of course, he's a handsome devil, if you're into that sort of thing. Naturally, Hope was."

"Of course," Nightmare murmured, and he noticed that outside the cabin, it was getting darker.

"Well, you know how young love goes." Storyteller paused, eyeing Nightmare. "Well, perhaps you don't."

"I know love," Nightmare protested.

Storyteller chuckled and waved a hand to placate Nightmare. "Mayhap you do. But understand, what those two felt for one another on first sight dove off the cliff of real love and landed in the dark ocean of obsession."

Nightmare shuddered. "I've sent 'mares to the Feed for less."

Storyteller snorted. "As amusing as that would have been, these are Walkers of which we speak, and Water has always been in contention for the most powerful Walker among us. He is a great warrior, a fanatical protector, and constitutes a massive network of connection. He feeds the ground, the soil, the creatures. He is the Lady's vehicle to spread her magic and enrich the land.

"With Hope at his side, they were an unstoppable force. He had her. One of the strongest and most connected beings in the universe had Hope. She was practically invincible. It is said their love was as true as it was implausible, and I will at least give them this much: they were equally obsessed with each other." Storyteller lifted the carved bird to his face, squinting at it. The carving was intricate for one done so quickly, and he set it and the knife aside, rising and going to a cupboard.

"In all great love stories, there comes a moment of cost and separation. We're at that point in Hope and Water's story, and it also happens to be the moment our world was unmade."

"How?" Nightmare asked.

Storyteller went to the door carrying a deep blue pot. He uncapped it, dipped his fingers within, and began to draw familiar sigils on the wood. "One day, Hope looked up at the sky and saw Nothing eating a piece of the broken sun. Now, he was doing this because it's his job and so that the Lady can remake things bigger, better, and brighter, but when Hope saw Nothing at work, she panicked. She fled to her lover, made him see what was happening, and Water, having a longer memory than Hope, understood that Nothing would come and find Hope, eventually; take her from him, and though her cycle would forevermore continue and she would, in effect, be reborn anew, he could not bear the thought of a single hair on her head being changed. Nor could he think to wait until Hope fell to the ground once again. What if she was different enough that she was no longer his?

"It wasn't all selfish, though. At least, not entirely. Water loved Hope, and he could not abide her fear and her terror of being unmade."

Storyteller lowered himself onto his haunches, joints creaking as he painted more symbols. "Now, I happen to know that ol' Zee can make the experience of getting chewed up and broken into pure energy rather pleasant, on the whole. He's a conscientious unmaker." Storyteller huffed a little laugh. "But the kids didn't come asking me for advice. Instead, they did the unthinkable.

"Water told Hope that he knew where she could go to stay safe, and he knew how to keep her out of harm's way. He told her his plan, she agreed, and Water summoned a massive amount of power. The rivers and streams dwindled or dried up in that very instant, and they've not been replenished since. But Water would need every ounce of magic he had in his possession, for he aimed to sunder Hope's corporal form from her essence. He'd keep her body and take her essence and send it through a very particular kind of Veil, one that no Walker had used in eons. The kind of Veil that can be shut forever once it's used, and it would transform the individual who went through it. The Lady used those things millennia ago when critters from various worlds would dally too long here and not want to return to their own land. Thought for sure that Nothing had eaten them all, but evidently not. At any rate, the magics of this rare Veil could send Hope into a body on the other side of the Veil.

"Now, Water had to be careful where he set this rare Veil to go. Send her to a few lands, and she'd turn insubstantial. Into others, she'd be so changed by the physics of the land that she would no longer be Hope. In others, her power would decimate the world, and she would be no more. So he had to find a world that was safe for a time and that also would give them the chance to be together as they were. Can you guess where he picked?"

The answer rose immediately in Nightmare's mind. "Earth."

"Precisely so. Water would send her into the body of a human child. She'd be safe – Earth contains plenty of power, but not so much that she'd be in danger. But she would also age, and, if Water didn't get to her in time, she would die a mortal death."

"By the Fear," Nightmare gasped, utterly horrified.

"I know." Storyteller used a nearby shelf to rise to his feet, the markings on the wood nearly complete.

"And she agreed to this?"

"She did. She trusted Water with her body and soul, and so it was done. Water split Hope's essence and sent half of it through the Veil. The plan had been for Water to join her, eventually."

"Wait," Nightmare interrupted, unable to help himself. "If a Walker that powerful was sent *out* of this world permanently, then..."

Storyteller nodded. "Water's plan was to fix the wrongness he knew would befall the world once she left, and then he, too, would leave."

"The arrogance," Nightmare said, aghast.

Storyteller waved his hands. "What can I say? Teenagers. Water was just a kid, basically, and he was deranged. Mad. Sick. He utterly overestimated his power and underestimated the devastation he would cause. When that Veil shut, a quake unlike any other struck our world. Our land literally and metaphorically tipped with a force that leveled cities and took many lives before Nothing could save them for the Lady. Nothing was enraged. Never seen Zee so angry. The man doesn't really do anger, but he was pissed off at that moment, I tell you. He was too busy salvaging damage to do anything to Water, and soon, well, the rest began to happen. The balance was gone. Light could no longer cycle. Our connections to other worlds was jeopardized. The Lady could not remake as fast as things were being destroyed, and then the Horrors came."

"Where did they come from? What are they?" Nightmare demanded.

But Storyteller sadly bowed his head. He sighed. "Walkers wilt in the aftermath of what Hope and Water did. We decay." Storyteller met Nightmare's eyes. "We forget."

Nightmare hugged his empty chest and followed Storyteller's gaze when Storyteller looked out the window. The trees were gone. The footpath had been swallowed by the grey, whirling mass, and the mist was practically at the Storyteller's porch. Silent. Deadly. Cold.

"I'd tell you more, but we are out of time," Storyteller said while gazing at the encroaching Horrors. "You know enough to do what must be done."

"Which is?" Nightmare asked.

"You must pass through a Veil, find Hope, bring her home, and begin putting our world back together."

Nightmare thought of all he could do, and he found himself unable to fathom his ability to accomplish such a massive undertaking. "I'm not sure I possess the strength."

"You must find it."

"How will I seek out or locate Hope?"

"You will have help. Zee and me, we are paranoid creatures. Cautious by nature. We had devised a system should the end times ever draw near, and son, they are as nigh as they can be and still have us speaking to one another. Zee is like me in some ways;

I'm everywhere there is time, and he's everywhere there is shadow. On Earth, he touched a woman. Strong spirit and a mind open enough to understand some of our universe in crisis. I'll make a Veil here that will send you to her. The timing, it had to be perfect. The seven have just now gathered, and this woman, she knows you're coming – Zee's seen to that – and she knows something of our lost Star. She will—"

The cabin was uprooted and pitched violently to one side. Nightmare tumbled and slammed into the wall, which was now the floor. He covered his head, and the drawer of the bedside table struck him. With a great, shattering crack, the wailing screams of the Horrors broke through the Storyteller's spell. It was deafening, soul-leeching, and it turned Nightmare's limbs to lead.

"You have to go!" Storyteller yelled over the din. He was curled into a ball at Nightmare's side, between Nightmare and the door.

"What of you?" Nightmare boomed in the voice he used to summon his 'mares. The Horrors ate the volume, softened the power of it, and their screech grew impossibly louder. Millions of claws and nails scraped the cabin's sides, tore at the last shreds of Storyteller's spell, ate of their current reality.

"Zee. I invoke thee, you creepy bastard." Storyteller yelled the words, and Nightmare convulsed with the desire to run. He did not – he *could* not.

"The Shadow!" Storyteller yelled. "I will go to the Shadow. It was planned." He pointed, and Nightmare braced on an arm to look. A deep, dark, fathomless pool was sliding down the corner of the cabin, high up and opposite where they lay sprawled. It looked like ink. It smelled like winter, like orchids, like hearth and home and—

"Mal'uud!" Storyteller bellowed, and Nightmare snapped out of the trance. "To the Veil!" Storyteller sliced open his palm with his whittling knife and slapped his hand on the carved backside of the door. He spat on the wood and spoke words in a fast murmur. Instantly, the door caved in on itself. With a tremendous noise that blotted out even the Horrors, the door twisted, and the hinges shot off and struck the opposite wall. The world behind the door shimmered, faded, began to spin, and the door got sucked into an incandescent whirlpool suspended in midair.

Unable to stop staring at the ever-creeping Shadow, Nightmare stayed on his side, frozen in dull terror. Storyteller grabbed him. Shook him. "Find Hope! Bring her home!"

The cabin shook, and the boards bowed as hundreds if not thousands of white, wailing, pink-slime tentacle creatures cracked another layer of spell and began to strike, to push, to gain entrance. A thing the size of Nightmare's leg and covered in sickly pink scales flopped onto the ground near Nightmare's foot. The sight of it broke Nightmare's trance. He got onto his hands and feet, threw himself into a leap that cleared Storyteller's body, and looked back in time to see the inky, midnight pool consuming Storyteller's feet. Terror and outrage like that of which Nightmare had never known tried to strike him still and leave him for dead.

"Even weakened, he is everywhere the light dares not go," Storyteller said, oddly calm and crazily loud, despite the hungry harpy screaming that threatened to drive Nightmare mad. Nightmare caught Storyteller's eyes. Laugh lines crinkled, and the Shadow reached his throat. "He makes it... pleasant... even when rushed. Fear not, son, I will rise again. The Lady will remake me, for she likes a good story." The darkness had risen to Storyteller's torso... shoulders... "Go, Mal'uud 'au Keen. Go. Remember. Save us all."

Nightmare put a fist to his breast, bowed his head, and spoke the words in the old tongue that swore him and his honor to the quest. The earth shook, and jagged edges of rock tore free of the ground and split the side of Storyteller's former home. The cabin flew apart, the white of the Horrors was blinding, and the last thing Nightmare saw was Daanske the Storyteller, Walker of Time and Veil, shutting his eyes, being overcome by darkness, and vanishing completely, as though he and the Shadow that had consumed him had never existed.

With a mournful sob, Nightmare spun and plunged through the Veil.

Chapter Eleven

The moment Mercutio left the room, Helen dug the little white pill out of her mouth. It was small enough to hide between her teeth and cheek, and when she spat it into a tissue, she sighed in relief that it was mostly intact. This pill would make her sleep. The one at dinner would keep her mind calm. The one at lunch would regulate her appetite. The ones at breakfast would help her blood and bones and heart and guts.

But none of them kept the darkness at bay when it needed to tell her something.

That afternoon, she'd dozed on the couch while Tio read a murder mystery, and she'd seen what she needed to do. The pictures had formed in her mind like paintings, complete with brush strokes. As she'd watched, she'd silently asked, *How are you here and doing this when you live on the other side?*

The painting continued for a few moments, and she didn't think the darkness would answer at all, but eventually, in her mind it said, *I am everywhere that shadows rest.*

It was answer enough, and when Helen had woken, she'd worked to hide the buzzing energy in her breast as she'd sipped her afternoon tea, eaten her dinner, watched her shows, all the while never letting Mercutio know that a flock of birds now lived in her heart, and their song was *"Go, go, go."*

The lights went out in the living room – darkness now outlined her bedroom door – and soon, Helen heard the front door open and then shut. She tossed aside the covers and changed her clothes. Tio hadn't even thought to check to see if she'd swallowed the pill. He never did, anymore, though Helen knew that if she got caught tonight, he'd check every day. He'd check at every meal. And if he thought she was resisting, it was possible she'd find herself tethered to the bed with a needle in her arm. He'd drown her in the pill's darkness to keep her safe and contained. And really, he was free to do that, so long as she did this one, last thing.

She couldn't be caught before she finished the task the darkness had painted for her. She had to be careful and she had to *move.*

Keeping to the shadows, Helen slowly opened her bedroom door and tiptoed into the main room. She ducked beneath the edge of the front windows, fearful that somehow she'd be seen in silhouette. She slid on her shoes and leaned against the front door.

Mercutio parked near the dock in the employee lot. He always went by the front of the house to get there. He'd drop inside to give a report on her condition to Daddy or Miss Teedee, sometimes. Other times he just went to his car. Either way, his path took him west and away from the stable, which meant Helen couldn't go that way to get to the museum. It would have been the most direct route: across the front lawn, across the driveway, follow it down toward the road, and there she would have been.

But the front of the house had security lights and spotlights on Andrew's garden features, not to mention a front porch where people might sit and drink and talk and spy her sneaking through the grass. And if someone caught her, they'd lock her in the main house rooms or even in her own apartment until morning when Tio would be there with more pills and admonishments.

She'd have to go the long way around. She'd sneak down the steps to the ground floor, turn due north to the outbuilding mostly hidden by trees and Andrew's handiwork. The outbuilding was where Andrew kept all his equipment. It was big enough to provide plenty of cover. From there, if she could make it to the woods, she could take the state park path through the woods to the opposite side of the main street, and then cross back again to the museum. The museum would be closed. Traffic would be light, and headlights would clearly tell her when someone was coming. She could time it just right.

Helen dug into her pocket – the little one inside the big one of her jeans – and pulled out a key to the museum. It was Monica's spare. Helen had stolen it that afternoon right before daring to run upstairs and talk to Jason. That way, the conversation with Tio had been all about how she'd wanted to talk to the new boy, and did she think he was cute, and what did he say, and how did he seem to be doing instead of, *Where were you just before I lost track of you and found you upstairs? You weren't picking keys off the pegboard, now were you?*

Letting go of a shaky breath, Helen gripped the key in the cup of her palms. Everyone was going to be furious with her if she was caught. And there were so many places for eyes to see her: on the steps leading down, from the garden as she ran toward the storage building, from the house as she ran to the woods. There might even be late-night walkers on the path. She'd have to hide from them, as well, and time would keep tick-tick-ticking, and she'd be late-late-later.

A rumble shook the apartment, and Helen's eyes went wide in the dark.

Thunder – that was thunder. Which meant –

Rain began to hit the roof, soft at first, and then in a loud and louder drone. And rain would obscure vision, drive people inside, and limit prying eyes.

Helen ran to the closet and grabbed a small flashlight and her raincoat, grateful it was deepest green. She put up the hood and tucked the key back into the tiny pocket of her pants. She undid the locks on the front door, counted to three, and thrust herself outside.

Quick and quicker, she raced down the steps. The moment her feet touched the ground, she turned and ran toward the storage building. It seemed to move farther and farther away the closer she tried to get, and when she was finally behind it, she leaned hard against the siding, gasping with a stitch in her side. She waited, straining to hear shouts of concern or warning, but she heard nothing but the thick patter of the fat raindrops pouring from the sky.

Helen looked toward the rock wall that lined the edge of the property and kept the woods barely at bay. For a second, she remembered her age and how long it'd been since she'd exercised. Her heart hammered away, clearly shocked at having to work so hard. A heart attack would definitely keep her from finishing this quest. She took some deep, slow breaths, and before she lost all her nerve, she began to walk briskly to the wall. She kept to the shadows as much as she could, wondering if the darkness knew her. Wondering if it would obscure her, let her slide into it and not be seen, even if someone was close. She whispered a little prayer asking for as much, and then she had to climb over the wall. It wasn't high, but it was still a wall, and Helen struggled on her first attempt. She cussed – said all the words Daddy would be shocked to hear – and then found purchase, found a way, and she was up and over and landing heavily on the other side.

The rain poured now, and Helen made for the spaces between the trees. The rain slackened some with the overhead cover. She concentrated on the ground, and as soon as she dared, she turned on the flashlight. Its light was weak, but it was enough to prevent her from twisting an ankle on underbrush and tree roots. It took longer than she remembered to find the walking path, and for a second, panic threatened to overtake her. She was lost in the woods, and no one would find her, and if they did, she'd never see the woods again, and there'd be needles and drugs and her daddy's sad, sad eyes—

Her tennis shoes landed on pavement. Helen wiped rain off her face and headed left. The path was dotted with benches and restroom shacks, all of which were lit, so she could keep her flashlight off most of the time. She jogged as much as she could, but the stitch in her side grew worse, and her knee began to complain. This was taking too long – it couldn't be more than, what, half a mile at most? Helen tried to calculate how long it'd take to walk that far in the rain and in the dark. She kept coming up with amounts of time that she was sure she'd already spent. She walked faster, trying to ignore her body's complaints, the fear of what would happen if she arrived too late driving her ever onward.

Finally, the trees to her left began to thin, and ahead, she saw where a branch of the path split in a turn to cross the road. There was even a sign – blue and gold and filigree letters: FISHERMAN'S SHACK MUSEUM – COME LEARN ABOUT THE TAYLOR POINT SOUND. Helen followed the sign, edging close to the road with caution. She took a deep breath and then ran across the four-lane road, just waiting for the sound of screeching tires and car horns, but of course, there were none. No headlights came on, no warning alarms rang – Helen made it to the museum's parking lot and around to the back of the building without incident. Her fingers were slippery and cold, but she managed to work the key into the lock by the light of the dim safety bulb, its glass fixture half-filled with the carcasses of dead bugs. The door gave inward, and Helen stepped inside to a shock of air conditioning and the muffled noise of thunder and rain.

The museum was a maze of counters, floating walls, and exhibits in a space too small for all it contained. The path through the maze was barely wide enough for two people abreast, and it'd been so long since Helen had tried to navigate it that she got lost twice before she found the steps leading up to the second floor. The stairs were roped off with a sign warning that the second floor was for EMPLOYEES ONLY. Boxes were stacked against the stairwell's sides, and Helen paused with her flashlight trained on the rope barrier. Thunder boomed and vibrated through the walls. She'd not been past this point since her mother had died twenty years ago. The steps seemed to go up and up forever into pitch blackness. Anxiety twisted through Helen's guts, and then, faintly, she heard a thump.

Heart in her throat, Helen stepped over the rope and dashed up the stairs, automatically avoiding the two places where she still knew they creaked. It was hotter up here. The air conditioning was not really meant to handle this much space. Merchandise sat in boxes and on shelves. There was a desk where her mother had once sat, and now Monica occupied it to do bills and take phone calls and go about the business of running the shop. Helen passed a counter with a coffee maker and an empty box of donuts, and next to the single-occupant restroom, she found the stair ladder heading to the attic.

When Helen's mother had been alive, these stairs had folded up into the square in the ceiling. At the time, though, the second floor had been a gathering area for book clubs and church groups, so most of the stock was stored in the attic. Becky had complained of having to yank down the steps over and over, and so Darryl had fixed them so they stayed down. He'd replaced the panel at the top so it operated as a trap door – to keep the HVAC system from working too hard and to keep the insulation in the attic, not the room. They'd put a rope on *these* stairs, warning people to stay out of the storage room.

Now there was no rope. The steps led to the closed trap door, and as Helen stared up at it, she heard the soft thuds of footfalls as someone walked around in the attic above her.

It was a testimony to how much she trusted the darkness that whispered to her that until that moment, it had never occurred to Helen that in the attic could be anyone or anything other than the King of Nightmare coming through a Veil. She'd seen the painted vision, clearly – a glowing portal, a monster crawling through, a monster growing human skin, and then a man standing in what was unmistakably the attic of the Fisherman's Shack Museum. Helen had known by the trunks and the windows and the boxes marked, "Becky's Things."

But now, as she stood with one foot on the bottom attic step with water dripping into her eyes and puddling on the floor, she wasn't so sure. The anxiety in her gut now had teeth, and they bit into her, tearing away at her resolve. She started to back away and then she heard something – a soft, so soft, moan of pain.

Growing flesh would hurt, Helen imagined. Carefully, she crept up to the top of the stairs. She knelt and spoke to the trap door. "H-hello?" she said.

Immediately, all sound ceased – so fast that Helen now wasn't sure there'd been any noise at all. She listened to the rain and found her courage. "I'm Helen. The darkness spoke to me. I'm here to help you."

A dragging sound spilled from above, and the trap door flexed with weight. Helen's heart skipped beats, and her mouth went so dry, she had to lap rainwater from her face and fingers to make her tongue work. "You're on Earth – the Blue World, I think the darkness calls it. You're in the attic of a museum. It's near the Taylor Point House, where the seven have come together again. You're looking for a woman who isn't a woman at all."

A light knock on the trap door – one for yes? One to let her know he heard? Helen couldn't be sure, but she pressed on. "I taught school before I saw the cracks between worlds. There was a girl who wore the face of a dead child in one of my classes. She was strange and bright and beautiful. All the things the darkness said she would be. Now she's a woman who lives off men. Even Miss Teedee says she's lost, so she must be *her*. I think. I think she's your—"

Another sound startled Helen, and this one came from the floor below her. Panic took full flight. "Madeline Banc," Helen said in a hasty whisper. "She stays at The Water's Edge – it's a fancy hotel. You have to go there and find her before it's too late.

Stay until I'm gonc – until I'm gone and whoever is downstairs is gone. I'm..." Helen touched the trap door and could swear she felt heat coming through it. "Thank you."

Another knock, this one stronger, and Helen fled down the attic steps just as she heard something crash from the floor below. She heard a man's voice cuss, and she wanted to cry with the idea that maybe it was Daddy. If it was, she was doomed. It was all over, this sliver of life she'd managed to cling to for so long.

Helen reached the top of the stairs and started down them; there was no point in hiding or waiting out the man below. She had to get out of there – had to get *him* out of there – so the King of Nightmare could walk the world and save it. Halfway down the steps, she spotted a tall, very tall, figure with the ridge of a growing-out mohawk for hair. When lightning flashed, Helen saw the whites of Jason's eyes; they were so wide with shock or horror or both. Helen walked down the rest of the stairs and over the rope, casting a furtive glance to check and see if the King of Nightmare was standing at the top of the stairwell. He was not, thank goodness.

But when Helen approached Jason, he backed up a step, and Helen knew, then, that Jason wasn't seeing *her.* He was seeing something else – something out of the darkness's world. She bit her tongue, but she wanted to ask if Jason had seen the King of Nightmare in his dreams. Or maybe one of the other Walkers. He'd definitely seen things that she had not, but they'd both seen the same *kind* of things – those that were from other worlds. She'd recognized a kindred soul the moment she had laid eyes on him that first night at dinner. She wanted to explain the Taylor Point House, the seven, the Veils, and why nightmares grew so big and bold, here, but he was visibly shaking when Helen turned on the weak flashlight. He flinched and put a hand up near his eyes. "Jason," she said.

"Helen?" Jason asked after a moment.

"It's me," Helen said. "I meant to tell you earlier that I like your new shirt."

Helen's eyes adjusted to the gloom quickly, and so she saw Jason's mouth work on a reply. "Got it at Goodwill," he mumbled. He shook his head. "Helen. Shit. I'm sorry. I thought I... I saw you run off for the woods in the rain, and I was worried, so I... but I just... I've been..."

"Having nightmares?" Helen asked.

"Maybe. I think I was awake. And just now, I saw..."

"What did you see?" Helen asked, coming closer.

"An old man. I thought you were..." Jason looked to the stairs and then back at Helen. "I saw an old man coming down the stairs, but then it was you. Not that I think you look like an old man. Not at all. You're beautiful. I—" Jason abruptly stopped speaking.

"It's okay," Helen soothed. She didn't know any old man, which meant Jason was seeing other Walkers that she had not. "Who else have you seen?"

"Crazy that you ask that," Jason muttered. "Not a 'who' but a... I was in the garden, and I thought I saw... this... there was a lot of..."

"Worms?" Helen asked.

Jason met her gaze and studied her intently. "Yes."

A fist squeezed Helen's heart. The worms were the worst. She didn't know what they meant, but they left her terrified. She'd seen them in empty pots and pans, in the bottom of her closet, in the bathtub, and, once, in her freshly empty cereal bowl. She couldn't eat Cheerios anymore. "Was it the thing that looks like a tree or the little girl with black eyes and hair and too-long bangs?"

Jason's face twisted, and Helen feared she'd gone too far. She waited for the hysteria. It would be wide and deep, and it might drive Jason to do crazy things. Like grab her hand and run for the water. They'd jump in and sink and sink, the water rushing and cold around them. Everything would get bluer and bluer until it was black and suffocating and stealing their lives out of their bodies. The thing was, Helen wasn't sure she'd fight him on any of those choices. They might be the more peaceful way to go.

After a long sigh, Jason rubbed at his eyes. The hysteria didn't come. He seemed calm. "Did I say the wrong... are you okay?" Helen asked, not sure what else to say.

"I used to share a bed with Judith and this kid, Rage," Jason offered, if inexplicably. "Victor was his name, but we called him Rage. And he wasn't a kid, like a child. He was older than me. I just called him 'kid.' Because Judith did."

"Okay." Helen clutched at the flashlight, afraid to move and break the spell that was making Jason talk.

"They were in that band together – remember the one I told you about? It was called Judith's Hell, and Judith and Rage were the two key members. I was with them. In like, a relationship, you know? And it should have been crazy weird, but it wasn't. Anyway." Jason shifted, his arms crossing over his chest. "Sometimes we'd all have the same dream. We'd wake up, and Judith had one part, I had the middle, and Rage had the ending. They wrote songs about it. Judith even used to say it was because of me. Nobody dreamed that way before me, but we could dream that way after I joined the band. It was good for a long time, the three of us. Everybody loved each other and the dreams."

"So you don't think it's strange that we've seen the same monsters?" Helen asked.

"No," Jason said. "I'm just happy to find somebody else who sees them."

Helen saw Jason in a sliver of light, as though a doorway had opened in the dead of night – a way back to the safety of one's bed when one was lost after a trip to the bathroom. "I came here to help a... a friend."

"Yeah?" Jason said. "What friend?"

Helen wet her lips with a sticky tongue. "I don't know, exactly. I know him as the Nightmare King. He's related to the Lord and Lady."

"The ones you told the story about at dinner?"

"Yes." Helen studied Jason, but he didn't seem to be running as fast as he could toward the land of disbelief. "He came here to find someone else. Someone important. And we have to help."

"How do we do that?"

Now it was Helen who faltered. Even with all the proof, all the visions, all the urgency – there was still doubt. "You'll think I'm..."

Jason's face softened with a tenderness that Helen could almost taste. "I don't believe in crazy. Not really. There's always truth in the insanity. Or we just don't understand what the so-called crazy person means, yet. They thought the guy who discovered gravity was nuts. Or the person who said the earth wasn't the center of the universe – I think the church really wanted that guy to shut up."

"The earth isn't the center at all," Helen said.

"Right," Jason agreed with a smile.

Helen took a deep breath, and the hair on the back of her neck stood on end. She could feel him – the King of Nightmare. He was out of the attic. He may even have been watching them. "We have to stick together and we have to remember who we are. Some of us will have to discover it. Or find it again."

Jason cocked his head. "To help your friend, you mean? That's what we have to do?"

"Yes."

"Well, that doesn't sound so bad."

Helen envied Jason, then – deep and wide and to her core. To think that sorting oneself out didn't sound like the most impossible thing in the world. What was that like?

"It'll be—" Helen began, but the shop was flooded with blue and red. A blat of a siren came from right outside.

"What the hell is that?" Jason asked, the fear spooling from his mouth like silk.

"Come on," Helen said. She grabbed his hand. They ran to the door, opened it, and were blinded by strobing lights and headlights and all the suspicious light of the world. Helen threw an arm up over her eyes to shield them, and Jason put himself between her and the disembodied voice coming over a loudspeaker. She couldn't understand what it said. She put her hands up, the rain in her eyes.

"Helen?" asked a woman, the voice unfamiliar. "Helen Taylor?"

"Yes?" Helen called, chin tucked to her chest. It was so bright, so loud, and the rain was drowning them.

"Keep your hands where I can see them," the woman ordered. Helen thrust her arms higher, but then she realized the woman had meant Jason, who was tall and tattooed and a stranger in this town.

"He's my friend," Helen tried to explain.

"What are you and your friend doing breaking into the museum and tripping the silent alarm?" the woman asked. Now there was a flashlight in their faces, marring the view of a shadowy figure in a poncho.

"I...I..." Helen couldn't find words, but thankfully Jason fetched them from where they scattered on the ground.

"She was showing me the museum," Jason said. "I just got here, and so she—"

"At night? In the dark?" the woman barked.

"It's spookier that way," Jason explained.

"Mmhm. And who are you?"

"Jason Hart."

"He works for my father," Helen explained.

"Your father," the woman repeated, not a question.

"Darryl Taylor. He owns the Taylor Point House." Helen didn't like the silence and the light and the pause. "He's my adopted father."

"He is?" Jason asked, shocked.

"Yes, but he's been that since I was a baby, so I don't think it should matter, now. And Monica is my step-girlfriend, and she cleans the house, and she needed help because she used to be hopeful, but now she's exhausted, so Jason—"

"Okay," the woman interrupted. The light dropped, and Helen gasped in relief. The poncho came closer, and now Helen could see it was a woman with very dark skin. The poncho had a security company logo on the chest. "Murph, call Darryl Taylor and tell him we found them."

"Found us?" Helen asked, shards of glass in the pit of her

stomach. The walls of her world were shrinking and soon they would suffocate her.

"You two mind getting in the back of the vehicle, please?" the woman asked.

"No, ma'am," Jason said. He and Helen followed orders, and soon they were dripping on the leather back seat of the security company's car. A man sat shotgun – Murph, Helen supposed. The woman climbed behind the wheel. They didn't bother with small talk as they made the short drive to the house. Actual police cars were in the driveway. Everyone was on the side porch, and when Mercutio saw the approaching vehicle, he dashed down the steps and ran to the car's rear window, a jacket over his head like a small tent. The lights of the house were all blazing, which made it easy to see him as he pointed at Helen through the window. He carved the air with his finger in a quarter circle and stabbed it toward the front of Helen's home. And then he pointed emphatically at the ground. Helen understood he meant, *Get out right now and up there immediately,* but she feigned ignorance.

"What's his deal?" Jason asked as the woman security officer climbed out and said something drowned out by the pouring rain on the top of the car.

Helen knew the consequences of her choices would soon be laid clear, but there was still work to be done, even if she wasn't the one who could do it. "Did you know he's in love with Andrew?" she asked, watching calmly as Mercutio tried to open her locked door and failed.

"Uh, I, ah, no...?"

"He is." Helen drew an invisible heart on the inside of the glass while Mercutio ordered her out of the car *right this instant.*

Murph climbed out of the passenger seat and popped open an umbrella. "Sir, please calm down and let me get the door open."

"You should tell him," Helen said while Murph hit a switch and the doors unlocked. "Andrew, I mean."

"Okay?" Jason agreed, but was clearly confused. With a sigh, Helen climbed out of the car. She was ushered onto the porch, where Darryl, Miss Teedee, Monica, and Andrew had gathered. Inside, Helen could see an anxious cluster of guests, some with coffee cups and enjoying the show more than maybe they should. The family was speaking to a man in uniform, who was closing a notepad.

"There she is!" Andrew cried, as though he'd been the first to spot Helen.

"Looks like you won't be needing that favor, after all," the policeman said.

"No, Chuck – and thank you for stopping by so late and in this weather," Darryl said.

"It's not a problem. I would have done the same thing."

Time warbled. Helen was placed in a spot where all could see her, and she stood there, praying the Nightmare King was out of the museum and gone. She hoped he had taken advantage of the chaos and that the alarm wouldn't trip again. Miss Teedee spoke to the guests, who dispersed. The policeman and the security team talked. Paperwork was signed. Eventually, the guardians in uniform had gone, leaving the family to reconvene on the porch.

"You hid really well!" Andrew said. "But you should have told us you were playing hide and seek."

"Andrew, hush," Monica ordered. She was dressed in a long skirt and nice shirt, her Managing Customers attire, and her wooden heels made *clunk-thump-clunk* sounds on the floorboards.

"They searched all over," Andrew said in a loud whisper.

"Pretty lady," Mercutio said, never looking at Andrew, and Helen could always tell how much effort that took. "I'm sorry I was so harsh when you were in the car, but, Lord, you gave me six heart attacks."

"How'd you know I was gone?" Helen asked him.

"I went back to get my scarf," Mercutio said. "And you weren't there, honeydew."

"No, she was not," Monica interjected. Her tongue had grown razorblades. "What on God's green earth were you two thinking?"

"Enough," Darryl said, pulling Helen into a hug. He smelled like a sweaty bear spritzed with drugstore cologne. "You had us worried."

"Sorry, Daddy," Helen murmured.

"It's okay. You're home, and you're fine. That's all that matters." He kissed her hair.

"Like hell it is!" Monica roared. "We just spent the last hour and a half thinking she was lost, hurt, or dead!"

"And she's none of those things, thank God," Darryl said, but he was using his nearly-yelling voice.

"Don't you raise your voice to me, Darryl Taylor," Monica retorted. "You wanted to call the hospitals and the morgues and get God knows who else. Thank the Lord that Chuck's a family friend, that he answered his phone, and maybe this scandal can be kept to a minimum."

"Probably not if you keep yelling loud enough to wake the dead and the rest of the town," Darryl said, and Monica's eyes flashed red and dangerous.

"Okay, okay," Miss Teedee said, stepping between them. "I understand you're concerned, Monica, but we explained to our guests what was going on, and they're all up in their rooms safe and sound and knowing the crisis is over. If it was ever a crisis to begin with."

"If it was ever a crisis to–" Monica spluttered and then wheeled on Jason. "And you! What the devil were you doing?"

Jason looked like a wild animal in a trap.

"I trust you, and *this* is how you repay me?"

"What are you even talking—" Jason started.

"We thought you'd kidnapped her!"

Jason's eyes bulged. "You thought I'd *what?*"

"No, we didn't think that," Mercutio said, exasperated.

"Oh, so it wasn't you spouting off about men in vans snatching her up out of her own bed and other hysterical ideas?"

"Mmhm," Mercutio said. "That's right, Miss Thing. Aim those lasers at me and my crazy-worried babble. Jason didn't do any—"

"He was with her in the museum in the dark, and you seriously think that—"

"Nothing happened!" Jason cried.

"You call this nothing?" Monica exclaimed.

"Mama! Too loud!" Andrew rubbed his shoulders and chest, clearly distressed by the emotions zinging through the air and starting to dance from foot to foot. Mercutio inched closer to him, still not looking, but drawn like a bug to a zapper.

"You're upsetting your son and the rest of us while you're at it," Miss Teedee said to Monica. She wiped her hands on her apron. "We were all worried and said crazy things in that worry, but now we can all calm—"

Monica pointed a sword finger at Jason. "I'll ask again: what the hell—"

"Mama!"

"—were you two doing?" Monica managed to lower her voice.

Jason steeled himself, steady in the face of Monica's outrage and clearly feeling not a small amount of his own. "I was in the garden, and I saw her going for a walk in the rain. I decided to join her, and we ended up at the museum."

"Which you broke into?" Monica demanded.

"I had a key," Helen said.

Monica's eyes bulged. "You took the key to the museum, went to it in the middle of the night in a storm, set off the alarm, and did, what, exactly?"

"Just looked around," Helen said.

Monica scoffed. "Sure."

"Look, it's true," Jason said. "I'd never seen the place, so Helen was just—"

"At night?" Monica interrogated. "You decided to do this at night?"

"When else could I have done it?" Helen roared back, shocked at the volume. The group collectively flinched.

"You guys own the place, right?" Jason asked, as he looked at all of them in turn, and the crease between his eyebrows judged each one crazier than the last. "I'm sorry about the alarm. The last person who wants to make any trouble is me, but what's the actual big deal?"

"Helen doesn't go anywhere without an escort," Darryl said, and Helen hugged her father and then pushed him away. She knew he cared, but his love was a tidal wave that would bury her head in the sand alongside his.

"Ever?" Jason asked, and Helen loved his horrified high voice.

"Ever," Mercutio confirmed, taking his place directly at Helen's side with one gentle, unmovable hand on her elbow. "It's not safe."

"But..." Jason fumbled. "Okay, but she was with me, so..."

"And you think that's even remotely comforting?" Monica asked.

"Monica," Miss Teedee gently admonished.

"What the hell do you think I would do?" Jason asked, genuine in his confusion, and it pained Helen to hear it.

Monica put her back to him and spoke to Helen. "Okay. So you decided to go for a midnight stroll. He wasn't with you initially, so tell me, Helen, what was so important that you went out in the dark and in the rain to the museum? Mm?"

Everyone was watching her, now. Daddy and his infinite forgiveness because he thought himself a poor substitute for the birth parents who gave her up and then the mother and wife they'd lost. Monica and her frayed nerves and exhaustion. Mercutio and his watchful gaze, ever ready to do whatever needed doing, even if it was distasteful. Andrew and his shaded eyes that saw everything and nothing at the same time. Miss Teedee and her catlike soul, watchful, interested, but distant.

And Jason, with his upended roots that sought stable ground. Looking at him, she knew she had to tell the truth. There was no other way to cast him out of the shadow of her family's fear. "The fallen star is searching for her way home. I had to get a message to the Nightmare King. He's going to take the star home."

Monica made a gesture of triumph. "I damned well knew it. More of your crazy—"

"Well," Mercutio said loudly, cutting Monica off. "We'll all be happier once you're safe and sound in your own little star nest."

"It's always some fool thing with her. That's the big deal. That's the problem. And she drags all of us down into her insanity with her!"

"Let her be, Monica," Darryl said. He was marshmallows and cream most of the time, but there were knives hidden in the fluff.

"Let her *be?*" Monica repeated. "I was working, making money for us and for our business, and then this fool wanders off, and you're running around frothing at the mouth! Once word of this gets out, the entire town is going to be calling, thinking she's dead."

"The town can fall into the ocean, for all I care," Darryl huffed.

"Oh, you'd better care. Those people and the referrals they give are our livelihoods." Monica pointed an accusing finger at Darryl. "If you weren't nose-deep in a bottle, you'd see that."

"I was at a meeting!" Darryl yelled, and just like that, they were continuing an old fight that had nothing to do with the current one. "I know I was late to come in tonight, but I trusted that you and the rest of my staff could handle things."

"*Your* staff," Monica sneered. "Which you manage, do you? Day in? Day out?"

"Monica, I know you do the lion's share of—"

"Just tell me one thing," she drew closer to Darryl, as though to whisper a secret. "Did you buy yourself a celebratory bottle on the way home from that meeting?"

Darryl turned red about the ears. "You don't speak to me like that, woman. I'll—"

"You'll what?" Monica challenged. "You'll do nothing, that's what. You already let her run wild and keep this family in chaos."

"Chaos?" Darryl said. "What chaos? She's home, and she's—"

"She's what, Darryl? Got everything she needs? Is perfectly provided for? Yeah, okay. Sure she is. Let's do the thing where I try to talk about reality, and you avoid it. Let's just forget the fact that not ten minutes ago, you were wailing and beating your chest."

“I was not—”

“You *were*. You do it every blasted time she wanders off to do her crazy act, and you did it this time, and you’ll do it again because, mark my words, she will do it all again.”

“Monica—”

“And yet you refuse to see that something needs to change. She stays here, where she could take a wild hair and wander into the ocean and drown—”

“Monica!” Darryl yelled between clenched teeth.

“But why worry, right? I mean, why put her in a controlled facility trained to handle cases like her, when she’s got a nurse who can’t even make sure your daughter doesn’t go wander the woods, much less the streets, the town, the entire fucking planet?”

“Monica, I know it’s hard to see from your high perch of inhuman perfection, but the rest of us are human and make mistakes,” Mercutio said, far calmer than any of them. “But I assure you, and all of you, that I will adjust my hours. We’ll talk this through and figure out how I can better serve Helen and this family in the future.”

“You’re damned right we will,” Monica said.

“I would have made sure nothing happened to her,” Jason tried.

“Oh, now that’s a comfort.” Monica nodded in the scary way that meant she was doing anything but agreeing. “A drifter has my Darryl’s only crazy child alone in a dark building doing God only knows what, God only knows where, for God only knows how fucking long.”

“An hour and a half!” Andrew yelled. “You just said, Mama. We know how f-ing long it was.”

Monica’s mouth tightened. “Andrew, why don’t you coil up that garden hose over there next to the shed?”

“No.”

“Andrew.”

“Nothing happened like... like that.” Jason was so red in the face and his eyes were so wide that Helen worried for his heart.

"Of course not," Miss Teedee said firmly.

"You say that like you know something about this kid," Monica accused.

Miss Teedee stiffened. "I know plenty to understand that your personal history is clouding your judgment, but this is neither the time nor the place to hash that out."

Monica threw her hands into the air. "You people are delusional. Every goddamned one of you."

"Mama!" Andrew yelled, clapping his hands over his ears. Mercutio cracked and rubbed Andrew's broad back between the shoulder blades with one hand. Andrew faced Mercutio with his chin tucked to his chest.

"I'm not delusional. I'm hopeful." A vein pulsed in Darryl's forehead, and his neck was getting splotchy. "Something you seem to have forgotten how to be."

"Easy to find hope when all you can see is the bottom of the Scotch."

"Monica, that's quite enough," Miss Teedee said.

"You know what, maybe you're right." Monica had gone from a firebrand to an icicle. "Maybe this time, it is more than enough."

Miss Teedee was unfazed. "You'll feel differently when you've gotten some rest." She hooked her arm through Jason's. "Come along, dear. Cleaning's a great way to wind down after a mess, and I've got a pair of yellow rubber gloves with you name on them."

"Oh no, you don't." Monica whirled so fast and so hard that she made a groove in the grass. "If you think I'm letting him go back to work after the stunt he just pulled, you're insane."

Jason went from pale to stark white, and Miss Teedee patted his hand. "Monica, you're overreacting. Go for a walk, dear. Cool off." Miss Teedee tugged Jason in the direction of the house.

"He is not working for me," Monica declared.

"Fine," Miss Teedee fired in retort. "He'll work for me."

Monica gave each of them a mean, fearful look in turn, made a disgusted noise, and finally headed for the parking lot.

"Okay, then. Bye," Andrew said. Helen didn't watch Andrew retreat, though, or even Jason, who was slumped to listen to Miss Teedee, as the pair of them walked toward the porch with Darryl in tow.

Instead, Helen watched Mercutio, who stared with worried longing at a sweet gardener currently doing his best not to cry into his rosebushes.

Chapter Twelve

The stall was nice enough, for a public bathroom. The walls and door were two inches off the ground, and they were painted a shade of cobalt blue that Madeline found soothing. The doorknob was painted gold, the toilet was relatively clean and shiny black, and there were plenty of hooks to hang bags while you did your business. The tile was blue and black, and not so bad for sitting. Good thing, too, since Madeline had no idea how long she'd been there. Her legs and ass were numb, but that was something of a blessing. Everything else ached.

Music lulled and roared as women came and went, but no men came looking for her. Especially not the one who'd shared her with his friend in the VIP lounge and had given her pills. Usually that and alcohol helped dim the nightmares. But as she'd sat there on the plush sofa, drinking and smiling on cue, the music's thump seemed to deepen. It turned into an erratic heartbeat that tugged at her own rhythm. She'd begun to sweat, her underarms and thighs ever more slippery. The colors of the lights swirled, brightened, and then all turned to a violent shade of fuchsia. The pink-red pulsed, and with every hit of the beat, the shadows lengthened. Swelled. Grew teeth.

When the fear threatened to black her out, Madeline had stood and stumbled out of VIP. She'd heard the faint complaining of the men – the outrage, the confusion. But every noise grew muffled. All she heard was the rushing in her ears. The world had transformed into Madeline's conch shell, and she was trapped inside it, deafened by imaginary oceans.

She needed sleep. Madeline couldn't remember the last time she'd shut her eyes sober and found peace instead of mayhem. She was so tired that she was numb. Yesterday she'd pricked her finger with the tip of a knife blade, and she hadn't felt a thing. The sweet man had been back, and he'd sucked at the wound for her before he left her to go vacation with his wife and kids. Madeline had changed and showered and gone shopping – buying anything her hands could find and taking as long as she could to avoid having to go back to the hotel. She'd changed into a short, red dress and sky-high heels in a dressing room, paid for the purchases, and sent the packages back to the Water's Edge by delivery service. She'd gone looking for music, drink, drugs, and sex, because normally some part of that combination worked to hollow her out so the fear couldn't take root.

But not tonight. Maybe not ever again.

The bathroom went dead quiet. Madeline's ears popped, painfully, and the music grew distant until it faded to nothing. She put a hand in front of her face to check to see if she could still feel her breath. It was there – but faint. Her hands were so cold. She scratched at her skin until she drew lined of welts and a bit of blood and barely felt a thing. Panic rose.

And then, faintly, she heard giggles.

Watery giggles.

The air went dark – deep black and blue and shimmering, like she was underwater.

Madeline scrambled to her feet, clumsy with her half-numb

body. She banged her knee on the toiler paper dispenser – cut it on the edge – and still, no sensation. Nothing.

The giggling grew louder. And closer. The shadows shifted under the door. Madeline climbed onto the toilet seat, balancing precariously on the balls of her feet in the ridiculous shoes. The door to the stall jiggled.

"*Maddy-lynn...*" giggled a little girl's voice. The rattling grew more urgent, insistent. And the voice grew louder, angry: "*MAAAAADDY-LYNN!*"

Madeline covered her mouth with both hands so she wouldn't scream. The door bowed on its hinges – and through gap she saw a single, hollow eyesocket. And then the voice changed – not a little girl at all, but deep, resonant, hollow, like steel on rock.

"*MADELINE. LET. ME. IN.*"

"No," Madeline whispered, tears pouring down her cheeks. "No, please, no, no, no—"

A painful constriction of anxiety to the soundtrack of her thudding heart, and then another pop. Music flooded the room. Women's voices. Faint, but clearer. The eye, the voice, the giggling – all gone. Madeline crouched, trembling, and her whole body tingled with muscles coming alive once again. She clamored off the toilet and flew out of the stall. The women called after her, "Are you okay?" But Madeline ignored them. She needed out, and she need out *now.*

In the hallway outside the bathroom, Madeline paused. She wiped her face. She tried to think. To the right were the club and a sea of humanity that moved like waves in the middle of a storm. Threatening, especially since somewhere in that sea were the two men who had already had her once, and they had hungry friends. To the left were the men's bathroom, a door to the DJ booth, and an emergency exit guarded by a bouncer. The man was huge, and he only got bigger as Madeline approached. His black T-shirt was stretched across his broad chest and linebacker's shoulders. His scalp was shaved and tattooed, and mirrored sunglasses hid his eyes.

"Can I help you?" the bouncer mountain yelled when Madeline got close enough to disturb him.

Shakily, Madeline mimed lifting a cigarette with two fingers to her lips. She made herself smile, she tossed her hair, and the bouncer smirked down at her. As he dug in his back pocket, Madeline made her smile widen into a grin, and the bouncer handed her a single, slender cigarette. Madeline frowned at it, and she touched the bodice of her dress, making sure her arm nudged her breast and made it strain against the fabric. She shrugged, tilting her head, and the man handed over an orange lighter. "Bring that back," he ordered.

Madeline nodded. He flicked a lever on a panel on the wall behind him, slammed a fist into the emergency door's bar, and pushed it open for her. Madeline escaped onto a concrete platform with a metal railing and five steps leading down to an alleyway between the club and the solid wall of a parking garage. The platform's edge and steps butted up against a tall chain link fence with dumpsters on either side and barbed wire across the top. The garbage reeked. It was dark except for the safety light over the club's door and a single light mounted on the corner of the garage at the mouth of the alley. Both the club and the garage were on the busiest four-lane street in this part of town, and cars zipped back and forth beyond the sidewalk. Madeline could probably find a taxi to take her home. At the bottom of the steps, she turned toward the open end of the alleyway to see an SUV block the exit and a man climb out of the back.

A familiar man. The one who liked the sound of her crying.

Madeline turned to run back inside, but one of the man's guards came out the emergency exit, blocking the path. He climbed down the steps and grabbed her. He knocked the lighter and the cigarette from her hands. She didn't fight. It was useless.

Her cruel lover asked a mean question laced with insults and venom, but Madeline's ears had already begun to ring. It didn't matter what he said or what she would have answered. He casually struck her across the cheekbone. Madeline twisted, pain blooming, and she had a moment to be happy about that – she could feel it – but then she was being walk-dragged toward the chain link fence. Rot filled her nose, and nausea threatened. Something went around her wrists and attached them to the fence. Plastic – a zip tie. The kind police used as quick handcuffs.

Her lover still spoke, but her ears were full of water. She understood he'd seen her inside in the VIP lounge. Or someone had, and they'd reported her to this lover. He was jealous when he wanted to be, and tonight, he was in that sort of mood. He wanted revenge. He wanted her to understand this was the sort of thing that happened to women like her. To women who disappointed him.

He hit her – several more times – but the sensations were dampened. Icy cold filled her limbs. She felt heavy and exhausted. She tried to struggle, but it was so pointless. Her skirt was shoved high, and her underwear torn away. She thought she was crying, probably she was begging. Her face and neck were wet. Tears, she hoped, and not blood.

The ocean in her head was so loud, Madeline wondered what would kill her first: that noise or all the men. There were a half dozen of them, and she knew exactly what each of them was going to do to her. Maybe until there was nothing left of her to do it to.

Pressure against her back, something awful between her legs, and the weight of rage blanketed by helplessness dragged her downward, into herself and against the fence. She shut her eyes.

And then everything stopped.

The shock of cessation forced Madeline's eyes open. She could see the guard – the one who'd blocked her exit back into the club – and his eyes were wide. Too wide – visible whites all around the rim. His mouth was open and drool dribbled out of the corner. He flinched, jerked like he was made of wood. His eyes bulged, and his mouth grew impossibly wider, like he was screaming, but in total silence. Then he slumped to the ground like someone had cut his strings.

Behind her, that man fell, too. She yanked away from the fence as much as she could and saw all the men were on the ground. They twisted and flailed, as though electrocuted, until at last they went deadly still.

"Hold steady." The words were mere sounds strung together in a pattern her brain recognized, but they were crisp and clear. Madeline still heard the water, but she also heard him, the newcomer, and then her wrists were free. She shoved down her dress and stumbled backward, away from the man she could so clearly hear and from the bodies of her fallen attackers. She shoved herself into a crevice between the dumpster and the fence. She pushed backward until the wall of the club stopped her. And then she waited, huddled in on herself while her heart skipped beats and stole the breath from her lungs, and she stared at the figure looming over the fallen men.

The man was tall with plenty of muscle. He wore a long, leather coat that shone like hematite. Madeline saw shaggy, coal-dark hair, wide-set, midnight eyes, and pale, pale skin. Beneath the jacket, he wore only pants made out of the same material as the coat and heavy black boots. Across his chest and belly were tattoos that showed his anatomy. Madeline could see his veins, his lungs, his guts, his liver, his ribs... He had a crack in his sternum. Above his collar bones were fainter, lighter etchings of bone and sinew that swept up his throat and outlined his jaw and the sockets of his eyes. And when he moved and crouched, his organs seemed to shift with him, as though they were real and not drawn. He didn't speak, he didn't blink, and Madeline had all the time in the world to study him and realize he felt familiar.

"I know you," Madeline whispered, as the ocean water in her ears faded away to nothing. She heard cars, distant voices, the thump of music, and normal sounds of night.

The man tilted his head slightly to the right. He nodded, once and only once.

"Are you... will you hurt me?" Madeline asked, though she already knew the answer.

Slowly, the man shook his head.

"You saved me."

The man merely studied her.

In a trance, Madeline licked her lips. She tasted tears, snot, and blood. "Are you my... are you the One?" She asked before she felt too sane to speak the words. But the man shook his head again, a negative, as though he knew she would ask and knew whom she meant. "You're not my Blue. The one I hear in my dreams. The one in the water." Again, another headshake to confirm what she knew. No reprimand. No demands for clarification.

"Then who are you?" Madeline asked.

The man rocked onto his heels, elbows on his knees, and his hands folded. The inked bones of his fingers gleamed in the light, and they didn't seem like tattoos at all. "I am Mal'uud 'au Keen," the man said, in a rough-grit voice that didn't register to Madeline as human. Animal, feral, alien, all those things, but not a man. Not a normal anything.

"In the language of Fear, my true name means, 'He who walks.' I am the King of Nightmare, one of the last Walkers of the Veil, and I have come, Madeline... Hope Star... to take you home."

Madeline held her breath and waited for the terror to return. She waited for his words to drive her mad, for her heart to burst, for her aching stomach to heave. She should have wanted to run, and she should have thought he was even crazier and more awful than the comatose men who had tried to ruin her.

Instead, Madeline took a deep breath and discovered she could breathe. It stung, but she could do it. Her face throbbed, her side hurt, and her wrists were on fire, but she wasn't scared of Mal'uud, and what he said made the most sense of anything Madeline had ever heard in her entire life. Everyone else in the world had been speaking gibberish that Madeline had to translate, but this man—

(creature)

—spoke true.

"Are you some kind of priest?" Madeline asked.

Mal'uud shook his head. "No. I am a king."

"A king of what?"

"Fallen ideas, goals, and dreams to which I give bodies. I rule these Nightmares while they live, and I rule their Bone Ghosts when they die. We reside and I control the Undermaze in which they dwell."

In her mind's eye, Madeline saw endless, dark hallways that felt like memories instead of imagination. She could feel heat on her skin – the halls were always warm, too warm – and the things that lived there... Heinous. But also harmless. At least, to her. "Where is that place?"

"Via'rra. A plane in the center of all planes, all worlds. My home." Mal'uud paused. "And yours. Are you hurt?"

"Yes." Chimes were tolling in Madeline's mind. "Did you say my home?"

"I did. May I aid you?"

Madeline was not afraid, but she was tired, small, and cracked open like an egg. "Please don't hurt me."

"Never," he said, like an oath made in blood.

If he had been going to do something terrible to her, likely he already would have done it. Madeline nodded. "Okay."

Mal'uud stayed hunched and hunkered, and he crammed himself into the space in front of her, crawling close until he sat cross-legged on the ground. And that was when she noticed he had no nipples. There were no scars that she could see, only a blank canvas where such human body parts had never been. "You smell like a camp fire," Madeline whispered, staring at his chest.

"When we Walk, we must look like the creatures native to the world. The skin I wear on this side of the Veil burns my real form. That is what you smell." Mal'uud retrieved a small leather bag from inside a pocket of his coat. He unwound its binding string and carefully spread the top.

"Doesn't that hurt?" Madeline asked.

"Yes." Mal'uud scooped a finger of moss green, glittering goop out of the bag. It shone as though it was radioactive, and it had the consistency of Hollywood ectoplasm.

"What is that?" Madeline asked, bracing as Mal'uud reached for the bleeding scrapes on her wrists.

"Healing salve. It is precious to me and mine. I do not share it lightly, but it will fix your hurts." Mal'uud touched the green gunk to her wounds, and Madeline gasped.

"Does it pain you?" Mal'uud asked, frowning.

"No." Madeline swallowed. "But I can feel it..." Madeline's skin crawled. Literally. The frayed edges were reaching for one another, and it itched. "Mending me, I think." While she watched her wounds vanish, more doubts that what he said was true evaporated, and the sheer relief made her limbs go to jelly. She moved closer, letting Mal'uud have access to the places that hurt.

"Good." Mal'uud continued to touch the salve to sore places. He was fearless when it came to blood, debris, or torn flesh.

"You said form. So this isn't what you actually look like?" Madeline's brain was full of mud, and she slung it away from her thoughts and her questions, as though searching to see if she'd find horror. And all the while, her fingers ached to touch him. She curled them into fists.

"Correct. This form is the one I adopt here. It is not what I really am."

Madeline wiped muck off a bad dream about a man with horns. She stiffened and pulled away. Mal'uud's hand hovered mid-air. "Do you..." Madeline tried to ask, but her voice got stuck in her narrowed throat.

"Do I?" Mal'uud repeated.

When she shut her eyes, she saw *him*, and she scooted away. "Are you bigger? With horns and shadows that move around you? That *are* you?"

"No." Mal'uud's eyes were huge and black but oddly also kind. "You describe the Lord of Nothing."

Madeline gulped. "Who is he?"

Mal'uud considered. "He is the Great Unmaker. The Eater of Worlds. He is as inevitable as your death, but more fearsome, for his destruction is calculated and his meals make the energy for Lady Creation."

Again, what should have been gibberish made complete sense. The facts clicked in her brain as though they'd been waiting for her to figure them out. "And you're... You're definitely not him?"

"I am not."

"Okay." What else could Madeline do but believe Mal'uud? This was all crazy, this talk of kingdoms and intangibles and unmakers. Any word of this conversation would send them both straight to the loony bin. Madeline wondered if she didn't mind because she was so sleepy or if she didn't mind because she believed it. Both, maybe. After all, the man might look like a gothic punk no older than twenty-five, but he had no nipples, his tattoos moved, and he carried green slime that made wounds vanish.

Nearby, one of the downed men whimpered, and Madeline suddenly panicked because she'd almost forgotten that they were still there, though they hadn't moved since Mal'uud had arrived. "What did you do to them?"

Mal'uud glanced at the limp bodies. "I made them dream."

"What do you mean?"

"I mean what I say, Madeline Banc. I made them dream."

"Okay, but how?"

Mal'uud slouched, as though figuring out how to explain it. "I reached into their minds, called forth their worst thoughts, and I set their terrors free in their conscious brains. They are consumed by them."

"Will they ever get better?" Madeline couldn't stop whispering.

"No. They will have moments of clarity that will only heighten their fear. They are chased and hunted in their mental, private lands, and they will be imprisoned in them until their bodies give out." Mal'uud faced Madeline, again. He swiped salve on her throbbing cheek and next to her mouth. The pain evaporated. "Did they hurt you elsewhere?" Mal'uud asked. He started to reach for her, between her knees.

Madeline gave a soft cry and grabbed his wrist. "No. *No.*" Mal'uud didn't fight her, but his wrist was solid beneath her hand, and hot as though he had a fever. "My side," she said, turning and unzipping her dress just enough. "It hurts."

"Then that I shall fix."

"How do you know?" Madeline blurted. The alleyway was beginning to spin and to blur, and she blinked back tears.

"Know what?"

She couldn't look at him or the dreaming men, so Madeline stared at the strange leather of Mal'uud's coat. "That I'm, what did you call me? The Hope Star?"

Though Madeline still gripped Mal'uud arm, he slowly reached for her as though Madeline's strength was little more than a breeze. Madeline choked down a sob, not even sure why it felt as though any second now, she would explode. And Mal'uud was somehow making it worse, with his tenderness. The salve left dust behind on her skin as it sank below the dermis to heal the tissue and bone beneath. The relief was instantaneous and awful, because each healing was a reminder that her brain was trying to crack into pieces.

"I was told of you." Even Mal'uud's voice was careful, and Madeline started to shake all over. "I've heard your story from another Walker. I know what you've lost, and I know the great sacrifice you made coming here. A woman messenger gave me your human information. She said you came from the woods wearing a dead girl's face, and that she taught you in school."

Madeline had only been in school a short while before her adopted parents chose to teach her at home with tutors. And even so, there'd only been one teacher who'd ever treated her with kindness – the sort of kindness later combined with a type of madness that might lead her to telling a creature of another world, of Madeline's real world, where to find her in this one. "Helen Taylor," Madeline gasped.

"Yes. The Lord of Nothing touched her; let her see some of the other sides of reality. She sees more than most, and it is tearing her asunder. Human consciousness is so simple. You are easy to touch or to break, either by my hand or by your own chemical imbalance. Walker minds feel differently. They are more complex, existing on at least two planes at once, and sometimes on more than one timeline. They are defended – feel like fortresses instead of wide-open planes – and intricate. And that is how I found you, when you were not at your residence. I cast my net and tested minds and felt yours some distance away. And that is also how I know you are a Walker, Madeline." Mal'uud gently touched her forehead with one finger, squinting as though he studied the intricacies of her brain. "You are fractured, only a piece of yourself, and yet still I know what you are."

Madeline curled into a ball. "So I'm different? Than other people?"

"Yes. Very. You are not 'people.' You are Walker."

"And I don't belong here?"

"No. You never have."

Madeline strangled on a sob. "You're going to take me somewhere else?"

"Yes."

"And I belong... there?"

"Yes. Our world is dying, and we need you."

Madeline shoved the heels of both her hands against her mouth. She wanted what Mal'uud said to be true so badly that she didn't care about anything else. She didn't know until right then that every second of every minute of every hour of every day had been spent yearning to be somewhere else. To be *someone* else. All the times she'd felt alone, isolated, strange... She'd been the wrong kind of revered for being too attractive, too odd, too beautiful, too perfect. And yet so empty. She'd felt so very vacant and lost. She sought men who'd tell her she was all they dreamed of, and for a while, being that for them was a way to fill her up. When that failed, the booze and drugs did the trick. But not forever. And really, not at all.

Because all the while she'd been dying for someone or something to come to her, to take her hand, and tell her it'd all been a terrible mistake. It'd been a test of some sort, but she had passed, and now the bad dream was over. She didn't need to suffer anymore. It was time to go home.

Mal'uud could be leading her to a cardboard box under a bridge and, once there, he could tell her she was the goddess of the trolls. As long as she was with someone who understood her and didn't hate her for what she was, Madeline would follow him anywhere.

"Oh, God." Madeline panted for breath, and she could feel heartache bubbling up, ready to boil over. "I'm sorry, but I think... I think I'm going to cry."

A hot hand stroked her hair, and Mal'uud drew closer. "I would weep, too, were I you, for all I'd have lost and had to live too long without."

Madeline glanced up and into a face full of kinship, and she flung herself against Mal'uud. She buried her face against his neck and wept, and Mal'uud, without a word or a sound, wrapped her up in his coat and held her. She felt safe, held, and wanted. *Truly* wanted – not for sex or beauty or power, but for herself.

"We must go." Mal'uud picked her up as though she weighed nothing, and she clung to him.

"What about them?" Madeline asked, pointing behind Mal'uud's back to the sprawled men.

"They are not our concern, anymore."

Madeline thought they'd be someone's concern, and that someone might come after Madeline, but she kept her mouth shut as Mal'uud carried her to the alley's entrance. "We'll need a vehicle," he said, and he started toward her cruel lover's SUV.

"No," Madeline said, squirming. Mal'uud set her down on her feet. She'd lost both her shoes, and the pavement was warm and rough. "We can't take their vehicles. We don't want them finding us."

"Agreed," Mal'uud said. "We want nothing following us. What do you suggest?"

At that moment, a truck swerved off the street and out of the main flow of traffic. It came to a halt with a screech of brakes directly in front of them. A little boy with a Halloween mask perched on top of his head leaned out of the passenger window. An older man – white hair, scruff of beard, work shirt over a white-tee – was behind the wheel. He didn't even look their way.

"Get in," said the boy, reaching to open the extended cab's door. "Hurry," he added, when Madeline's feet refused to unroot themselves.

Mal'uud approached and leaned toward the boy. He drew close enough that their noses almost touched, and the boy didn't flinch when Mal'uud didn't waver. He went so still – too still; no breath, no pulse, no movement. At last he pulled away and held out a hand to help Madeline into the truck.

"Do you know them?" Madeline asked.

"I sense Shadow on the child," Mal'uud said.

"Like Helen?" Madeline asked.

Mal'uud dipped his chin in a nod.

Madeline climbed into the truck, and Mal'uud followed her. He shut the door and the driver immediately pulled into traffic. He flicked the rearview mirror down. His vivid blue eyes met Madeline's. "Where we goin'?"

"The Townsende Trail," Mal'uud answered. "The start of it, near the water."

The driver grunted and adjusted the mirror so that all Madeline saw was the wad of chewing tobacco being worked behind thin lips.

"This is Vern," said the boy, turning himself in the front seat so he could see the rear passengers. "He's my friend who can drive. I'm Toby."

"I'm Maddy," she said.

Toby grinned. "I know. And he's a monster."

Madeline flinched, but Mal'uud didn't seem to take offense. "And so is she," Mal'uud said.

Toby grinned wider. "I know. She's the dead girl from the woods."

Mal'uud swiveled his head to study Madclinc. "What does this mean?"

Images rose in Madeline's mind: dirt, the snout of a dog, the cold, hard plastic of a chair in a room full of people in uniform. "I was an orphan," she said. "They found me in the woods on private property. A hunter's dogs sniffed me out."

"This is when you were born, here?" Mal'udd asked.

Madeline swallowed the bile that rose when she was forced to talk about it. "I-I don't really... I wasn't a baby when they found me. They guessed I was about four or so."

"You don't remember?"

Madeline tore away from Mal'uud and stared into the headlights of oncoming traffic. "No. I remember the dogs. They were big and wet and had coarse fur." She paused. "And I know that when the hunter who owned the land caught up with his hounds and saw me, he screamed."

"Why did he react this way?" Mal'uud asked.

"He said it was because he knew me. That I was his granddaughter who had disappeared years before." The headlights were blinding, mesmerizing. So she said more than she normally would have said. "I was soaking wet. He said he'd found me, years before, drowned and dead. Said he'd buried me, that I couldn't be alive, and then he ran."

"And were you his kin?"

"No. Of course not. The girl who'd gone missing would have been the same age as I was when he found me, and when he calmed down, he noticed there were differences." Like her eyes, Madeline didn't say. The man had said his granddaughter had sweet brown eyes, and Madeline's were pale. Too pale. Devil eyes, he'd said in the police station. He'd yelled for all the world to hear: *"That girl has devil's eyes!"*

"They put me in foster care." Madeline shrugged. "Mr. and Mrs. Banc adopted me."

"*Such a gorgeous child*," Mrs. Banc had gushed at the sight of the girl who'd been found in the woods. The woman wore pencil skirts and furs like she was stuck in a rich nineteen-fifties uniform, and she doted on Madeline. Called her perfect. And God help Madeline if she strayed from that image. "*She just glows, doesn't she?*" Mrs. Banc would say. "*Like she's lit up from within, the precious child.*"

"Why are we going to the hiking trail?" Madeline asked, noting that Toby didn't interrupt like most kids. He watched them speak like he watched a play.

Mal'uud eyed Vern and didn't answer.

Madeline chewed her lip and tugged at her skirt. "Can we go by my place, first? I'm a mess and I'd like to—" She had to stop when she felt ties around her wrists and pressure between her legs as though it were happening all over again. She breathed. "Change."

Toby vanished below the front seat. A second later, a duffle bag dropped onto Madeline's foot. "I stole it from Mama," he explained. "She's not shaped exactly like you, but..."

Vern wheezed a chuckle and shook his head, though he offered no further commentary. "Thanks," Madeline said. She unzipped the bag and saw jeans, a shirt, socks, a plastic sleeve of hair ties, and hiking boots. The shoes even looked close to her size. Madeline grabbed the jeans, and Vern yanked Toby down and into the seat, facing front. Madeline took a second to appreciate the gesture before she went to work getting dressed. The top was loose enough that she could put it on and then undo the dress and yank it off. The shoes were big, but the socks were thick. She laced them up tightly.

Madeline had just managed to loop a few of the ties onto her wrist and tie her hair back when the truck pulled off the road near a sign for the trail. Quickly, Madeline took the diamonds out of her ear lobes. "Here," she said to Toby. "Give these to your mom, if you can. Tell her..." Madeline didn't know how to finish.

"I will," Toby said solemnly. He took the earrings into a careful fist. "Please go save the world with the other monsters, okay?"

"I'll try," Madeline said. Impulsively, she leaned forward and kissed both their cheeks before climbing out of the truck. Vern took off, and Mal'uud took Madeline's hand.

"Why are we really here?" she asked.

"Because it is close to where the Veil is," Mal'uud answered, and Madeline both understood this to mean that a place to cross over into other worlds was close and simultaneously wanted to tell him he made no sense and had to be crazy. "As you said, we want no one following us." Mal'uud swiftly crossed the street, and they nearly jogged down it and into the parking lot of the Fisherman's Shack Museum. The Safety lights flickered and died as Mal'uud approached and opened the museum's rear door. He ushered Madeline inside, shutting the door behind her. Quickly, Mal'uud went to a panel on the wall and punched in a code. The screen stopped glowing.

"How did you—" Madeline began.

"I heard the humans in blue uniforms speak the numbers that would silence the cry of the alarm. Come. We must go quickly."

Madeline had only been to the museum once, and she'd been a child, so she was grateful that Mal'uud knew his way through the exhibits in the dark. They climbed roped-off stairs, crossed a room, and climbed into an attic. The only light came though a series of high, dirty windows, and it took a moment for Madeline's eyes to adjust to the gloom. The room was finished with rough floorboards, and it was full of boxes and shelves. In the middle of a cleared space was an odd, black ring, like gunpowder over a burned mark. Mal'uud let go of Madeline's hand to kneel next to the ring. He spoke unfamiliar sounds in a low, inhuman voice that set every one of Madeline's hairs standing on end. The very air crackled, and Mal'uud cut his palm with his nails with a wicked show of force. Blood rose from the wound – but it was slow to come and deep, dark maroon. He spilled it in the middle of the ring, then spat, and immediately the ring began to undulate like a coin trying to settle on one side if the coin was made of water. The ring was hollow in the middle, and floating in the air in the center of it, a light began to glow. The light quickly turned into an expanding patch of fuchsia edged with darkness. Madeline staggered backward into a wall, reeling away from the strangeness.

If there had been any doubt that Mal'uud was anything other than precisely what he said he was, it died as Madeline watched the Veil begin to open.

Which that also meant that she was what Mal'uud said she was, too.

Part of Madeline – the human part – began to scream. Watching her reality rip in front of her eyes was doing terrible things to her mind. A migraine pulsed in her skull, and for a moment, the pain was so intense, she wondered if this was what an aneurism felt like.

But the pain ebbed, eventually, and the part of her that believed the creature who could make people dream studied the Veil and felt like she was watching something she remembered. Like watching a movie she'd forgotten she'd seen. Her human side told her she was dreaming – this had to be a dream. But the rest of her understood clearly in that moment that the illusion was the men and the flowers and the shopping and the mean looks at the dead girl from the woods.

And reality was gods, monsters, and portals among worlds.

Mal'uud suddenly drew away, and the Veil took on a different tone: it melted from fuchsia to sickly green to cirrhosis yellow to a pink-cream that made Madeline's stomach churn. "What's happening?" she asked.

"It's unstable," Mal'uud replied, frowning. He glanced from her to the Veil, and Madeline read his fear.

"What does that mean?"

Mal'uud shook his head. He drew closer to the rip in time and space and put a hand close to it. "It's only happened to me once, when a war in the Undermaze destroyed a Veil. When I crossed, I didn't arrive back in the same place from which I left."

"So you don't know where this leads?"

Mal'uud looked at Madeline. "I do not."

Madeline took a shaky breath and drew closer. "Can't we just stay here?" she asked, in a small voice. The one she had used when she asked the police if she was dead and asked her social worker if she had to go live with the Bancs.

Mal'uud drew away until he stood next to Madeline, shoulder to shoulder. "If we stay, then we lose the chance to help rebalance the worlds."

"What unbalanced them?"

"The Hope Star was taken from one and put in another through a rare kind of Veil that we thought had been destroyed."

"And I'm...?"

"You are the Hope Star, or at least part of her. You were split into two pieces when taken from our world."

Madeline heard waves again. "Who did that to me?"

"Your lover. Water."

Madeline heard mournful singing – lonely, lost notes floating in darkness. "Is he my Blue?"

"Yes."

Tears ran down Madeline's face, and she wiped them away. "What happens on the other side of the Veil?

Mal'uud met her gaze. His eyes were no longer human. They were deep pits of darkness with faint specks of light in their centers. Fear lanced through Madeline's belly, but she locked her knees and didn't pull away. "I do not know what will happen."

"But if we stay, then everything ends?"

"Yes."

Madeline glanced away and stared at the boxes marked "Becky." Boxes full of someone's life – the little things someone saved. If Madeline died – if this was the end or if she were already dead and this was some kind of delusion of an oxygen-deprived brain – it'd be the small things she missed most. The feel of soft sheets on Saturday morning. Ice cream eaten straight from the carton in the middle of the night by the light of the refrigerator. The sun's heat in summer and the first chill of autumn in the breeze. Rain. Campfires. The way people smiled when they thought no one was watching. Baby giggles. The purr of a cat. The joy of a dog fetching a ball.

She'd miss those things if she was gone, and that meant those were things worth trying to save. "Then we have to go," Madeline said, and the Veil grew – multicolored with jagged edges. Around them, the Shadows deepened, began to whisper.

Madeline didn't wait for the King of Nightmare to answer. She walked to the Veil and passed through it.

Chapter Thirteen

Jason opened his eyes in the darkness because someone was right behind him. The nightlight in the bathroom was on, filling the room with a puddle of weak yellow. Jason could hear moist breathing and soft, pained sounds of distress. Slowly, he rolled his head on the pillow, and he came face-to-face with Andrew, who was crouched next to the sofa, staring at Jason with shining bat eyes.

"Shh!" Andrew shushed Jason, one finger to his lips while the other arm hugged his knees more tightly to his chest. Andrew pointed to his ear, and he pointed to the door.

Dutifully, Jason remained still and strained to hear what was bugging Andrew. At first there was only the whir-clink of the ceiling fan and the creak of the old house. Then there was a thump, a muffled yell, and a slam, like a door behind many other doors had just been shut in somebody's face.

Jason wriggled closer to the edge of the sofa cushion and Andrew. "What's going on?" he stage-whispered.

Andrew's mouth twisted into a frown, a pout, and finally a thin, tight line. "They're fighting."

"Who is?"

"Mama and Darryl."

"About Helen and all that?" Jason still felt so guilty and so prepared to be evicted at any moment.

"About everything." Andrew pressed his mouth against his T-shirt's long sleeve. The corners of his eyes were damp.

"Hey." Jason struggled to sit up, shoving pillows behind him. He awkwardly patted Andrew's shoulder, and Jason was ten, again, and at that God-awful survival camp Papa Jack had sent him to. It'd toughen him up, Papa Jack had said. Make Jason strong. All it had done was teach Jason that other boys cried just as much as he did when the lights went out.

"It'll be all right, man," Jason said.

Andrew sniffed, chewed on his sleeve, and sat down hard on his ass next to the couch. He leaned his head on the cushion. "I'm glad you're here."

Jason heard more slamming. It was hard to tell where it came from: next to them or above them. "Me, too."

Andrew turned big eyes on Jason. "You care for people, even if they're strange."

But never enough to save them.

The crash of glass reached Jason's ears through the walls, and Andrew started to hum "Can't Get No Satisfaction." Jason joined in, and they stayed in hoarse harmony until the house grew too quiet once again.

"What do you think of Tio?" Andrew asked.

"Who?"

"Mercutio. Helen calls him 'Tio.' I like it."

"He seems like a cool guy," Jason said, remembering Helen's parting words before she exited the security car. "Why do you ask?"

"I dunno." Andrew went back to gnawing on his shirt. He was going to chew through it at this rate. "I dream about him, sometimes," Andrew whispered.

Jason was pretty sure he wouldn't want to know, but he asked, anyway. "What about?"

"It doesn't make much sense."

"It's a dream."

"So?"

"So, they usually don't?"

Andrew pursed his lips, a wet spot the size of a man's palm staining his shirt. "My dreams make sense. I want to know more about my father, so I dream about old guys with guitars. I miss my mama, so I dream about her making waffles and bacon. I'm tired of winter, so I dream about the garden in spring."

Jason couldn't argue with Andrew or, it seemed, ever accurately predict what the hell would come out of his mouth. "Okay, well, what is it about your dreams with Mercutio—"

"Tio."

"Tio, then, that don't add up?"

Andrew looked left and right, got feet under him and scooted until he sat facing Jason, though he kept his butt on the floor. Andrew rested his head on Jason's forearm, and, on impulse, Jason patted Andrew's hair. Just once, and it was awkward, but Andrew sighed and the weight of his head grew heavier.

"We're in a garden, but it's overgrown and dead. It's snowing, but I'm not cold. I think there's a castle and a river, but I can't see them, just sort of sense them. The Stones are always playing on an old record player, and sometimes he sits in this huge chair and reads to me out of this big black book and sometimes we dance."

"Sounds nice?"

"It is. Right until I have to wake up. Everything goes darker than dark, and I get scared. It's like... losing him. Losing all of it, when I never, ever wanted to be anywhere but there. It's awful just for a second, and then I'm here. And everything's fine, but it doesn't feel right for the rest of the day."

Jason envisioned torn flesh and guitar strings. He shied away from an invisible pool of congealing, remembered blood. "I've had dreams like that. The ones that tip everything else off-center."

"What do you think the dreams mean?"

"I'm not sure they mean anything other than you like Tio."

It took Andrew a few seconds to whisper a reply. "Yeah."

"And maybe he likes you, too."

Andrew's frown threatened to turn into a scowl, and Jason silently took Helen's name in vain. "So, do you know how you like him?"

"How does anyone like anybody?"

Jason laughed. "So true, man."

Andrew's frown quivered at the edges. "Am I wrong?"

"About what?"

"I don't know. Liking Tio?"

"Why would you be wrong?"

"I don't know." Andrew was trying to work out what to say, and Jason watched the facial contortions that went along with that process. "How many other people have to think you're wrong before they're right and you're not, anymore?"

Jason scratched at the side of his neck. "I think it matters more how you and Tio feel than anybody else."

"Oh." Andrew was crestfallen. He slumped and started chewing on his other sleeve. "Oh. I don't think Tio feels at all."

"Bull," Jason said, and he tried not to squirm when he once again had every ounce of Andrew's considerable attention. "I've seen the guy. Heard him, too. Tio's the kind of person who feels all kinds of things and isn't shy about sharing them."

"I know." Andrew put his head down again. "That's how I know he doesn't feel anything about me."

Jason was still working on how to comfort Andrew when a knock came at the door. Andrew hissed and grabbed Jason's arm when Jason leapt off the sofa to answer, but Jason shook Andrew off. Jason opened the door to find Miss Teedee on the other side, white purse strap over her arm and mouth drawn. "You're not dressed," she said.

"Should I be?" Jason replied.

Miss Teedee's frown tipped upward into amusement. "It's five a.m., lovie."

Jason craned his neck to look at the clock on Andrew's mantel. "Holy sh—er, cow. It is. Let me throw something on. I'm sorry."

"It's all right." Miss Teedee stepped into the room while Jason grabbed a pair of jeans. She clucked her tongue and held out her arms to Andrew, who got up and threw himself into them. "You hungry, sugar pie?"

"Uh-huh." Andrew said, muffled and nodding while comically bent to bury his face against Miss Teedee's narrow shoulder.

"Well, you come on up with Jason, then, and we'll get you fed." She patted his head. "You've got a busy day of making things grow ahead of you, don't you?"

Andrew wiped his nose on his arm. His head tipped backward, and he whispered at the ceiling. "Can you hear them upstairs?"

"Not a peep."

"Oh." Andrew sighed. "Oh." He grabbed a flannel robe covered in ice caps and playing penguins, and together, he and Jason followed Miss Teedee out of the bedroom, to the central staircase, and up to the main floor. It was pitch black in the house, but Miss Teedee moved as though she could see in the dark.

The kitchen lights were on, much to Jason's relief, and Miss Teedee stowed her personal belongings and pulled out two aprons. She tied one on herself and tossed the other to Jason. "Today, you learn about biscuits and eggs," she said with an impish smile. "Let's get to it."

Andrew sat on one of the stools at the island, drinking orange juice that Miss Teedee poured for him. Meanwhile, Jason discovered that the fastest way to make Miss Teedee happy was to obey her with a kind of fearlessness that Jason had never previously encountered in the kitchen. If Miss Teedee handed him some dough and told him to knead it, he'd do exactly that, never having kneaded dough in his life. If she told him to shake flour into a bowl, he did, not knowing how much or how to shake it properly. In the space of an hour, Jason kneaded, shook, cut, rolled, formed, sprayed, and half a dozen other baking tasks that he'd seen done or heard of someone with skill doing, but had never tried.

And it would have been a disaster if Miss Teedee didn't think anything he did was marvelous. Jason spilled half a bowl of flour onto the floor, and Miss Teedee laughed and told Andrew to get some wet towels. Jason didn't know buttermilk from regular, and he didn't know where the actual butter was stored. He dropped three eggs, and he ate three blueberries without washing them first, but Miss Teedee's smiles only grew wider and her instructions kinder.

By the time the eggs were in the pan and the first batch of biscuits had gone into the industrial oven, Jason was dusted with white and grinning hard enough to hurt his cheeks. "That was awesome," he said.

"I know." Miss Teedee beamed in return. "I get to do it every day, and now? So do you."

"I like you two at the stove together." Andrew twirled on his stool and started to sing "Ruby Tuesday." Miss Teedee joined in with a pretty soprano, and Jason with tenor, but they hushed when they heard a door open and close. A moment later, Helen appeared. She wore a white nightgown under a robe, and her hair was a billowing halo of curls. Her feet were bare and she had grass sticking to her toes.

"Morning, gang," Mercutio said, stepping around Helen. He wore jeans and a baby blue scrubs top under a cardigan that reminded Jason of Western sunsets. Mercutio had dark circles under his eyes and a coffee thermos in hand. "Nothing would do the pretty lady this morning but to come see y'all when we saw the lights on."

"They have you on all-nighters, again?" Miss Teedee asked, heading for the coffee pot.

"I'm sure changes are coming, but I wanted to stay with Madam Butterfly after her woodland adventure." Mercutio shot Jason a raised eyebrow. Jason poked the calm sea of eggs, butter, and milk heating in a pan with a spatula, trying not to break his eyeballs with his strained, sideways glance at Helen, who was tugging Mercutio down to whisper.

"Well go on, then. It's just us here, love." Mercutio nudged Helen toward Jason, and Mercutio slid onto a stool next to Andrew. "Well look at you with your penguins."

"I have to go." Andrew shot up and dashed around the island, head down and shoulders hunched.

"Okay, sweetheart." But Andrew was long gone by the time Miss Teedee turned around.

"Something I said?" Mercutio asked.

"Oh, I doubt it. Monica and Darryl have been at each other's throats all morning."

"Well, hell." Mercutio sighed.

"Be nicer to him," Helen said to her nurse, padding over to Jason and the eggs. She peered into the skillet.

"I'm always nice to him."

"That's why I said 'nicer,'" Helen muttered.

"Tio, honey, can you reach this top shelf for me?" Miss Teedee asked, huffing at a cabinet. "Somebody went and put the spare coffee tins all the way up top."

"Sure Miss Tee."

Mercutio went to help Miss Teedee, and Jason focused on the eggs. Helen was right next to him. He could smell grass and dew and roses. She put their shoulders together so they stood like two people crammed into a subway car, not a spacious country kitchen, and she covered his hand with hers on the spatula handle.

"How were your dreams last night?" Helen asked quietly.

"Fine. No nightmares."

They stirred the eggs, which were finally hot enough to start scrambling. "You're in the right place, here with Miss Teedee. Sometimes you'll feel like you're not where you should be, but I want you to know that you are. I know it in my bones just like the way you feel in yours that you've found family, here."

Jason's eyes burned, and he blinked and nodded to show he heard. Sometimes his growing affection for these people felt like fear.

"You remember what I said our part would be to help the Walkers of the Veil?"

"Remember who we are, right?" Jason replied, as they both stirred the eggs so they wouldn't brown too much on one side.. It didn't bother him that Helen liked to speak in symbols. Or that maybe they weren't even symbols at all. Judith and Rage used to trip and talk in trances, sometimes. The things they'd say usually didn't make any sense, but occasionally they did. They predicted a bad gig or someone who would betray them – right down to the date and time and circumstance.

There were all kinds of things that Jason didn't understand in the least, but he did know that if speaking of Walkers or friends or symbols that stood for parts of Helen or even the people in her life, helped Helen in some small way, then he was completely game. Anything to feel more like he belonged and less like he was a burden.

"No, not that tin," Miss Teedee said loudly from across the room. "The one behind it."

"I don't see one behind it, Miss Tee," Mercutio said, standing on tiptoes and pushing canisters left and right. "You sure it's all the way in that corner?"

"I'm sure."

"I gotta get the stepladder if I'm going to get that beast."

"Well, it's in the pantry."

Mercutio huffed but went toward the swinging door.

Helen's voice dropped to a whisper. "The Hope Star is back in Via'rra. The Nightmare King saved her. You saved her. *We* did it. The last Walkers are on the path to heal themselves, but we've got to set ourselves to rights on this side, too, or Via'rra Walkers won't be able to restore balance. If they can't restore what was lost, then everything is lost. Including you and me."

"No." Jason gave in to impulse and touched his lips to Helen's curls. "That's just not going to happen," he said, because it wouldn't. Not if he could help it, and it didn't matter if Jason understood everything Helen said or not. He didn't want this woman to hurt. He didn't want anyone in this house to hurt.

Helen stilled their hands and looked Jason in the eye. "I believe in you. But you should know that here, in our world, everything will shatter so it can mend. Everyone will be forced to focus on themselves and what they've lost. It'll hurt. A lot. But you, most of all, must stay strong."

"I can take it," Jason said, though he wasn't sure he believed himself. "And I'll help in any way I can."

Helen kissed him. Quick and light and with a smile afterwards that was brighter than the sunrise lighting up the house. "I know. Cook with Miss Teedee and get Andrew and Mercutio to see one another. It'll get clearer after that."

"What will?"

"Everything." Helen sniffed. "The eggs are burning."

Cussing, Jason lowered the flame, and Helen was gone from his side and over to the island. She fidgeted with the tie on her robe until Mercutio got the ladder and the tin and handed both over to Miss Teedee when he was done.

"I'm tired," Helen said, and Mercutio waved over his shoulder as he followed his charge out of the kitchen and into the early morning beyond the windowpanes.

Chapter Fourteen

Madeline smelled earth, soot, decay, and sulfur. She was Santa Claus caught in the chimney descending to hell's furnace. The air clogged her lungs, and she coughed. A dull razor had scraped all of her skin and she ached all over like she had the flu. Moaning, she clutched at her head, which pounded in time to the colors dancing behind her eyelids.

Did she drink too much last night? She must have.

No, wait...

She remembered: the men in the alleyway and the thing that saved her. The light and the feel of power on her skin as she walked through—

A Veil.

—a passageway. So brave, she'd been, marching into the unknown without letting herself think too much on it. But the moment she was halfway into the Veil, she'd felt her entire body shift. Her entire world view. Everything she thought she understood and took for granted – all gone up in so much smoke in an instant. She'd been compressed, squeezed, then thought she'd come apart. She'd screamed and screamed, until she was hoarse and deaf, and she'd fallen, been caught, and...

"A dream," she whispered. "Just a dream."

"I fear not," said a raspy voice from very nearby.

Madeline opened her eyes, not wanting to, but knowing she could not stay in the darkness forever. A man-thing, a creature made of black, rotten ribbons painted over bone, was crouched next to her. His bony, raw elbows were resting on the bare muscle sinew covering his thighs. The muscle was shiny black and the tendons dull matte. His chest was cracked open, the ribs broken off and the sternum missing, as though something inside him had erupted and left him in this ruin. There was nothing inside him that Madeline could see, but there was a swirling green mist like a visible floating pearl of static electricity. She could hear it hum, oh so faintly. And his eyes were sunk deep into wide sockets. Barely visible, the irises were black ringed with red and the pupils were a bright dot of white dead center.

She wanted to cry, because this wasn't what the other world was supposed to be. Her Blue should be there, waking her with a kiss and a gentle caress. They'd swim in warm waters until the sun set and the stars came out.

Stars.

Suddenly Madeline stood on the edge of unimaginable loss – teetered and knew if she toppled into that abyss, she wouldn't survive it. The pain cut through her, and Madeline wanted to scream for all new reasons, but her throat felt like it'd rip and bleed if she did, and instead all she could manage were wet, raspy sounds like muted sobs. She scrambled backward until she struck a wall. The kneeling creature by the bed tilted his head, and Madeline suddenly knew this was Mal'uud. She knew this was the same man who looked like a boy with living tattoos when he was on the other side of the Veil. She knew he would not hurt her, because of what she was, but she couldn't quite remember who that was supposed to be. And when she tried, every part of her hurt. Madeline pressed her hands to the sides of her head, hoping the pressure would ease the agony.

"You are not whole," Nightmare said. Madeline thought he might have sighed. "That isn't good."

The urge to run crashed through Madeline's body, but a hand wrapped around her wrist. Mal'uud was hot – tropically warm – to the touch. "Try to calm yourself. We're safe, for now."

Madeline forced herself to stop crying and tried to take stock. She was in a bed in what appeared to be a bedroom in a dilapidated, rotting house. The ceiling was cracked and black mold crept across the plaster. The light fixture dangled from wires snaking out of a hole in the ceiling, perilously close to falling at any moment. The furniture was broken down and covered in dust so thick it looked like snow. Mildew offended her nose and, beneath the smell of damp, she smelled smoke and cinder.

"Is something burning?" she asked.

Mal'uud grunted and stood. He was tall and wide and made the room seem miniature. "The flesh I wore on the far side of the Veil," he explained as he settled next to a foggy, cracked window. "The Walking burns such forms away."

Madeline frantically looked herself over, but she saw only the borrowed clothes on her familiar body. She yanked up her pants leg and saw only her skin. She groped her face, neck, breasts – all the same. "Then how am I still like this? Shouldn't my form have burned away, too?"

"I fear I cannot answer that."

Fighting down another wave of nausea, Madeline pushed upright and leaded against the bedframe. Exhaustion overtook her, and she rested for a few moments before finding the energy to ask, "Is this how I look? Over here?"

Mal'uud's black lips thinned, as if pained. "I don't think so."

"But you don't know?"

"If we met when we both were whole, I do not remember it now. When this happened," he gestured to his torso while studying whatever was outside, "many of my memories left me. It is one of many reasons I went to the Storyteller; I thought he could tell me all of what I'd forgotten."

An image of an old man transposed onto a young man's face filled Madeline's mind in a flicker and then was gone. "Please, tell me everything that happened before you found me?"

Mal'uud dipped his chin, and as he told her of waking in the throne room of the Undermaze, of his 'mares, of his Bone Ghosts, she remembered in bits and pieces in flashes that simultaneously made perfect sense and no sense at all.

Adimoas was the King of Nightmare's commanding general, friend, comrade in arms. When Madeline tried to describe him, Mal'uud confirmed her memory was accurate. Madeline knew that Adimoas was a fallen paradigm: a complete way of life and thought. At one time, some world worked the way it did because Adimoas had existed.

But that'd been centuries ago, and Madeline didn't understand how she could remember *centuries*. Just like she didn't know why the Storyteller sounded like an old friend and a stranger. Or how, when Mal'uud told her of the tale of the Star and Water, it was like hearing an old, familiar bedtime story that filled her with images that felt like memories of someone else's life that she was borrowing.

Madeline shut her eyes and remembered blue scales, strong hands – five fingers, long-nailed – and the sensation of a man deep inside her; moving, pleasuring, clasping her skin, for hours and hours and—

With a gasp, Madeline leaned forward and swallowed bile. The undiluted love she felt for her Blue competed with the sense of unending betrayal and loss, and she was going to tear in two. She couldn't live like this. She couldn't stand this. So much rage. So much hate. So much fear. So much pain. The emotions ignited in colors, red-gray-black-yellow streaking through her vision. She clawed at her throat, unable to breathe, at her face, unable to scream, at her chest, at her heart, trying, begging, pleading, needing.

A hot form wrapped around her, and she was small in Mal'uud's lap. Her strength was no match for his, and when she stopped trying to fight him, he merely held her and stroked her hair. She rested her head on his torso and discovered the sinew gave more than she would have thought. She let herself be comforted by a creature that ruled monsters, and slowly, the memory of her Blue faded.

"I thought that simply bringing you here would mend you. I was wrong."

"Clearly," Madeline said with a harsh laugh. She sighed. "And can I say, I still can't quite believe all this."

"Mm," Nightmare intoned, climbing off the bed and going once again to the window. "That's because your humanity persists. Or perhaps you ensure that it does."

"Why would I do that? *How* would I do that?"

Mal'uud considered. "Perhaps it isn't you doing the deed at all. It may be that since you were created as you are now with power – with the force of a Veil – that it will take the complete undoing of that power to make you whole. And until then, the power persists."

"Meaning the reason I'm the same as I was back on Earth as I am on this side of the Veil is because the power made me that way?"

"It's an idea. Possibly the only explanation we have with the information we currently know."

Madeline sighed. "So we've not yet broken the witch's evil curse?"

Mal'uud chuckled, and were she not sure that he was absolutely an ally and not a foe, the sound would have sent Madeline fleeing from the room. "In so many human terms, yes. If you were rent in two, then we need to find your other half."

"How do we do that?"

"We must seek answers from someone who might have them. Someone versed in power, in Veils, and in this catastrophe."

"A Walker, then?" Madeline asked. Her heart skipped beats. "But you said Storyteller knows everything, and he was eaten by..."

Madeline had to stop. She saw swirling galaxies, looming night, and a cold so final slithered through her, she couldn't move.

"The Master of Shadows," Nightmare said softly.

Madeline curled in on herself, teeth chattering. "The same thing that spoke to Helen and touched Toby?"

"The same," Mal'uud agreed.

A different coldness weighed down Madelien's limbs: dread. "Can you see them out there? The Horrors?"

"Not exactly," Mal'uud said. "I can't see anything but fog."

Madeline chewed her lip. "Can't we just stay here for a while? In your house?"

Mal'uud turned to her. "This isn't my house."

The world tipped onto its side. This entire time, she'd assumed they'd been safe because they were in Mal'uud's kingdom. "This isn't the Undermaze?"

Mal'uud slowly shook his head. "No. We came through the Veil downstairs. I carried you up here to this room. There are others."

"Rooms?"

"Yes."

"Show me?"

Mal'uud extended a hand, and Madeline took it, allowing him to help her to her feet. After a few steps, she was steady, but she clung to Mal'uud's hand as he opened the door and ducked out of the room. She followed him into a hallway. The red runner rug was in tatters, and the wooden floor below it was scratched and faded. The picture frames on the walls were empty, hanging lop-sided, and dozens of clocks were frozen in place, telling different times. There were, indeed, more doors. Behind the open ones, Madeline saw more rooms that looked like bedrooms.

And all of it seemed somehow so familiar.

They walked along a landing, and when Madeline saw the Center Hall and the paneled stairwell, she knew where she was. "This is the Taylor Point House."

Mal'uud said nothing, but followed Madeline down the stairs and into the front lobby. She went to the front door and peered through the glass panes. She could see the front porch, the looping drive, some of the grounds, and then beyond that was nothing but a dense, swirling, gray fog.

"What's that fog?" Madeline asked.

Mal'uud peered through a window on the other side of the door. "It comes with the Horrors."

"Then how do you know we're safe here?"

Mal'uud drew closer to her. "See the edge of the property, there? A ring of power divides this place and keeps out the fog."

"How?"

Mal'uud didn't answer for many seconds, and Madeline turned to face him. "What is it?"

"The Taylor Point House," he said. "Is that where Helen Taylor resides?"

"Yes," Madeline replied.

"How many others?" Mal'uud asked, quickly.

"Who live there?" Madeline struggled to think. "I only went there a time or two."

"Could there be seven?"

"Sure. I mean, Darryl, Monica, Helen, Miss Teedee, everyone knows them. But I don't think Miss Teedee lives there. Or that nurse guy. I can't remember his name. He looks after Helen but he doesn't—"

"But it is their place, is it not? Perhaps not where they sleep at night, but where they are most times?"

"Sure, yeah. Yes."

"And it's close to the Fisherman's Shack Museum?"

"It's on the same property."

"Ah." Mal'uud looked around. "Then this place is protected because we are standing in a Veil's construct."

He seemed so pleased with himself. "Am I supposed to know what that means?" Madeline asked.

Mal'uud knelt into a crouch, elbows on his knees and fingertips together in a peak. It put his head level with Madeline's chest. "All of creation comes from seven key ideas, Hope Star. Many worlds say three or nine or twelve, but there are seven. Throughout the worlds are places wherein seven entities embody these ideas – they align with them by power, by design, or entirely by accident, but align they do. When this happens, a portal is made between Via'rra and the world wherein the alignment has occurred. And in Via'rra, a mirror of the place is created. This construct, as it is called, is a Veil that needs little power to open because it is the alignment of the other world with Via'rra that keeps the passage clear. That's why I am less drained than I anticipated after making the Walk.

"There were once thousands such constructs, and Walking among them was easier. You and your sisters shone brightly onto all constructs, through all Veils, and penetrated the worlds beyond them. The Walkers traveled and spread their power and their gifts, keeping balance among all worlds. Now, I fear we may be standing in one of the last constructs, and it is a mirror of your world's Taylor Point House."

Madeline glanced out the window at the looming fog. "How long does the construct last?"

"For as long as the entities embodying the ideas are linked."

"And you said that fog was bad news, right? Does that mean the people at the Taylor Point House are in danger?"

Mal'uud tipped his head side-to-side. "In ways, possibly. The occurrences here and there are not precisely like-for-like, but they are linked. As this world spins, so too shall theirs, and events may mirror one another because the door swings both ways. At one time, this was considered a miracle. A blessed thing."

"But now there are Horrors."

"Yes." Mal'uud rose. "And the sooner we reform you, the sooner we can eradicate the Horrors and perhaps prevent ultimate tragedy from touching Earth and all other places in time."

Madeline felt suddenly made of lead. "I don't think I can save anything. Or anyone."

"Not as you are, no." Mal'uud took her hand. "Which is why we must go."

"I don't—" Madeline began, but the floor shook beneath her

feet. Mal'uud staggered, and Madeline fell hard against a wall. Books, pictures, clocks, and figurines crashed to the floor. The furniture groaned, and the stairwell creaked as though it may break. It was over almost as soon as it began, but Madeline's heart felt permanently lodged in her throat.

"The Horrors may sense us, here," Mal'uud said. "And be trying to destroy the protection over this place."

"What happens if it falls?"

"The Horrors would invade the construct and..." Mal'uud didn't need to finish. Madeline saw the chaos of an ending world clearly in her mind.

"Stay close to me," Mal'uud said, and he opened the front door. The air outside was stagnant and cool. Her heartbeat was loud in her ears and her breath fogged in front of her. Madeline drew closer to Mal'uud's warmth as they descended the front stairs and walked across the grass, which was soft beneath her boots and gave just like the soil did on Earth. It would be easy to mistake this place for home were it not for the creature walking ahead of her, hunched forward, as though about to pounce or strike. Mal'uud extended the hand not linked with hers to his side, and she saw nasty claws slip from the ends of his fingers. They glittered black.

"Anything?" Madeline whispered as their feet crunched across the driveway.

"No," Mal'uud murmured back. Then, he shushed her as though trying to figure out where might be a safe place to cross. The fog was a dense, gray, swirling wall beyond the ring of protection. Cautiously, they approached the edge, and then Mal'uud changed directions, following the line back toward the house and to where the Taylor Point Sound and dock would have been. After a few minutes, he paused. "Wait here."

"No," Madeline said, still quiet but urgent. "You're not leaving me here."

Mal'uud gave her a calculating, cold look. "I need to see where this fog thins. It will be where we make our exit. I can move faster than you if I move alone."

"No," Madeline said around a whimper, but Mal'uud had already let go of her hand and stalked away, using the full stride of his legs. She watched him bound across the parking lot and around the house, out of sight, and she wiped tears from her cheeks. "Shut up, Maddy," she said to herself.

"It's okay, Maddy girl."

Her kind lover's voice was clear and close and Madeline jerked toward it on instinct. It happened so quickly, but adrenaline slowed the world by degree enough that Madeline saw her foot cross the ring of protection. The moment it landed where the ground should have been, she discovered there was nothing there.

She fell, the protective barrier shocking her like an electric fence. Her cry of pain was cut off when she landed, hard, on solid ground. Warmth engulfed her. It was warmer—

Topside.

—here than it had been inside the construct. The ground beneath her was covered in grass, but it was the wrong color: purple, not green. The very air was a purple-magenta-blue haze that shaded everything it touched with the deep end of the rainbow, as though the gods of this world had begun with an entirely different color scheme.

Scrambling, Madeline rose to her feet and looked behind her, immediately backing away to make sense of what she saw. The construct floated several feet above the ground on which she now stood. Far enough back, and it'd look like a snowglobe, maybe, the barrier was so thick and obvious. Fog encircled it, but it hadn't closed in down here – on the ground surrounding the chasm created by the floating construct. Below the floating land was nothing but air – a hole, as though this place's earthen crust were only a few feet deep. Down below in what appeared to be starry nothingness, Madeline saw tunnels that reminded her a bit of hamster habitats, though they were brown and black like snakes, and Madeline had to turn away. The difference in this place versus Earth was too much and she stagger-spun away.

Around her, Madeline could see wave upon wave of purple grass. Straight ahead of her, beyond the circle of the elevated ground and for as far as she could see, was wave upon wave of purple grass. The ground swelled in the distance into hills, and maybe those lines that looked like etchings were roads or paths cut into the grasses, but Madeline couldn't quite tell. The hills eventually drifted into the foot of a mountain range that must have been hundreds of miles away. Its peaks were capped with white, purple-grey, and pink, as though somewhere there was a setting sun that Madeline couldn't see. But how anyone could tell what light came from which heavenly body in the sky above, Madeline didn't know.

The sky was full of thousands of golden, glittering stars, some far away and twinkling, and some near enough that Madeline could tell they were shaped like jagged meteors. She could make out the points and some were big enough to see their craters and crumbling edges. There were distant planets ringed with white, and closer there were moons and chunks of golden rock. All the heavenly bodies floated in a field of deep, deep gray, not black. While Madeline watched, the sky spun lazily by, but not like Earth spun around the sun or the moon around the earth. This sky was like a dome, and at the very top of the dome was an invisible spindle, and someone was turning that spindle and setting the universe into a lazy sideways spiral. The planets and stars and hunks of rock spun *around* her not *over* her, and watching them, Madeline grew dizzy and faintly ill.

She tore her eyes away from the sky to watch a drifting mote of pure white light zip by her face. Faster than an insect could move, it crackled like electricity – similar to the barrier – and was gone in an instant. More motes sparked near and far, lighting up the hazy air, and she saw they weren't only white. The sparks were magenta and shimmering gold. Some were small like the ones near her and some so big, they resembled ground-to-ground lightning. They lit the patchy fog that dipped and slinked among the hills. Slowly, Madeline turned, watching the bursts, and she saw they lit up the fog that lurked in the woods.

Beyond the construct in the direction opposite the purple hills was a horseshoe-shaped forest. The trees twisted in curls and knots that grew tall toward the sky, but every one of the trunks had been split and hacked as though struck over and over by lightning. No leaves were left, no foliage, though the forest bed was rich with broken roots and scorched moss. The tree trunks were black, dark brown, and gray, and they were smooth, as though they weren't wood, but glass. Madeline followed the fractured lines of trees upward, and she gasped. A bank of pure white clouds blotted out the sky above and beyond the bottom bend of the forest. A thunderstorm the likes of which Madeline had never seen was approaching. Lightning lit up the thunderheads, too, but inside the white clouds, the lightning was black, not magenta or yellow-white. There was no thunder. Instead, it was dead quiet. Even the breeze was silent and the movement of the grasses was barely a whisper.

The air smelled and tasted of minerals, like a hot spring. Her eyes burned and she rubbed at them. The hair on her arms, neck, and legs stood on end, and she was suddenly intensely aware of her lack of cover and that the fog around the construct and dotting the landscape now spilled onto the land nearby.

It was moving. And getting closer.

"Mal'uud," she whispered, starting to jog backwards, unwilling to take her eyes off the fog. "Mal'uud!" she screamed. Could he even hear her in the construct? Would he know she was gone?

The thunderstorm had now caught up to the fog, and the lightning within it sparked over and over, its thin lines like pulsing black veins. Madeline strafed to the right, moving away from the cloud and fog bank and jogging along the ground beneath the construct's edge. "Mal'uud!"

"No," came a voice, deep and distant as though it carried over vast distances that could not be measured with such simple things as eyesight or physics. "Know this..."

"What?" Madeline glanced around and spied a black rock – small and no bigger than her hand, but it cast a shadow.

"He... He cannot..." The voice rose and fell, tired and growing quieter with each syllable. "He does not know... that which he does not wish... to remember."

Air that was so hot it burned cold kissed Madeline's skin. The bank of white was mere feet away, blotting out one half of the world, and Madeline threw herself away from it. She crab-walked backward as fast as she could, not daring to take her eyes off the crackling storm. The bank of fog was dense, more a solid wall than cloud. And something was moving inside it. Something that undulated... slithered... rippled...

"Mal'uud?" Madeline whimpered.

A little girl appeared to her left, and Madeline screamed and rolled away. She stopped mere inches from the white cloud, and when she tried to retreat, the girl blocked Madeline's path.

The top of the girl's head was level with Madeline's chest. She was plump and pale, and she wore a white dress that was blackened at the hem and the edges of the sleeves. She had long, thick black hair that swung at the girl's waist. Her eyes were huge and black and... wrong. They shone, but not with life, but with the reflection of it. Madeline saw herself in those eyes, saw everything that had ever hurt her and relived every moment she had ever been powerless and hopeless. Madeline was in the police station with someone screaming she was an abomination. She was in a minivan, asking the boy to stop touching her, please, she just wanted to go home. She was Madeline Banc, crying on the ground in a strange world that couldn't possibly exist.

"Hi, Maddy," the little girl said in a chilling childlike voice completely devoid of humanity. She was closer and closer, and so were those eyes... looming... growing... expanding. The entire universe and all within it were only those eyes. "Do you want me?"

Madeline tried to answer, but couldn't, and the girl's face transformed. The jaw unhinged, the lips split bloodily as pointed teeth formed into rows, and the girl reached for Madeline. The fingers weren't fingers; they were *roots.* White, bulbous roots dripping with sap.

"WHY DON'T YOU WANT ME?" screeched the monster, close enough that air blew back Madeline's hair, and Madeline couldn't move. She was in the alleyway. She was going to get raped. She was going to get eaten. She would die. She was—

—in the shadow of something flying overhead. It shrieked, landed, and the storm cloud shrank away from the horse with six legs. Taller than a Clydesdale, the horse reared, its whinny a battle cry, and it trampled the little girl beneath hooves swarming with green fire. A spray of hot warmth flew into Madeline's face, and she gasped in outraged fear when she realized it was blood. The little girl... thing's... blood. Madeline kicked until she found purchase, and she got clear of hooves and carnage, rolling and desperately cleaning her face.

The horse pulverized the girl and trampled on what looked like an umbilical cord connecting the girl to the fog. The cord, when cut, whipped up into the air, spraying and writhing, and a scream ripped through the air that made Madeline's ears ring. The horse's hooves struck the ground and demolished what was left of the girl.

The storm retreated, just slid away like a receding dungeon wall that'd been about to squash them, and the horse spun and came for Madeline. She saw that its skin was not skin, but black sinew over bone. Its eyes were black and red. Its teeth were white and sharp. And when Mal'uud knelt, Madeline climbed onto his back and threw her arms around his corded neck, buried her fingers in his coarse mane. He took off away from the storm and the blood-soaked ground.

"What was that thing?" Madeline called.

"Horrors." Mal'uud's raspy voice was thickened around a bigger tongue. "Those were the Horrors."

"Will they chase us?"

"Yes."

"What do we do, then?" Madeline wailed, tears streaming from her eyes from the wind and the fear that was so big, she thought it'd eat her faster than the little girl from the vein cloud.

"We go to find our answers," Mal'uud said, kicking up grass as he galloped toward the mountains. "We go to see my father."

Madeline squeezed tightly and hung on.

Chapter Fifteen

Monica left at half past six, and Darryl sat on the edge of the bed for a while after she was gone. He smoothed the sheets, wishing he could smoke and dying for the oblivion that having just one (it was never just one) drink would give him.

"Our bed," he muttered to himself, and he coughed his way through a chuckle. It'd been shared with exactly two women, and Rebecca had been gone for twenty years. Monica should know; she was here when Becky had finally gone home to the hopefully-merciful Lord. Monica had been one of Miss Teedee's finds, and Miss Teedee had been one of Becky's. The women in Darryl's life had always run things. His sisters had started that trend when he'd been a boy, and it wasn't a tradition he'd ever cared to break.

Becky had been one of the best God had ever made. So Darryl hadn't raised a single question when Becky had brought a sad woman who'd been about Darryl's age to the Taylor Point House. The woman had seemed capable and smart, but she hadn't wanted to say a thing about her past. Darryl had let that slide, and Miss Teedee had turned out to be a godsend of so many sorts that Darryl had lost count. And so it was that when Miss Teedee had brought in a terrified, overwrought woman carrying a sleeping little boy, Darryl had welcomed the newcomer and her son to the family. That'd been a quarter of a century or so ago, now, and though Darryl's mind struggled to accept that fact, his bones felt every second of every year.

They'd been happy for a while, back then, with Becky, Monica, and Miss Teedee as the Three Musketeers Who Could. The House had more staff, and had owned a marina to moor boats as well as guests. Monica and Miss Teedee had been instrumental in getting the museum opened and running. Becky had supervised and sat behind the counter with her head scarves and her smile for the first few months they did tours. Little Andrew had gone to local schools and consistently freaked out teachers, a source of great amusement to Darryl and greater anxiety to Monica. Around then was when she'd finally told Darryl that Andrew's father had been an abusive, drunken, one-night stand that seemed closer to force than pleasure to Darryl. He'd said so to Monica and though she hadn't agreed, exactly, she had told him the white lies she'd fed her son about the father. Darryl had embellished a detail or two, and together, they had created the Legend of Andrew's Daddy. Nowadays, Darryl was pretty certain that Andrew was on to them, but somewhere along the line, the boy had learned that occasionally children had to take care of their parents by letting them lie.

Yeah, they'd been happy. But Becky hadn't been long for this world, and two years after the breast cancer took his sweet wife away from himself and his adopted (though he rarely ever thought of her that way; only when he'd caught Becky rubbing her lower belly as though wishing the parts had worked just once like they should) daughter, Monica had shared this bed with him for the first time. She was too young for him, barely older than Helen, but she put up with him, and they'd been sharing pillows regularly ever since. Monica always said everything would be all right if they kept hope and faith alive. Considering her past and all she had been through, Darryl was awed and humbled and determined to be worthy of her.

Helen's creativity and grief, however, had sent her further and further into herself and farther indoors. Nurses joined their house staff. Little Andrew had grown into Big Andrew. Guests had come and gone. The marina had been taken out in that huge flood, some years back. Miss Teedee had never shared her secrets, but as time put distance between her and them, she'd started to smile more often and more crowsfeet had formed at the corners of her eyes. Darryl had gotten a belly and tingles in his toes that his doctor told him were caused by the sugar disorder.

Darryl hugged a pillow and breathed in Monica's shampoo. All the years and all the struggles, and if he'd asked Monica where her bed was, she would still say in her room. If he asked her where they liked to sleep and sometimes do the things with their bodies that made for sweeter rest, she'd say his bed in his room. There'd always been space between them. Some of that space was for Monica's demons, which had sprung fully formed out of the fists of a father who hit, a step-father who neglected, and a series of boyfriends who had followed in their footsteps.

The other hunk of space between himself and anyone he loved, well, that was for Darryl's demons: Miss Ginny Tonic, Mr. Scotch Neat, TQ Shot, and Whiskey Sour.

Darryl called it the Barrel Bottle. Because a bottle at an alcoholic's lips was anybody else's gun barrel. When he was off the wagon, he was Barreling. When it was bad, he was Doing a Little Russian Trigger Pull. When it was really, really bad, Darryl would hope that some night soon, his buddy Alcohol would load the chambers of the Barrel's gun for real, and when he took a slug, it'd be the last one he'd ever take.

He'd been sober for ten years. It'd taken a decade to get well and truly away from the booze after Becky had been taken from him. She'd kept him together and the two of them apart from influences that could break them. When she was no more, he'd spent some time in a facility because the shadows had gotten so dark and long that he had started thinking fighting them wasn't the way to go. Monica had picked up the pieces, and Darryl had always wondered if Monica had done that on Becky's orders. Neither woman had ever said, but they'd been thick as thieves at the end. Whether or not it'd been a plan, Darryl couldn't do enough in a single lifetime to thank them both. Monica had helped remind Darryl why he kept the Barrel lowered. With her by his side, it'd stayed locked away out of his reach, even through the times when Helen had been so bad; in and out of programs and screaming about nightmares and kings and shadow things and screaming louder that they all knew what she was yelling about, to stop pretending and stop faking it, because what Helen saw was part of all of them. More than once, Darryl had wondered if Helen was right. There were terrible potentials in everyone, after all. What if only she could see them?

Eventually, Helen had gotten as stable as she was likely to get. The Barrel was cold and dusty. Darryl had his family, his hotel, his clocks, and his sugar-free Miss Teedee cookies.

And then Darryl had the dream, again. The *damned* dream. The dream that had been with him for as long as he could remember, and Monica had found him at the kitchen island with an opened bottle of wine and a full glass of red. It wasn't the first time the dream had made him walk, but it was the first time Monica had caught him.

"The hell do you think you're doing?" Monica had sounded like a little girl trying to be tough, and Darryl hadn't been able to give her an answer or an explanation. He'd just stood there, wiping away tears because he'd scared his sweetheart and petrified himself.

Darryl ran his palms over his unshaven cheeks. He got up, one hand helping his lower back to straighten. Last night, his mouth had been dry and there'd been no lip prints on the edge of the glass. His breath had smelled like stale toothpaste. That had been true for all his nocturnal Barrel binge attempts so far, thank God, but Darryl couldn't help but wonder how long it'd be before Monica wouldn't find him standing and sober but prostrate and drunker than Satan on a tub full of souls.

"You're a dumbass," Darryl mumbled to himself, locking his bedroom door behind him. "Now shut up, Darryl."

After giving Monica's closed bedroom a long look, Darryl left through the door next to the furnace and laundry room. It was going to be another blister of a day. By the time he got to his old pickup, he was sweating. He started up the Ford, got on his way, and waved at Andrew as he passed. The kid was clearing out some brush in the median on the road to and from the Taylor Point House. Andrew didn't seem to be paying any attention to the world that existed outside his garden, though. Kid was shirtless and hard at work, and Darryl had no idea how the kid avoided poison ivy and oak. Hell, he even managed not to get sunburned and mosquitoes didn't bite him. Crazy kid. Beautiful and special to Darryl in almost all the ways Helen was special, and just like Helen, the boy was a quarter off plumb.

He cranked the radio, blasting Clint Black out the open windows and singing when he started to think too much. He followed the roads that twisted alongside the Sound, heading for the other side of town. Vern Kuller's place was a hodgepodge house on the edge of a Nature Preserve and at the end of a sandy driveway. Vern was seventy-five if he was a day, and he didn't like to do much driving. He walked to his favorite fishing spots in the Sound, and he used the Preserve's trails to hike when the fish weren't responding to his lures. He was a skinny man with little use for words. In his heyday, however, Vern had loved liquor more than he'd loved anything else, so that gave the two of them plenty in common.

Darryl bounced to a stop at end of Vern's driveway. Vern, in a white undershirt and overalls that showed off his hairy, stick-thin arms, got up from the bench next to his mailbox. The box was shaped like a grinning fish complete with teeth. Vern popped open the fish's lower jaw, stuck a letter inside, and yanked on the fishing-pole flag to alert the mailman there was something inside. Then Vern climbed into the cab and shut the door with a slam.

"Mornin'," Darryl said.

Vern spat the last of his chew out the window.

"Thanks for answering the phone and coming with me to the early meeting."

Vern smacked his lips.

"I know we usually do the ten a.m.-er. And I know you'd rather be out with the fish. I don't like this meeting much, either. Too many people trying to get right before their day starts. They always run out of coffee before I can get my third cup."

Vern finally looked at him, and his eyes asked the questions.

Darryl sighed. "You'll think I'm nuts."

Vern wheezed.

"More than you already do."

Vern leaned his head against the cab's rear window and made a *carry on* motion with his left hand. The joints were swollen and the nails yellowed. When Darryl did nothing but stare, Vern stomped the truck's floorboard with one foot.

"Yeah, yeah." Darryl dropped the truck into drive. "Mind if we take the long way?"

Vern shrugged.

"Thanks." Darryl wanted to talk because it might take some steam out of the dream, but he'd never put everything together out loud to someone else before. Monica knew the most of what went on in Darryl's mind, and Randal, Darryl's sponsor for two decades, knew almost as much, but nobody, least of all himself, knew everything. Darryl sat around putting people and experiences together like he put together clocks. He tinkered until the damned things ticked true, but sometimes it took an awful lot of hammering.

"You ever feel like you live next door to the crazy shit?" Darryl blurted. "Not literally next door, I guess, but figuratively speaking?

Like it's there and it's close enough that it's messing with you, but you can't mess back 'cause the rules don't work that way?"

Darryl glanced at Vern to find him watching Darryl with one narrowed eye open. Darryl knew enough about Vern to have faith in Vern's ability to tell him to shut the hell up if what he was saying bothered Vern's sense of propriety. When Vern didn't do anything, Darryl continued.

"I have this dream. Everybody dreams. I mean, even Monica has nightmares. She wakes up in cold sweats and paces the hallways. I asked her once, and she told me in her dreams, she's in the sky, if you can believe it, hanging out up there, dangling off the tip of the moon or some strangeness. She says that part's not so bad, and sometimes that's all the dream is. But other times, she's falling through space just like Alice down the rabbit hole. Sometimes she falls and falls and she wakes up screaming. But in other dreams, she lands in this water that's too hot. She says it always feels like returning to the womb, if you even want to imagine what that'd be like. Tight fit, if you ask me. Anyway, she drowns in the water most of the time. And when she doesn't, she says she gets put on this stone slab next to some freaky kind of doorway, and that's where she stops talking, but I think some man comes in and does her harm."

Vern grunted.

"Yeah," Darryl said. "That's about how I feel about it. She's had some version of this dream for years, but I think it's worse, now. Maybe not just for her, either. The whole house seems off. Even Miss Teedee looks tired, and when I asked, she blamed it on her age and guilt of all them banks she must have robbed." Darryl chuckled to himself. Miss Teedee acted like she'd done a wrong so wrong there would never be a right, but Darryl knew better. Miss Teedee was bedrock; the foundation that kept everything moving and ideas fresh. And no one like that could ever truly be a monster.

"And Helen wandered off last night. Went for a walk to the damned museum, if you can believe it, with the new kid we hired."

Vern spat out the window and wheezed a sound that could have been an affirmative or could have been the natural reaction to bouncing on a bony ass over a pothole in the road. "It might not have been such an ordeal, but..." Darryl sat up straighter in the driver's seat, finally getting around to the point he needed to make. "Monica caught me sleepwalk barreling."

Vern's entire head turned so he could look at Darryl. "I know, I know." Darryl patted the air in Vern's general direction. "Hear me out. Like I said: Monica's not the only one with a bad dream that's been haunting her a while.

"Mine starts with me in the kitchen in somebody else's house I've never seen, and I'm mixing drinks. Then this woman comes in. She's the kind of beautiful that turns atheists into believers, 'cause nothing can be so pretty and not be divinely planned. She's in red, and somehow she's there to see me. I make her a round or two, and I'm thirsty. I'm so fucking thirsty. But I don't drink, and she doesn't talk, though she does smile at me. It's sad, though, like a good-bye kind of smile." Darryl paused. He didn't much want to talk about what happened next. "And then I wake up, and I'm not in bed. I'm in the kitchen with a bottle of whiskey or wine and a full glass.

"I don't drink," Darryl said, firmly. "Though I must be pretty desperate for one. You know Miss Teedee keeps the wine and spirits locked up, so I've got to be doing some real entertaining shit in my sleep. And this has happened pretty much every night for the past little bit." About the time the new kid showed up, but Darryl didn't say that; wasn't the kid's fault. "I pour whatever it is out or back in the bottle. I lock Miss Teedee's cabinet and go back to bed." Darryl also left out the part about how he'd be so sad he'd usually cry himself to sleep. "The crazy thing is, the next day? I feel better. I guess it's because I resisted temptation. But I also think it's 'cause I got to see her. The woman in the dream, I mean. And I know how that sounds, but, it's like I know her. Or knew her. Once, maybe. Past life shit or something. Not that I believe in that, either. I don't know, Vern. All I've got is a lot of questions, and the one person I want to talk to about it shuts me down before I get the first word out of my mouth. I can't say as I blame her, either."

Vern ducked his chin to his chest, mouth set in a vicious frown, and Darryl started to take turns that would get them closer to the basement of the liberal arts center. They might make it for coffee after all, despite the talk and the drive.

"I died once," Vern said, right as they pulled onto Hopover Avenue, a few blocks over from the center and heading toward the night club on the corner that the Concerned Citizens Association kept trying to shut down and the Tourist Board kept wide open. "Back in 'Nam." The way Vern said it, the word rhymed with "ham."

"Was mindin' myself, and blast took me out. Threw me 'gainst a tree. Knocked me 'round enough I stopped breathin' for a few. I saw some shit. On the other side. Weren't all human things, neither. When I came back, I figured seein' anythin' a'tall was better 'n not seein' nothin'." Vern met Darryl's gaze, his eyes entirely too aware for any one man to be. "We don't know how any part 'a this world works. We're just guessin'."

A stone sank into Darryl's guts, because the truth was a heavy thing, and when he saw the boy in the road, he got his foot on the brake just in the nick of time. The front bumper stopped maybe a bare two inches away from the kid's arm, and Darryl didn't have enough air to spare around the panic to speak. Toby Creed, the odd boy who liked to steal, streaked across the road and vanished into an alleyway. And it was about that time that Darryl noticed all the police cars.

No lights. Not anymore. But uniforms and non-uniforms were milling around next to the nightclub, where it looked for all the world like Toby had come from.

"What in the devil...?" Darryl asked, and he sounded like he felt: scared.

"Don't think he gonna tell us much," Vern said.

Darryl eased the truck into a parking space next to the sidewalk. He spotted Chuck Dobson, who'd been so good about coming out when they thought Helen had run off the other night. Chuck lifted a hand and headed their way.

Darryl rolled down the window. "Mornin', Chuck."

"Mornin'. Hey Vern." Chuck nodded to them both and leaned an arm against the truck's window ledge.

"You got yourself some early craziness today?" Darryl asked.

Chuck didn't say anything for a moment. "Everything settle okay at yours last night after I left?"

"Oh yeah," Darryl said. "Tucked Helen up in bed, and Mercutio stayed the night. Probably going to have that kid on more nights than he'd like, but we'll pay him."

"Good, good." Chuck sighed. "Must be a damned full moon."

"That'd explain the howling," Darryl joked. He knew better than to press Chuck about business. But he seemed to want to tell Darryl something, so Darryl played the long game.

It paid off. Chuck stepped away and opened the truck's door for Darryl. "Want to show you something. You too, Vern."

"You sure? Won't be messing with anything official?" Darryl asked, climbing out.

"Nah," Chuck said. "We've been here since the wee hours of the morning and are wrapping up. We'll block off the alleyway and the club's closed for the next two nights, but word's already out. Channel Twelve has already moved on to the hospital and took Channel Six with them."

Darryl didn't comment as he and Vern followed Chuck over the caution tape and into the alleyway. They crept between looming cinderblock and painted brick walls, the club on the right and parking garage on the left. At first, Darryl didn't see anything unusual, aside from police tags randomly numbering places on the ground: graffiti, trash, dumpsters, an old cardboard box; a loading dock with freshly-painted rails to match the club's spastic décor. A chain link fence barred the way halfway down the alleyway. The club's rear emergency exit platform stood about eight feet away from the fence, creating a shadowy nook between cinderblock and fence.

Insects buzzed, and the stench of human waste hit Darryl's nostrils. He pulled his shirt up and over his nose. Vern took out a handkerchief and covered his face, and it was about that time that Darryl saw what they were meant to see.

On the wall across from the loading dock was a mural, of sorts; a painting made with dull brown and red. It used the gray of the building, and there were white lines, too, and it took Darryl a moment to realize that someone must have used a knife or, God forbid, their fingernails to scrape away concrete. He was looking at a castle, judging by the turrets. And the brown-black hump things were mountains. Above the landscape and the castle was a big, black cloud with eyes chipped away in white. Darryl stared, half impressed and half horrified, and he would have sworn the cloud moved. Darryl felt a scream bubble in the back of his throat, but he choked it down when he saw all the flies stuck to the painting. They were trying to break free and creating the illusion of roiling skies. "Jesus," he muttered.

"Mmhm," Chuck agreed, standing aside and letting them look.

In the foreground of the montage, so large that Darryl figured a ladder had to be involved, was what seemed to be a horse-like thing with too many legs. On its back was a stick figure. The figure was a woman, her breasts crudely drawn and her mouth a big, muddy-red *oh*. Her arm stuck out to one side and floating above the five sticks meant to be her fingers was a white thing that might have been a snowflake. Or maybe a kindergartener's version of a star.

Darryl took a step back because the longer he looked, the more he realized the painting's parts were familiar. He'd seen that fortress-castle thing. He'd seen the horse with too many legs. And he'd seen lots of stars.

They were often the central focus of Helen's paintings and drawings.

"You don't even want to know what it was made with," Chuck said.

"I think I can guess," Darryl replied.

"We found the artists in the alleyway, spaced out and unresponsive."

Vern hummed. "Drugs. Bad drugs."

"We're looking into it," Chuck said.

The tableau was strange in ways that made Darryl sicker than the smell of bodily fluids could ever make him. The mural made his eyes hurt. He turned away.

"You all right?" Chuck asked. He was eying him in the way police do when they're keeping their cards close.

"Yeah, just stinks is all," Darryl said. "When did you find all this?"

"'bout two a.m. Bouncer at the club called it in."

The timing wasn't right for Helen's antics. No way could she have had any part in this – she'd only been gone an hour or so, which wasn't enough time to... Well, do what exactly, Darryl asked himself. Drive to the club, give drugs or take drugs with a bunch of people, paint this mural, and get a ride back? And not appear to be under the influence, herself, when she got home? And Jason's minivan had never left the parking lot, and nor had any other vehicle. So unless they called a car or a cab and did some tricky logistical maneuvering...

No, it wasn't possible. A coincidence and nothing more. And not something he needed to share with Chuck.

"The kids who did this gonna be all right?" Darryl asked.

"We'll see." Chuck sighed and ushered them away and down the alley. "Crazy mess," he said on the way back to Darryl's truck.

"It is. Sorry you're having to deal with it."

"Eh, keeps the job interesting. I'm sure you'll hear all about it on the news." Chuck hung back after Darryl was in the driver's seat again and Vern beside him. "Not sure why I thought you'd want to see all that." He rubbed his face. "Need sleep. Too much excitement for this town."

"Come by the House and get Miss Teedee to fix you something before you head home."

"Might just do that." Chuck thumped the door, and Darryl pulled away. He swallowed on a dry throat and calculated what stores that sold beer were closest.

"Trouble," Vern said.

"Looked like it."

"Noticed you didn't mention there were certain similarities 'tween that shit mural and Helen's stories."

Darryl rambled too goddamned much at meetings. "Naw. No way she did all that."

"Don't reckon she did. But I got somethin' I need to tell you."

Turning the wheel, Darryl resisted the bottle's barrel and pulled into the center's parking lot. "What's that?"

"Toby came to see me in the dead 'a night last night. Don't sleep no more, so I was up. Kid said somebody needed a ride and could we use the truck. I know he's got the Sight—"

Vern paused, waiting for the usual snort from Darryl. But honestly, after the nightmares, that mural, and Helen's strange behavior, Darryl didn't have much derision left in him for the unusual. He kept his mouth shut.

With a grunt, Vern continued. "—so figured I'd see what he wanted and then get him home safe. Woman needin' the ride was too pretty – blonde. She was that woman - the one who used to be the girl from the woods and now has all the boyfriends?"

"Madeline Banc," Darryl supplied. Everybody knew Madeline, especially every male body.

"Mmhm. And the man had a peculiar air 'bout him. Tattooed. Dark. Reminded me a little of the stuff I saw when I was dead."

Cold splashed in Darryl's belly. "She all right?"

"I reckon. Picked her and the guy up in front of that alleyway we just left." Vern took a breath. "Dropped 'em off at the Townsende Trailhead awful close to the Museum."

"The Fisherman's Shack?" Darryl asked.

"Mmhm. And ain't that where you said Helen ran off to last night?"

"Yeah, but it was... what time was all that?"

"'Bout half-past-two in the mornin.'"

"Why the hell you go and do such a fool thing?"

If Vern was offended or alarmed by Darryl's yelling, he didn't show it. "Toby had clothes for the woman. Knew right where they'd be and when. Even had me drive a little so we'd be on time."

"He's just a fool boy, Vern."

"Mmhm. I know that's what you think. Which is why I'm tellin' you all this. Maybe you ought to check the museum. Just to be on the curious side of things."

"Damn right," Darryl said. but when he started to shift the truck, Vern put a hand over his.

"After the meetin.'"

"But—"

"Place is locked up, ain't it? Got an alarm?"

Darryl didn't answer, his face hurting from its scowl.

"It go off last night?"

"Not after Helen's thing, no."

Vern gave him a look and nabbed the truck's keys on his way out of the vehicle. Darryl sighed. Monica was going to kill him, and for some reason, he felt like the trouble had only just begun.

Chapter Sixteen

For what felt like miles, they traveled in silence. At first, Madeline was too concerned with her racing heart and receding terror to lift her head and open her eyes, but the drone of Mal'uud's hooves was comforting and the steady beat of him running beneath her was calming. Mal'uud's mane was black and thick, and Madeline wrapped it around her hands before daring to sit up.

In all directions was a massive, flat, dark purple plain. On the horizon to the left were the distant bumps of pumpkin-orange plateaus. Plumes of smoke dotted them and drifted skyward in perfect miniature tornado shapes. To the right was a forest that rose to cover rolling maroon hills. Far behind them was the construct and the Horrors, and from this vantage point, she could see the top and sides of the fog bank. It didn't reach as high as the ever-spinning sky, and the fog was generally circular in shape; cylindrical. And it seemed...

Hungry.

Here and there, Madeline saw scorched patches of earth with low-lying clouds that were not clouds at all hovering over them. Once, they passed close enough that Madeline could see the pale pink tentacle things slithering from the bottom of the foggy Horrors, reaching for the dirt below. Anywhere they touched, fires burned and ashes flew. Madeline began to think of the spotty fog as the decaying entrails and missing finger bones of a much larger creature. A white thing that loomed and destroyed and pulsed with black veins. When she noticed that here white roots infested the ground, especially in the scarred circles, Madeline shuddered, envisioning the little girl's fingers reaching for her and getting closer.

A gust of wind brought the smell of death. It got worse when they crested a hill and tore across a plain that was matted with what seemed to be black tar. "Battlefield," Mal'uud said, without Madeline asking. "Here, creatures fell in the struggle to stop the Horrors."

"So, the sticky stuff is..."

"Yes," Mal'uud said sadly.

A pang resonated within Madeline, too. She had put her head down until they'd ridden beyond the bloodied field.

On and on they ran. Though it was ever-present, the fog wall never encroached upon them like it had earlier, but Madeline thought she could feel the icy tendrils of awareness reaching for her across the land. Mal'uud was hot to the touch, and she burrowed against him for warmth and the strangest sort of safety Madeline had ever known.

Their speed dried out her eyes and made them water, tears streaking down her cheeks. When they raced into the steady breeze, it was hard to breathe. Gradually the ground changed from tall, waving meadow grass to desiccated, hard-packed mud cut with cracks and gullies. Mal'uud slowed, trotting as though the ground hurt him to touch. The soil was grey, not red or brown, and deep blue, bony shrubs and strange grey trees erupted from the widest wrinkles, their branches thin, claw-like;

hooked as though grasping for air or water or life, itself. There were no signs of life, and yet Madeline felt watched. A sense of foreboding dread rode with them, and no matter how much Madeline breathed deeply or swore to herself that she was safe for now, her heart stayed lodged in her throat and prickles broke over her skin again and again. It wasn't just the Horrors that haunted them. The ground — the very air — seemed to have eyes or at least a sense that something was traveling across it and through it. Somewhere, some*thing* was following their progress. Like it was waiting. Patiently and inevitably... waiting.

The only sound was Mal'uud's panting and the drumming of six feet, and the only smells were sickening copper and burning amber. It was as though at the beginning of time the god of this world had lit a mountain of incense in a pool of blood and the scent still lingered. The sky above them had no clouds and no sun. It was impossible to tell time or get a true sense of direction, and Madeline gave up trying. She watched the earth change and clutched at Mal'uud's flanks with her aching thighs as they surged over a rise and began to descend into a dead, dry valley echoing with shrieking winds. Tiny pebbles and bits of sandy grit dug at Madeline's exposed skin, causing stinging welts to rise. The electrical charges were bigger, here. Huge bursts of magenta lightning exploded all around them, filling the air with a low-humming static. Mal'uud didn't seem concerned about the lightning balls, and any sound was a relief after the oppressive quiet, though Madeline ducked and jumped every time a magenta bolt fizzled near them.

In the valley, Madeline saw ruins. Once, people of some variety had lived here. She saw the stone piles of their homes and the rings of fire pits long gone cold. There were roads of sorts, and Mal'uud followed one that took them directly through the middle of the valley and up the other side of the basin. It should have been a long ride, and perhaps Madeline slept during some of it, because it seemed like she blinked and they were heading out instead of going in.

On the far side of the valley, there was a low maze of rock and brick that Madeline realized had once been a castle or much larger common building. There were big round things that could have been cannonballs, and there were silver metal structures that could have been weapons or high-tech gadgetry. The machines dotted the landscape, too heavy to be moved by the breeze. Madeline couldn't divine their purpose, and couldn't find a thing that told her about the people who had been here and gone. She saw no bones, no remains, nothing of the inhabitants at all.

"Who lived here?" Madeline asked as Mal'uud navigated the rocky path that followed the lip of the valley.

"The creatures of Topside," Mal'uud replied.

"I know, but who were they? What were they? What is this place?"

"I do not know who they were or what, as such."

Madeline remembered the Shadow's whispers. "Tell me what you do know, then," she suggested with care.

Mal'uud slowed to a steady walk, and Madeline ducked lower over Mal'uud's back, both to hear more and to try and avoid the wind. "Via'rra spins to form bridges among worlds. Once long ago, it was thought that the wisest and luckiest of beings would and could cross through this land on their way to the next."

"And what about the Walkers? How did they get here?"

"We are created individually. We are made of the Lady's clay, planted in her garden, and harvested when we are ripe, fully formed with everything we will ever be. Our world is the Lady's dominion."

"And that's why people thought it brought them good luck," Madeline heard herself say. Her lips and tongue were moving on their own accord; speaking as if from rote memory that she didn't think she had. "For Lady Creation takes Nothing and makes all. Everything is possible, here. Every story, every legend, every inspiration, every being who ever was or ever could be first began life here. Even thoughts and dreams can live here. They are the wind, the rain, the cosmos, and the trees. Everything lives and loves. Fights and wins; loses, falls. When they've served the length of their usefulness, they go to other worlds or are destroyed. Potentials and ideas wither and fade. Those shades go below, to the..."

"Undermaze," Mal'uud finished. "Yes. You remember."

"No." Madeline shook her head, and Mal'uud's mane scratched her cheek. "It's like I'm quoting someone else."

"I believe you are quoting yourself. Your *full* self, whom we seek."

Madeline both wanted to be whole and wanted to continue to exist as she was, even if it meant being afraid all the time. She wasn't sure she could join the ranks of these Walkers. She didn't know what that would mean. She didn't know if she was cut out to be so important.

Mal'uud walked on, carrying Madeline with no apparent effort. On the other side of the valley, the road disappeared. Now they traveled over a bed of rock, much of it marked with oily black char. The land was flat and wide with nothing to obscure the view except the hint of mountain peaks far, far away. The sky was so broad and so strange that it made Madeline sick to look at it. So she leaned forward and closed her eyes.

When she opened them again, they were walking at a brisk pace. Madeline took a deep breath and inhaled smoke. Her eyes watered and she coughed. "What's burning?"

"Everything."

Madeline scrubbed her eyelids with the heels of her hands. Her ass and legs were killing her, and her groin was numb. She coughed more, and when she could see, she saw smoke rising off the barren plain. Seven, eight, possibly a dozen tracts of fire cut across the land in lines. Bits of white fell, and she plucked ash off her shoulder. "The Horrors?" she asked, though she knew the answer.

"Yes."

Madeline frowned and tried to find a comfortable position. Again, she tried to speak with caution. "Isn't it strange that you don't know what monster is doing all this destruction?"

"In some ways yes, and in some ways, no. I don't concern myself with Topside. My domain is the Undermaze."

Madeline wished she had something she could put over her nose. "But isn't there history or something? Has this happened before?"

Mal'uud stopped so abruptly that Madeline had to scramble to hold on. He turned his head and one red-ringed eye glared at her. "No," Mal'uud said, almost angry, before facing front and beginning to walk again.

"So this is the first time with the Horrors and the smoke and the missing people?"

"No."

"But you just said—"

"I don't know," Mal'uud said.

"You mean you don't remember or you never knew?"

"It is as I said," Mal'uud said, tone sharp. He began to run again. "Apologies, Hope Star. But these are not questions for me. These are questions for my father."

"How can you have a father if you were made in a garden?"

Mal'uud chuckled. "All Walkers have the same father. He is your father, too, after a fashion."

A ball of ice formed in Madeline's midsection. "'The Lady takes from Nothing... Nothing." The ball of ice turned into a wall of freezing pain and pure fear. "That's... that's..."

"Him. Yes. Lord Nothing. The one who lends his power to the Lady so she can make. Our father, for lack of simpler term."

"No." Madeline's mind was full of horns and shadows and unearthly eyes. Before she knew what she was doing, she had swung her legs to one side of Mal'uud's back. He slowed, and Madeline leapt to the ground. She hit, crumbled, rolled, and came to a stop on all fours. She'd scraped her knees and hands, and she was so sore from riding that she couldn't stand.

"What are you doing?" Mal'uud asked.

"We can't." Madeline started to crawl, and Mal'uud patiently followed her. He resembled a centipede more than a horse from ground level.

"What can we not do?"

"See... go to... No." The ground was so dry. She had grit wedged painfully under her nails. "I won't. I can't."

Mal'uud blew air through his nostrils. "I thought you understood when we left the construct that we were traveling to see Lord Nothing."

"No! We talked about how he ate the Storyteller!"

"It was necessary."

"Then he'll kill us, too!"

"Probably."

Madeline whirled and sat down hard on her behind. "That doesn't bother you?"

"Death holds no fear for me, no, especially a death the Lord of Shadows brings. Such a death isn't final. We'll be remade by the Lady's hands, assuming she is still alive."

Hopeless resignation stole Madeline's breath. "The Lady... she's...?"

"Look around you, Hope Star. Do you see evidence of life or dawning creation? No, you see disorder and destruction. All of the land is barren, which means the Lady is either gone or incapacitated. She would not stand for this."

"So, you know her, do you?" Madeline laughed. "On a first-name basis with God?"

Mal'uud pawed at the ground. "There is not a god, here, Hope Star. There are many. The Lady is a kind of god, yes, and in this land, she rules all. But she does not do it alone. She needs power. And that power lies in the mountains at the edge of the world. That power is wise and older than anyone, save the Lady, herself. If anyone knows the answer to your questions, it is he. So we will go to him, the Eater of Worlds, and we will ask for his help and counsel. And if he chooses to destroy us, then so be it. Because this I know to be true: if we remain out here in the open, the Horrors will find us, defeat us, and we will die a death that lasts for all eternity."

Madeline heaved a great sob and only then realized she was crying and shaking. She was too hot and too cold. Her skin was too tight and her head ached. She wanted to curl up in a knot and wait for the Horrors to find her. "You killed that one, though," she all but whispered. "That Horror. The little girl."

"A mere half-creature. Not the whole of anything." Mal'uud slung froth from his mouth and stamped his hooves. "I have enough energy within me to get us to the Fortress beyond the mountain pass, and then I will have to feed or I will begin to fade. I cannot fight a war against a legion horde. I can barely carry you across this desert. I am tired, but I am a king who will not forget his subjects. So we will go to the mountains and we will find Lord Nothing."

Madeline put her head on her knees. "I'm scared."

"You are a Walker."

Mal'uud's faith in her was humbling and enough to make her numbly struggle to her feet and onto Mal'uud's back when he bent so she could straddle him. Behind her was certain death by Horrors. Ahead of her was at least the possibility of learning more about Water. What he did. And also what she truly might be. She knew she had no choice, and she hated herself for her pathetic protests. "Sorry," she whispered.

"Strength, Hope Star."

Madeline wrapped her arms and hands up in Mal'uud's mane, and willed herself to sleep. She dreamed of a blue pool at the bottom of a cavern as deep as time. She heard whispers, singing and when she was on the verge of understanding the words of the song, which would explain everything and tell her all she ever needed to know about her life and its meaning, she woke up predictably too soon. And she was still on Mal'uud's sweaty back, riding toward her doom.

Time and distance didn't work right in Via'rra. She slept more and woke up when they were on a road leading them by a row of twisted, gnarled trees. She dozed and woke up as they were passing the ruins of an enormous building that was shaped vaguely like the Coliseum. She studied the pile of stone until the building was an indistinct lump to their south. Mal'uud never paused to eat or drink, and Madeline knew she should have been hungry or thirsty, but she wasn't. To her body, it felt like only minutes had passed, but her mind knew better. They'd traveled across half the known world and it had taken them months and also only seconds. A fleeting thought danced through her mind that the reason time was strange was because there wasn't *a* sense of time in Via'rra; there were *many* senses of time. A tree in one timeline was a sapling and in another timeline it was as big and vast as a country. In one time stream, Madeline was as she appeared. But in another, she was dust. Time flowed around them as fluidly as the grass and the constant wind, and it paid no mind to creatures who tried to measure it.

When the ground around them began to swell into foothills, the temperature dropped. They found a path made of broken rock. It cut through the hills and lead straight into a narrow chasm that carved a dividing line in the mountains. On and on they walked, and the mountains grew impossibly large. Soon they blotted out the sky and cast deep, dark shadows in the light thrown by bursts of magenta lightning. Madeline shivered on Mal'uud's back until the path grew so steep and broken that he could not navigate it as a horse. He told her to get down, and he shut his eyes. In less than a single moment, the horse melted and Mal'uud morphed into the bone man version of himself. He was thinner. His sinew was sparser and the ball of energy whirling beneath his broken ribs was smaller.

"Should we rest?" Madeline asked.

"We cannot." Mal'uud's dwindling energy didn't affect his speed, and Madeline ignored her screaming muscles to keep up with him as they climbed.

The road leveled out just as Madeline was sure she would collapse. Her palms were bleeding and her shoulders were killing her. It had begun to snow, and a film of flakes covered the ground. "There," Mal'uud said, nodding. "The tunnel."

They stood on a flat piece of ground jutting out from the side of a mountain so tall it disappeared into a misty snow cloud that blotted out the sky. About a hundred feet above their heads, a crack had formed in the mountain, looking to Madeline like lightning had struck the mountain and split it like a tree trunk. The crack widened into a crevice that opened ahead of them into a carved tunnel big enough for a train.

Two statues of broad-shouldered, muscular men wearing scale covered armor flanked the gaping dark mouth of the tunnel. Each figure was twice as tall as Madeline and made out of the same shiny, black rock that formed the sides and roof of the tunnel. Both statues had four arms, though, not two. One set of arms held a round shield in front of their bodies and a sword aimed at Madeline and Mal'uud. The other set of arms held aloft a dull, black gate the size of Madeline's former apartment building.

"What are they?" Madeline whispered.

"Two of the Lord's Shadow stone army," Mal'uud answered softly.

"He has an army?"

"Hush," Mal'uud cautioned. "Everything here has eyes and ears, Hope Star. Let us speak in low tones of reverence."

Madeline didn't like that Mal'uud's voice had traces of fear in it, nor did she fail to notice that he'd not taken a single step toward the tunnel. "Can those things drop that gate?" she murmured.

Mal'uud didn't respond for a long moment punctuated by a whirl of snowflakes. "If they haven't by now, I don't think they will. This way."

Madeline, teeth chattering, followed Mal'uud into the tunnel. The relief from the wind and snow and oppressive sky was immediate and wonderful. Madeline started to ask if they could rest, but Mal'uud put a hand on the wall, and Madeline gasped. Hundreds of tendrils of pure white light came to life in the rock, itself, and floated toward Mal'uud. They swirled under his palm, each mote of light making a shimmering trail. It reminded Madeline of silver glitter, and as Mal'uud began to walk, he kept his hand on the wall.

The light followed them, illuminating their path. Madeline went to the opposite wall and tentatively touched the smooth surface. She could see crystals beneath the rock's surface, and she expected it to be cold, but it wasn't. The lights began to glow brighter, and when the lights reached her hand, the stone warmed. Madeline leaned against the wall, pressing her bare arm and cheek to it, and she sighed when she could feel all of her fingers.

"You feel the cold when you should not," Mal'uud said softly. "As a Walker, it will not touch you."

That couldn't happen soon enough. Mal'uud was kind, but she was weary of hearing all the things she should be and was not. Madeline walked with both hands on the wall leaving wakes of silver sparkles. They were halfway through the tunnel before the earthquake struck.

Screaming, Madeline fell to the floor with her arms over her head. Immediately, Mal'uud was beside her, shushing her, and Madeline gnawed her lip to trap her next scream in her mouth. She waited, tasting the acrid flavor of fear, and Mal'uud eventually shook her shoulder.

"We must go," Mal'uud said.

Not obeying, Madeline dared to look and saw that the tunnel behind them was now blocked. Darkness engulfed them. "The gate," Madeline whispered, groping for the wall and its silver trails.

"Yes," Mal'uud said. He was crouched next to her, staring at the way they'd come. "He knows we're coming."

Madeline put her forehead against the tunnel's side and watched the beautiful dance of light beneath the rock's surface. The tunnel wouldn't be such a bad place to spend her last remaining days. She could watch the rock's stars until she grew sleepy. She could rest, and soon enough the cold and the end of this world would take her.

Instead of ordering her to stand, Mal'uud hauled Madeline to her feet. She went limp like a protesting child being dragged by her parents to someplace she didn't want to go. Mal'uud trudged forward, and Madeline reluctantly found her footing and followed him.

The light at the end of the tunnel was blinding white. When Mal'uud yanked Madeline forward and out of the tunnel, Madeline shut her eyes, fully anticipating that she would be struck dead instantly. When she was still breathing a moment later, she dared to look.

They stood on a ledge overlooking a valley enclosed on three sides by mountains whose peaks disappeared into roiling storm clouds. The valley had been terraced. The walls of the terraces were made of the same black rock in the tunnel, and each of the gradually widening terraces had been made into a garden. There were swings and seating areas covered in snow piles. Black, twisted vines studded with enormous thorns spilled over the rock walls. Dead trees with pure white bark and corkscrew branches swayed in the gentle wind, and the snow fell continuously. Tiny flakes spun to land and blanketed the valley in utter silence.

At the bottom of the valley were the ruins of a castle. Madeline could see the decayed stone walls of the wide, flat outer court. As the external courtyard flowed toward the heart of the structure, the ground climbed in elevation. Wide stone steps outlined the way to the inner castle walls. The gate, if there had been one, was gone, as were three-quarters of the walls. Remnants of turrets and pillars all open to the sky dotted the castle, most of which had been built into the mountains, themselves. The rooms in the shelter of the mountainsides remained, the giant windows gazing at them like hollow eye sockets. The stone of the castle was white and grey, not black like the stone of the tunnel and terraces.

"What is that place?" Madeline asked Mal'uud.

"The Fortress," Mal'uud replied. He sounded stunned. "Or, it was."

"Was it attacked?"

Mal'uud shook his head. "The only way in is through the tunnel. Clearly he could have blocked the path." Mal'uud took a few steps toward the edge of the topmost terrace upon which they stood. The steps leading down were worn but solid. "He must have consumed it."

"Why would he eat his own home?"

"I don't know." Mal'uud scowled. He reached into his chest, and Madeline had to look away. Watching Mal'uud fondle his empty insides was more than she could handle. "Perhaps. Though the Lord of Shadow's consumption is usually complete. This isn't."

Mal'uud's features tightened. He lingered for a few moments more on the topmost terrace, and then he began to descend into the valley. The path was wide, well-traveled, and for the most part, easy to navigate. Here and there, it was overgrown with vines or prickly brush. Mal'uud walked through these brambles without losing speed, but Madeline was slower wading through the dead landscaping.

Mal'uud remained quiet, evidently lost in thought, which suited Madeline. She wasn't in the mood for conversation. She feared the answers to any questions she had, so she kept them to herself. She concentrated on putting one foot in front of the other.

The eerie quiet seemed to walk with them for a while, but when they'd climbed a third of the way down, Madeline realized she'd been hearing a sound for some time. At first, it'd seemed far away. Faint, like a distant echo. By the time she realized it'd gotten louder and closer, it sounded like it was coming from right behind her, and a jolt of adrenaline shook her. It was a heavy noise. Grating. Like a massive pestle scraping the sides of the universe's largest mortar. "What is—" Madeline began, and she came up short so she wouldn't collide with Mal'uud. He stared behind them, and his eyes were wide.

Slowly, Madeline turned. Through the blowing snow, Madeline saw figures standing on the edges of the terraced walls. They hadn't been there when she'd gone past, she was sure of it. Now, though, they loomed. Still and huge and terrible. They weren't flesh, but stone; the silver sparks of Shadowrock danced across the surfaces of their forms. Some were humanoid, with two arms and two legs, and one head, but many had wings or serpentine necks or multiple sets of the standard limbs. Some were on all fours, and many of them perched like enormous birds on the edges of the terrace walls, their talons the size of Madeline's head.

All of them wore armor. All of them had weapons. And hundreds of flat black eyes stared at Madeline and Mal'uud.

"More of his stone army?"

"Yes. Shadow Guardians."

"Don't they, I don't know, take orders from... you know, *him*?"

"Usually."

"What?" Madeline's heart hammered in her throat. Nothing in the valley moved or made sound, and Madeline held her breath.

"It is possible that they were left behind to keep out anything unwanted." Mal'uud took a measured step backward. The statues stayed where they were. "Or they were to trap anything daring to enter the valley and destroy it."

"Should we try to tell them we aren't enemies?"

Mal'uud's thin lips twisted into a sardonic smirk. "I would not like to stay long enough to discover if they speak. Come."

They walked backward for a few more steps, and the Guardians made no move. Mal'uud spun before he tripped over the next set of stairs leading to the lower terrace, and Madeline reluctantly faced the husk of the Fortress.

After they'd climbed down another level, Madeline glanced over her shoulder. The Guardians had doubled their numbers without the pestle-and-mortar warning noise, and they were several terraces closer than they had been.

"Mal'uud," Madeline whispered, urgently.

"Walk steady," he said. "If we run, they will run, and we will lose the race."

"Can't we reason with them?" Madeline tried not to trip down the next flight of stairs. Mal'uud tightened his hold on her wrist.

"They are stone statues, Hope Star. What do you hope to make them understand?"

Only six more terraces to go, but they were the widest ones. "That we're Walkers," Madeline gasped between ragged breaths.

"If that was the coin in the balance which would make the difference between life and death, they never would have revealed themselves."

There was no shelter or cover or weapon to be had. The gardens on these levels had all been low, elaborate flower beds. The stone benches had dissolved into piles of pebbles. The decorative edges around the beds were piles of rocky dust.

They cleared the fifth terrace. The fourth. They were halfway to the third when Madeline heard the grinding stone sound directly at her back. She couldn't help the scream, and the moment the sound flew from her lips, a Guardian landed in front of them to her right. It was at least ten feet tall, wide-shouldered and hunched like a troll. Its helmet covered a boulder-sized head, and it aimed its spear directly at them.

Mal'uud grabbed Madeline and swept her to the side. They jogged away but another Guardian landed with a ground-shaking thud to their left. They appeared as though they were chess pieces controlled by an invisible hand. The Guardian on the left was a winged creature, thin and lithe, with a sword in each of its ten hands. This time, while Madeline watched, the Guardian moved so fast it tricked her eyes into thinking she'd blinked and suddenly all ten blades were raised to strike at her. The grinding sound filled her ears. She blinked and the swords were in stop-motion. She blinked and saw moving legs. She blinked and the monster's beak had spread, and she was running before Mal'uud bellowed, "GO!"

Madeline willed energy into her exhausted body and streaked across the terrace. The stone sounds were a nauseating roar. She heard Mal'uud yell, heard something strike the ground, and Madeline dared to look once she had climbed down the last of the stairs onto the outer courtyard.

At first, she thought the six-legged scorpion-cat thing was a Guardian, but the sinew flexed and the red eyes gleamed, and a dull light glowed in the scorpion's thorax. The head was like a big cat's, complete with tusk-like fangs dripping with frothy saliva. The body was like a scorpion's, and the tail and stinger struck at lightning speed. Mal'uud didn't penetrate the troll Guardian, but he did strike hard enough to knock the rock statue backward several feet.

Mal'uud spun, skittering toward Madeline in a blinding rush. She didn't think. She didn't reason. She merely leapt and landed on Mal'uud's back. The thuds of landing Guardians echoed and boomed directly behind them, and a deafening crack signaled the beginning of an avalanche high above. A gust of arctic wind hit them, and Madeline's screech was lost beneath the boom of Guardians and the tumbling tons of snow and ice. Mal'uud dove to the left, dodging a landing eagle-shaped Guardian. Mal'uud's tail lashed and drove the thing backward, and on he ran. As they gained some ground and Mal'uud dashed forward, the body beneath Madeline morphed into the six-legged horse. Their speed doubled, and the Guardians fell further behind.

The stairs leading to what had once been the gate were wide enough for Mal'uud's hooves to find traction. Madeline could only cling in sheer terror, and she screamed again when a Guardian landed on the stairs. Its weight was too much for the crumbling stone to handle, and the thing fell along with half the stairwell. Mal'uud leapt, and four of his legs landed on the inner courtyard. The back legs kicked wildly for a heart-stopping second, and then they were inside what remained of the castle walls.

"Where is he?" Madeline yelled. Her fear of Lord Nothing had dimmed in comparison to the tangible threat of the Guardians. If they found the Lord of Shadows, he could call off his damned dogs.

Mal'uud slowed, stumbling with exhaustion to the left and then the right. His big head swayed as though trying to figure out options, and he and Madeline saw the rear gate at the same time.

"There!" Madeline pointed to an empty archway that had at one time likely led into the sprawling manor protected by the castle walls. The rightmost wall of the main wing still stood, its white stone gleaming and its windows still with glass panes intact. A rockslide had demolished the left wall and side. Madeline thought – no, *knew* – that at one time, the Fortress had been much more than a fortified castle. It had been an immense and ostentatious manor. Its inner rooms would have been lavish beyond comparison, decorated in gold, silver, silk, and elaborate tapestry. Fireplaces would have grown from the marble floors of every room. Paintings in frames would have covered the walls. Baths that would have been the envy of any Roman emperor would have been in every living suite. Ballrooms, libraries, gardens, atriums... all who had ever ruled would have wept and knelt in the face of such splendor.

It had been a palace home to a Lord who loved to live like the grandest of kings.

The vision of the Fortress as it had been danced before Madeline's eyes and vanished in the next instant. Mal'uud shot through the open archway and galloped across checkered, glittering tiles. They hopped over half walls, sped through grand, empty chambers swirling with snow, and finally entered what must have once been an indoor garden. They wove through barren fountains and kicked up littered scraps of fabric and splinters of what was left of the furniture.

Madeline shot a look over her shoulder and didn't see anything but empty rooms. "I think they've stopped following," she said just before Mal'uud's startled whinny sent icy tendrils of pure terror through Madeline.

The Fortress had been built between two mountains, and the rear wall of the estate must have at one time been entirely made of glass. And through that glass Lord Nothing would have had a view of the cosmos and space.

The floor of the indoor garden ended at the edge of the world. Beyond the jagged lip of the broken marble were floating bits of tile, glass, and ice lazily turning, end over end out into the void. Via'rra's sky, full of its strange hunks of meteors and with a view of distant, ringed planets, continuously spun beyond the walls of the mountains that braced the rear of the Fortress. Mal'uud had slid to a halt not six feet from the edge, and Madeline could see the roots of the mountains trailing off into space. Though she grabbed his mane and tried to pull him back, Mal'uud cautiously approached the edge. Madeline caught a glimpse of the Fortress' subfloors before nausea got the better of her. She climbed off Mal'uud's back, staggered away, and dry heaved on all fours. She sucked a breath and burst into angry, terrified tears when the boom of a landing Guardian vibrated the floor beneath her.

"The Ring," Mal'uud whispered. He'd transformed into his usual self, though he seemed smaller. He braced himself on a fountain. "Water and the Ring are gone."

To Madeline's consummate horror, Mal'uud began to weep silent tears. They streaked down his leathery cheeks, and they did not stop when the next miniature earthquakes signaled more Guardians approaching.

"Mal'uud..." Madeline went to his side, took his free hand, tugged it. "Mal'uud!"

He didn't acknowledge her, and the booms grew louder behind them. The sound of grinding stone reverberated through the ruined Fortress, and Madeline fought down bile. "Mal'uud, we have to go."

"Go," Mal'uud repeated. He blinked, frowned, and looked at Madeline. "Go," he said again.

"Yes," Madeline hissed. She glanced at the door to the garden and back at Mal'uud. "We've got to hide. Don't you hear them?" She desperately tried to drag Mal'uud away from the fountain and toward a doorway leading into a room buried in the mountain to their right. "Please!"

Mal'uud stumbled a few steps, got himself together, and clapped a brutal grip on Madeline's forearm. It hurt, but the reaction was better than watching him cry. "Come on," Madeline urged.

"Yes," Mal'uud agreed calmly. "We have to go."

And with that, he began to drag Madeline to the edge of the world.

"What are you doing?" Madeline shrieked. She struggled and kicked at him. "Mal'uud! Stop! For the love of God! Stop! You have to—"

Mal'uud didn't heed her warnings or pay any attention to her fear. He strode to the place where broken tile met floating debris free of gravity. He yanked Madeline to him with enough force that the air knocked free of Madeline's lungs. They stood there in a fierce embrace with Mal'uud's bony toes hanging over the rim of existence, backlit by absolute darkness and with the sounds of Guardians now echoing in the garden.

"Please," Madeline wheezed.

And then they fell over the edge.

Chapter Seventeen

When Becky had died, Monica had waited a week before packing her best friend's belongings into airtight plastic storage containers. Drawer after drawer, shelf after shelf, into the container went clothes, knick knacks, journals, and shoeboxes full of letters. Then, one by one, Monica had hauled the bins to the Fisherman's Shack Museum and stored them in neat stacks in the attic. No one had helped her. Most had scorned her for attempting to put Becky out of sight and mind so quickly. It had started at the funeral.

"*She was that family's greatest source of hope and comfort, but it was all to take the man after the wife was finally out of the way.*"

"*Becky's barely cold in the ground, and already that woman's packing her away like she never even existed!*"

No one had asked Monica how she had felt about it. They assumed she had been and still was a husband-thieving, callous bitch. But Becky had said, "Don't let that stuff sit around and collect dust, Monica. It'll drive you nuts."

Becky was always right. After Becky was gone, Monica had done as Becky had asked, not realizing until it was too late that she was a *hurting* callous bitch who was grateful to put away the reminders of a friend who'd been dying not for those last days in hospice care, not for the last two weeks when Becky was in and out of consciousness, but for two full years of not being Becky. Not really. Becky sometimes emerged from the cancer-morphine cocoon to smile and make requests or attempt jokes.

"Ice chips, God, what I wouldn't give for a vodka tonic."

But then she'd gone away again. The disease had taken Monica's dearest friend bit by bit, part by part, and when it was finally over, Monica had been grateful. Guilty and grateful. *Angry* and grateful.

Monica had been mad at everyone because it was as though they'd only seen death in Becky at the very end. Monica had wanted to scream at them all, and had, actually, screamed more than once, that death had been there – right *fucking* there – squirming beneath Becky's pallid skin for years.

It had taken many hours sitting in Doctor Spirrell's office for Monica to stop referring to her loved ones as selfish pricks. Spirrell had pointed out that Monica didn't truly feel that way, the angry part of herself who was grieving over her lost friend did, and though eventually Monica had moved beyond the anger, she never was too sure about Spirrell's theory. Monica was pretty sure most people naturally suffered from a chronic case of me-ism. Her loved ones were no different. And neither, she'd eventually understood, was she. There were many ways to grieve, and just because Monica's way was the best way for her, it was not the best way for everyone. She'd seen that, in the end, but not before giving in to impatience and telling everyone to hurry the hell up and get on with living because years of waiting on death to call had taken its toll.

Monica sighed and caressed the unopened bottle of whiskey in her lap. Her ass was going numb from sitting on the floor, leaning against the wall. The mid-morning light coming in through the attic's narrow windows was cheerful and warm. It made three yellow rectangles on the attic's wooden floor, each of them dappled with tree limbs swaying in a summer breeze. The stacks of Becky's belongings were to Monica's right. Tax forms and crates of old clothes and trunks dating to the previous century were to Monica's left. The Halloween and Christmas decorations were across the attic in a pile. Jack the Pirate Pumpkin King was resting his orange head in the life-sized Santa's lap. Monica wondered what a Pumpkin King would want for Christmas. A world-wide knife ban? The declaration of pumpkin pie as cruel and unusual baked goods?

Andrew would know. If he'd been there with her, she could have asked him what Jack could want, and Andrew would have had a dozen ideas. He could have told her the scientific name for the pumpkin vine or plant or whatever it was. He could have told her the best ways to grow pumpkins, and he would have gotten excited over the idea of growing the biggest one in the world.

Andrew, her son, her beloved strange baby boy, who was in love, though Monica wished such a thing were impossible.

Monica twisted the cap off the whiskey bottle. She brought the open neck to her nose and took a sniff. She winced. The stuff smelled terrible, like rotten animal urine. And yet, her Darryl loved it more than life with his family. Loved it more than his daughter, than his business, than any reality in which he had to face the truth. He'd take a bathtub of whiskey over the truth any day. He'd take a lake of whiskey and drown himself in it before he'd ever agree he needed help. Real help, not only the "Hi, I'm Darryl and I'm an alcoholic" help but "It all started when I was five and Mommy said I couldn't go to the circus" kind of help.

Darryl didn't see things the same way. He'd rather take that lake of whiskey with a side of powdered donuts that shot his blood sugar so high, it'd come out of his mouth like a crystal-encrusted rainbow. Monica could see it all clear as a bell in her head. He'd be standing on the lawn vomiting up rainbows, and Miss Teedee would stand on the porch and shake her head. Helen would chew the ends of her hair and make up a story about a man who died when a rainbow landed on him. Andrew would prune a rosebush and think the rainbow was pretty. Only Monica would worry, because Monica was the only one who ever did. Monica the Responsible. Monica the Helpful, the Hopeful... the fucking exhausted.

After Becky was gone and her belongings were stored and Monica had more or less stopped thinking of everyone as selfish ghouls, she'd started running the Taylor Point House. She'd fired lazy staff members. She'd taken over the cleaning schedule. She'd balanced their books and made them stop hemorrhaging money. She'd made sure she had a spare handyman on speed dial for the times when Darryl was too lost in his thoughts or his clocks to fix anything. She organized an ad campaign to get them more visitors. She'd single-handedly run the museum, and after two years of being super woman, she'd collapsed.

When she'd woken up from her three-day nap, she'd gone to see Spirrell, who had informed her she was attempting to make up for the family's loss by being perfect. She was, in effect, taking on all the responsibility so everyone else could grieve and she wouldn't have time to. She was overcompensating and avoiding, and though she'd been so tired she hadn't argued with her shrink, for once, there'd been no real time to do anything about his suspicions because Monica had started sleeping in Darryl's bed, and Helen had gone nuts. Darryl insisted one had nothing to do with the other. Monica wasn't so sure. She continued to be unsure, even eighteen years later.

The first time Helen had wandered off to find the people from another world, she'd been gone for a full day. Darryl had been losing his mind, and the rest of the family wasn't far behind him. The local police wouldn't take their missing person assumption seriously, but that changed when the State Trooper had shown up with Helen in the back of his car. She'd been found miles away in the middle of the interstate holding up a cardboard sign that had read, "HAVE YOU SEEN THE MISSING STAR?"

When they'd gotten Helen inside, they'd all listened patiently to her story of people from another world or dimension or whatever the hell.

"I have to find them," Helen had said. "I'm the only one who knows. I'm the only one who can do this."

She hadn't been able to hold still. She wouldn't sleep, and she wouldn't shut up. It'd been Monica who'd called her shrink and had him call in a prescription for a sedative. It'd been Monica who had to give Helen the pill. Darryl had gone off to drink, Miss Teedee had believed the spell would pass, and the rest of the staff had steered clear.

Over the next six months, they'd found Helen in a motorcycle bar, an abandoned building squatting with heroin addicts, and a dentist office reception lounge, among many other interesting places. It'd always been Monica who'd gone to fetch her. It'd been Monica who'd asked her therapist what to do. With Darryl drunk and Miss Teedee watching Andrew, Monica had driven Helen to the psychiatric facility and checked her in. Helen had screamed that Monica was a controlling, destroying, evil bitch worse than Banshee ever could imagine being, and Monica had driven home in time to catch two hours of sleep before she was to begin her cleaning shift.

They'd called her brutal. They'd said she had changed. That losing Becky had killed the best parts in her, too. Monica had faced her accusing family, the uncomfortable guests, and the whispering staff with a poker face she'd learned to make while growing up in a house with a man who enjoyed violence. She took care of Andrew, put him to bed, and then cried by herself and for herself. She told her therapist that she saw no other way to cope with what was happening to Helen. No one offered any other solutions, least of all Darryl. Helen's father was lost in his own grief.

In those days, when Darryl would stumble home, it'd been Monica who'd put him to bed. It'd been Monica who'd called his sponsor. And it'd been Monica who had learned to accept how nobody in the Taylor Point House seemed to remember any of the tragedies after they were done and gone. Darryl never talked to her about his battles with recovery. Nobody reflected on how often Helen lost her mind. There was no discussion about the past Miss Teedee refused to acknowledge. It was simply accepted that occasionally Miss Teedee would see a photograph of young men in a fashion magazine and hide in the pantry to cry.

They didn't talk about the chaos in the house. They gave it a key and a room and the run of the grounds. And it was up to Monica to clean up in chaos's wake.

Monica tentatively took a sip of whiskey. It was disgusting. She spat it on the attic's floor, sealed the bottle, and set it aside. She'd find no safe haven in alcohol; she couldn't abide the flavor. She'd given up smoking because there were too many guests who were sensitive to it. She'd stopped eating chocolate because she had a milk allergy. She didn't have time to exercise, and she'd not dared to try to find a fast fuck because the last one had left her nearly dead and entirely knocked up.

"Trust me," Monica whispered, thumping her head against the wall at her back. That's what Darryl had told her the day they'd sat in his office in the Taylor Point House. Andrew had been in the kitchen with Miss Teedee. Becky had still been well enough to supervise the cleaning rounds in the rooms above them. Staff had been buzzing around, and guests had been laughing loudly in the central hall.

Monica had been in and out of bad hotels and in between jobs for a solid month. No matter what she'd done, she hadn't been able to catch a break. She'd lost her job as an administrative assistant at a paving company when she refused to suck off her boss. She'd lost the job before that because Andrew had one ear infection after another and there'd been nobody to watch him, so she'd missed work and gotten fired. The infections had been so bad, they'd ruptured his ear drums more than once, and he'd scream and scream for hours. The night before Monica had run into Miss Teedee, they'd been at the emergency room again. The doctor had told Monica that her son might be deaf because of the frequency and severity of the infections. Monica, sleep deprived and buried in so much discord she couldn't find where harmony was hiding, had contemplated killing herself because her death might give her son's hearing back and let him live a normal life. She'd driven and driven while Andrew finally slept in the backseat, chock full of antibiotics that Monica had bought with the last of her cash, and she'd wound up in a town on the water.

She'd still been thinking of wrapping her car around a telephone pole when Miss Teedee had knocked on her car window, invited her into the diner, bought her coffee, and told her about a job in a B&B nearby.

"Trust me," Darryl had said after they'd chatted about her work history and desperate life. He'd smiled without judgment, and it was the nicest thing anybody'd done for Monica in possibly all of her life. "We need you," Darryl had said, "and you'll be taken care of here. You and Andrew."

The safe haven had saved her life. Monica hadn't cared what the people in the haven had asked of her, she'd felt the tasks were her dues to pay. For years, she'd felt like that, as though there were a tally being kept somewhere and eventually, maybe, if she was lucky, she'd do enough to repay the blessings in her life. Nothing was ever free. She didn't care what Spirrell said on the subject.

For the longest time, her payback system worked, too. She ran the house and it made a profit. She provided food, clothing, shelter and even a job for her little boy. Darryl struggled with alcoholism for years, sure, but Monica had managed the shitstorms, and he'd been sober, now, for at least a decade. So long as she paid her dues and did anything asked of her, everyone's stability, including and most of all Monica's, would last.

And then she'd woken up to find Darryl missing from bed. Thirsty, Monica had crawled from under the covers to go to the kitchen for some water and to see if she could find Darryl. She'd found him, all right. She'd found him standing at the kitchen island with a glass full of wine and a guilty expression.

Oddly, her first thought had been that Spirrell had been right, after all, and damn him. He'd told her that it was impossible to exert control over every aspect of life. He'd tried to explain that thinking of existence as a series of checks and balances was futile. Shit happened and no amount of good behavior could prevent it. One could not, through sheer force and capability of duty, stop cancer from killing, stop bullies from hurting an unusual child, or make an alcoholic save himself.

Monica hadn't wanted to believe it. She'd thought it was bullshit because her life was proof positive that Spirrell was wrong. Nobody did hope and willpower like Monica. Whatever else she had to do, she'd do it to prevent the chaos from winning.

Monica never suspected that she had limits. She never thought she'd be weak in the face of new challenges. She'd never anticipated that there'd be a day when she'd want to walk away.

It turned out that her breaking point was seeing her may-as-well-be-husband looming over a drink and babbling about sleepwalking and barreling. And her second thought after thinking Spirrell had been right was, "I can't do this." The words had felt and sounded like a castle gate slamming shut against the advancing enemy. She'd stormed downstairs wondering how anybody ever trusted anyone ever in this life. Darryl had followed her, of course, and they'd begun fighting their usual fight – Darryl, see somebody about your shit; Monica, I would never stoop so low; Darryl, I've seen someone for years; Monica, there's clearly something wrong with you, with me it's just the booze, and I've got AA for that; Darryl, that's obviously working so well for you, would you like another glass of dream liquor for the road? – and then Darryl had the audacity, the sheer unadulterated balls, to say those two words to her again.

"Trust me," he'd said, sitting on the bed in his shorts and undershirt and looking ninety, not sixty-five, "You have to trust me. I need you to believe me."

The fight that had followed had been their worst one in eighteen years together. Darryl was trapped in a prison of his own making, and Monica was done trying to show him doors.

And then the text message.

Darryl had gone off to the early AA meeting – a show of good faith and an attempt to maintain sobriety. And that's likely all it was, a show, because who knew how often he "sleepwalked" and drank? Monica had been going about her business, because she evidently was the only one who knew how, when her phone had gone off.

"EVERYTHING OKAY? HOUSE AND MUSEUM?"

Monica had stared at that for two minutes, seeing plainly what was between the lines. The fact that he was asking about the house and the museum meant he was worried something would be discovered at one of them. Monica immediately went and checked the liquor stores. They were all accounted for, and under lock and key. The rest of the house was in order – she knew because she'd put it that way. So she took off down the road to the museum. It wasn't open today, so she had the place to herself. The doors were locked, the windows intact, and the exhibits appeared untouched. Upstairs, her rough workspace was in as much order as it ever could be, for all the neglect it faced. The museum had been Becky's project. Just another thing Monica kept going maybe way longer than she should have.

After checking everywhere, she'd gone back to the car and retrieved the bottle she'd brought with her. God knew why. Maybe she was trying to understand. Maybe she just wanted to escape like everybody else seemed to be able to do. She went up to the attic, where she found a weird, dusty ring, and it smelled like smoke and ash.

Somebody was hiding something.

One more thing she'd have to deal with on a list with too many to count.

Monica drew her knees to her chest and rested her forehead on them. The position strained her back and squished her boobs, but she could fall asleep like this, no problem. She was so tired. Fuck Darryl and his liquor. She had a son, a child in the body of a man, to think about.

At her last visit to Spirrell's, she'd told him Andrew was in love. "How do you know?" he'd asked.

"A mother knows."

"Did he tell you?"

"He didn't have to."

"How do you feel about it?"

Monica and Spirrell had been together too long for niceties. "I feel that he has to understand it won't work."

"How do you know?"

"Because he's Andrew. You know Andrew."

"Apparently not as well as you know Andrew, if you can predict his entire future."

"I know Andrew couldn't possibly understand what love means; what being in a relationship means."

"He knows you love him."

"That's different."

"It is," Spirrell had agreed. "But it's also the first foundation upon which we build our structure of love."

Monica had snorted. "If I'm his example, then he already knows love doesn't work out."

"Because you think it didn't for you?"

"Because of how it *did* for me."

"His father, you mean."

"All of them, I mean."

Spirrell had folded his hands. He thought he was on to something when he did that. "How are you and Darryl?"

"Fine. I take care of him, he does what he wants, and we're fine."

"You don't feel taken care of?"

"I feel like we're out of time."

"How so?"

"Literally," Monica had said, gesturing to the hour hand.

Monica sighed and rested her chin on one knee. Dust motes swam in the sunbeams, and for once, Monica was content to let them be. Back at the house, the ground-floor side door would be cracked. The hallway outside her room would be empty, her bedroom door would be shut and locked, and inside the room, her suitcase was packed. Waiting.

She wanted to feel self-righteous and justified. Those sensations came and went in shimmers. They shook her, filled her up, made her yell threats and make demands, but then they were gone in the next instant. Guilt, dread, and weariness remained. Exhaustion was her constant. Regret was her companion. And fear. Of change, of staying the same... Of going or sticking around. It seemed to her on days like this that everyone existed in a bubble, floating along oblivious, and Monica was on the actual ground, wearing herself out against it, forever walking, forever pacing, forever go-go-going.

"Going, going... gone." Monica stood and stretched. She'd been moping for long enough. She'd shed her tears and she'd tried to speak her mind. It was time to act on a decision she should have made years ago.

Monica climbed out of the attic, folded the ladder, and padlocked the latch. She walked down the worn, narrow, wooden steps and smiled at the sparkling clean display cases. She locked up behind herself, sighed, and climbed into her car to drive to the main house. She didn't see a soul. She parked in the bend of the circle drive off the road in case guests needed to get by. She glanced left at Helen's apartment, feeling observed, and quick-stepped to the side door. She trotted to her room, grabbed her suitcase, and locked another door behind her. She briskly paced to the garden hallway through which she'd entered and to Andrew's room. And Jason's, now, Monica supposed, the lost boy who had come into their lives and wreaked havoc. Maybe she was being unfair, again, but everything had started to change after that boy had arrived. She fetched down Andrew's suitcase and started filling it with clothes.

"Mama?"

Monica jumped and spun. "Andrew," she gasped at her son, who stood sweaty and covered in grass. He held garden gloves in one hand and his ball cap in the other. The doorway gave him a white picture frame. "I didn't hear you."

"I'm quiet." He frowned. "What are you doing?"

"Packing your suitcase."

"Why?"

"We're going to take a vacation."

"Oh," Andrew said. "Oh! But..." He came over and fidgeted while standing next to the bed. "Don't we need to ask for time, first?"

"We don't need to ask anyone else for time. I say we get time, so," Monica folded a pair of jeans and forcefully stacked them on top of Andrew's favorite t-shirts, "we get time."

"But Mama—"

"Get your shoes," Monica ordered, but Andrew didn't move. He stood, looming over her with a crease between his eyes like a hill between two canyons. He'd gotten his father's height. Luke had been tall and big with huge, angry hands. Andrew's hands were gentle, but they had strength in them that Monica didn't like to feel. When Andrew had been little, he hadn't wanted to be touched much. As Andrew got bigger, he grew out of that, for the most part, but then it was Monica who didn't like him hugging her. Every time he did, she could remember Andrew's sperm donor pinning her and dragging her to the floor. "Andrew, I said get your shoes."

"Mama, I have work."

"You can take a break."

"No, I really can't. I need to make money." Andrew's eyes widened and his mouth formed a silent *Oh.* He'd said too much.

"Why do you need money?"

"I..."

"What do you need it for?"

"Things, Mama, just things."

"Like what?"

Andrew danced from foot to foot, like he had to go to the bathroom or was fighting the urge to run. "I like making it," he said because her son didn't know how to lie. "The money, I mean."

Monica slapped the top of the suitcase over the piles of clothes.

"You want money so you can fill up your scooter and go cruising around town?"

A beet red blush broke out over Andrew's cheeks and neck. He crossed his arms, hugging himself, and he studied the ground. "You knew?"

"Of course I knew." Every nosy neighbor in a thirty mile radius had felt duty-bound to call Monica to tell her that Andrew liked to scoot around town in the early hours of the morning.

"I'm careful, Mama. I promise. And I'm not skulking."

"Good boy." The suitcase thumped on the carpet when Monica dragged it off the bed. "You're my good boy, which is why you're going to come with me."

"But I need to plant things, Mama. They help people. Like the woman who makes men happy, the man who works nights, and the lady used the gun and her blood went on the walls."

Fear rippled through Monica. She'd always known, in her heart of hearts, that she didn't understand her own child. He was gifted with a way of seeing the world that was at once alien and yet beautiful. "Is that why you need money? Because you're helping those people?"

Andrew fidgeted. "Not those people."

Monica knew Andrew was keeping the whole truth from her. She wanted to cry. She wanted to yell at him. She wanted to wring answers out of him and tell him she couldn't protect him if she didn't know everything. It was her job to know all and be all for him, and she wanted to ask him when he'd decided her love and protection weren't enough; he had to go out and try to get it from strangers who wouldn't understand him. People would hurt him. He was too good and too pure, and the world would use that up and spit him out in pieces.

Heart breaking, Monica said in her best soothing, authoritative voice: "We'll talk about this later. Right now, I want you to get your shoes and your bag. We're leaving."

Monica had made it to the door before she heard her son say, "No, Mama."

"Andrew," Monica warned.

"Hey." Jason scuttled backward after almost running into Monica. "Sorry."

"What are you doing here?" Monica asked Jason. The rings under his eyes had lightened, and the bags were gone. He'd lost the starved puppy look, but he was still thin and awkward.

Jason shoved his hands into his pockets. "I came to find Andrew," he said. "See if he wants lunch."

"Yes," Andrew said.

"No," Monica rebutted. "We'll get something on the way."

"The way to where?" Jason asked.

"Mama, I said I'm not going."

Jason glanced from Andrew's stubborn stance in the middle of their shared room to Monica at the doorway. He turned and saw her suitcase leaning against the wall. "Listen, I should give you two some—"

"Yes," Monica said to Jason. "You should. Andrew. I said. Let's. Go."

This time when Monica stalked out of the room and down the hall, she heard her son following. They exited through the garden door, and Monica began to trudge up the gentle slope leading to her car. She hadn't made it off the lawn when Mercutio bounded down the external steps leading to Helen's apartment with Helen floating behind him. The sound of an old engine made Monica glance to see Darryl in his truck pulling into the circular drive and stopping in front of the house, and from behind Monica, Miss Teedee called from the main floor's side porch.

"Yoohoo!" Miss Teedee said, hands cupped around her mouth. "Monica? Andrew? Jason? Lunch is ready, loves."

"Mama?" Andrew said softly at her back.

"No, Andrew."

"But—

"Andrew I said—"

Andrew clasped her upper arm, and Monica had to stop or risk a scene wherein she yanked away from her baby boy. "Mama, listen, okay? I can't go. I have to get the flowers tucked in before nighttime. I have to finish blowing the old grass off the asphalt so it can rest in peace. I have to get rid of the mean weeds taking over the baby blooms in the median so they can grow without being worried about making anything angry. And Jason wants to learn how to dance. Or, well, he needs to learn how, even if he doesn't want to just yet."

Dizziness spun Monica like a top. She slowly turned to face her son and saw Darryl scrambling out of the vehicle. Miss Teedee was on the porch with her hands on her hips, and Jason had slinked away, as though not sure where to stand. "Andrew—"

"And what if Miss Teedee's back goes out again," Andrew said breathlessly, "and she can't take care of her home garden this fall? If I don't pick those veggies, they'll go bad, Mama. And nobody likes bad vegetables."

"Monica?" Darryl said, as he jogged through the side yard as fast as his body would let him.

"Lunch, I said!" Miss Teedee repeated. "These cheese cubes aren't going to eat themselves!"

"Where you off to, Madam M?" Mercutio asked, hand-in-hand with Helen who said nothing, but Monica could swear Helen had peered into Monica's mind and deemed what she'd found to be lacking.

Monica couldn't catch her breath. She shut her eyes and let go of Andrew's suitcase, but she couldn't pry her fist off her own. The suitcase roll handlebar in Monica's palm was unnaturally hot. It seemed to her then, with everyone in her life yelling something at her, begging her to do the very thing that was killing her, that the suitcase didn't hold clothes and her laptop, but bricks. Bricks from this house, bricks from the house where she grew up scared to speak, and bricks from the hotel where a big man had held her down and hurt her while planting Andrew inside her. Maybe she'd said that once to him, and that's where his oddness about flowers had started. Maybe she'd been too soft on him, and that's why he was so strange. Maybe it was those drinks she had before she knew she was pregnant or the cigarettes she sneaked puffs from when she thought she'd throw herself down a flight of stairs to spare the baby in her belly a life with the likes of her.

Monica wanted to let go of that handle. She wanted to launch herself up, up, up into the vast expanse of the sky.

Instead, she whirled and grabbed her son by the front of his shirt with one fist. She tugged until he bent so their faces were on the same level. "People don't come from a garden," she said quietly, urgently, and in a voice she barely recognized as her own. "They don't want to be tucked in. They don't want peace. And no matter what happens, somebody's always angry."

"Mama," Andrew whispered, and his eyes were filling up with tears.

"You want the best of yourself to exist in others, and Andrew, it just doesn't. You hear me? Love uses people. It doesn't save, and it doesn't heal, and it doesn't grow. It eats you up and gets mad when there isn't any more."

"Oh," Andrew murmured. He sniffed and a tear rolled down one cheek. "Oh. Mama. That's not true. That's not true at all."

"Get in the car, Andrew," Monica whispered.

"No, Mama."

"Now, Andrew."

Andrew pulled away from her. "I love you, but I'm not gonna leave him."

Andrew whirled and took off running toward the Sound, and above them, though there wasn't a thunderhead in sight, the sky rumbled.

"Monica," Darryl panted when he got within speaking distance. "What's going on?"

"I've..." Monica pulled her eyes away from the vision of her son's retreating back. "I've got to go."

"Go?" Darryl asked, panicked. "Go where?"

"Anywhere but here." She threw a look at Darryl, telling him without words what was his fault and what was hers. She dragged her suitcase to her car.

"Monica, let's talk about this. Please."

"Nothing to say." Monica loaded the case into the trunk and slammed the lid.

"I swear to you, I didn't drink."

"I don't care." It may have been a lie, but it was an easy one. She climbed behind the wheel.

Darryl stopped her from shutting the door by grabbing it. "We need you around here. You give this place life. You give *me* the hope to go on after—"

"You're going to have to make do without me."

Darryl's chin wavered, though his eyes stayed dry. "I need you."

Monica sighed and the breath tasted stale, like it'd been lingering in a part of her lungs she used so rarely that it was dusty when stirred. "I know."

"When will you be back?"

They stared at one another. When Monica didn't answer, Darryl finally lowered his gaze and let go of the door. Monica closed it, locked it, and turned on the car. She glanced in her rearview and saw Jason standing behind her car. He bent, put a hand with splayed fingers on her dirty rear window, and did something with the other hand that Monica couldn't see. When she realized he was writing, Monica put the car into gear and drove away.

Later, when she'd put some distance between herself and the Taylor Point House and when she had to stop for gas or else she'd be running on empty, Monica saw what Jason had written.

There, in the dust next to the insignia on her trunk, Jason had scrawled:

I GET IT. SO WILL TH

Monica read the words over and over until another customer in line for her pump honked. She wiped a hand over the message and started to fill up.

Chapter Eighteen

Madeline thought she'd fall and fall, maybe hitting an asteroid eventually, if she lived that long, or maybe never hitting anything at all. She'd fall forever, screaming into a vacuum until she could scream no more.

Instead, she skidded across rock. Vertigo flip-flopped her stomach and spun the world away from her. Pebbles abraded her skin and dust filled her mouth. She tumbled, thought she was done for, and then she landed hard on unforgiving dry ground. She coughed and heaved. She spat out wads of wet dirt and didn't dare look up or move.

A few seconds later, Mal'uud landed next to her, but gracefully in his crouch. His fingers dug into a crevice and clung, and he panted for a moment. When the Shadow Guardians didn't appear to tear them apart, Mal'uud adjusted his balance and knelt next to Madeline. "It worked," he said on a long breath.

Madeline spoke between gasps for air. "You mean... you didn't know... it would?"

"No."

"Then... What... What did... What just...?"

Mal'uud stared ahead of them but gestured behind them. "Go and look for yourself."

Madeline's head felt stuffy and heavy, as though she balanced on it. She glanced at Mal'uud and hastily shoved loose tendrils of her hair behind her ears. Unwilling and perhaps unable to stand, Madeline rose onto all fours. The ground beneath her was scaled like a lizard, dry and hot. Her palms and knees hurt where she'd fallen, but she ignored the pain. It was getting easier to do.

Without lifting her head, she inched slowly in the direction she'd come. She found the edge of the world again, but when she lifted her eyes to see beyond the rim, everything was upside down. Confusion made her brave, and she peered over the edge to see crumbling rock, floating pebbles, and dust. She stared, not blinking, until she heard the grinding of a Shadow Guardian high above her. It shrieked an inhuman cry. The ground vibrated with the stamping of its hooves or talons, and Madeline backpedaled. She spun to land on her knees and gazed ahead.

Miles and miles of flat, barren land stretched out before them. Above her were faintly glowing stars and more broken chunks of orbiting suns and planets. She took a breath and then another and the more she took and the more she told herself the ground was down instead of up, the less her head ached. Her eyes watered, and she wiped grit from them. Daring to stand, she observed column shapes that bloomed at the top like giant trees dotting the landscape. Some were huge, like cylindrical tornadoes. Others were skinny, and now that she was paying attention, she heard a whispering sound like someone pulling silk through a tightly closed fist. Ten feet to their right she saw a thin column, and when she cautiously approached it to investigate, she discovered it was sand. Or, well, not just sand, but all kinds of grit that emerged from the crevices in the ground and fell *upward* to form a column of glittering dust. The dust rose toward the sky and dispersed into threadlike tendrils, floating out into space, twinkling.

"What is this place?" Madeline asked softly.

Mal'uud approached her and the dust and put a hand into the column. "This is what remains of the Sea and the Ring. The Sea was your Blue's domain. It circled the world. It fed the streams and the land. The Ring was the Lady's protection and power stores. It, too, encircled the world in a field of magenta light. It provided the Sea its warmth, helped Water to multiply and endlessly flow. That is Water's power, the ability to multiply himself. He could manifest rain and storms and split his particles into millions of new ones. This world never lacked for water." Mal'uud withdrew his hand and cupped a palm full of dust. He tipped his hand and let it run between his bony fingers.

"Where did the Ring and the Sea go, then, if they're not here?"

"I do not know, but I do know that if they have vanished, then the Lady and Water are lost."

"Lost?" Madeline's heart leapt into her throat. "You mean dead?"

Mal'uud frowned. "I cannot imagine the Lady can die. But her power is gone." He sighed. "We must find the Shadow Lord. Then we will have our answers."

"Okay, then. Where is he?"

Mal'uud peered into the distance. Madeline waited, listening to the quiet with such intensity that she thought her eardrums would rupture. "He is here," Mal'uud whispered at last.

"Where?"

"Everywhere."

Madeline hugged herself and stood on her toes. She saw sand, dust, and an endless bizarre sky. The air here was darker than it had been on the top of the world; a deep blue twilight thick enough that when Madeline licked her lips, she expected it to have flavor.

When Mal'uud took several cautious steps forward, Madeline did, too, and when Mal'uud grunted in surprise, it was all Madeline could do not to shriek. "What?" she asked.

"There." Mal'uud pointed to the crevices in the ground. At first, Madeline couldn't see what Mal'uud wanted her to see. The cracks were deep and wide. In some places, they were so wide, Madeline had to step over them else one of her feet would get lodged.

She watched, waiting and holding her breath, and then she saw it: the shadows hiding in the earthen cracks... *moved.*

The movement was more sinuous; almost sensual, as though the shadows stretched and reached and, if she dared to put her ear to the ground, she could have heard them sigh in soft contentment. Slowly, slowly the inky darkness slithered deliberately in the cracks of the dried seabed. It was odd how she could see those shadows so clearly in comparison to the gray murk that lurked in the other cracks. Before she knew what she was doing, she was kneeling, bending, attempting to study the sentient Shadow. With her face hovering inches above the ground, she saw the Shadow wasn't true black. It was richer, darker, and shimmered black, gray, dark blue and even with threads of silver and the faintest hint of glittery gold. It moved like mercury, like thin, tarry magma, but faster. The gloom spread and soon a road of darkness rose before them, coming to life like a creek bed after a sooty rain. The path shot off into the distance at dizzying speeds.

"Don't touch it." Mal'uud caught Madeline's wrist, and to her horror, she discovered she'd been lowering a fingertip between the edges of a wide crack as though to caress the darkness that shimmered like oily black water. "Unless," Mal'uud continued, "you wish for him to touch *you*."

"No." Madeline scrambled to her feet, careful to plant them on solid ground. Her imagination conjured the sound of a deep, rumbling chuckle barely within range of her hearing. It thrummed through her like bass at a rock concert, and when Mal'uud shuddered, Madeline suddenly wasn't sure if she'd imagined the sound after all.

"Let's go," Mal'uud murmured, but after only a handful of paces, he staggered.

"What is it?" Madeline asked, steadying Mal'uud with one hand. His sinew was cool to the touch and not slimy in the least.

It was dry; soft and leather-like. It reminded her of her adopted grandmother, who'd been ninety-five when she'd died. Her skin had been so thin, so papery, so close to bone.

"I do not have much left in me." Mal'uud sighed. "The shifting of forms, the fighting, the running." He shook his head and ran a hand over his bare skull. When he could stand on his own, he reached deep within himself and removed the same jar of salve that he'd used back in the alleyway to heal her wounds. Madeline bit her tongue asking him where, exactly, that jar had been hidden. She merely observed as he uncapped the jar, scooped a finger into the salve, and put it in his mouth, sucking at it like an infant at the breast. It seemed to help steady him, and Madeline let go of a silent sigh of relief.

Though the tributaries of the Shadow river were below the ground's uneven surface, and though Mal'uud carelessly walked across the ooze-filled cracks, Madeline kept her eyes on her feet as she followed Mal'uud through the desert. At first she counted her steps to keep her mind occupied, but when she lost track of their paces in the low hundreds, Madeline gave up and let her thoughts drift. She thought of her grandmother, of the day the woman had died, and the funeral that had followed several days later. It'd been springtime, and she'd gotten stung by a wasp. Her adopted mother had shaken her when Madeline had begun to cry with the pain. She'd been told to be quiet, to hush, though later, at the house, her adopted father had brought her ice for the swelling.

Had there ever been bees in Via'rra? Wasps? She almost asked Mal'uud, but thought better of it. He was ahead of her, walking deliberately while slowly eating the salve, and when Madeline began to contemplate how a being who had no internal organs could digest or absorb anything, she quickly tried to think of anything else. The texture of a rose petal. The smell of the ocean. The feel of sand between her toes. The hiss of rising sand and dust grew louder, and they passed through a veritable forest of dust columns, all thin but tall enough to brush the sky. The hair on Madeline's neck stood on end, and she grabbed the end of her ponytail just in case she got confused about which way gravity worked on the underside of the world. She didn't want any part of her to drift toward space. Though, surely, she should be more concerned about where she was and who they were going to see more than she was about walking upside down. She tried to conjure fear, but the best she could do was dull trepidation. She didn't know if that meant she was in shock or denial. Maybe both.

Or it could be that after getting chased by monsters across a land inhabited by tentacle beasts that hid in banks of fog that were trying to kill the King of Nightmare who had no skin and no innards but who could turn into a scorpion-cat and a six-legged horse, heading toward a mysterious Shadow Lord seemed normal. More normal than a day at the beach back on Earth seemed, now. More normal than sex or sleepless nights or eating at a restaurant. That life was more than distant. It was fading like it had been the bad dream, not this. Perhaps she desired to belong somewhere and her certainty that she did not belong on the other side of the Veil, but she was becoming surer of herself. She could hope that was part of this becoming whole process that Mal'uud so wanted for her.

Maybe she did belong here. Maybe Lord Nothing could tell them what they had to do next. Somebody in this forsaken land had to have a plan, and if Mal'uud thought Nothing was the most likely candidate, then Madeline had no choice but to trust him. She didn't know how to return to Topside. She didn't know how to fight off the Horrors, and if she chose to stay here until she rotted, she had no clue what God-awful things would attempt to kill her in this desert.

So Madeline walked, listening to Mal'uud suck his fingers clean of salve and to the sound of trailing dust. As before when they had traveled, time played tricks. She blinked and the scenery changed. Hunks of broken earth floated above the seabed, slowly turning like enormous, jagged, disembodied stalagmites. The cracks in the ground grew so large at certain points that

Madeline and Mal'uud had to jump across them. And though she had to run and jump to keep up with Mal'uud, she wasn't winded and her heart didn't pound with exertion. Her body ached, though, and at one point she got so tired she nearly fell. She wanted to curl up and sleep and sleep, but one look at the shimmering darkness hiding just below the packed earth's surface changed her mind. She found her willpower and used it to keep going.

"Look."

Vaguely, she could see shapes in the distance, and slowly they came into focus. The irregular, oblong tunnels appeared small this far away. Twisting through the air like a floating ant colony, they cut through and climbed toward the outer space above.

"The Undermaze," Mal'uud said. "A piece of it, at any rate."

Trying to follow the line of the Undermaze passages hurt Madeline's head and eyes. "The physics of this place escape me."

Mal'uud chuckled as he pressed ahead. "We are Walkers, Hope Star. We create the rules of physics, they do not dictate to us."

"Okay," Madeline said, thinking conversation might make the passage of time easier to measure. "How does it work, then? Via'rra's flat and once had a Sea that surrounded it and then the Lady's Ring enclosed the Sea?"

"Yes." Mal'uud nodded. "And the place the two met created huge founts of steam. The beaches around the edge of Via'rra were the most densely populated. Water was plentiful and bred much life. The rain was warm and frequent. The comfort of the Lady's power was near and tangible. It was paradise for many."

"But you never went there," Madeline said. "You never saw it, yourself?"

"No, but the Fallen ideas remembered. Once they were given form in my kingdom, many would talk for days of their time spent Topside. Long ago, we would have feasts for new brethren. We'd eat and drink and fight and fornicate and then bathe in salve before doing it all again."

"I'm sorry," Madeline said after a moment. "For what you've lost."

"Thank you."

Silence descended once again, and on and on they walked. They paused to rest more than once, usually by a wide column of dust so Mal'uud could run his hands through it. Madeline wasn't so brave, but she enjoyed watching Mal'uud gather the falling sand before letting it travel on, out into the strange galaxy beyond.

The Undermaze tunnels gradually came into view on all sides. They did resemble bones, now that Madeline thought of it, or perhaps scaffolding. They were evenly shaped and smooth, like black pipes crisscrossing the sky. Many were broken, their shattered pieces crumbling in the air, but many more were intact. Sometimes the tunnels would converge and form a cavern. Those had to be the rooms of the Undermaze, and she was heartbroken to see that almost all of those had cracked open. One broken room was low enough that Madeline could see bones spinning amid the dust and gems that had once made up the walls. Mal'uud shed silent tears, his face grim, and Madeline didn't know what to say, so she said nothing at all.

With her eyes on the sky, which was not the sky at all, Madeline didn't notice right away when they began to gain altitude. The incline was gentle at first but quickly and steadily rose to the rim of a depression. The rim of what had to be a basin was so wide, Madeline couldn't see the end of it in either direction. They climbed for what could have been days, had to scramble on all fours to ascend the side, and they had to use the seabed cracks as handholds to gain the last hundred feet to the top of the rim. The edge was wide and flat, thank God, and Madeline crawled onto it on her belly and sucked a gasp.

When she'd been thirteen, the Banc's had taken her on a tour of the western United States. Her father had drank and her mother had driven the RV. They'd fought almost the entire time, and it'd been an exhausting trip, but some of the sights had been breathtaking.

One such stop had been a meteor crater in Arizona. The crater was almost forty miles wide and surrounded for miles by cattle and dust. There was an observation area and museum, of course, and Madeline had made a beeline for the metal platform overlooking the massive hole in the ground. From the rim, she hadn't been able to make out what, precisely, had been at the center of the crater. She'd needed a telescope to see the bottom, and she'd stared through it at the six-foot-tall astronaut manikin next to the United States flag. Without the telescope, she hadn't been able to tell that he or the flag were there.

The crater on the underside of Via'rra was similar in size, though the sloping to the bottom wasn't as sharp a grade. Swirling, cavorting black sand that sparkled even in the gloom like snow in sunlight filled the basin. Though there were plenty of columns of normal sand all around the rim that were rising toward the sky, none of the black sand was similarly affected. It roiled in an invisible and constant wind, gently creating hills and valleys.

It seemed to beckon to them. It whispered, hissed, and Madeline could almost make out words. The harder she tried to listen, the more distant she felt from the ground below her feet and the world around her. She covered her ears with her hands and next to her, Mal'uud did the same.

At the bottom of the crater, smack in the middle of the murmuring sand, was a rock formation made out of black, glimmering stone. Since she could see its walls and tell it was made of more of the Shadowrock, the formation had to be the size of an apartment building; ten, maybe even fifteen stories. Wedges of stone bloomed at regular intervals from a flat black center like petals, their edges gracefully scalloped and so smooth they gave the appearance of being soft.

It looks like a black rose.

Looming above the stone rose and also above their heads was a cavern of the Undermaze that also appeared to be made out of Shadowrock. It glistened against the backdrop of stars and hunks of meteors. "The Feed Room," Mal'uud said. "That's the..." He glanced from the Undermaze above to the stone rose below, and he visibly trembled.

The inky blackness that had led them through the desert slithered past them at speed. The path raced toward the sand and cut through it, creating oily veins through the dunes. The tendrils darted toward the stone rose and vanished once they touched the Shadowrock, absorbed.

Clearly, there was only one place to go.

"Mal'uud?" Madeline whispered.

"Yes?" he replied at the same volume.

"If I were wholly myself, the real Star, would I be this scared?"

"No." Mal'uud gingerly put a foot on the sloping basin's sides, testing his balance and maintaining it. "The fear would be worse."

Mal'uud could only know that based on his own terror, and as she watched him begin to descend, Madeline screwed up the courage to start to climb down the crater's side. They both slipped and slid, resorting to a crab crawl when Madeline slipped too far and Mal'uud caught her by the arm. Just as Madeline despaired that they'd never make it to the bottom of the basin alive, all the sand in the entire crater came together in a line before them. It whispered, the sound tickling Madeline's nerves. All of her hair stood on end, and the sound was arousing to the point of painful. Only Mal'uud's steely grip on her arm and the spectacle of the sand kept her from getting the hell out of there.

The sand formed stairs, very similar to the terraces ledges in the Fortress' Valley. Mal'uud tested their measure first, and he nodded at her, silently telling her that they would carry them. When Madeline came to stand beside Mal'uud, however, the stairs began to move. Whirling tendrils of sand worked below the platform on which they stood, acting like wheels and gliding the platform downward toward the bottom of the basin. Mal'uud went into his crouch for balance, and Madeline landed on her knees.

When the platform came to a stop, the stone rose was as big a stadium. The sand, having done its job, rushed toward the platform exactly like the oily darkness that had led them to the crater had done. The sand flowed into the air and instead of making a dune, it formed the shape of a throne. The sand appeared to expand and then it solidified into Shadowrock. The entire process took maybe thirty seconds, and Madeline reminded herself to breathe.

"Where is—?"

"Coming," Mal'uud intoned, and he flinched. "Forming," he corrected himself. "There."

Mal'uud and Madeline stood at least a hundred yards from the edge of the stone rose sculpture's base. The Shadowrock throne was as tall as a building inside the stadium-sized rose. Every inch of darkness rushed toward the throne. Only when the Shadow moved did Madeline realize it'd been there all along, lurking in the blue-gray twilight. The basin's bed became visible, more cracked and ragged earth, and she gasped at the sudden color in the landscape.

Madeline's ears ached with a change of pressure and inside the stone rose, the Shadow began to take form. Next to the two front legs of the throne, Madeline identified feet. Then calves. Then bent knees and seated, heavy thighs. She saw hands resting over the ends of the throne's arms, a wide torso, broad shoulders, thick neck, and finally an oval head and a face with only the hint of features. From the sides of the head sprung horns that slowly grew over ears and curled upward into wicked points.

Madeline had an urge to wet herself, but she'd not had anything to eat or drink, and though the urge was in her mind, it was not in her body. This land was changing her, and attempting to figure out if that was a good or bad thing allowed her to stay still without fainting.

The Feed Room of the Undermaze hovered over Lord Nothing's head like a flat disc crown. The stars shrouded his shoulders like a cape. Madeline could see no distinguishing characteristics, only the vague outline of a darkness, a sentient, ever-moving, vast darkness deeper and darker than any and all reality around it. The edges of his form hurt her eyes to see; they were blurry, wavering like a mirage in desert heat. Lord Nothing was outlined in invisible fire.

"Now we kneel," Mal'uud said under his breath, and Madeline dropped to her knees with Mal'uud. She stared at the titan before her and was frozen in place when Lord Nothing began to stand. He'd be too large when upright, impossible and overwhelming. She'd beg him to destroy her before he reached his full height. Fear choked her and dread rippled through her, but as Lord Nothing rose, he began to shrink. When he took a step toward them, he diminished in size. Like a shadow responding to the rising sun, Lord Nothing grew smaller and smaller as he came toward them, and as he approached, more of his features became visible.

By the time Lord Nothing was merely ten feet away, he was a man at least seven feet tall clad in a long fur cape that trailed the ground. The fur was white as fresh snow; it gleamed iridescent as it moved. He wore heavy, black, knee-high boots, dark leather-like pants held in place by a belt with a silver buckle, and a plain shirt the color of moonlight that was open at his throat. Lord Nothing's skin seemed to form as the Shadow drained from it, leaving him pale like frost. The Shadow retreated into swirling lines on Lord Nothing's exposed skin that looked like tattoos, but Madeline thought they were—

(*cracks in his skin; seams of darkness holding together his humanoid form*)

—something else. His black hair was short, curly, and streaked with pure silver. His nose was long and beakish, his mouth wide and thin, his chin strong and his jawline pronounced. His cheekbones threw pale blue shadows on his long face. His ears were tall and pointed, pierced with silver rings, and his horns were carved ebony, so shiny Madeline could see her reflection in them.

When Madeline met Lord Nothing's eyes, she made a soft, involuntary sound. The eyes were large, too big to be entirely human. The sclera was gray and the iris and pupils were swirls of blue, gold, black, and white. They turned like lazy galaxies fixed in Lord Nothing's head. Or, perhaps, they reflected what he could always see. He blinked and a more human dark pupil appeared and widened, as though until that moment, he'd seen them with every other means aside from his actual eyes.

"My Lord of Nothing, Master of Shadows, Eater of Worlds, Lover of Lady Creation." Mal'uud paused, steadied his voice. "Father. We have come to you in need."

Lord Nothing sighed, and Madeline's ears popped, relieving pressure. He opened his arms as though movement was difficult. He stood there, inviting Mal'uud to him like a statue that could wait millennia, and eventually Mal'uud went to him. Lord Nothing embraced Mal'uud with an affection Madeline would never in a million years attribute to a god of death and darkness.

When Mal'uud drew away, Lord Nothing caught Mal'uud by the jaw. They locked eyes, and Mal'uud sagged. Lord Nothing shoved a thumb into Mal'uud's mouth and bent so Lord Nothing's nose touched the craggy bone where Mal'uud's once had been. Madeline floundered forward, as though she could somehow stop Lord Nothing from eating Mal'uud or hurting him. Mal'uud didn't resist, caught instead in a strange embrace. Lord Nothing pursed his lips, exhaled, and whispers rose from around them, some shrill, some low, some almost laughing. Black and green Shadow poured from Lord Nothing into Mal'uud's mouth. Mal'uud shuddered, in pain or ecstasy, Madeline couldn't tell. When it was done, Lord Nothing released him with the same tenderness Lord Nothing had used to hold him.

The green energy ball inside Mal'uud's cracked chest was bigger, thrumming once again, and Mal'uud was steady on his feet. "Thank you," he said.

Lord Nothing inclined his head. "It is a weary journey, when the paths of the familiar stray into the unknown." His voice was resonant, if oddly hollow. He fixed his preternatural gaze on Madeline. She wanted to shrink into the seabed. "Hope," Lord Nothing said. "Diminished Star, you come with His Majesty,

Mal'uud 'au Keen, King of Nightmare seeking Eeadian, Water of Life."

The true name of her Blue rang bells in Madeline's mind, and her vision swam. She couldn't make her voice rise to the occasion, but Mal'uud stepped in for her. "We seek reasons why the Star isn't the Star, my Lord Nothing. She's returned to this world but is not yet a Walker."

"As I said, you seek Eeadian, Water of Life and Imprisoned Warrior."

"Imprisoned?" Mal'uud asked, his formal tone replaced by alarm. "Water is imprisoned?"

Lord Nothing continued to stare at Madeline as though weighing and measuring each of her parts toward an unsatisfactory sum. "I was mortal once. Human. I dwelled in the realm to which you escaped. I felt you leave our land, your home, and go to that place. Since I was once a resident of that land, I could and did send motes of my essence after you. I attempted to thwart the sealing of the Veil. I tried to stop Eeadian's plan, but I failed, for you were not contained. My motes, they survived and they followed you to the Blue world. They found the souls of interlopers between our realms; human visitors to Via'rra. Those who dreamed of this place, and who planted seeds here to grow. Seeds that have likely since been destroyed.

"My motes, they spoke to these humans, one a woman who was and is near you. They told her of all that would and did befall this world. Their infection of this individual's soul could not be helped, nor could my touch's spread to those around her to whom she tried to explain what she knew, what lurked then and continues to fester now in her consciousness." Lord Nothing lifted one of his hands, palm up. "My touch, it is heavy."

"Thank you for Helen Taylor and the boy, Toby," Mal'uud said. "Tell me, what of Daanske?"

Lord Nothing briefly closed his eyes and licked his lips, as though savoring a flavor still on his tongue. "He is with me, the Storyteller. His essence is companionable. His poisoning is slow."

"He harms you?" Madeline asked, visions of a man alive and well but dying by inches in the belly of a great beast filling her mind.

"All who and that dwell in me for too long rot, Star of Light."

"Why is he rotting?" Mal'uud interjected. "Why have you not passed what was once the Storyteller onto the Lady?"

Lord Nothing didn't acknowledge Mal'uud. "I am meant to bring the sanctuary of darkness and rest to any and all that has passed its prime. I am meant to consume that which my Lady requires; her mistakes, her attempts, her chosen power sources. Containment is not my purpose. Transformation is. The rot of that which cannot be transformed leeches strength from me as surely as the Horrors diminish me by destroying the places over which I might cast my arm."

"But you ate him anyway," Madeline blurted.

The cracks in Lord Nothing's skin shifted, as though he were restless beneath his human form. It felt like impatience to Madeline. "I do not eat," Lord Nothing intoned. "I absorb. And I can only hold the Storyteller because he allows it to be. Eeadian would not have permitted thus."

"Then where is Water?" Mal'uud persisted.

Lord Nothing took his time to answer. "Fear makes fools of all who succumb to it."

Mal'uud bowed his head, the teeth, which were visible through the sinew holding his jaw in place, gnashing. Madeline reminded herself to breathe.

"Fear," Lord Nothing said, "as with all things, is balanced in our land. It must be. Via'rra is a pivot point wavering between chaos and order. We give dreams and magic to the realms in which such gifts are welcome and even some in which they are not. No dream and no magic are wholly made of either chaos or order. All things are dual. Even you, Mal'uud."

When he dropped into his characteristic crouch, Madeline could tell Mal'uud was losing patience. "Please," she whispered, "tell us what happened to Water?"

"Your nature, Hope Star, is even further divided than ours," Lord Nothing continued as though he hadn't heard Madeline and as though the land around them wasn't actively and quickly being destroyed as they dallied in this desert. "All of your nature is necessary, as it is part of an intrinsic cycle that balances not only our world, but all worlds, so even when one seventh of your existence left us, we were forever tossed into unbalance until such time as you could be reclaimed."

"The Storyteller himself told me as much about the imbalance she left behind when she went through the Veil. She has returned, Father. Why hasn't she recovered her power?" Mal'uud growled. "I did as I was bid to do. I brought her here."

Lord Nothing was no more flustered by Mal'uud's threatening tone than Madeline would have been by a gnat. "You have returned a piece of divided Hope. Her intrinsic nature, her soul, to use that old word, lies elsewhere."

Mal'uud's eyes widened. "Water. He has the rest of her?"

"He holds her memories, yes, it is so."

"Then where is he?"

Again, Lord Nothing did not answer the question directly. "At times of great unbalance, a force awakens to right the wrongs. This force targets. Aims. Finds the heart of disturbance and rids our universe of it."

"So the Horrors are after Eeadian?" Mal'uud asked.

"All who are responsible for maintaining balance are in danger."

"Everybody," Madeline whispered, comprehension dawning.

"All the Walkers," Mal'uud said. "They are not just after Hope and Water. They're after all of us?"

"It." Lord Nothing held up one graceful, pale finger. "Not they. The Horrors as you call them are merely the manifested power of a single force whose nature is to separate and seep through the world." Lord Nothing gazed at Mal'uud expectantly, but when Mal'uud merely stared back, Lord Nothing's features showed faint surprise. "Of this, you are blind."

"We are all less than we were," Mal'uud said.

Lord Nothing frowned. "The opposing side of a warrior's courage is a coward's fear. Eeadian was lost. He forgot that all things must cycle and change. He wished for stagnation, and such a state would and is trying to crack the nature of our existence. Eeadian's self-deception was so powerful that he, too, would have left us or he would have fought the rebalancing force until his death.

"I could not abide this, for the Universe would topple. I would have stopped Water, I would have used Power to force him wholly into myself and allowed my Lady to carve him anew, but my Lady..." Lord Nothing slowly lowered his head. The edges of his body wavered as though it temporarily took all his concentration to maintain the shape. The whispers returned. Their volume was low at first but escalated into a deafening trill of grief that roared through the basin and then went silent as fast as it had begun. "My Lady was the first to fall. Trapped in a prison web of reflection and brilliance so none of my motes can reach her, the key to her freedom was gone from this world when Eeadian shoved her through the Veil."

It took Madeline a moment to realize that Lord Nothing meant she was the key to unlock the Lady's prison.

"But the Lady lives?" Mal'uud asked. "Hope can free her?"

"It is so."

Mal'uud rose. "Then we must make Hope whole and go to the Lady. She could stop the Horrors."

"These are two of many things we must do, Mal'uud." Lord Nothing lifted his arm out to one side, palm down. The Shadows slithered toward his hand. At the same time, pure darkness rose from the ground as though it'd been waiting there to answer his call. The blackness joined the rest of Lord Nothing's Shadows, and began to gather and swirl into a spinning globe the size of a basketball. "While I waited for my motes to plant seeds on Earth, a necessary sequence formed. This sequence was left for me to engage, and it is made of defenses against the Horrors. It is a sequence that has been long in the making, and in the waiting, I have been weakened. As I weaken, so too does my Lady, for without me, she starves, and without her, I languish and decay."

"There is only one way out of this war, then," Mal'uud simplified. "And it's this sequence of yours."

"But," Madeline said, shying away from Lord Nothing's raw power. "But what about Eeadian? You said he was a prisoner. Did the Horrors take him?"

"No, Hope Star. Eeadian is my ward. To save him, I shattered into heart and body and imprisoned him. Anything less, and he would have recovered and continued his path of destruction."

Madeline was rendered speechless, but Mal'uud was practically stalking in his impatience for action. "And where is this prison that holds the Warrior?"

"I have been sustaining myself by consuming that which was mine to make—"

"The Fortress," Mal'uud said in revelation. "That's why it's only partially destroyed."

"—as what I made with power bestowed upon me by my Lady and transformed into my design will not poison me. The rations have kept me as you see me. They gave me strength enough to spare Daanske a Horror fate, but I must limit myself to guard my wards. My reach goes no farther than this basin below and the ruins of my Fortress above."

The ball of power had steadily grown in diameter until it resembled a shining black beach ball. The whispers chattered, and the ball stopped spinning. Lord Nothing gathered his fingers into a point and touched their tips to the top of the ball. He spread his fingers and the ball shot downward into the earth, burrowing with liquid force into the seabed. Effortlessly and silently, the ball drilled a hole toward Topside.

"Water is a ward of the Fortress dungeons?" Mal'uud asked.

Lord Nothing gave a single, deliberate nod.

Madeline hugged herself for comfort. "But the Shadow Guardians chased us. If we go back, won't they...?" She looked to Mal'uud.

"They ushered you to me," Lord Nothing said.

"They nearly *killed* us," Madeline protested.

Lord Nothing appeared faintly amused. "If they had attempted to end you, then you would not have survived unscathed. They will not harm you, now, for they've done their duty."

The whispers suddenly stopped their susurration. Stepping to the hole in the ground, Lord Nothing gazed into it. His blurry edges grew more indistinct, as though the invisible flames were consuming him. His features melted into smooth darkness, the cracks in his skin widening until he was not a man but a man-like shape. Tendrils of power licked across the ground toward Madeline, and she jumped away from them as they reared and writhed through the air.

The whispers rose again in ferocious volume and pierced Madeline's ears like static feedback. "Come," they said, and Lord Nothing's voice was grainy and distant. "Water and the last pieces of the Star await us."

The air pressure crackled. Lord Nothing's form stretched and narrowed. Black sand hissed through the seabed's cracks, and Lord Nothing dove into the hole and vanished.

Chapter Nineteen

Jason stared at the place where Monica's car had been and thought somebody should go after her. Not him, obviously, as what could he do? Other than write not-so-comforting memos in the thin skim of dirt on her trunk, Jason was at a loss.

Knowing it wasn't his place to help didn't stop the urge to get in his van and chase Monica down. Maybe buy her some coffee. Maybe tell her that he completely understood needing to leave a situation even if nobody else could see why it was killing you. Why it was clouding up your head and making you think you'd never be any better than a servant to somebody else; a caregiver, overworked and never thanked.

He jerked away from the light touch on his arm, and he met Helen's deep, dark eyes. "Go," she whispered.

The hair on Jason's neck stood on end and dread knocked the wind out of him. Helen's features softened. She cupped his chin in her palm. "Not after her," she said, turning his head toward the road, "after him." She faced him toward the water.

"Shouldn't he be the one who—" Jason started to say with a glance at Mercutio.

"Not yet," Helen whispered. She backed away toward her nurse's ever-attentive care. "Go," she mouthed.

Mercutio put an arm around Helen as though he needed that anchor not to run off to destinations unknown, himself. Darryl stood with his eyes fixed on the ground and hands in his pockets. He looked thirty years older than he was. Miss Teedee had vanished off the side porch, no doubt to serve food to the guests and the customers in the Solarium. Jason's job was done, there. He'd already helped her prepare trays for lunch. He was free to follow Mercutio and Helen inside or to do as Helen had asked and go after his strange friend. Jason gnawed his lip.

Unable to conjure any words that might comfort Darryl and not wanting to appear contrite or uncaring, Jason clasped Darryl's shoulder before continuing in the direction Andrew had taken. He checked the gazebo for signs of Andrew life and found none, nor was Andrew in the garden's swing. When he got to the dock and the walking path that ran along the Sound's edge, Jason peered east toward the guest parking lot and the remnants of the marina. He didn't see a lone figure that way, and, after lingering a moment listening to the slap of water against wood, Jason took a chance and went west.

The paved path was narrow and in need of maintenance, its blacktop crumbling along the edges. Jason avoided stepping in duck crap and narrowly missed squishing a panicked chipmunk heading for its hidey hole. Humidity doused him in a sheen of moisture that the light breeze dried on his skin. The paved path was part of the Townsende Trail, which ended at a Nature Preserve some miles away from the Taylor Point House. They went through the historic shopping district, carved their way through several of the oldest communities in town, and when Jason encountered the first man wearing walking shorts and carrying a walking stick, he asked if the man had seen a tall kid running in dirt-stained clothes. The man said yes, and he pointed out a rougher dirt trail that cut closer to the water's edge.

The trail quickly moved away from the walking path, and woods sprung up between the trail and the path. Jason's shoes crunched over pebbles, sticks, leaves, and sand. The sound of lapping water filled his ears. Small vessels floated out in the sound, some working and some purely for pleasure.

Soon, Jason found Andrew sitting on a large, moss-covered rock with a view of the Sound and an old metal train bridge that Jason hoped was no longer in use under all that rust. The trees blocked the sunlight, offering deep shade and cooler temperatures, and Jason plucked his shirt away from his sweaty chest.

"Hey," Jason said to announce his arrival. When Andrew didn't respond, Jason climbed onto the rock and sat next to Andrew. It was wet and a clingy kind of cool that seeped through his shorts.

"You scared a snowy egret," Andrew said sadly when Jason had settled.

"Sorry."

Andrew shrugged. The water grass rippled, breaking the surface of the shallow water. Moss clumps floated in miniature bogs. Despite the mud factor and the proximity to shore, the water was a soothing shade of deep blue.

"Mama's gone," Andrew said.

"She'll be back," Jason reassured him. "She just needs time to think."

Andrew slowly shook his head. "You heard them. Mama and Darryl. It was bad, Jason. Real bad."

Jason didn't say that Monica and Darryl's fighting was positively civilized compared to what he and Judith used to do. Or he and Papa Jack, though those fights were over far faster what with Jason being unconscious and all. "Couples fight, Andrew. They get over it."

Andrew mashed his lips together and yanked off his ball cap. He spun it slowly in his hands. "Mama doesn't think I can love somebody."

"What?"

"When she left and she was talking about love and people... She thinks that I can't love somebody."

"I'm sure she didn't mean it like—"

"It's not exactly what she said," Andrew pressed on, "but she doesn't believe in people, that they can be good on the inside instead of twisted, which means she never really believed in love. Because you have to accept all parts of people to accept all parts of yourself so you can love them and love yourself."

"Well, hang on," Jason interrupted. "You don't necessarily want to accept all parts of all people, right? I mean, I hate to rain Hitler down on this parade, but..."

Andrew squinted at Jason as though Jason were speaking a foreign language Andrew more or less understood, but it pained him. "Not all people are people, Jason. Some are more purpose than people. And they choose that purpose over their human parts, and that purpose can be whatever they then choose to make of it."

"Oh," Jason said, for lack of any other way to convey that he'd need to ponder that one for a while.

"I'm talking about people who are mostly people and not other stuff, like big, mundo purposes and destinies. Mozart, Hitler, Jesus. You know."

"Did you just compare..." Jason shook his head to clear it. "Nevermind. I think I'm with you."

Andrew hummed a single note of satisfaction that his point had been received, and he went back to watching the water. "So it works back and forth, right? Vice-a-versa. If Mama thinks people are only out to hurt, she thinks people only hurt each other. Which means people have only hurt her. Or, oh." Andrew blinked a few times. "Oh. People have hurt her in ways that left marks. Scars. Places she can't get past because it hurts too much. So she doesn't love Darryl because she can't, not in the way she wants, and she doesn't know how to love me, though she tries, and she thinks I'm going to end up just like her – hurt and scarred – because she only knows what she understands about herself."

Flabbergasted, Jason tried to follow Andrew's line of thinking. "People also have bad days. Days when they think that the people-only-hurt-others kind of thing is more true than it is. So maybe your mom doesn't believe all that, but today she does because she had a fight with Darryl and she feels helpless."

Andrew fixed Jason with the closest thing Jason had ever seen to anger. "You think I'm dumb, too, don't you." It wasn't a question.

"No," Jason answered immediately. "I don't. Really. I think you're probably one of the most enlightened people I know. I mean, check out this conversation. But I think your kind of knowledge can be dangerous, too."

"Why?" Andrew demanded.

"Well, because when somebody thinks another person has a part of life's bigger picture figured out, occasionally that person fears the one who's done more work to understand. That fear usually doesn't go anyplace good. It can get violent."

Andrew scowled. "Mercutio would never hurt me."

"Wait, what?" Jason shook his head. "Since when are we talking about Tio?"

"You know we were." Andrew pulled his long legs to his chest and put a chin on one knee. "Don't play dumb."

"I don't have to play." Jason chuckled. "I'm not sure what's getting talked about, here."

"Oh." Andrew sighed. It was quiet for a long moment and then Andrew suddenly straightened. "Oh! You're enlightened, too. And you've been hurt for it!"

"Huh?"

"You've been hurt like Mama's been hurt."

"Oh, no, I've not been—"

Andrew spun toward Jason and grabbed his arm. "Mama was hurt 'cause she always tries to show people how they could be and you were hurt 'cause you see people as they are too well."

The ghost of a memory strangled Jason. He was in the studio with Judith and the band in the middle of the night. Jason might not be able to sing a note or play a chord, but he knew what sounded good and what didn't. For whatever reason, Judith valued that particular opinion. They'd do a cut, and they'd wait for him to give it a thumbs up or down. It was positively Roman, the way they'd kill an entire piece of music if Jason, the Emperor, voted to end its life.

Jason always had this role, especially there at the end, this veto power, but some days it was far more urgent than others. He could tell by the way Judith would stand in front of him in ragged fishnets, tops with pit stains that somehow managed to be sexy and not gross, and would stare him down, waiting for his answer.

"*What do you think? How did it sound to you*?"

On those days, the urgent days, she wasn't asking about the music. She was asking how she sounded. How she was. How she performed. Dozens of people around with more knowledge and weightier opinions backed by years of experience, and she wanted to know what he thought.

"*I trust you, Jason. You always know.*"

So there had been days when Jason had told her she was good even when she wasn't. He told the lie while gazing right into her eyes, because he knew if she didn't hear what she wanted to hear, she would never listen for his opinion again. His voice and the power he had to kill the truly awful crap that came out of the studio would be gone. He'd be the one vetoed, and she'd be even less merciful with him than she was with the music.

Jason was too hot beneath his clothing. "I guess."

Andrew gave Jason's arm a little shake. "You have to tell me your bad stuff."

"I have to what, now?"

"Tell me your bad," Andrew repeated with deadly seriousness. "Mama has bad stuff, and I thought I knew about it. Like my dad. He wasn't in a band and he didn't die but he hurt her and he left her. Today I realized I didn't know that her bad stuff is still hurting her. It's making her think that everybody is going to hurt me instead of love me."

"So, you think her 'bad stuff' is making her believe things that aren't true?" Jason asked, trying to steer the conversation away from the murky waters of his past and back onto dry land.

"Not just the believing but the doing, too. She thinks people are or still want to hurt her or... oh." His scowl of concentration was brief. "Oh. Use her. She can't show who she really is to people, or thinks she can't, so people can't love her any more than she can love anybody else, 'cause she doesn't trust them. But worse than that, I think she's afraid what's happened to her has rubbed off, that she's going to hurt me or thinks she already has. But it hasn't. I'm okay! I see Tio. I visit his house and plant flamingos so they can grow into hope trees."

"Of course you do," Jason said after a beat.

"But that's not the point."

"Then what is?"

"The bad stuff!" Andrew laughed and threw his ball cap into the water. "There. You're safe here with me. I've sacrificed something of mine so the water won't tell anybody our secrets."

"Water does that?" Jason asked.

"Oh yeah. Water's all connected and emotional and stuff."

"Yeah. I can see it. Sure."

Andrew shifted on the rock. "So go for it."

"All right, seriously, let me catch up. You want me to tell you bad things about myself—"

"Or that you've done."

"—or bad things I've done so that you can, what? Determine if those things are still bothering me?"

"No."

"What'd I get wrong?"

Andrew smiled with sparkling white teeth and infinite patience. "I already know the bad things are still bothering you. They still bother *everybody*. That's what I said: I realized bad things were still bothering Mama. And if she'd told me, if she'd trusted me, though I know it would have been hard for her, then I could have helped her.

"So, what I need you to do is tell me all your bad stuff so that I can do something to fix it before it makes you leave me, too. Because I cannot think of a thing to plant that would help me in a world where I lose my Mama and my best friend on the same day."

"So we're best friends?" Jason blurted.

"Yes," Andrew replied, simply.

Jason was touched. "Andrew, I'm not going anywhere today."

"Or in the same lifetime," Andrew amended.

"Well, eventually people do..." Jason rubbed his temples while Andrew gazed guilelessly at him. "Andrew, even if I tell you... You can't... It doesn't work like that. You can't fix other people's bad things."

"Not in the prevent them or stop them in the past kind of ways, no, but I can fix them bothering you in the now way."

"How do you think you can do that, exactly?"

Andrew rolled his eyes. "By listening, silly. It's what the people who fix bad things always do. But!" He held up a finger aimed at heaven. "You have to tell the *right* person. Because while some people are people and some people are purpose, other people are magic. They can do things that nobody else can do." He beamed. "So." Andrew made a go-ahead gesture with one hand.

Jason floundered. "What do you want me to say, here?"

"The truth."

"I don't... I can't do this."

"Why?"

"Well, for one, it's not what you need right now."

"It's only partially about what I need. It's also about what you need."

"That's my point, dude. We should be focused on you, here."

Andrew's shoulders drooped for a microsecond of defeat before determination straightened them again. "You came out here to help me, didn't you? To find me and to make me feel better?"

"Well, yeah."

"Telling me will help me."

There was no cunning in Andrew, no manipulation. He was being as straight with Jason as he knew how to be. Which, granted, was pretty damned crooked. Still, the kid had made several highly insightful points in the last ten minutes, and Jason thought he'd be dumb to ignore them. The conversation had been a bit like watching King Arthur go for the sword, if the sword was the meaning of life, and Andrew was playing the role of the skinny knight with a good heart who had the inner strength to pluck up the sword of knowledge and put it to good use.

Jason ran a hand through his hair. "Just anything?" Andrew gave him a solemn nod. Jason almost protested again, but Andrew had that We Can Be Here All Day and I'm Cool With It look.

"I used to cheat on Judith." Jason scrubbed his mouth with one hand to make sure it'd been his lips that had done the talking. He glanced at Andrew, who merely waited for Jason to continue.

"I mean, kind of. She and I, we were together, and we were sort of with this..." The image of Rage and blood returned. Guitar strings that would never strum a note. A piece of paper that said "I'm Sorry." An overturned chair. Exposed muscle and bone. "Sort of with this other person, too, only that part of the relationship wasn't sexual. At least not for me. For Judith, it was. She slept with the other person. Rage. We called him Rage. And sometimes she'd do that while I was in bed with both of them. Sometimes she'd tell me I couldn't have what she had, meaning two people or anyone at all. She would say she kept us both, fed us both food for life, and she could stop at any time. When she'd talk like that, it'd turn Rage on. He got off on having her as his reason for living. So they'd be there, going at it on the other queen bed in some hotel room, and I'm watching and not supposed to... to do anything with what I'm seeing, and sometimes she'd asked me if I wanted it. If I thought I deserved it. If I was worthy of what she had and was willing to give away."

"You like watching me give it to him, don't you Jason? Look at him. Gone. He's gone to bliss, and you can't follow."

Jason shuddered until Judith's smile faded in his mind. "And then, I'd go a little nuts. I'd find myself wandering around hotel hallways or lobbies or streets. I'd find some girl, and I'd fu—er. I'd have sex with her. Then I'd tell Judith about it the next day or whatever, and she'd scream at me and throw things. She'd say I wasn't worthy, and I'd tell her I didn't care if she thought I was, and she'd throw herself at me. Apologize. Be like this bad kitten, this little girl, and God it... Um." Jason glanced at Andrew, and couldn't read the kid's poker face. "It did it for me. Her needing me. Then we'd have sex to make up. She'd be fine after that, and for days Rage would sleep on the couch. She'd say she needed me all to herself, and I'd be so happy on those days. We'd talk about the music. She'd sing for me or play for me, and I'd tell her how amazing it all was. It was during one of those happier times when I got the tattoo."

"Which tattoo?" Andrew asked. "You've got more than one."

"The tree one."

"Let me see it."

"What, now?"

Andrew gave Jason a long-suffering look, and Jason sighed. He spun around on the rock and yanked his shirt up so it hung around his neck. Between his shoulder blades was a fist-sized, withered and blackened but anatomically correct heart. Growing out of the top of it, the veins its roots, was a burnt tree, the branch tips still on fire. On the dying branches were tiny people hanging like dead fruit. The words JUDITH'S HELL were written in gothic letters around the edges of the dark heart.

Andrew touched a finger between Jason's shoulders. Jason didn't jump anymore. He'd become accustomed to Andrew's odd sense of personal boundaries. Kind of even liked them.

"Keep going."

Jason swung his legs around so he faced the water. "There was a lot of bad stuff between us," he said, pulling his shirt on. "Judith and me, I mean. Drugs. Sex. History. She'd talk about how she wanted to set the world on fire and one time, she said – now, she was high, but she said it – that I was her muse. I was her meaning and a gift meant for her alone to show her that her hellish way was the way to go." Jason considered, lost in a cloud of memory laced with Judith's perfume and the feel of her dreads in his hand. "I guess Rage wasn't the only one who wanted her all to himself. I wanted to be hers and nobody else's. I think everybody who met her did, a little.

"But even while I'm neck-deep in it, while I'm there and holding her at night and listening to Rage snore, I'm thinking, 'Dude, this isn't right. This isn't real. This isn't... love.' I tried to talk to Rage about it a few times, but he didn't like talking. He always told me I talked too much. I worried too much.

"So I guess I understand when you talk about how your mom doesn't know how to love 'cause of the stuff that happened to her and that she's afraid she'll hurt you because of it. For what it's worth, I think that makes her the best kind of mom. Rage and me, we didn't stand a chance of figuring out what real love is. Papa Jack, the guy who raised me? I never heard what happened to him or if he was just born with a real love of boxing, but he didn't know how to care about me, and he for darn sure didn't care if he hurt me in the process."

Andrew waited as though checking to see if Jason was done before he spoke. "Oh, oh. You got planted into the wrong family. It happens. The wrong person found you or someone who was supposed to find you didn't find you in time. A lesser person got to you first."

Jason blinked hard at the horizon. "I guess that's one way of looking at it."

"It is." Andrew nudged Jason with his shoulder. "You had to find the people you belong with, that's all. Your family wasn't it. Judith's Hell wasn't it. But we are."

Jason had to smile. "Think so, huh?"

"I wouldn't have said it if I didn't think it."

"No. You wouldn't."

"You're right. About Mama. She needs time. She needs to go make some and gather some, and then she'll feel better. And while she's gone, I'll think about how to show her that love won't hurt me because I understand it. I'm capable of understanding it because..." He chuckled, and his eyes shone with unshed tears. "If there is one thing we are very good at, here, it's loving those who are hard to love."

"Cool. I'll fit right in."

Andrew put an arm around Jason's shoulders. "Always."

Jason swallowed and tried not to squirm when faced with such naked acceptance. "Should we head back?"

"Not yet. The water's lonely and it likes us."

"Okay," Jason said softly. In that moment, staying to keep the Sound company was the best idea he'd heard since he'd followed the fisherman's summons and met Miss Teedee in the diner.

Chapter Twenty

Lord Nothing's absence was a tremendous and instantaneous relief, which turned out to be all-too temporary. Madeline stood a good ten feet away from the hole in the underside of the world contemplating whether and how to run or where to go, when tendrils of inky night shot out of the hole, snared her ankle, and dragged her across broken seabed.

Mal'uud's cry of surprised outrage echoed Madeline's and then down—

(*up*)

—she went. The hole was barely wide enough for her to fit. Her arms and legs and hips banged on the sides of the smooth walls, and their touch was cold enough to freeze her skin. Madeline thought she must be screaming, but the speed and the confined space stole the sound. The void swallowed it, just as she felt it was engulfing her, and for infinitely long, terrifying seconds, Madeline was sure her fate was to fall and fall. Her destiny was in the falling, and faintly, as though somebody else recounted the memory to her, she recalled another fall—

(from the sky, from her sisters, toward the ground, toward the infinite blue)

—and when she reached the other end of Lord Nothing's tunnel and landed on cool, stone floors, Madeline was crying hysterically. At once she floated out of herself, the grief and the pain too much to bear, and she stood apart from herself. Madeline saw her body sprawled on black stone. She observed her messy hair, her ill-fitting clothes, her broken, chewed fingernails. She saw Mal'uud leap out of the hole and land in a crouch, as though he was dragged through tunnels all the time. Mal'uud narrowed eyes at Madeline, who was screeching, babbling, calling out about exhaustion, fear, and loneliness. All the sorrows of all the lifetimes were in those incoherent words, and Madeline felt a twinge of pity. She wanted to go to that poor girl on the floor and tell her that she should accept the inevitable and stop feeling sorry for herself and what was fated to happen. Being too long with humanity had poisoned her, but that wasn't her fault, and soon she'd remember the way she was supposed to be. Soon what worried and bothered her would seem alien and distant, and until then, she didn't need to lay around screaming and crying.

Before she could move, go to herself and try to talk sense into herself, Lord Nothing manifested from the shadows. He crossed to Madeline, slowly lowered himself to one knee, and placed a wide, long-fingered hand on her head.

Madeline blinked, and she was back in her own body. Panic was gone. Fear had diminished to a mere dot on the emotional horizon. Her mind and limbs were pleasantly numb. Anesthetized. Like when she had to get her wisdom teeth out when she was eighteen, and she'd woken up in the recovery room with a mouth full of cotton and a head full of fluffy pink insulation. It took focus to use her eyes and to blink. She stared at Lord Nothing's boots until they flexed with movement. He walked away, and slowly, Madeline sat up. The estranged sensation was gone.

She was entirely one self, and the split-personality sensation was in her head as though she'd woken up from a dream. She remembered it, how calm that other version of herself had been, but that version of herself had gone back to sleep or had gone wherever she went when Madeline was in her right—

(*human*)

—mind. Now the only thing that mattered was where Lord Nothing's tunnel had led her. Looking around, Madeline observed she was sitting in a square chamber about fifteen feet to a side. There were torches on the walls at even intervals, and their flames burned green, not red. In an alcove to Madeline's right was a set of stairs that led up to a landing before turning a corner and presumably climbing higher. The ceiling was about twelve feet high, and on every wall were huge canvas paintings in heavy gilt frames. The paintings were of benign, if unusual scenes. Strange landscapes, odd skies with too many moons, houses, trees, they all appeared to be approaching human or familiar to Madeline, but not quite.

"Where are we?" Madeline asked in a sleepy monotone. She put her fingertips to her mouth to feel her lips move as she formed words. "And what did you do to me?"

Lord Nothing swept across the room, and Madeline wanted to warn him about the hole in the ground, but Lord Nothing crossed it as though it wasn't a problem. After he'd passed over it, the hole was gone. "Welcome to my underground keep," Lord Nothing said. He removed a torch from its holder. He was taller, here. His head almost brushed the ceiling. His eyes glinted silver and red in the green light, and he paused to stand on the far side of the room as though waiting for them to follow.

"He absorbed your hysteria," Mal'uud answered. He helped Madeline to her feet. "It is a great kindness."

Madeline wasn't so sure about that. In fact, she was pretty certain that Lord Nothing absorbing anything of her was an awful concept that she should avoid at all cost. She waited to be afraid or righteously indignant about the invasion, but all she felt was sleepy. When she walked, the room wavered as though she swam through reality. "I feel funny," she stated.

"It will fade," Mal'uud promised.

"Why do I feel funny?"

"Because," Mal'uud explained while Madeline leaned heavily against him, "he removed your emotions with a skilled blade. They are not merely diminished. Your fear, all your fear that you generated in that moment, is gone."

Madeline wanted to sit down and think about that for a while, but Mal'uud had other ideas. He led her to where Lord Nothing stood, and Madeline suddenly saw that what she had thought was a solid rear wall in the initial chamber was actually a corner. Around it was a hallway which extended for maybe eight feet before it took an abrupt turn to the right. The closest wall of the hallway in the initial chamber matched the continuing wall of the room in a perfect optical illusion.

"It's a maze," Madeline murmured.

"As are most things," Lord Nothing commented from ahead of them. He walked confidently though the identical hallways, taking turns that Madeline could not predict. Mal'uud and Madeline progressed at a slower pace, but they kept up. The last thing anyone would want would be to be lost down here. The floor, the walls, and the ceiling were all the same shade of gray stone. The seams of the stones were identical, impossible to distinguish from one another. There was no water stain, no mold, mildew, or even mineral growth, and though pictures hung on the walls, even they added to the confusion instead of alleviating it. All the frames appeared the same, despite their embellished gilt intricacies. The paintings were the same size and spaced precisely the same width from one another. Some walls did seem to have two paintings and others three or four, but invariably the paintings were set so that they appeared to be hung from two walls forming a corner of a dead end instead of one painting being on a short wall and the other being on a rear wall of a new hallway.

Never had Madeline felt such sympathy for rats in an experimental labyrinth. The lack of features combined with the murky green light would have had Madeline running into walls or convinced there was no way out even when there was. She had no bearings, no idea from which direction she'd come or in what direction they were going. Quickly, Madeline stopped studying the maze and started examining the paintings. They were beautiful things, clearly created with much skill. The brush strokes were thick and short, layering the image onto the canvas in a way that made it leap toward the viewing eye.

They passed a valley, deep and lush but surrounded on all sides by fire. Next was an hourglass full of water drops, not sand. In the bottom of the glass was an old man calmly sitting in a rocking chair who was unaware that he would surely drown. The next several paintings were portraits, though the subjects were not human. One woman was blue-green and dressed in fur. Another painting showed a nude man with human parts except for the addition of a tail and two extra eyes, one between the usual two and the other in his forehead. The background of these portraits was simple gray, but the next painting was different and, for whatever reason, made Madeline slow down to view it.

The little girl stood on what Madeline thought might be volcanic rock with glowing, red-hot lava flowing through the crevices. Steam rose around the girl's bare feet. In the far distance appeared a mountain range lit not only by runnels of lava but also by white lights, as though people lived in homes perched in the peaks. Like the other portraits, this girl didn't appear human. Her arms were impossibly long, hairy and ape-like, with her hands hanging around her knees. Her hands were too big for her body, and she had seven fingers per hand, not five. Her hair was curly and thick, standing out from her scalp in shiny waves. Her mouth was large with full lips, her nose was long, but her eyes were tiny; black beads sunk into the flesh. The effect should have been comical, even cartoonish, but Madeline was struck with a wave of misery and a vague sense of danger. If she lingered too long, played staring games with this creature one too many times, she would find herself in the painting and the girl free and laughing at her from the hallway.

Madeline reeled away from the portrait, hurrying a few steps to catch up with Mal'uud. When she looked back, the girl in the painting had moved. Her distorted face was mashed against the painting as though the canvas were a layer of glass. One hand was up, reaching toward Madeline, and seven claws dug into the invisible barrier that kept the creature in the painting.

"They're trapped," Madeline whispered to Mal'uud. Until that moment, Madeline hadn't noticed that Mal'uud walked the hallways with his eyes firmly fixed on Lord Nothing's cloak. He didn't want to look, and Madeline wished she hadn't. "The things in the paintings, they're prisoners, aren't they?"

"No more than you are a prisoner of your own reality," Lord Nothing said. The acoustics of the walls made it seem as though he spoke from beside her, not in front of her, and Madeline jumped. "The things you see in the landscapes I've frozen have made their cages."

"Frozen?" Madeline asked.

"Preserved," Lord Nothing added. "Made to stand still."

"They're his energy stores," Mal'uud chimed in. "Things he could not or has not yet consumed."

"Why not?" Madeline asked.

"Because my Lady did not wish to remake them, as yet," Lord Nothing intoned.

"Where did they come from?"

"Every and all where," Lord Nothing replied, almost dreamily. His lengthy sigh oozed over Madeline's exposed skin. She fought the urge to scrub at her arms with her nails.

"And these don't poison you, because they're not..."

"In me," Lord Nothing finished for her. "Correct, Hope Star. But even here, I feel their weight."

"But if you can freeze anything in a painting from anywhere, then why not freeze the Horrors? Stop them?"

"Because their weight would have been too much," Lord Nothing replied. "I am not the cage for that task."

Lord Nothing took a small step closer, and Madeline couldn't back up, else she walk into a painting and feel whatever entity it trapped clawing at her, trying to get out.

"We're sorry, my Lord Nothing, we—"

"Be calm, Mal'uud." Lord Nothing's gusty sigh stirred the hallway's green flames into a dizzying dance. "Hope Star, your questions remind me that the sequence I formed after the imbalance was one designed from loss of choice." To Madeline's utter astonishment, a silvery tear trekked down Lord Nothing's cheek. "I am tremendous in my existence, but that existence depends upon my Lady. Together, we are creatures of unparalleled symmetry. Apart, we are equally unarmed. The failsafe of Via'rra knows all there is of all of us. It had marked the Walkers as the enemies, for it was Walkers that upset the world, and it knew to take my Lady away first, rendering me powerless to fight directly. Without her to feed, I could no longer absorb. Without me to feed her, she could no longer create. What I could do, what I could save, I did. I live with the knowledge that it could never be enough.

"I have also existed in an imbalance wherein the Guiding Star could no longer light the path which I did not dare to take. You were no longer the guardian of what is good in this world, leaving me to choose as I saw fit. You abandoned your purpose. You succumbed to the fear of your one truest and most powerful believer.

"I do not resent you for this, for I understand your nature. I trapped Water because it is my nature to unmake that which serves no purpose. He had corrupted himself, and that corruption had no place in our land. What he chose did anger me. I lost my Lady because he wanted to keep that which was not his. He wished for stagnation in a reality that relies on endless change.

"But I am without resentment at this moment, however, as we stand on the brink of freeing Water. Such emotions are petty and short lived. We are all now less than we were. We have forgotten what it is to be whole. We must face our reality as it is, not as we wish it could be. My sequence and my power could mean the eventual righting of the world. But I cannot do it alone. I never could. We were not designed that way." Lord Nothing lifted a hand toward Madeline's cheek, though he did not touch her. "Do you understand more of my purpose and of the purpose you abandoned but which still awaits you, Hope Star?"

Madeline trembled so hard she nearly fell. She'd been thinking of this world and the Walkers as "other," even while fighting and surviving amid the chaos Mal'uud told her started because of the choices she made. She wanted to believe that everything had been her Blue's fault; that it was his madness that was to blame. But that wasn't entirely true. She, too, was culpable, here. The fact that these gods didn't blame her – didn't want to shatter her, trap her in a painting, or do worse – was a grace she couldn't believe she deserved.

And for the first time, she understood that Via'rra and all within it and all it touched was her home. If this place and these creatures needed her so badly that they would forgive her this much, then it was time to stop being afraid and start trying to be worthy of the faith they had in her.

Madeline started to fall to her knees and beg forgiveness, to thank Lord Nothing for his generosity, to apologize again to Mal'uud, but the actions and words would ring hollow here, in the ruins of a god's palace that had tumbled by her indirect hand.

Instead, Madeline met Lord Nothing's gaze and asked the question she should have been asking all along: "What can I do to help fix that which I helped to break?"

Lord Nothing favored her with the hints of a smile. "Continue to become more of yourself. Proximity to the last piece of your consciousness, which Eeadian possesses, has brought you closer to whole. Follow that path and have patience with your brethren whose pieces are scattered wider than even your own." Lord Nothing stepped to a painting of what appeared to be dense fog obscuring a strip of land. A distant shape and play of light suggested a house with somebody home. "Go into this cell and retrieve Eeadian and what he guards."

"Which is what?" Mal'uud asked.

Lord Nothing appeared sad. "More of the Star and the last piece of my Lady's power which I still possess."

"You left a shard of power with a prisoner?"

"It was necessary to create a cage strong enough to contain a force such as Water." Lord Nothing touched the edge of the picture's frame. The brushstrokes flattened, the painting deepened, and suddenly Madeline wasn't looking at an image but at a real place that existed beyond the frame's threshold.

"Go," Lord Nothing commanded, and his word was law.

Mal'uud went first, jumping over the painting's bottom ledge and vanishing into the thick mist. Madeline followed more cautiously, unsure of what kind of ground she'd find hidden by the fog. She extended one foot, found something solid, and put her weight on it. When she'd cleared the painting's frame, she expected it to disappear, but it and Lord Nothing remained.

"Are you coming, My Lord?" she asked.

"I cannot. If Eeadian senses me, it will do no good for our cause. Go to him. Free him. I will wait."

Nodding, Madeline turned and took several wary steps forward. She heard splashing, as though she walked through a puddle, and she bent to inspect the ground. Her reflection wavered at her beneath the shimmering, dark gray surface. She appeared to be walking on water. Madeline touched it, and her fingertips met the same resistance as her feet.

"Illusion." Mal'uud's voice came from her left, and it was closer than Madeline thought. She jerked in surprise, stood, and Mal'uud emerged from the mist. "It is a lake, I believe, but only in appearance, not substance."

"Why? I mean, what is this place?"

Mal'uud scowled. "I assume it's manifested by Water, himself, or perhaps built by Lord Nothing. It would not be the first time he built an elaborate illusion to serve as a prison."

"What do you mean?"

Mal'uud shook his head with a frustrated growl. "I am not sure." He gestured ahead of them. "Toward the music."

"What music?"

"Listen."

In the hush, Madeline strained to hear. At first, there was nothing but the distant, gentle lap of water against a shoreline. Then she heard what could have been a note. And then another. And another. She couldn't make out the tune or if it was, in fact, a song and not someone blowing single notes on an instrument without any melody.

"I hear it," she said. "And I hear the shore, I think."

"Yes." Mal'uud took her wrist in his hand, but not with force. "This way."

They walked side by side through the fog. Madeline could detect no source for the light reflecting off the white whorls. The air smelled stale. Faintly acrid. One day when she'd been a teenager, her adopted mother had decided to clean out the attic. They'd found a trunk full of old knitted scarves and blankets that had belonged to a former generation of Bancs. They'd smelled like this, like frozen time.

The shore appeared all at once. One second they were lost on a silent lake, and the next they had their toes in muddy grasses. They climbed up the steep bank, and paused when they'd reached level ground.

A bloated full moon hovered directly above them, casting the landscape into shades of gray, black, and white. About thirty yards ahead stood a simple, two-story cottage with white siding and lattice trim. The front porch was covered and wrapped around the western side of the home, and another porch came off the eastern side and stepped down into a modest garden. Someone had put up a fence around the healthy tomato plants. A scarecrow perched on a stick like a happy overlord, his big, floppy hat askew and his coat unbuttoned to show his straw insides. Big maple and oak trees grew around the white house, their leaves lush and green, and a tire swing hung from one low branch. At the apex of the roof, above one dormer window, a weather vane aimed south.

Warm yellow light filtered through the sheer lace curtains over the ground floor windows. A stone path flanked by more trees led away from the front porch steps and widened to become a lane that ended a few feet from where Madeline and Mal'uud stood. Off to their left, in the shade of a forked white birch, were a stone bench and a birdbath, as though this were the owner's favorite place to sit and watch the water.

Butterflies beat against Madeline's insides. Her skin went clammy. Chills raced up and down her spine, and she clasped Mal'uud's hand, the strength in it when he returned the favor was comforting.

Madeline took a step forward, but Mal'uud tugged her back. He lifted his free hand to point, and Madeline saw the woman in red. Madeline had no idea where the woman had come from. There was no car, no other visible point of entry to the fog house. Madeline hadn't seen her even a second before, walking along the side or through the garden or the trees.

Nevertheless, a woman with long blonde hair wearing a skin tight, blood red dress and matching four-inch heels slowly sauntered up the porch stairs. She didn't knock. Instead, she pushed the front door open and shut it carefully behind her.

"Maybe she lives here?" Madeline said in a low voice above a whisper.

Mal'uud put a finger to his lips and cocked his head. Madeline waited with him, and as the seconds ticked by, her anxiety spiraled up and up until she was choking on it. Her insides went loose. Adrenaline shot through her veins, and she fought the urge to turn and flee across the water. Being back in Lord Nothing's underground keep with the creepy paintings would be better than standing here staring at the house that was not a house. Madeline kept expecting it to waver, distort, and blur before reforming into a ruined castle in hell. The longer the image held, the more awful it became to stare at it.

Madeline tried to count backward, tried to breathe, and just when she thought she would lose her mind, snap and bolt, a man's unearthly scream ripped out of the cottage. The force and fear in the sound hit Madeline like a death blow to the gut. Madeline flung herself at Mal'uud, who caught and held her to his side, and she felt him trembling as the scream went on and on and on. It rose higher in pitch, pleaded and begged for something to stop, please, please, please stop. Frantic sobs tainted the next wailing scream which rose in volume to the point that Madeline wrapped an arm around her head, trying to drown it out.

The man screamed until it was no more than a warble followed by silence, his voice shredded. The woman did not come out of the house. Instead, all the lights in all the windows dimmed, the music stopped playing, and the weathervane slowly swung to point north.

When it was over, Mal'uud and Madeline clung to one another. Madeline couldn't stop staring at the front door. She kept waiting for the woman to appear, knife or other weapon in hand. Madeline wanted a target. She wanted that woman to reappear so Mal'uud could change into his scorpion-cat form and shred her to pieces. Any second now, and the murderer would emerge, thinking herself triumphant.

Nobody came out onto the peaceful white plank porch, but while Madeline watched, the front door slowly swung inward, opening into darkness.

"Wait," Mal'uud growled, but Madeline was already moving. Inside the house might be a murderous demon ready to bleed her one drop at a time or a vortex that would take her straight to a metal box too small for her to stand or lay down or any other number of horrors.

But she'd known that voice. Even full of terror and pain, she knew it. She'd heard the screaming man singing to her sweetly in her dreams. If he was hurt or dead, Madeline had to know. She had to *see.*

Madeline streaked across the yard and flew up the porch steps. She hesitated for half a heartbeat at the door's threshold before conjuring her last shreds of courage and stepping inside. She braced, waiting for an attack, but nothing came at her. The moon's light filtered in through the windows illuminating a small, empty foyer with bare walls. To the left was a living room with dusty hardwood floors, a cold stone fireplace, and a murky bay window. There were cracks in the sheetrock and a water stain spreading across the plaster ceiling. Madeline peered around a corner to see two open pocket doors at the far end of the living room. They led into what Madeline thought might be the dining room. A picture frame hung on a dingy wall, but there was no painting or photograph in it. Tatters of wall paper trim drooped from the corners of the dining area and wires stuck out of a hole where once might have been a light fixture. Madeline inched into the living area, sensing Mal'uud behind her, now, in the foyer. She made a *come on* gesture but stopped in her tracks when she heard the whooshing sound that accompanied a pilot light being lit.

Flames appeared in the fireplace and cheerfully lit the room. Cushions appeared on a couch-bench which was suddenly tucked into the bay window. A lush rug manifested beneath their feet. Wallpaper with tiny flowering vines unfurled up the bare walls until it covered them. A crystal light fixture grew out of the living room ceiling to dangle above a striped sofa and set of chairs facing the fire. A table popped into existence in the dining room. It was set at one end for two, complete with candles and fine china. A chandelier spun into place around the bare wires, and a picture of the house in springtime filled the formerly empty frame. Lemon polish and spices floated in the air. The fabrics and patterns and lack of electronics reminded Madeline of her grandmother's home.

A heavy oak sideboard emerged from the wall at Madeline and Mal'uud's back. As they stumbled out of the way, a middle panel opened, revealing a record player recessed in the sideboard. The needle was already set. Music started up as though the power had come back on, and the player resumed its tune.

"By the fear," Mal'uud whispered.

Billie Holiday crooned "*I'm a Fool to Want You*," and a man said, "Aw, shoot!"

Taking each step like the floor might crumble, Madeline tiptoed through the living room. She could feel heat coming from the fireplace and even from the lit candles on the dining room table. She smelled food, done almost to the point of burned, and she saw that the kitchen was in the very back of the house conveniently next to the formal dining room. A swinging door stood propped open with a jeweled doorstop, and Madeline watched a tall, slim man pull a baking pan out of the oven. He set the pan onto the stovetop, dropping the dishtowel he used to protect his skin. He wrung his hand as though the pan had burned him despite the towel, and he absently sucked a thumb as he went to the old fashioned refrigerator and removed a bottle of wine.

"You were always better at this than me," the man said with a laugh.

Mal'uud and Madeline flinched, and Mal'uud hunkered low. Madeline circled the dining room confirming it was empty, and she expected to find someone else in the kitchen when she crossed the threshold, but there was no one seated in the small table in the breakfast nook. There was nobody perched on the stools at the tiled counter. The pantry door was open, and there was nothing in there but shelves of canned goods and sacks of grain. On the left wall of the kitchen was a hallway leading farther into the house, but it was dark and empty. The door at the end of that hallway was shut and did not open.

"Oh well, practice makes perfect, right?" the man asked.

Madeline and Mal'uud exchanged glances. Nobody answered, but the lack of response didn't seem to bother the man. "Hello?" Madeline tried, her voice a hoarse croak.

The man didn't look up. He hummed along to the song, which had started over, and he fetched two glasses from the cupboard and a cork screw from a drawer. He was even-featured and handsome, though his hair was stark white and standing up in stiff waves. The style seemed intentional. He wore brown slacks, a crisp white dress shirt, and a navy blue suit vest and undone tie. His cuffs were rolled to show tanned forearms. His face was flushed from heat, exertion, or maybe a touch too much sun.

"Do you know him?" Madeline asked Mal'uud, who shook his head.

"You don't know him, either?"

"No," Madeline replied. This was not her Blue. Or, at least, it wasn't him in any form he'd ever taken in her dreams. "Could he be in his Walking form?"

Mal'uud climbed on top of the breakfast nook table and sank into a crouch. The white-haired man paid no attention to the perching King of Nightmare. "Perhaps," Mal'uud answered Madeline. "I don't know of any stories of Water going to other worlds, though he must have had the capability."

Mal'uud's logic made sense, though it appeared it'd been several decades since Water had traveled to the human realm. "Why can't he see us?" Madeline asked. She waved her hands in the air, trying to get the man's attention. The cork popped free of the bottle and he poured the wine until both glasses wee full to the rim. He swept around the counter and walked into the dining room. He passed within inches of Madeline's shoulder.

"I do not know," Mal'uud said softly.

A clock hanging from the kitchen wall ticked. It was five minutes until eight, and Madeline was sure time was running out. "How are we supposed to free him if he can't see us?"

Mal'uud climbed off the table and strode over to the white haired man. He lifted both his hands and tried to shove the white haired man. Mal'uud's hands made contact with the white haired man's back, but nothing happened. Mal'uud's bones and sinew flexed with the force he tried to exert, but it didn't seem to matter. The man didn't flinch or move, continuing to set down the salad bowl and make minute adjustments to the silverware.

"I used the fine china," the white haired man said. "Your mother's. You always loved these plates. They're just dishware, but..." The man trailed off and traced the edge of a dinner plate with his finger.

"I can touch him," Mal'uud said. "But I cannot affect him."

Madeline mentally flailed. "What about everything else?"

Mal'uud reached for a wine glass and successfully scooted it away. When Mal'uud let go, the glass snapped back to its original position as though yanked by a tether. Not a drop spilled. Mal'uud picked up a plate and threw it across the room. The plate bounced, spun in midair, and returned to its place in the blink of an eye. The man continued to pay no attention whatsoever.

"What in the world..." Madeline's voice trailed off to a murmur, and the man rushed by her, heading to the stove. He smelled like sweet aftershave and, faintly, of cigar smoke. A strange combination of déjà vu and nostalgia crept through Madeline to mix with the ever-present fear.

"It seems we cannot affect this plane of existence," Mal'uud said.

"But we have to, don't we? Otherwise, won't whatever is happening just keep on happening?"

"Again, I do not know, Hope Star." Mal'uud went into the living room, and Madeline left the oblivious man in the kitchen.

"We are to retrieve a shard of power, your essence, and Water," Mal'uud said while gliding one hand across the fireplace's mantel. "See if you can find a clue that may lead to any of these things."

Madeline went to the sofa and managed to remove a couch cushion and glance under it before it flew out of her hands to return to its place. "What would the shard or my essence even look like?"

Mal'uud felt along the coffee table. "What do you remember of your dreams? Were there any clues?"

"Clues? Like what?"

"Like an idea as to where the man in your dreams might hide an object dear to him?"

The clock in the kitchen struck the hour with a cheerful ringing of chimes. Panic flooded Madeline and froze her in place. "I don't know."

"Or perhaps where he'd hide himself? Where he'd go?"

It was getting hard to breathe. The heat from the fire was suffocating. The music was deafening. Madeline thought she might faint. "I... I don't..."

"Think."

The chimes began to count the hour. "I'm trying."

"Perhaps try harder," Mal'uud suggested.

The clock finished its count, went silent, and the front door opened. "We're too late," Madeline whispered as the woman in red walked into the house. Madeline staggered around a chair and stood next to Mal'uud in front of the fire. A moment ago, it'd been too hot. Now the fire still blazed, but without heat. A chill had stolen into the air.

The woman paused in the foyer to smooth her dress. It hugged her curves and showed off her breasts. Her blonde hair spilled across her shoulders, and her blue eyes were huge in her heart-shaped face. She seemed at once familiar and utterly alien; human but not, a friend but also someone who'd backstab her own mother. She smiled at them, or maybe not at them, exactly, but in their direction. Her teeth were straight and even, sparkling white beneath her blood red lipstick.

"Honey?" the white haired man called. "Is that you?"

The woman didn't answer, but she strolled into the living room and stood in front of the sideboard. In unison, Madeline and Mal'uud inched closer to the dining room to get away from the woman. She filled the room with a miasma that would rival Lord Nothing.

"Be on your guard," Mal'uud murmured to Madeline, and the woman in red shot Mal'uud an icy glare.

"She sees us," Madeline whispered, suddenly afraid to move an inch.

"Or perhaps understands that we are distortions in her world," Mal'uud replied.

The white haired man hurried into the dining room to set a pan of pot roast and vegetables on the table. He smiled at his guest, and his welcoming attitude made Madeline want to weep. He should be going for the knives at the sight of this woman, not gazing at her like a love sick puppy. "Just in time. I made your favorite."

The woman returned the smile but said nothing. The white haired man joined them in the living room. He bit his lip and crossed his arms. "Yes, I know. I never cook. But it's a special occasion."

The woman tipped her head, not speaking, but the man clearly heard something because he spoke as though she had. "I have a confession." He took a deep breath. "The doctor called this afternoon while you were out." Actual tears filled his eyes, and his grin split his face. "Positive. The test was positive, my love. The treatments worked."

The white haired man approached the woman in red, and Madeline started to go to him to stop him, but Mal'uud grabbed her and held her.

"We're going to be a family," the white-haired man said. "Oh, honey." He opened his arms and went to the woman. She clasped his forearms, stopping him just shy of an embrace. "Sweetheart?" the man asked. "What is it? What's wrong?"

The woman's smile didn't waver when blood began to rush between her teeth and run down her chin.

"Oh my God." The white haired man yanked off his vest and reached as though he'd wipe up the blood, but a precise, thin line sliced across the front of the woman's throat. A gush of red struck the man square in the eyes, and the woman kept smiling as the man let out a startled cry.

"No," the man said, wiping his face while dark, black blood began to spill out the woman's nose. "No, no, no, no..." he chanted, again trying to go to her, to put pressure on the wounds, to try to help.

The woman jerked backward as though she'd been shoved. She spread her arms and legs as though being splayed by invisible bonds. Her head flopped backward, the gash in her throat cutting cleanly through muscle and severing bone so a thin hunk of meat held on her head. Gore glistened and with a sickening crack, the woman's arms and legs came free of their sockets. They snapped backward at the elbows and knees and then again at the shins and forearms, thighs and upper arms. Madeline didn't know when the man had begun to scream, because she was screaming with him. She and Mal'uud were huddled in the corner of the living room. The music's volume amplified, the words drilling through her eardrums alongside the white haired man's futile wails for mercy.

In the end, the woman began to vibrate, to shake like a paint can in an automatic mixer, and Madeline ducked her head to her chest. She heard the woman explode or rupture or whatever awful thing happened, and hot spray struck Madeline's naked arms. She was too horrified to catch enough breath to keep screaming, so she heard the white haired man say, in a voice so raw it was like listening to water dash against rocks and form words: "I just wanted a normal life and you."

And then the music stopped, the warm stickiness on Madeline's skin vanished, and the house was still, silent, and empty once again.

Chapter Twenty-One

In the chilly, gray aftermath of the illusion's violent conclusion, Nightmare braced to endure the Hope Star's hysteria. It seemed the closer she got to the missing piece of herself, the more courage and strength she found, but she was still frail. Nightmare's hopes that Lord Nothing would fix her as easily as the Master of Shadows had renewed Nightmare's energy with but a single kiss had been fleeting. His secondary hope that upon entering Water's prison they would quickly find what they needed to restore Hope, free Water, and get out of Lord Nothing's domain as fast as possible was also dying on the vine. It was not Lord Nothing's way to give direct and concise instruction. His father's mind simply did not think in linear lines but rather in concentric circles. Nightmare and the Star would have to find their own understanding of the painting's strange circumstances, and they would have to do it together.

Tentatively, Nightmare nudged Hope's shoulder. She uncovered her face and resumed her ragged breathing. Nightmare sympathized. He had to admit, the illusion had been monstrous. He'd seen his fair share of tortured souls and endless agonies and battles between creatures that would ruin the peace of any warrior, but the very environment in Lord Nothing's prison was toxic. Each and every passing second they spent in the painting's world destroyed another molecule of Nightmare's resolve. There'd been a moment upon observing the white-haired man in the kitchen in which Nightmare had completely forgotten why they were there. He'd been lost trying to recall how it was that he knew this odd man and how, precisely, Nightmare had come to be a guest for dinner.

Nightmare didn't believe Hope was similarly affected by the illusion, but he couldn't be sure until she spoke or moved. "We must act," he said, standing up and hoping she would follow his lead without him having to bodily drag her. "The illusion will begin again any second."

"I know." Hope's voice was thin and threadbare.

Nightmare helped her to her feet. "We must complete our mission."

Hope nodded just as the cycle began once again. The thrum of the power needed to restart the prison's illusion quaked Nightmare's bones. He and Hope raced to the kitchen. There was the man, his wine, and his banal one-sided conversation.

"A shard of power," Hope murmured.

"Yes," Nightmare said. And a piece of her, as well. But where? And how?

Beneath his feet, he swore he felt a tremor; one that had to come from the very foundation of Via'rra. A storm was coming. Possibly something worse.

Hurry, he thought. They had to hurry.

Frantically, Nightmare began opening and closing all the cupboards in the kitchen. He and the prisoner danced around one another, the force of the man knocking Nightmare to one side or the other.

Hope searched the dining room and living room. The music stopped, started, and stopped again. Around them, the house shook as though it were about to fall. Plaster crashed to the floor from the ceiling. Dust flew. Madeline screamed from the living room, and Nightmare stood in the kitchen, frozen. For a moment, there was utter silence.

The prisoner broke his pattern and slammed a fist onto the counter. His shoulders hunched and bunched and were distinctly inhuman; so unlike the flustered man-husband he wished to portray.

"You… are… *ruining it.*" He suddenly wheeled on Nightmare. The prisoner's eyes had reptilian, vertical slits. They were brilliant yellow and green. The prisoner took Nightmare by the throat and slammed him against a wall. The house shook in earnest. Nightmare clawed at the prisoner's hand, but it was no use. The man was strong. So very, very strong.

"Mal'uud!" Hope yelled, coming around the corner.

"Stop ruining it!" the prisoner bellowed in Nightmare's face. His breath was hot and acrid. Spit flew and burned Nightmare's flesh. Nightmare cried out, struggling.

"Leave him alone!" Hope grabbed the prisoner's arm, and instantly, he let go of Nightmare, who crashed to the floor. His throat was on fire and he could smell his sinew melting where the spit had struck him.

Venom. It's his venom.

"A family," the prisoner moaned at Hope. "I just… I only… a family, a life, with you. Oh, why… Why could it not—"

The ground trembled in prelude to a bigger quake. Nightmare struggled to his feet just as the woman in red entered the house. Her eyes were ablaze. His hands formed fists. She was furious and stalking toward them.

"Hope Star," Nightmare warned, and from the corner of his eye, he caught a glint of brightness. A very specific magenta brilliance that he knew, even though he couldn't quite remember what it meant.

A vial on a chain that had come out from beneath the prisoner's shirt during their struggle. Brilliant pink-magenta-whiteness danced inside the glass. Nightmare opened his mouth to tell Hope, but she'd seen it, too.

The woman in red screeched a deafening wail.

The prisoner wept.

Hope grabbed the necklace and yanked.

The chain broke.

The house vanished.

Nightmare crouched, prepared for battle. Nothing came at him. It was dark, it was murky, and they now stood in warm, shallow water. It lapped at Nightmare's knees. From somewhere too close, a sigh blew like a slow tornado. It knocked Nightmare back several steps. He sat in the water, and without thinking of why, he splashed some on his face. At last, he'd found an antidote for the venom. He reached to touch his cheek and found a hole in his face.

"Mal'uud?" Hope whispered.

"Here," he answered in the same tone.

"Where are we?"

That was the question, and it was one Nightmare could only partially answer at best. He didn't sense his father, so they were still in the painting, in the prison, but the hell that Water had made was gone. The ground was solid, if wet, beneath his feet, but his eyes, attuned to darkness, could see nothing. He touched them to ensure he still had them. They watered, and he blinked. "I cannot see."

"But I thought you could see in the dark?"

"I can."

"So why can't you, now?"

Only one thing made sense: this was another kind of illusion. If that was true, then only one thing would break it. "The vial, do you have it?"

"Yes."

"Hold it up."

Nightmare heard a rustling and a faint tinkling of chain. Murky red brilliance filled the chamber. It flashed too bright, temporarily blinding Nightmare. He held up his arm, waiting, and when he could, he opened his eyes.

Before them was a wall, twice as tall as Nightmare stood. And then the wall moved. So not a wall at all, but a *coil.* Scales glinted in a beautiful rainbow of green, blue, gold, and pink, all tinged different shades by the Lady's trapped power. Nightmare staggered backward, trying to see more, to look higher.

The coil wound around on itself. A mountain of scales rose from the shallow depths, dwarfing even Lord Nothing's mountain pass. It was too large to comprehend; too much to see. Nightmare ran, not in fear, but in dire need of better perspective. Hope chased after him, and he could hear her panicked breathing. They found no walls, only more water, more mist and humid, dank, darkness broken by the gleam of the vial. As they drew away, the vial glowed all the brighter, until Nightmare couldn't even glance in its general direction. Not that he tried very hard. He was too fixated on the roving coils.

The scales gleamed as they slithered, slowly, so terribly slowly. Another sigh whipped through the cavern, and a giant arm ridged in scales reached out from the top and center of the coils. A human hand with scales on the knuckles hooked and held onto the coils as an anchor.

And then the rest of Water emerged from the center of his coils.

A great head with a massive, golden lizard fan rose atop a thick neck erupting from a pair of shoulders so wide they filled Nightmare's entire range of vision. Viciously sharp scales raced along Water's spine. His chest was iridescent with scale armor, but man-shaped. His torso was impossibly long and morphed at the waist into a serpent's body. His face was narrow, with a flat, almost non-existent nose and ridges over his enormous eyes. A thick streak of hair parted his scalp, pale blue and purple and gold, but each strand was distinguishable; could be counted at a distance. Water's mouth was wide, his lips pale and thin, and when he parted them, Nightmare saw fangs lying flat against the gum line. They elongated as Water took another deep breath. They dripped with the venom that had eaten through Nightmare's sinew.

Rarely did Nightmare face a foe that inspired in him the urge to flee. Water, even broken and tired and trapped, sent a thrill of pure terror through Nightmare. He broke it into tiny pieces and swallowed them. Nightmare stood firm, and Water slowly lowered himself until his hands were on the ground and his face loomed in front of them. It was all they could see: Water's head and eyes and fangs in all their terrifying, powerful beauty.

Beside Nightmare, Hope didn't scream. She made no sound at all, in fact, and Nightmare wondered briefly if she'd fainted. Then the light of the vial moved, lowered, and changed angles. Hope had set it down. The water muted the glow, but Nightmare saw Hope walk toward Water.

"Eeadian," Hope said. "My… my love?"

Water's eyelids closed sideways. A mournful, defeated sound echoed in the prison, and Nightmare trembled with its volume.

Hope's throat clicked with a dry swallow, clearly audible in the utter silence. "We're here to free you. We have to go. The world is dying. It needs you. It needs us. And I need… I need you, my Blue. I need what you have of me."

Giant tears welled where Water's eyelids met. They rolled and dropped, and Nightmare realized that was the liquid in which they stood. Tears. Wretched sadness stole through Nightmare. He desired nothing more than to lie down in this shallow water, drink it and go to sleep forever. The universe was too much. Living was too great a torture. Nothing and no one were meant to be.

Water lifted one of his hands. It was closed into a loose fist, and he opened it. In its center, a tiny, glistening shard no larger than Nightmare's finger rested. While they watched, it awakened and floated into the air, hovering.

"Is that… me?" Hope asked.

In answer, the shard shot across the cavern and struck Hope squarely in the chest. Her hands flew up to frame the wound, and she gurgled. The shard pierced the leather of her shirt and also her skin, burrowing. Hope frothed with white foam at the lips. She shook, jerked as though she would fracture into a solar system of broken parts, and her arms and legs splayed with a force that held her aloft. It was eerily similar to the way the woman in red had risen before she'd dissolved.

But Hope didn't transform into red mist. Instead, the veins beneath her skin began to glow white. Slowly, they widened, as though she were cracking in a million places at once. Silvery-white liquid light leaked from the glowing crevices, swarmed over her arms, her chest, the tops of her breasts, and up her neck. Her eyes stared sightlessly at the sky as the light took her, and as the last tiny bit of it enclosed the Hope Star, the world started to rock. The violence of it threw Nightmare against Water, who flailed as well. The ground shot up in great slabs. Nightmare stood firm, but Hope and Water were knocked off balance, sliding away. Water bellowed in disbelief and pain.

"*RUN*."

The voice was not Water's, but Lord Nothing's. It seared Nightmare's ears and burrowed to his core. He obeyed the directive without thought. He scrambled in the direction of Lord Nothing's voice, and he used power to transform into the Mare. He galloped, full speed, toward the picture frame that sat like a pinprick at the end of a tunnel.

It was only after he'd changed forms that he gave pause to consider his companions, the one he was to help and the one he was to rescue. Without stopping, he looked and saw Water on his right, some distance away, but slithering as fast as Nightmare ran. To the left was a silver blur that could only be the Hope Star. Blinding magenta brilliance danced around the chamber, a kaleidoscope of every shade of red and pink that existed, and that had to be the vial of the Lady's power.

Nightmare could see Lord Nothing ahead, framed by the portrait. They were close. They would make it.

A catastrophically loud eruption exploded above their heads.

Dark chunks rained down, splashing into the water and disintegrating into wriggling snakes. A trilling shriek echoed through the chamber, and a maggot-like branch burst into the prison. At its end was a giant puppet doll of a girl. She had no eyes. She was screaming.

Water pivoted. His coils pushed him forward, and his torso lifted off the ground. His head shot toward the writhing root of the Horror, and he bit it. His fangs sank deeply into the flesh, and the Horror's scream of pain made Nightmare stumble. The root fell from the ceiling and crashed behind them, but the hole above them remained. More roots, tens, dozens, hundreds, poured through, and Water abandoned his enemy. He dove downward, tearing through tendrils with carelessness.

They charged for the portrait, for Lord Nothing. Nightmare was slower than Water and the Hope Star, who shimmered in silvery glow tinged by the light of the Lady's vial. Nightmare let loose a stallion's cry and poured all his effort into driving his legs faster, faster. Behind them, more roots struck the ground. Nightmare didn't dare turn to look.

When they reached the exit, Hope went first. She zipped through the opening in a silver dash. Nightmare followed, leaping over the rim, and he craned his neck to see how by the Fear that Water would escape. He shouldn't have doubted. Water, in man-form, with legs and scales and that lizard-human head leapt out of the painting.

"This way."

Again, Lord Nothing's voice boomed, and all Nightmare could do was follow it. Around them, the catacombs were pulsating with the Horrors. Wormy threads cut through the stone. They were silent in their destruction, hungry. They were eating everything, devouring the portraits. The prisoners beat against the invisible barriers, desperate to escape, and as they passed through a hallway being ripped to shreds, Lord Nothing paused. He urged Nightmare, Hope, and Water ahead of him, and he waved a hand. There was a chorus of muted whisperings, Lord

Nothing's power, and Nightmare knew his father had unleashed a horde of trapped monsters to fight the Horrors. Shouts, warrior yells, cries of pain, and the crushing crash of destruction filled the narrow chambers. Nightmare's ears rang, but on they ran.

One moment Lord Nothing was behind them, the next he was in front. Tendrils of Shadow chased him. They surrounded them, flickered on the walls. They were keeping the hallways intact long enough for them to get clear. A Horror burst from a wall, a shrieking puppet at its end, and Water tore it from its moorings. He ripped the puppet in two, spilling filth and gore with careless abandon. He tossed the husk aside, and still they ran. The slope of the floor began to rise. The ceiling drooped. Nothing shrank to fit, but Nightmare and Water had to duck. With another chorus of spine-tingling whispers, Lord Nothing sent his Shadows ahead. They punched through the solid surface of a wall. One minute, they were in catacombs and the next, they had spilled out the side of a mountain. Snow and ice crunched beneath Nightmare's hooves. Horrors pulsed pink in earthworm runnels across the ground. To their left, a Shadow Guardian lifted a massive axe to cleave one Horror, only to be overtaken by hundreds of smaller ones. They ripped the Guardian apart and absorbed its pieces through hideously pale suckers ringed with teeth.

"Go."

Lord Nothing's command was law. They ran, Lord Nothing and Hope Star gliding over the ground without touching it while Water slithered and Nightmare galloped. He didn't know how long they fled, but it seemed too soon when exhaustion set into Nightmares bones. He staggered, changed his form into one less taxing, and with him, the others stopped to catch their breath.

An earthquake shook the land. They stood in a rolling field, cold but without frost or snow. The hills rippled like someone shaking out a carpet. They staggered and turned as a group, watching as in the distance, now, a great white peak snapped, shattered and fell. For a moment, the mountain stood, headless, but then it succumbed. With a noise like the roar of a collapsing cosmos, the entire range disintegrated. It took only seconds to level the gardens, the terraces, the ruins of the palace, the Guardians, the tunnel, the gate and its keepers.

The Mountain Fortress, Lord Nothing's home, and one of the Lady's finest creations was no more. The Horrors had overtaken it, their triumph sung not in song but in terrible silence, all-consuming in the wintry landscape shrouded now by a dense, ominous fog.

Lord Nothing stood stoic, his cloak flickering without a breeze. His tendrils of power drew close. The ground beneath him was darker, and the Shadow he cast was crumpled at the waist with its hands to either side of its head, as if it wept though Lord Nothing could not.

"Give me the shard," Lord Nothing commanded.

Water opened his hand and the brilliant pink shard floated to Lord Nothing. He cupped his hands over and under it, closing them gently. There was a bright flash of magenta and the shard was gone; absorbed by Nothing. He held his hands over his heart and stared at the wasted landscape.

"Can you do anything?" Nightmare asked Water, who stood to Nightmare's left.

Water shook his head. He collapsed to his knees. He spoke like a human, breathless and dying in a white bed with machines pumping artificial life through veins. "There are too many. There is too much that has been destroyed." He glanced with baleful eyes at Nightmare, and then lowered his chin as though in penance. Or prayer.

The Hope Star stood apart from them. She was whole, now, a Walker. Her skin glistened like wet diamonds in deep mist. At first glance, she seemed solid. Upon another look, she was smoke trapped by a female outline, small and curvaceous, but with cracked skin that leaked glimpses of light. They were bright enough that Nightmare understood if he was ever caught in the full force of one, he'd likely vanish.

Hope turned her face toward them. Her features, like the rest of her, were suggestion. "We did this," she said simply.

"I am… sorry," Water wheezed through tears.

"I know," Hope said to her lover, her voice gentle.

"What are we to do?" Nightmare said when it became clear Lord Nothing was not going to speak.

"The only thing we can do," Hope Star said. "If it's not too late."

Dread churned in Nightmare's aching body. He looked to his father, who gave a single nod and a great sigh.

"We go to free my Lady."

Chapter Twenty-Two

By the time Jason and Andrew made it back to the Taylor Point House, the day had faded into the gray of twilight. The house glowed on the other side of Andrew's gardens; windows were illuminated with yellow light and the Solarium bustled with the dinner crowd. Night bugs had started to sing from the branches and shrubs, and the water against the dock was calm. It seemed so picturesque that when Andrew dropped the arm he had slung around Jason's shoulders and froze, Jason thought Andrew had stubbed a toe.

"What's wrong?" Jason asked.

Andrew frowned. He put a hand over his stomach. "I don't feel so good all of a sudden."

"You're just hungry. Come on."

"No. Oh. Oh! I am hungry. Starving. I can smell Miss Teedee's fresh bread from here, but the sick in my belly isn't that kind of sick. It's another kind."

Jason marveled how well Andrew knew himself. "It's probably

just because you've had a hard day, man. Your mom and all. You know."

Andrew's features smoothed for a second and then clouded once again. "No. She had to go. I understand that. Just like she will understand I couldn't go. I'm not her boy, anymore. I'm her man. This is… I think there's…"

He didn't finish, choosing instead to take off running. Jason cursed and chased after him, running past trees and flower beds and the first hint of lightning bugs. They circled the house, Jason wondering what on earth could happen now, and he nearly ran into Andrew, who came to a sudden halt.

There was a large white van in the driveway parked behind a beat up black sedan. The car had obnoxious orange lightning stripes along its sides. It was the kind of car that had been sporty about twenty years ago but now looked sluggish and out of place.

"Oh. Oh," Andrew whispered.

"There you are!" said Mercutio. At first, Jason couldn't tell where the voice had come from, but then he spotted Mercutio leaning over the front porch railing.

"Miss Pretty wouldn't budge from her chair 'til she knew you two were back." Mercutio's smile was easy, but his body was tense, biceps flexed beneath the short sleeves of his scrubs top.

Andrew headed for the front stairs, and Jason followed, but when he passed closer to the van, he stopped.

The license tag read, JDTHEL2.

Jason's heart froze in his chest and frost crackled in his veins. His back began to itch beneath the leaves and trunk inked on his flesh. He didn't breathe until Andrew grabbed his wrist and hauled him away from the van.

"Not good, no, no, no," Andrew murmured as they ascended the porch.

"Who…?" Jason choked on the word and pointed to the vehicles. Mercutio came closer, arms crossed.

"The car? Oh, that's Jennifer's thug BF, don't you know?"

Jason shook his head so hard he made himself dizzy.

Mercutio's eyes lit with sympathy, but he didn't answer. He looked to Helen, instead. She sat in a rocking chair, her ankles crossed and tucked under the front cross-rail so the chair didn't move. Her hands were folded in her lap, and her dark eyes were endlessly enormous and black in the dull light.

"They're here," Helen whispered.

"Who?" Jason asked.

"Oh. Oh." Andrew danced from one foot to the other in a manic shuffle. Like he had to pee. Or he was fighting the urge to run.

Mercutio made an exasperated little sound. "Our new guests, that's all. They showed up a little while ago and started moving in their things. Remain calm ladies and gentlemen, they too shall pass from this place in due time."

Though Mercutio's demeanor helped slow Jason's pulse, fear still fluttered deep inside him. Helen gestured to Jason. He knelt in front of her, and instantly Mercutio was looming over Helen's shoulder, ever watchful. Helen waved Jason even closer, and Jason leaned until Helen could speak in his ear. "The Fortress Fell. The Horrors are everywhere. Only you can stop them."

Jason jerked away as though she'd struck him. A silver thread of pure panic squirmed through him, though he couldn't say why. What Helen told him made no sense, and yet, it did. Ever since he'd arrived, he'd been waiting for the other shoe to drop. Impending disaster was always on the horizon, and now it had set upon their driveway and was lurking inside his safe haven.

"Someone's here who shouldn't be," Andrew said, as though translating, and with that he spun, flung open the front door, and went inside.

Jason rose, and Helen caught his wrist. "Only you," she repeated.

Mercutio clucked his tongue. "Miss Lovely, why don't we stop freaking people out and get you some grub?"

"She's not..." Jason shook his head. It was pointless to explain that Helen wasn't and didn't bother him. He understood her, and she was trying to warn him. He glanced at the van, at the door, and steeled himself before going inside.

Maybe it wasn't what he thought. Maybe God wasn't that cruel. Maybe he wouldn't have to run.

The air was cool past the front threshold. The doors to the library on the left and the front parlor on the right were open, and guests milled about sipping from wine glasses or water bottles. The drone of clocks drowned out the conversation, and ticking filled Jason's brain. The foyer in front of the check-in desk was crowded with music equipment and trunks. The one closest to him was blood red and covered in stickers. One read, WELCOME TO TENNESSEE, THE VOLUNTEER STATE. It was garish orange against the red trunk, and Jason remembered—

"Don't put that on there. Jesus." Jason laughed.

Judith tilted her head to look up from where she crouched in the gas station parking lot. Rage was inside the QWIK-EE Mart buying smokes and beef sticks. Judith had made Jason unload her trunk, which was heavy as all hell, out of the back of their dark green van. It was dark green because white was for molesters and dog catchers, or so Rage had insisted and Judith had accepted. Besides, the green one had been cheaper by a grand. It also had a rust hole in the back big enough to see the road pass by as they sped down highways. But what did that matter? It was theirs.

While Jason had struggled with the luggage, Judith had slinked inside the convenience store. She'd come out a moment later with the sticker tucked into the front of her pants. She never paid for anything.

And now Judith was hunkered down next to all her worldly possessions. The beads and threads in her hair glittered in the sunlight, and her teeth flashed white when she grinned. Still staring at Jason, she slapped the memento onto her luggage and smoothed it into place. "Don't you want to know where we've been?"

"I know where I've been. I don't need a goddamned sticker to remind me I had to come back."

Judith traced the edges of the sticker with a tiny finger tipped with a lethally pointed nail. "Breadcrumbs, darling. I want to be able to find you if I ever lose you."

Jason snorted. "You won't ever find me here."

"We all go home eventually."

"Yeah. Well." Jason sucked on his cigarette. "Home sweet fucking home." He thought to himself that it just went like that, didn't it, life? Try like hell to get out of Dodge and get dragged back to it on the circular road of fate.

Every time.

—when she'd put it there. Just like he remembered the vanity plate they'd all sprung for to hang on the back of their illustrious tour van.

JUDTHEL1

The state hadn't allowed the second "L" for anti-profanity reasons, so they just went with the one. Jason swallowed around the lump in his throat and swayed on his feet. He glanced around, looking for Rage's ghost.

Instead, he saw Jennifer looking even more shrunken than usual, her shoulders wrapped in the beefy arm of an enormous man with brown hair and goatee. He had a paunch under his t-shirt, just starting, and his work boots had left tracks on the polished floor. His eyes were small and mean in their deep sockets tucked in with folds of flesh, and though he sneered at Jason, he said nothing. Neither did Jennifer, though her cheeks flushed a deep red.

In front of the counter, two more men stood. They wore identical jeans, black shirts, and shoes, and Jason had to blink several times to make sure he wasn't seeing things. It wasn't just their clothes that were the same; they were twins. They had the same weak chin, chubby, stubbly cheeks, and shock of nearly black hair. They flanked a petite woman with waist-length, straight black hair. She was too thin, with a pallor to her skin. She wore a black and white dress made out of a fabric that made it look wet, like paint, and when she turned around, her breasts strained against the cloth, the outlines of the nipple rings clear. She had more face piercings than the last time Jason had seen her, and her bangs were too long, but her eyes were the same: a feverish, intense, almost clear color that was not blue or green or even gray but somewhere in the middle of all of them. When asked for their color on paper, she wrote, "Ghost."

Judith's grin split her face. She was beautiful like death to a terminal patient on a morphine drip. "Hey lover."

"Jason." Darryl came around the counter. He had circles under his eyes a mile wide. "This woman says she knows you."

The thousand times Jason had known Judith lit up his head. Every time he'd been inside her while she clawed at him, urging him to bite her, mark her, pinch her nipples harder. He saw himself cuffing her, spanking her, taking her any way a man could have a woman and a few he was still convinced they'd made up. She only liked sex when it hurt. She'd laugh afterward, say her cunt was killing her and give him a kiss of gratitude. One time, when he'd refused to cut her with a razor blade, she'd tied him up and done it herself while riding him. She'd made shallow wounds all over her body until she looked like a patchwork doll splitting red at the seams. He'd been horrified and high and under her spell, thinking this was what it meant to love, really fucking love; like life depended on it.

And then there were the lost times, those moments when Judith wouldn't come out of a bathroom or a closet or a dressing room or tour van. They'd miss a show and the club would be screaming at them from six directions, but Rage and Jason hadn't cared. Let the masses wail. Their queen was in pain. They'd park themselves outside Judith's door, begging and pleading for her to come out. Rage had been better at that game. He could rock and roll with her death wish, and Jason could never quite give up enough of himself to find that particular abyss.

Judith would cry that she was blank, empty, hollow inside. Rage would tell her everybody was; Judith was simply more honest about it. He'd encourage her to write it down, spill it out of her. He'd pass her pen and paper beneath the door. Or he'd pass her a safety pin so she could prick herself. They'd found her poetry on tile written in sticky blood more than once. They'd copy it down and leave it. They'd take pictures and put it online; make posters out of it. Judith would come out of those black moments with an armful of ideas. She'd share her pain with the fans, on stage into a mic—

"So last night, I wanted to die again. Rage brought me back. I can't live without him."

—or writing it online for the world to read. Their names might have been blacklisted at a hundred small clubs, but the rest loved to see Judith's Hell on the Coming Attractions board. No matter how badly Judith seemed to screw it all up, she came back stronger than ever. People loved her more and more. Jason had been no different. There was a time in his life where her opinion of him was the only thing that existed in his world. Her smile, her disdain, her body, her voice. He'd wept backstage when she'd sing Rage's praises after he'd talked her down and gotten her to speak to the crowd. Hadn't Jason been more important? Or at least equally so? Wasn't it him who gave her everything she needed? Anything she wanted?

Except, maybe, a will to live at times when she didn't want to anymore.

That last time, the one that had broken Jason and gotten his feet moving toward the door, she'd finally said it:

"Nobody will love me ever again."

They'd both been in the bathroom. She'd let him in, a witness and also a victim. The light over the mirror had flickered, so she'd seemed like an apparition. He'd stood right there, a heartbeat away, and he'd been suffering just like she had been. Papa Jack had died a month ago and now Rage was dead. Gone. Destroyed.

"What good are you?" Judith had asked. "You just don't understand me. You never did. Only he did. And he left me."

"He left us."

She'd smiled a cruel little smile. "Is that what you think? Stupid boy."

She'd said other things, but Jason didn't remember them. He remembered walking away, hitching to the next town, and getting clean in a ratty hotel that didn't care if a man occasionally screamed in the middle of the night. It'd been him and the roaches and the nightmares for the days and weeks he'd spent at rock bottom. It'd taken all he had to move on. She'd hollowed him out, and he'd had to fill up again with something new but slower.

And here she was again. Full circle.

Fuck fate.

If Andrew hadn't been standing right behind him, Jason would have turned and gone straight for his van. If Darryl hadn't been staring at him, if Helen hadn't warned him, if they all hadn't been watching, his new family that he so desperately wanted to love him and to love, he would have run.

Their eyes and the anger kept him fixed on that specific spot of floor as though he might never walk again. A great wave of anguish and pain and fury rose in him. When it crested, it shorted out his internal fuse. Suddenly he was stock still and empty. There was nothing. He was rooted and frozen solid in the dead of emotionless winter.

"Happy to see me?" Judith asked Jason.

"The band all together in the same room," said the Left Twin. He smacked his gum. "It's a party."

"Jason?" Darryl asked. "Are you—?"

"How?" Jason asked in his winter voice. "Why?"

"Oh, it's a fabulous story." Judith's laugh tinkled. "After I lost touch with you, I was adrift, you know? Floating in the wind. And I met Cain and Abel, here," she gestured at the twins, "and they got me through. You remember that, don't you? You. Rage. Getting me… through?"

Jason remembered: an infinity of drowning kisses. He glanced at the twins. Cain and Abel. Probably more like Henry and Brett. Something plain and inconsequential made powerful through Judith's influence. Jason remembered her light; like a black light, making all the impurities glow in the night like they led somewhere other than destruction.

He thought his knees would buckle, but Andrew was there. He held Jason up by an elbow and stepped forward at the same time. He seemed to fill the room's gaps and crowd Judith and her crew. "You're not welcome here."

"Andrew!" Darryl admonished.

"And you are?" Judith asked Andrew.

"I'm the gardener. I make things grow."

Judith's eyes gleamed. "I'm thinking the gardener doesn't have the power to throw me out, especially not when I have a reservation."

"Andrew," Jason rasped. "It's..." Well, it wasn't okay, so Jason didn't finish the sentence. "How did you find me?" he asked Judith.

"By not looking for you! It's cray, right? The boys convinced me that I needed music back in my life, so we hosted an online audition to replace Rage. We had hundreds of applicants, can you believe it? But Gruff, here, he won by a landslide."

"Gruff?" Andrew asked, confused.

The man draped around Jennifer spoke up. "Billy. That's the name, but she said it made her think of—"

"Billy Goats Gruff." Judith laughed. "It was on after that. The band was going to pull a full phoenix. We were set to meet in the big ATL, but then he told me that his girl, there, told him that she'd seen a familiar face at this little hometown motel. So we just had to come. I mean, I couldn't *not* see you."

So that's why Jennifer stared but didn't speak. It wasn't fear that her boyfriend would be jealous, or, at least, not only that. Jason saw the scene clearly in his mind. There was Gruff, packing and delirious with excitement, and there she'd been, getting left behind. If Gruff was to her even a fraction of what Judith had been to Jason, then Jennifer would do anything to make him stay for just a little while longer. Selling out the new help would have been a no-brainer. Tell the seductive girl with the tattoos on the

Skype screen that her long lost muse was cleaning toilets. Have Judith come there instead of Gruff going to her. Buy some time to figure out a way to go with him, sneaking if necessary, because God, Jennifer couldn't let him go. She wouldn't be able to lose him. It'd mean letting all of herself go as well, and Jason knew what it took to fill a body back up when it'd been stuffed to the brim with someone else for too long.

"I'm sorry," Jennifer said, her gaze on the floorboards.

"What're you sorry for?" Gruff asked, shaking her in what Jason guessed was a gentle way but looked all too violent with Jennifer so much smaller. "This band breaking up was the worst thing in the history of rock, babe. You, like, helped get it fixed."

Protest tried to escape Jason's mouth, but Judith was quicker. "No, no. Not fixed. There's history here, kids, and we all know it. I'm just happy for the chance to see you, Jason." She walked closer, the mobilized embodiment of Jason's private pain, and she took his hand. She squeezed it. Her skin was warm. "We've been through so much."

"I'm sorry," Darryl said, interrupting, thank God. "I can't seem to find Monica's notes on your reservation. She handled all that. Handles, I mean. She's on a short vacation."

"I spoke to her, myself," Judith said. She never stopped staring at Jason. "Sweet woman. Is she yours?"

Darryl seemed taken aback, and Andrew spoke. "She's her own."

"My kind of lady, then," Judith said. "She said we'd be in rooms with flower names."

"Daisy, Iris, Lily, and Rose are open," Darryl said.

"Cool. Cain?"

The Right Twin with the first murderer's name removed a wad of cash from a pocket. "This'll do it, right?"

Darryl looked at Jason. Andrew whispered, "No, no," but all Jason could think about was Papa Jack saying money was the grease in the wheels of the world. The Taylor Point House needed guests. They were its food. They were the way it provided for the permanent residents. Jason cared about those people and the house.

Only you can stop them.

What was there to stop? Judith from staying? That'd hurt them all, wouldn't it? Maybe Helen didn't mean stop them. Maybe she meant fix them. Fix himself and Judith. Repair the damage. Change was another kind of fix, wasn't it? And their history was an ocean of jagged rocks and hidden icebergs. If he could find a way to mend bridges over that water, then maybe Judith would have her music and leave Jason in peace.

"It's fine."

For a second, Jason thought he'd spoken, but he realized it'd been Darryl. "Come the rest of the way in, everyone. I'll show you the rooms."

"Perfect." Judith smiled at Jason and let him go.

"No," Andrew said, nearly a shout. "No, no! Darryl-Dad, you don't know the story. Jason told me his story. You can't let them—"

"Andrew, that'll be enough." Darryl's voice boomed through the foyer. Darryl took a calming breath. "I'm sorry, folks. He's had a rough day. His mother, ah, had a family emergency."

"Oh," Judith said sympathetically while her twins gathered their things. "I know all about those."

"Darryl-Dad," Andrew choked, as though they were the only words he could find.

And Jason knew all about how this tiny woman could make anyone lose the ability to speak, think, or reason. Silently, he and Andrew watched Judith, Cain, and Abel go up the stairs. Gruff and Jennifer vanished into the library, heading for the kitchen, most likely. Andrew wheeled on Jason, who expected to have to explain himself or make excuses for Judith, just like in the old days. But Andrew wasn't angry. Tears flowed down his cheeks. The sight shocked Jason almost as much as Judith.

"He can't hear me. Why can't he hear me?"

"Because he can only hear what Monica said when she was leaving," Jason blurted. He wished he hadn't said it, but he knew it was the truth.

Andrew's chin quivered. He barreled past Jason, who gave chase, but Mercutio caught him. "I've got this one."

"What?" Jason asked, wondering now if he was dreaming. Judith couldn't really be here. He'd run and hidden and walked and driven thousands of miles to get away from her. She couldn't possibly be right upstairs unpacking her black thongs into antique dresser drawers.

"I'll go get him," Mercutio said.

Jason tried to focus on anything but himself. "But Helen—"

"Will be just fine if her new friend Jason sits with her."

"No, it's…" Jason wanted out of the house. He needed to get away. "I can—"

"You went after him once today, already." Mercutio was firm. "Let me give it a go. I know where all his favorite spots are."

"You do?" Jason asked. Defeat settled in to stay. He wasn't going to get away. Even if he ran now, he would have to come back. There was too much tying him to this place. Helen thought he had something vital to do here, and he hoped she was right, because it felt like all he was good for was destruction.

"You just keep my girl happy and help her get fed, and I'll be back in a mere twinkle of time."

"Okay."

"Good man." Mercutio thumped Jason on the back. He went to Helen, kissed her hair, and took the steps off the porch two at a time. He headed for a glittery black Jeep in the gravel parking lot, and Jason watched until the taillights winked out of sight down the driveway. Then, with complete lack of other options, he sat down next to Helen, one rocking chair over. She took his hand and together they rocked in time, waiting.

Chapter Twenty-Three

Hope stared at her own hands, watching the way she shimmered beneath the illusion of her silvery flesh. She made a fist and for an instant, she was both the Star and Madeline. The duality passed in a breath, and then she was Hope, the Walker Star, and she knew, as Madeline had known, that she would always be fractured. Without her six sisters, she was small. She was alone. That was the way of things. Too much of her in one place was too dangerous. Too little was too crippling. By cycling through the constellation of Light one at a time, everyone would have their share of the best in the universe. So her place in time and space was to fall, to land, to guide, and to leave when she was weakened. She would fade, would go, would die, and another of her sisters would touch ground.

But the cycle had been broken.

She remembered.

"You hurt me," Hope said.

Water wept.

They stood in the middle of a barren, scorched field. The Twilight around them and the burnt grasses beneath Hope's feet called out to her. She was to show the way. Help them, help everything and everyone, to heal and grow. Give them strength to hope that everything would get better. She was to give herself, freely, to all who desired her. They needed her.

But the Horrors were here. Their fog distorted the distance. She could no longer see the place where Lord Nothing's Fortress and mountains had been. The world merely ended in a plume of impenetrable fog.

Emotion pulled at her. She wanted to cry, and she remembered how Madeline had cried so much. She could recall herself as Madeline, her human form, and wasn't that strange? All that soft, supple skin and terrible mortality. How did Nightmare do it? Of all the Walkers, he was the one who Walked the most, and he loved Earth. When the universes that spun around Via'rra didn't provide him with new children, his favorite way to swell the numbers of his 'mares was to bring home the forgotten, the abandoned, or the abused human thought. Their lives were so swift, so much came and went, and the intensity of every thought, ideal, pattern, and process was rich. He gorged himself.

Did he not remember?

Hope looked at Nightmare with his shattered sternum and fading green light. No heart. It was gone, and with it, his purpose. She thought to ask him, *Do you remember going to human homes in the dead of night and listening to their dreams? You'd touch their foreheads, over the place where long ago a third eye had seen, and you'd spindle from them the ideas they no longer needed. You'd steal what you judged they wouldn't miss; what they so desperately wanted to forget. You'd tuck the threads on their black spindles away in your coat and return here, to your Undermaze. There you'd hang the threads from the ceilings of your caverns. You'd watch those threads swell, the cocoons growing under your tenderness, and new 'mares would be born. And you'd take their tales to the Heart cavern and tell all to the one who meant the most.*

Do you remember King of Nightmare? Do you recall what you've lost?

She didn't ask. She knew the answer. She knew it just like she knew how she'd gotten to where she now stood. As Madeline, her sundered self, she'd known so little. Sympathy bubbled in her chest for her fellow Walker. He didn't know. She couldn't tell him. He wouldn't believe her.

"Come," Lord Nothing said, as though sensing she were on the brink of speaking that which could not be spoken. "We have our task."

"Wait."

Lord Nothing paused at Hope's request. He needed her, and she would fulfill his need, but not yet. She had Madeline in her bones. Her human form that should never have existed, that she had stolen from a grave of a dead child, haunted her like the Bone Ghosts haunted the Undermaze. She was Hope's fallen human ideal. She deserved to have her say.

Hope went to Water, her lover, who knelt. He was weakened. Madeline felt pity. Hope felt cold.

"You called me to our favorite place," Hope said.

"Please..." Water begged. His tears flowed.

Hope was not Mercy. Her sister might have stopped. Hope never would.

"I'd been in the Lady's garden. She liked having me there, and I loved to whisper to her fledglings. That morning I'd whispered to the king of a new civilization the Lady was growing that he could be great and good. He could lead his people to righteousness. He was tiny, you understand, just a seed in her soil, but I could hear him. He was afraid. He knew his task was massive and he was small before it. I know all about being tiny and facing the enormity of purpose. I am the littlest of my sisters, did you know? But I am also the brightest.

"You called to me, and I left the Lady and went to you in our cave. Our beautiful, glittering cave. You gathered all the prettiest stones and put them in the walls. We made mosaics out of emeralds and diamonds. Our bed there was the softest fur, piled high on the stone floor, and warm, so very warm. You took me in your arms. You shed your tail, you came to me as a man, not a warrior, and you made love to me. I wept, and you smiled, and when I was lazy beneath you, weak with happiness, your face changed."

"We had agreed of the path we would take together," Water sobbed.

"We had, it's true. But not of the method. You tore at my chest. You ripped out my heart. You crushed it in a fist until it was tiny, and you fashioned it into a pendant. I watched, bleeding and unable to move. Do you remember what you said?"

"That I loved you."

"You opened the portal. You pushed me through. I woke in the dirt on the ground beside a grave. Madeline doesn't remember how she got there, but I do. My memory was fading so fast once I was on Earth. I claimed a body, the closest I could find. I clawed up and out. I figured out lungs and heart and human parts. I cried and tried to keep myself, to hang on to Hope, but I slipped away. Madeline was alone. I couldn't whisper to her. She was born of a garden, but there was no Hope to tell her she would be all right."

Water's mouth parted in a silent cry. He doubled over, his great head touching the ground. Hope wanted to feel satisfied. Instead, she was too hollow and exhausted.

Lord Nothing came to stand by Hope. "I wish we had the luxury of time to create a space for forgiveness, but we must journey to free my Lady."

"I don't think I can travel with them," Hope whispered.

"You won't need to. They have their own task."

"And what is that?" Nightmare asked.

"You and Water will journey to the Undermaze to rejoin Water with the rest and last of his power."

"What?" Nightmare asked gruffly in disbelief. "The Undermaze? The essence of Water is there?"

"I broke him in two. One part of his strength guarded the Lady's power shard in the illusion. The other part of his strength I sundered sent deep in one of the most heavily guarded places in Via'rra."

Nightmare's eyes darted back and forth. "The Scrying Cavern. You buried the rest of Water at the bottom of that pit."

A Madeline memory swarmed through Hope: the dreams of a lake at the bottom of a chasm; a lullaby sung in a lost, lonely voice. Some part of her had known what had befallen her lover. Across Universes, they had connected. A bond so strong and capable of so much destruction. Quietly, she wept.

"I did." Lord Nothing nodded. "The last of Water is now being watched by your most powerful."

Nightmare considered the information for mere seconds. Hope admired his ability to adapt and accept. "After I take Water to the Cavern and he regains his power, what will we do?"

"We will finish saving our world."

"How?"

Lord Nothing closed his cosmic eyes, but only briefly. "By doing all that we can."

"Father, that's not—"

"You will be summoned. You will know. Now go. We have precious little time."

Nightmare dragged Water to his feet. "Let's go. I don't have the strength left to change forms again, so you will have to be the swift one."

Water, his head bowed in defeat, stood to his full height. His legs melded, elongated, and soon his Nāga form loomed over them. He wasn't as large as he'd been in the illusion, because there was no need. But he was big enough that Nightmare could climb onto his back. Nightmare threaded his fingers into Water's ropey hair. He cast a glance at Lord Nothing and Hope, and his mouth opened as though he wanted to speak. Maybe he wanted to wish them well but knew their chances of fixing their world were getting smaller and smaller with each passing moment. Instead,

Nightmare stayed silent. He gestured toward the east, and Water took off in that direction.

"He was deranged," Lord Nothing said, breaking the silence that fell in the wake of Nightmare and Water's departure. "He could have fought Banshee and the Horrors, but instead, he chose to stand aside. Had they taken him, there would have been no chance for our future. We had already lost you. We couldn't stand to lose another."

"You did what was best for the world, My Lord. Capturing and hiding him may have saved us."

Lord Nothing's shadow swelled with a sigh his body did not betray. "I did much of it out of malcontent."

"Understandable."

Lord Nothing gazed down at Hope, his expression made of granite but his eyes oddly kind. "Your comfort is appreciated. However, it is a concept lost upon me with my Lady not at my side."

"Where is she?" Hope asked.

"Imprisoned." Lord Nothing began to shrink. His humanoid form dissolved into pure darkness. "I will show you the way," his voice murmured. The hiss of his power surrounded Hope, and she watched a crevice in the grasses appear. It was a line leading to a destination. Her final one.

Steeling herself and calling upon the last of her power reserves, Hope willed herself to travel. As a part of Light, she could keep up with the Lady, who traveled at the speed of creation, or Lord Nothing, who was everywhere Shadow could be. The only one of the Walkers who could ever outrun her had been Storyteller. Anywhere Hope would be, Storyteller had already been. Likely he'd already met her, spoken to her, and done what they needed to do by the moment she caught up with him.

In a fraction of a fraction of a blink of a mortal eye, Hope was at the end of Shadow's path. Hope paused and while Lord Nothing reformed next to her, she stared at the landscape before them.

Hope stood on the edge of a sheer canyon cliff. The bottom of the canyon opened onto the bottom of the world. She could see the shattered cosmos spinning far, far below. Once upon a time, Water would have filled the void. A great lake had been here, infused with the Lady's energy and tipping the blue waves the bright pink of a sunset.

In the center of the canyon was a floating island. Gentle hills made up the landscape, and though it seemed small, Hope knew it was larger than it appeared. That was the way of any of the Lady's places of refuge. It would be bigger, denser, more complex up close.

It was impossible to see any of those details, now, however, not because of the Lady's power but because of Banshee's.

"What is that?" Hope asked Lord Nothing.

"The walls of my Lady's prison," Lord Nothing said.

String. Hope saw a string, faint and only occasionally catching the dim Twilight, and hanging from the string was a series of slim mirrors. They glimmered, reflecting the world back on itself. The string didn't section off the entire island but seemed instead to be haphazardly placed. Faintly, Hope heard a tinkling noise. She squinted and saw that bells had been attached to the string in between the mirrors. Invisible wind blew them, and they rang out in song.

"It seems so breakable," Hope said. "I don't understand."

"It is a maze," Lord Nothing said. "Banshee led my Lady into its heart and strung the bells to confuse her. Their noise is enchanted. They make my Lady believe she is always close to the way out. The mirrors obfuscate the true path, shining back on itself. She has wandered there, lost and starving and crying out for me."

"Why can't you go to her?"

"Because Banshee stole a piece of the sun and put it in the mirrors. They reflect light. There is only one way to my Lady. The wrong ways lead to pure light. I would not be permitted to pass. Traveling the maze would have shredded me. There wouldn't have been much left by the time I found her, and I would not have been able to show her the way out. We would have been trapped, though we would have been together."

Hope's heart hurt. "But both weakened to the point of powerlessness."

"Yes."

Hope weighed her words before she spoke. "You are weaker now than you seem, aren't you, My Lord?"

Lord Nothing's pupils dissolved into stars and spinning universes. "On the underside of the world I had saved a heart of my own power. That is where you found me. To escape Banshee and my maze and to destroy the illusion that held Water, I used some of what was mine. Now there is enough of me to bring you here. But yes, I am diminished. I am poisoned."

"The Storyteller," Hope whispered.

"He is a great part of it, but it is not only him. What I had consumed that did not go to the Lady is eating me alive. I have fear, Hope Star, that I am too poisoned to feed my Lady. I fear that what I can give her will be nothing but blackness, and she will not be able to take it and remake it."

A terrible chill shook Hope to the core. If the Lady could not be fed, if she could not escape and regain power and thus restore Lord Nothing and the world, then...

"But we must try," Lord Nothing said. "I have brought you here because Banshee built this prison with only one key, and that key is you. Only the Star can shine the way out of the maze. And that, Hope Star, is what you will do."

A tendril of Shadow unfurled with a whisper of power, and the Lady's magenta shard floated to Hope. She opened her palm, and the shard hovered over her skin. "My Lady used all her power trying to find a way out of an impenetrable maze," Lord Nothing explained. "She could not create a way out of it, for the mirrors only refracted the way, making them infinitely smaller. She was not being fed more energy, and thus, had no stores of power after her reserves were expended.

"You can and must use that shard to break the string, and you can use the mirrors to light the path of escape. I ask you to please do this. For me, for the Lady, and for this world upon which all others depend."

Hope gazed upon the magenta shard. It contained pure creation power: destructive, explosive, volatile. Without the Lady to guide it, the shard was a bomb, and in Hope's hands, that was exactly what the shard would be. Hope understood in the pause before action that this was how she repaid the world for her mistakes. She should never have become so infatuated with a single Walker. She should never have become so close to Water that his love turned into fanaticism. The lines between her fault and his were blurred, and she loved him enough even now that if doing this would also clear his name, then she would throw herself into the task with everything she had left.

And afterward, she knew, she'd be making another sacrifice. She foresaw her future in the nightmares of her past. Madeline wanted her to wait, to stall, to think things through. Madeline was terrified; so afraid.

Hope couldn't afford to be scared. It had been fear of loss that had led them into this catastrophe. Hope couldn't let fear win.

Without even fully understanding what would happen, Hope clasped the shard and willed herself to travel over the canyon. Suddenly she stood on the island, and it was a vast land of rolling hills covered in row after row of strings. They set at odd angles, made triangles and shapes and dead ends. Threatening eyes watched her from the mirrors, dozens of them looking at her. She didn't heed their warning. She didn't hesitate. She took the shard and touched it to the nearest string. She winced, expecting an explosion or worse, but instead, the string severed, and the shard dissolved into so much dust. The string didn't fall, but wavered in the air, its frayed ends floating in an invisible breeze.

Thunder exploded in the sky. Chunks of the shattered moon and sun broke off and crashed into one another.

A shriek that struck pure terror into Hope's heart sounded from far, far away.

Banshee.

Hope picked the closest mirror and dove for it. She felt herself bouncing, each reflection like a punch to her body. Dozens and dozens of blows landed everywhere. The path pummeled her until she cried out, and her call died only when she was deposited on top of a sloping hill amid soft, short, bright green grass. Green, like Earth, not Via'rra. Emerald hills sprawled in every direction. She couldn't see the canyon or its cliffs at all. Stunned and disoriented, she noticed that the air here was not Twilight. This was the light of a summer day on Earth. It was warm on her skin, almost cloying and uncomfortable, as though the light was a giant tongue lapping at her.

Shakily, Hope rose and glanced around. She saw mirrors and string everywhere. The clearing where she stood was barely large enough for her to take three steps, and it was roped off on seven sides. She glanced behind her and saw the path. To her, it shone. Her essence made the mirrors gleam, but it was fading. She had to be quick.

Spinning, Hope despaired as she didn't see a thing. The space was impossibly small. She had expected to find the Lady, broken and cut and bleeding. She was looking for a body, but instead she saw empty space.

"Lady Creation?" Hope cried. There was no answer. She strained to listen and heard absolutely nothing. The bells had fallen silent when she'd severed the string. But she also didn't hear Banshee's wail or Lord Nothing or anything else. Terror struck her. What if while she stood here failing in her task, Banshee was consuming Lord Nothing? What if nobody was waiting on her when she returned, with or without the Lady? And if she came back empty handed, and Lord Nothing had managed to fight Banshee off, then what?

He would look at her. He would know she failed. Again. She'd be the reason the world would end. Her sisters would weep. The sky would fall. The Universe would crumble.

And it'd be all her fault.

Choking on sobs, Hope fell to her knees. She felt around, blindly searching for something, anything, and the first few fistfuls offered only grass. She cried and cursed and crawled, and then her hand closed on something solid that was not grass or dirt.

Hope was so desperate, she nearly dropped the object in her haste to pick it up. She fumbled and clasped it in her cupped palms. It was warm. It pulsed with vibration in a rhythm. Slowly, Hope opened her hands.

Hope held a seed. Its shell was a deep blushing pink. With every thrum of its life, a magenta light lit it up and transformed it into a beautiful rose shade. It was shaped like an eye and on its husk were even the faint outlines of a pupil. As she studied the seed, she shifted it in her hand, and the pupil moved.

It was looking at her. It saw her.

No, not *it.*

The Lady.

Hope's breath caught. "I've got you," she whispered, struggling to stand. "It's going to be all right. I've got you now. And he's waiting. Your lover is waiting for you on the canyon's edge."

Hope's hand was suddenly damp and she realized with a sob of her own that the seed had shed a tear. The eye beseeched her from where it rested in her hands. "I'll take you to him. I will. I swear it. We'll go right now."

Cradling the Lady protectively to her heart, Hope turned and ran for the mirror. She dove and flew, fervently wishing with all she had that Lord Nothing would be there on the other side.

Chapter Twenty-Four

Andrew's favorite hill on the Shady Field Golf Course had a view of the wisteria-entrenched club house, which was lit tonight by the solar-powered safety lights lining the walkways leading to and from the doorways. The vine was in full bloom, along with the night jasmine and the gardenia. The scents floated around him, trying to make him feel better. The Bermuda grass under his butt and hands and feet was rich and green and soft. It tickled him, knowing he liked it.

"I think I did bad," Andrew whispered to the grass.

It swirled with a light wind, and Andrew understood that the grass did not agree. It should have comforted him, because grass knew evil. Lawn mowers. Weed eaters. Pesticides. Chemical burns. Drought.

But Andrew's upset was stubborn. It wouldn't let go of his guts, where it clung like a stressed out koala in a tree. "I made him talk about his Bad Stuff," Andrew murmured. "And then it appeared."

Conjuring evil should be harder, but all it took was intent and a name. The wicked were always in the wings, waiting for the cues, and the good were always tired and nodding off backstage. And it had to have happened on today of all days, because evil came with friends. His mama had to take off. Jason talked. And then the she-devil had appeared with her gang of look-alike demons.

"My fault…? Is it?"

A scurrying beetle crawled over Andrew's hand. It pinched him. Clearly, that was a no from the insect world. Well, that was something. The grass and the bugs both couldn't be wrong. He would have liked to ask the Four-O-Clock's (*Mirabilis jalapa)* whose home was a nearby land feature, but they were in deep discussion amongst themselves. They'd not yet bloomed, but they were thinking about it. Their buds were babies with adult consciousness. They knew timing was everything.

So when would it be his time?

The evil appearing had distracted Andrew from his earlier melancholy, but it was still there, rising like bile in the back of his throat. Mama thought Andrew's time was never and Andrew hoped it was now. He wanted to sprout. His outer shell would crack and out he'd come, probing the world around him for fertile soil in which to settle. The dirt would be his partner, his lover and guide; feeding him as he fed it and together, they'd grow.

But could he, should he, put down roots when there was a woman in the house with longing in her eyes? She'd see anything fresh and shiny and new as a target. She'd go for the throat. Oh, but Andrew did not like her. Not after what Jason had said. Not after how sad she had made him.

The wind blew, stirring the scented air and ruffling Andrew's hair. His mind went quiet for a little while, until he remembered the flowers left untucked and up past their bedtime. A flash of guilt brought water to his eyes. He wasn't good at balancing himself *and* balancing others. Usually he didn't have to do the first, which meant he could focus freely on doing the second. It wasn't like him to be so caught up in his sad thoughts that he didn't hear the trees warning him that somebody approached.

Andrew's heart ran up his throat and clung to the inside of his mouth when Tio stopped next to him and then dropped to the ground beside him. Tio wore black scrubs with hot pink trim, a thin, wispy, silver scarf, and big boots that covered his long toes and slender feet. There was a bracelet around his left wrist and a silver ring around the middle finger of his right hand. Andrew wanted to touch it, to see if it was as smooth as it looked, but he clutched his hands together in his lap.

"*You* came," Andrew said. The lightning bugs twinkled around them, ablaze with Andrew's awe.

"Somebody had to," Tio said.

The bugs all went dark at the same time. Sadness overtook Andrew, and his heart crawled back into his chest to beat a melancholy rhythm. "Oh. Oh."

Something about the way Andrew spoke invoked a heavy sigh in Tio. The air gusted between his perfect lips in a long rattle. He ran his hands over the burr of his scalp. He bent one long leg and propped an elbow on his knee, cupping his face in his hand. He studied Andrew, and Andrew felt the weight of what Tio was about to say before he uttered a syllable.

"I thought we should talk."

A few of the bugs began to glow again; pinpricks of light in the dark. "Oh. Oh?"

"Do you know what the biggest part of my job is?"

Andrew pictured Helen climbing a mountain and Tio in the harness under her, ready to catch her when she slipped. "Maybe," he said.

Tio snorted softly. "Well, I'll tell you. The biggest part of my job is being invisible everywhere at once."

The enormity of that kind of responsibility stunned Andrew. He sat with his eyes unblinking and dry in the breeze thinking of how hard Tio would have to work not to be noticed. He was so big in the scheme of so many things, not just Andrew's perspective, but life's. "You must be really sleepy," Andrew said.

"Oh, honey," Tio said around a chuckle. "I am well beyond sleepy and into zombiedom, but that's just part of the territory. See, I have to be in all the places that my sweet, fragile girl might go or wander about. I have to hear all the things that might affect her. I have to know all the answers to the questions she might ask about any old thing at all. I know what Miss Teedee's gonna cook for meals, 'cause my pretty girl will want to know how much she can eat, and I need to know where Miss Teedee stores all her wares, 'cause my girl needs her cream and her real butter and her lemon pepper. I keep track of what projects her daddy is doing, when he moves boxes of gears or when he finally fixes one of them clocks, 'cause my girl is fixated on time and what her daddy does with his. Even if it's fighting with the missus. She'll want to know how many rooms Monica cleans on a Thursday or how many guests are due to arrive on a Saturday. She'll want to know when you come and go so she can watch you with the roses. And lately, she's been real interested in everything mister Jason gets up to. So I know he keeps his cash in secret stashes in his clothes. I know he don't much care for green peas, but he loves baking with Miss Teedee. He loves most things that woman does. And I know that even though he tiptoes everywhere he goes, the earth still quakes where he dares to tread. He is change, the kind that brings trouble, and she done showed up tonight. I know you don't like it, I know he feels helpless because of it, and I know Darryl is too numb to figure on how bad it might get."

"Real bad," Andrew said.

"Mmhm. Could be. I have to think about all that, the outcomes of sixteen futures, good and bad, 'cause I want to protect Helen until she can figure herself out. And for the record, I do think she will. No matter what her daddy might wish. I think that like it is with so many of us, stories will be her salvation." Tio paused to dig in a pocket for a sucker. He unwrapped it and popped it in his mouth. He did that so he wouldn't smoke.

"See," Tio pulled the sucker out so his speech wasn't garbled. "I can do all that shih tzu because my mama, she was real paranoid.

For so long as I can remember, she's been thinking somebody somewhere is out to get her. The cops, the FBI, the little green men, the neighbor, Lord mercy, you don't even know. I was six years old when I found her in her closet. She wouldn't come out, see, because she heard the Postman and thought he was a soldier gonna break into the house and have his wicked way with her. She told me, at that sunny, tender age, just what rape meant and looked like and felt like, and I told her that she would never have to worry. I'd be her eyes and ears and sixth sense. I'd run her errands and defend our castle from every dragon she could conjure.

"I got real, real good at being everywhere. And then I had to learn how to hide in plain sight. 'Cause the teachers and the social working people, they all thought helping her and me meant splitting us up. So if I was good at being everywhere, I got frickaseed fantastic at being unnoticeable. Plain. Bland. I pretended to be normal, though Lord knows I was in love with the neighbor boy from the time I was seven or so, and I knew I'd never be what the holy rolling Christians thought was right in the head. I was doomed to be different, just like my mama only not, but that was okay. We were all right. 'Cause I helped my mama be normal at the right times, too. We'd know a visit was going to happen, and she'd down her pills, and we'd practice our lines. Why hadn't I been in school? Walking pneumonia. I had weak lungs. I had a rash. I'd even take a scour brush and ruck up my skin 'til it bled so I could gross the do-gooders right out. Worked, too. I could spin a mean illusion. Bend reality the way it needed to go to keep me and Mama together." Tio paused for a long suck on his candy. He wasn't looking at Andrew anymore. He was staring out at the hills. The wisteria noticed. It waved at him. Andrew signaled for it to be still. This was important. Without even Andrew asking, Tio was telling his Bad Stuff to Andrew. He wanted to warn Tio that today was a day for dark magics, that speaking ill might make it appear to infect them, but he didn't want Tio to stop talking. It was selfish, but there it was.

"But, see, in time Mama got fat, real fat, and too scared to go even to the curb. Then she got the sugar sickness. And sometime in there, I was in night school and working two jobs to pay rent and keep her in medication. When she'd forget it, she'd scream bloody murder and the only thing that would calm her down was gin and me telling tales. Her favorite one was me talking about how our house was a Fortress surrounded by snow and guardians and nobody would ever find us out there." Tio considered for a moment, hesitant as though weighing Andrew's worth to hear what he'd say next. Andrew held his breath.

"I'd dream about that place, see? That one and a lot of other ones. Caves and palaces and anywhere that wasn't that tiny little house that smelled like Mama's feet and muscle ointment. Lord how that stank. And Lord, how scared I was when I knew Mama was getting bad off enough that I couldn't handle it and live, too. But, as it turned out, Mama made the choice for me. The one thing I think she did for me, whether or not it was conscious, was to say to me one day, 'Mercutio, sweetness, I think I need to be in a place with bars on the windows and bolts on all the doors.' And I said, 'Mama, you sure? There ain't any coming back from that.' Because I knew, selfish basset hound that I am, that if I got the weight of Mama off me, I wouldn't ever want to feel it again. But she looked at me and smiled and said, 'Son, I need a real fortress and an actual army.'

"So off she went the next week to that fancy Home up the freeway. And 'bout that time I started working at the Taylor Point House, and I figured out right quick that the way to stick around when no other nurse-man or woman had been able to do so was to use all the skills I'd had to learn for Mama. The Good Lord and mystery, they're so tangled up you can't ever tell end from end." Tio chewed his sucker, grinding it into bits and swallowing the sugar. He dropped the stick on the ground and Andrew had to tune out the ants' cry of joy from a nearby colony.

"So, see, honey-Drew, nothin' but nothin' gets by me. Hence how I knew you'd be here, not on that rock by the water that you like so much, and not in that old treehouse over near the park that you found a couple years back, and not near Toby's, ready to gossip about stealing or finding or whatever it is you boys find common ground on." Tio cocked an eyebrow and fixed Andrew with a one-eyed corner gaze. "So tell me, Drew-boy, what else do you think I been noticing about you?"

Andrew's mouth was full of cotton. His throat was clogged with sand. His eyes were glued wide open, his lashes stuck to the skin beneath his brow. His lungs burned and his hands were hot enough that the grass under them tried to get away, lest it be set ablaze.

What did he know? Tio who noticed everything, knew everything that needed to be known, what did he know? Had he seen the million lingering stares? The way Andrew would watch him walk, mesmerized by the runway model hip sway? Andrew had tried to mimic that walk once in his room. He'd fallen over. His lower half wasn't made that way. Tio was fluid; liquid chocolate. Andrew was a pack of Skittles; hard and scattered and prone to leaving rainbow stains on any hand that held him too long.

Or so he imagined. Had imagined. Often. Being held. Held close. Touched. Did Tio know that? About the dreams and the long showers and the box hidden way, way in the back of Andrew's closet that contained a set of scrubs that had gotten dirty, been washed, and then stolen by Andrew's fast hands before Miss Teedee had gotten around to the folding and returning?

Did Tio think him sick? Stupid? Slow? Or worse, cowardly? For being quiet all these years and skulking, (*sorry, Mama*) instead of walking proudly where Tio and everyone else could see him?

The silence grew longer and longer, and Andrew started to shake. Was this it? Was this the chance that Andrew had been waiting for without knowing he was treading water and time? They were here, alone, at night with only the wisteria and the grass and the four-o-clocks to see them. And the lightning bugs. But all of the above could keep secrets. They weren't like the gossiping daisies or the rumor-loving, old-biddy irises.

Tio put a hand on Andrew's shoulder. "Honey-Drew, it's okay."

There it was. Permission right from the mouth of the man, the singular man, who lived in miniature in Andrew's mind. Ever-present and always there, Tio was a constant source of comfort. And if that was okay, then the world had finally righted itself on its axis.

Andrew found breath and twisted. He grabbed Tio by the shirt and hauled them closer. He planted his lips on Tio's in a chaste, dry kiss that was over too fast because Andrew had to catch Tio, who was knocked off balance. He nearly tumbled face-first into Andrew's lap, but Andrew caught him and set him up again. "Sorry," Andrew gasped.

If Tio had been born with wings, they would be all a-flutter.

"I forget I'm strong," Andrew said apologetically.

"Mmhm." Tio's hand flitted near Andrew's wrist and encircled it. He didn't try to pull Andrew off him, but it might happen. It could.

"I'm sorry. Should I be sorry? I've had a long day. And you were sharing your Bad Stuff. Like Jason did, but I don't *want* Jason. I like him. I want to teach him how to dance. But you already know how. You could teach *me* some things, and I—"

"Andrew, honey, slow it down."

"I don't know how."

Tio nodded. He disengaged Andrew's hold on his shirt but took Andrew's hands in his. He sighed and when he spoke, it was breathless. "I was going to say I appreciate the graveyard of martinis past and the cash in the cookie jar, and then I was going to sort of lead into this, but clearly I should have lead with the crush and worked my way backward to the cash."

The world lit up red, and it scared Andrew but didn't stop him from yelling, "It's not a crush!" Tio flinched, but Andrew was a juggernaut. He was a tornado. He was a flood. "I am grown. I am not a boy. I know my mind. I know the seasons and the names of the life all around me. I know how to make life grow. I know how to give it hope to thrive. I *know* I fucking love you!"

Tio's eyes were big and white and his mouth was open in a silent oh. He licked his lips and hesitantly touched Andrew's shoulder. "Drew-baby, I'm—"

Andrew didn't know what came over him, but reality blurred like the images through a window on a rainy day. When the pictures shifted into focus, he and Tio were tangled up on the hill, Tio staring up at him. They were both breathing fast, and Andrew couldn't get over how now he knew what Tio's tongue and teeth tasted like.

"Okay," Tio said, his dark eyes full of galaxies. "Not a crush. I can see that, now."

"I don't plant things for just anyone," Andrew said. He was ashamed and enflamed and wondering what came next. Or maybe not *what* but *where* and *how.*

"I know. And I've known. I mean, I've seen you. I've wanted to…" Tio swallowed. "But my job. And your mother."

"She's gone."

"For now."

"A part of her is gone for good."

"How do you know?"

Andrew took a deep breath. "Because the part of her that thought I was still little died today when I didn't obey her. I'm not her boy. I'm her man. And men choose. I would never choose to hurt her. But I do choose you."

Tio shut his eyes. "I'm so going to get fired."

"No," Andrew said ferociously.

"But—"

"No. You will not. I will not let you. I will not let them. They need me. And they all need you. I just need you more."

Tio's face split with a grin. "And maybe you need slightly different sorts of things from me?"

Andrew's face caught on fire. His ears were open flames. An entire photo album of such things flipped through his mind, and he chewed his lip.

Tio chuckled in a way that sent a chill up Andrew's spine. "My house is a wreck. The Taylor Point House is worse. And we need to get back there sooner rather than later, so a hotel for the night is out. So where do we go?"

There were fireworks in Andrew's brain. "Go?"

Tio did that thing with his hips that Andrew could not do. "To continue our bodies' conversation."

Now Andrew's neck was steaming, but he tried to think. "Oh. Oh! The treehouse. It's not far. I have sleeping bags. And snacks."

Tio shoved Andrew off him and stood up, helping Andrew up after. "My car's that way. I'll drive."

Turned out Tio was a very good driver.

Chapter Twenty-Five

Hope crashed onto the ground and pain sang through her right shoulder and echoed throughout her body. If she'd been younger and stronger, not broken and remade, she'd never have felt the impact. But she was old, nearly powerless, and weary, so the best she could do was shelter the Lady against her belly and hope no harm came to the Seed.

Resting with her cheek on the purple grass, Hope shut her eyes, just for a moment. She breathed. She listened. At first, Hope thought the sound she heard was the rushing of her own life in her ears. When she dared to squint and look around, she discovered it wasn't in her head at all. The sound was coming from above her.

She was listening to the sound of darkness and power.

Shadow tendrils lanced through the purple hazy air, striking Banshee's roots. The battle was blotting out the shattered shape of Via'rra's destroyed sun. The fight was silent except for pops and sucks and impacts. The air was raw with the stench of rot. Banshee's roots darted and dove, trying to escape Shadow's reach and find purchase. One root plunged into the dirt near Hope, and she screamed. Chunks of the ground sprayed and got into Hope's eyes. She rolled away, cuddling the Lady and feeling Lady pulse against her. When Hope could see again, she watched Shadow rip across the field of her vision and strangle Banshee's root. Pieces of the root fell to the earth, flailing and spewing pale white blood. A Shadow on the ground sought them out, blanketed them, and then they too were gone.

Chills overtook Hope. She lay staring, helpless, as roots and Shadow battled. When another dug into the ground nearby, Hope struggled to her feet and staggered away, only to fall to her knees. The ground was quaking with the impacts, the air crackling with power, and soon all Hope could do was curl on her side and cover her head. One of Banshee's roots sliced open her leg. Hope screamed into the void, the noise swallowed like she was being smothered in open air. Pain roared and light poured out of the wound. Hope crawled away, whimpering and concentrating on closing the gash. It took everything she had, every last shred of power and concentration, and still she bled. When the next root struck next to her head, Hope couldn't even twitch. But Shadow was there, swallowing up the root in an instant.

After an eternity, the silence cracked and a scream reverberated across the land. A monstrous and yet somehow piteous wail, Banshee's bellow confirmed that she was losing the fight. For now. Her voice didn't come from nearby, but far away. These were merely roots, not Banshee herself. The rise of whispering power soon drowned out the scream. Hundreds of Shadow tendrils flew. They met one another, laced together, twisted and braided in mid-air, and soon Hope rested on the ground, curled with her knees to her chest, and above her was a solid black dome. She trembled, bleeding still, and studied the pinpricks of light twinkling in the far distance of the night painted by Shadow. She knew if she looked, if she tried, she would be able to see galaxies. She would lose herself exploring those worlds. She'd come apart and join the darkness, never to be remade.

Hope sat up. She blinked to get the stars out of her eyes and searched for Lord Nothing's body. She found him nearby, humbled to his knees with his head bowed. His cape flowed, no longer even trying to appear as fabric but only as the ripple of his Shadow. It spread along the ground and rose to form the protective field around them. But it wouldn't last. As Hope watched, Lord Nothing shrank. He would grow smaller and smaller as his power diminished. Until he was nothing but a speck of darkness without form.

Hope rose to her feet and went to her companion. He was ashen; Banshee was poisoning him. "My Lord," she said, crouching in front of Lord Nothing. He was mumbling to himself. It was a language Hope did not know. "My Lord!"

Lord Nothing lifted his head. Hope held up her hands and showed Lord Nothing the Seed. "It's her, isn't it?" Hope whispered.

Lord Nothing's features cracked into an expression of anguished happiness that broke Hope's heart. Lord Nothing cupped his hands beneath Hope's, and Hope dropped the Seed into Lord Nothing's palms. The Seed lit up from within, glowing brilliantly pink, and Lord Nothing lifted the Seed to his lips. He kissed the husk.

"Can you feed her?" Hope asked. "Bring her back? Whole, I mean?"

In answer, Lord Nothing smiled. His power roared to life, the whispers suddenly so loud it was as though Hope were in the middle of a tornado. She staggered away, falling to the ground. She watched.

Lord Nothing's form dissolved. There was now only a great Shadow where his form had been. A tendril of darkness suspended the Seed in the air. With a suddenness that made Hope gasp, tendrils snapped in the air like whip cracks and latched onto the Seed. The Seed glowed so brightly that it was easy to see the Shadow tendrils snaking their way inside the hull. First there were a handful of tendrils, then more and more as the Seed began to grow. It swelled as though it would burst. Hope winced, shielding her face, and she flinched and cried out when the *crack* resounded through the dome.

The side of the Seed had split and from it a green form emerged. It wasn't a plant. It was more like slime. It oozed and grew larger and larger as the shell grew smaller in comparison. A smell struck Hope, like evergreen and cut grass and lemon trees. Slowly the slime split. It formed a shape: two legs and feet, a torso, arms that pulled away from the trunk with a sound like a shoe coming dislodged from muck. Finally, a neck and head appeared and the Seed dissolved into tendrils that were at first brown, then green, then infused with pink light that faded into deep magenta. They grew with a sound like wheat rustling in a field and formed hair as long as the Lady's body. The Lady was half the size of Lord Nothing. She was also not only a "she." Hope remembered this when the chest swelled with breasts and the groin swelled with both the lips of a woman and the length of a man. For a moment, the Lady hung nude and still forming, until the skin began to take color – pale iridescent pink – and her scales began to grow.

Deep red scales shot up the sides of the Lady's legs, covered her groin, and emerged from her tailbone in a long tail with spikes at its ends. The scales grew up along her spine, covered her chest and belly and arms, and formed a collar around her throat. At first they were white, then pink, and then deep, dark magenta.

In the cracks made by the scales, the Lady's eyes began to appear. Hundreds of eyes in all shapes, sizes, and pupil-types began to open. The protective film formed over them so they could shut to appear like lines of silver.

For now, they were all open, blinking, glancing around. Many of them watched Hope watch as the Lady's gigantic mouth first formed. The line of her lips stretched obscenely wide. A Joker mouth, Madeline would have said; a clown's horrible smile. The Lady's lips were thin, and Hope didn't bother trying to repress a shudder when the Lady acknowledged Hope's presence with a grin that stretched from one ear to the other. The Lady's jaw could unhinge and she could swallow many of her creations whole. Her teeth were razor sharp and in many rows. Now they clacked together in a feral smile that stretched across the entirety of her tiny, pixie-like face. Her little drop of a nose and the great caverns of her face-eyes appeared. They were nothing but hollow sockets at the moment; her face-eyes were her most precious; the ones that allowed her to see how one of her creations could grow. They were many-faceted, like jewels, and glittered all shades of light.

That was, when the Lady had them open. When closed, the Lady's face was dominated by two black holes. Hope had to look away. The Lady was her most armored and most terrifying to behold when hungry. And right now, she was starved.

When a hand touched Hope, she screamed, but cut herself off when she saw Lord Nothing kneeling beside her. He wasn't much bigger than Hope, now, but his cosmos eyes swirled with power. His face was gentler, kinder. His expression was one of regret as he said, "What I can give her is not enough, Hope Star."

Hope closed her eyes. She began to cry. The tears froze to her cheeks. She was suddenly cold, and when she grew brave enough to look, she saw that Lord Nothing held her hand.

"It's me, isn't it?" Hope took a shuddering breath.

"It was always you, Hope Star."

Hope cried all the harder. She shook her head in denial. Lord Nothing stroked her hair and it turned black in his hand's wake. "If... if you...?" Hope couldn't make herself speak the words.

"If I consume you, then yes, it would be enough for the Lady to form, for her power to rise, for this world to have a chance."

A duality of memory struck Hope in the chest: Madeline at a window and seeing the illusion of Lord Nothing's visage behind her, and, at the same time, the sensation of her heart being torn from her body by her lover's hand.

Hope gazed at the Shadow dome, trying not to get lost in the night sky. She could feel all of the Lady's hundred eyes watching her. The Lady hung suspended in air by the Shadow tendrils burrowed inside her, feeding her. The tendrils connected to the Shadow cape that flowed up and over them and also to Hope, where Lord Nothing wasted energy to form himself to speak to her, to hold her, to give solace where he could. It was a great kindness. But still, Hope wept.

"Will it hurt?"

"No."

Why, *why* couldn't Hope remember what it was like to die? She and her sisters had been born and lived and died and been remade for longer than any of them could remember. There was no beginning for Light, only existence when before there had been none; Purpose where there had been no form or function.

Hope had fallen to Via'rra uncountable times since she first understood her task. So why by all the cosmos, could she not remember what it was like to die? If she could recall just a bit of it, even if it was terrible, it wouldn't be so scary.

"I'm so afraid. I'm sorry."

"Hush, Hope Star, little one. Be still." Lord Nothing held her close, and Hope went cold. It did not quell the fear, but it slowed her form, made it sluggish. The tears stopped. Her leg wound ceased to throb. She was numb.

"You must call unto me," Lord Nothing said. "For you are the Light that governs our world, and I am but the Shadow which exists in between."

Hope thought of the Lady. She thought of Banshee, who had to be stopped, of Water who had hurt her so much, and of the King of Nightmare, who was the most broken of them all but the one who still managed to find the strength to attempt to save their lives.

She needed to be more like him. She needed to search within and find her fearless, infinite self. The part of her that could never be broken or ruined or harmed. The eternal piece. The part of her that was Light.

Hope took one last, deep breath.

"Lord Nothing, Master of Shadow, Eater of Worlds, whose name in the oldest of tongues, both in the language of Love and in the language of Fear, is Zee, meaning "the end's beginning," I call out to you. Consume me. Feed the Creator. Let me be free."

"Find your place in my cosmos, brave Hope. Have faith."

Zee's words were far away, and Hope floated. She was surrounded on all sides by stars and darkness. She wasn't warm, she wasn't cold, but she was content. For a trembling moment, there was nothing, and then there was everything.

Every life she had touched, in Via'rra, on Earth, and in all the other worlds, rushed at her. Lives and emotion, meetings and farewells, they spun around her in a whirlwind. Then her understanding exploded, expanded up and up and up, until she was higher than she ever thought she could be. She saw how Light was not merely Light, but also thread. Light lit up every living creature across all the galaxies, resided within them, and silver strings bound them. The universe was nothing but a great web, a blanket, a cocoon. It was cradled by darkness, safe and cold and eternal; ever-watchful, ever-present, ever-always.

Hope was so dazzled by the sight of the way of things that she almost missed the door. White and looming, it was in front of her, blocking all else. It opened when she willed it to and on the other side, she saw a field and trees and a bright sun. She heard laughter. She heard a great, chorus of delighted gasps.

"Sister!" they called.

And she was home.

Chapter Twenty-Six

"I'm going out," he'd said, as he'd stomped down the porch stairs and across the drive to his truck. He'd not stopped to kiss his daughter's head. She'd been sitting in a rocking chair, Jason next to her, and Darryl hadn't acknowledged her or Jason. He'd not asked where Mercutio had gotten off to, either. Mercutio never left Helen's side, not in all the years he'd worked for them, and now he and Andrew were missing. Miss Teedee had said so, with her hands on her hips while staring out the kitchen windows, and Darryl hadn't been able to speak a word. He'd wanted to care and comment, but his mind was elsewhere. There was turmoil brewing inside him, about to come pouring out his ears. It'd been all he could do to get that girl checked in, her and her thugs, and then the good kind of life had drained out of Darryl's body and been replaced with the sort of nervous energy he'd not felt since he'd been trying to give up the drink.

All he could think about was that Monica would never have let that girl, Judith, stay. Monica would have taken one look at those dead eyes and those sneering twins and told all of them to take a hike. Or, if they preferred, they could hang out until the cops showed up and be in for a real fancy escort out of town. Monica was like that. She could sense things and, what's more, she would act on them while the rest of humanity tried to convince themselves they were being too judgmental. Or cruel. Or just downright stupid.

That was the Monica Darryl knew and loved. She could illuminate the world, even the dark and ugly parts, and keep everyone safer for it. She could fix any problem, find any solution.

Which was why her leaving that afternoon hadn't made any sense. Darryl had spent the first hour she'd been gone convincing himself she'd be right back. He'd spent the second hour furious at her for leaving him and them, not to mention she'd gone off with all sorts of things undone. The cleaning wasn't finished, the books weren't balanced, the supplies hadn't been ordered, the list went on. Darryl'd done what he could and spent the third hour after Monica had left not thinking about the fact that she was gone, and the fourth hour had been spent with a rising feeling of guilt and shame he'd tried and failed to ignore.

He'd done this. It'd been his fault she'd left. He just didn't know precisely what he'd done or when or what the devil he'd been thinking when it'd happened.

And now here he was, on unlined back roads with it dark as aces and no moon in the sky, and he could sit with himself and somehow see the last twenty years clearly. He'd rumbled around town and on side roads and passed by fields, and he'd gone over every moment since Becky had passed. The years had played on the movie screen in his mind, and it was a damned wonder he didn't wrap his fender around a pole. He knew he was searching for the thing that would answer a question he didn't quite know how to form.

Where had it gone wrong? Had it gone wrong at all? How long had it been wrong?

He was right on top of the answers when he realized he'd come to a stop in a parking lot. The engine was idling. His gas tank was near empty. His headlights illuminated beat up Chevys and Fords parked sporadically between faded lines. He heard music, and he squinted in the face of too much neon.

The bar's name was Loose Ends. A few decades ago the owner, Bill, had splurged for a glowing sign that was supposed to be a knot of string fraying, it's split ends going off in all directions. It looked more like an alien hand ready to pluck something out of the ground. The words LOOSE ENDS were deliberately askew in vertical lines beneath the string. Tonight the second O in LOOSE and the S in ENDS were out. Lose End.

Darryl chuckled wetly and coughed. He hadn't felt good since the moment he'd woken up about to do a little barreling in his sleep and had met Monica's eyes over the open bottle. Actually, now that he thought about it, he'd not felt good for longer than that. Say, twenty years, give or take a few days? Ever since he'd stood in front of the open casket and thought, as he'd looked down, "That's not my Becky. She wouldn't be caught dead in that shade of lipstick."

He'd laughed and cried until they'd taken him into a small, dim room where he could "Get himself together." So far? No luck. For all he knew, he was still in that damned room, and the rest of his sprawling life had been a dream, and he'd be waking up any minute now.

Tears streamed down his cheeks. He wiped them hastily away. "A fucking bar." He sighed at himself. No wonder Monica had gotten out of there, away from him. He was dream-driving to goddamned bars. He was at the edge of the wagon, watching his feet dangle over the back and the wheels turn over the ground, and all it'd take was one good gust of wind to knock him off.

He had to get out of there. Darryl put the truck into drive. He started to go on his way but hit the brakes. He gaped at Monica's Camry parked under a yellow safety light near the side of the bar. He hadn't seen it until now because it was mostly hidden from his view. He told himself it wasn't hers. He ordered himself to go on and get. He tried, but he stopped again. Andrew had put pink heart stickers on Monica's windows. Not when he'd been little, but just last year. He thought her car had needed some sprucing after he'd finished washing it, and God help them but that kid loved pink. Monica had lit a fire under the boy's ass never to do that kind of shit again. She'd gone after those stickers with a razor blade, cut the shit out of the glass, and she'd scraped most of the stuff off, but the outline never had quite come away.

The light was hitting the windows just right for Darryl to see the outlines and the scratched glass. It was her, all right; like she'd gone to the place of Darryl's original sin and had just sat to wait until he showed up.

"Well. Hell." Darryl killed the engine and glanced at the entrance. He did a double take. For a second, he'd been sure Monica was heading for the door. His heart even tripped rhythm and banged around the inside of his chest. But it wasn't the woman who'd shared his bed for twenty years. It didn't even look like her. The lady was blonde, the wisps of dyed curls all piled high on her head, and she wore a tight red dress and heels. She went in without a backward glance, one hand smoothing fabric over her backside.

Darryl glanced at Monica's car. He'd found her. He hadn't known he'd been looking for her, but here he was and there she was and so. Darryl climbed out of the truck. His keys jangled too loudly in his pocket, and his footsteps seemed to echo on the broken pavement. The music grew louder as he approached. Two men with bikes parked near the front railing eyed him as he walked past. Darryl kept his head down and went inside.

Smells struck him: beer, vomit, urinal cakes. He nearly heaved and gulped down bile. It was gloomy, hazy, and not very crowded. The bar itself ran along the left side of the room. Pool tables were in the back, along with the emergency exit and the bathrooms. There were a couple of booths and some tables to the right. The door to the kitchen and storage and whatever else kept the place going was to Darryl's left. Big, round corner mirrors had been mounted near the shelves of liquor so the bartender could keep an eye on both the front and rear doors. Bill stood with his arms crossed gazing at a TV mounted on the wall that was playing a football game from the '70s. Darryl could tell by the uniforms. The woman in red was at the juke box, which had to be antique, and for her cash she bought the Stones, who started to sing about never getting satisfaction. Figured.

"Turn that shit off," said a familiar, angry voice.

The woman in red shrugged and sauntered over to the pool players. They seemed happy to see her.

Monica smacked the bar in frustration. There were only three stools taken: hers, and two others occupied by weathered men in trucker caps who stared at their glasses as if searching for answers to their prayers. They could have been brothers.

Darryl went to the bar and sat on a stool one away from Monica. She glanced at him, and her expression went from shocked to pissed to dismissive. She went back to staring at the bottles.

"Darryl," Bill said in greeting.

"How you doing, Bill?"

"Fine."

"Place looks good. Those new benches in the booths?"

"Mmhm."

Darryl sighed. "Club soda."

"Good." Bill relaxed. They saw each other at meetings. Bill was a sponsor, though he wasn't and never had been Darryl's. He filled a tall glass with fizzy water and set it down in front of Darryl. Then he went back to the other end of the bar and stared at the TV again.

"Go away."

In response to Monica's command, Darryl slid one stool over so they were next to each other. Monica glared at him like he was a gray hair she'd found in her crotch. "Do you remember the first time we made love?" Darryl asked.

Monica looked away. She sipped her drink. It was nearly empty. Instead of answering, she lifted her glass, and Darryl waited while Bill came over and filled it with more whiskey.

"Only thing I remembered how to order," Monica said when Bill was through. "I got here, sat down, and thought, 'Shit. I don't know what I want.' I couldn't even think of you and what you drank. Not *how* you ordered, right? Like you do this all the time and aren't some idiot fool. And then I remembered some surgeon with nice hair on TV saying, 'Whiskey, neat,' and…" Monica lifted her drink and drained half of it in one swig. "How long do you think my boy has been in love with our intrepid nurse man, Mercutio?"

Darryl flailed for the fly ball hurtling toward him from left field. He fumbled, only briefly, before catching it and throwing it back to her. "Years."

"Mmhm. I'm realizing that, today. I'm realizing a lot of shit. Like how it's not the house and keeping up with everything that's wearing me down. You want to know what is?"

He did, but he knew a rhetorical question when he heard it.

"Rage, Darryl. Pure, purple, undiluted rage. And it didn't even start with Becky. Oh no. It started about 40 weeks before Andrew was born. But then I had to push through. For Andrew. And then for Becky, Miss Teedee, you, and Helen. For guests I'd never met or would ever see again. For all the reasons in the world and none of them feeling like the right ones. All that therapy, and none of it stratched at that deep, dark well, and now the lid's been blown off its hinges. And it's that damned boy's fault."

"Andrew's?"

"No." Monica spun the glass in circles on the bar with her hands. "You called me Becky." She drank.

It took Darryl a moment to catch up. Or rather, to backtrack. He felt his heart grow heavier in his chest. It was his turn to stall with his soda water, but eventually he said, "So you did hear me."

Monica snorted and shot him a nasty look. "Of course I heard you, Darryl. You were on top of me and inside me and you called me your dead wife's name while you cried and fucked me."

Down the bar, Bill used the remote to turn up the volume on the TV. Or he must have. Suddenly the announcers were talking about fourth down. Darryl was too busy staring at Monica's flaring nostrils to dare a glance over his shoulder. "What did you think, Darryl, that I was so transported with orgasmic ecstasy that I just missed that one?"

"I hoped you had."

"Well, I didn't."

"You didn't say a word."

Monica's voice dropped to a murmur. "What did you want me to say?"

"Go fuck yourself?" Darryl suggested.

Monica's eyes widened briefly in surprise. Then she frowned. "She was my best friend. I owed her. I think I..."

"Think you what?"

Monica spun toward him, her dark eyes calculating. "Do you believe what they say? That it's genetic, being gay?"

"*Fumbled! He fumbled the ball! Intercepted*!"

Darryl tried to tune out the TV. "I don't think Andrew woke up and decided to like boys one day, if that's what you mean. I don't think it's a choice."

"So you do believe it's in the genes?"

Darryl waggled his foot where it rested on the barstool's rung. "I guess I never really thought about it. Andrew's the only one like him that I know. And he's just Andrew and whatever he wants to do is fine. What does that have to do with Becky?"

"Nothing. Something." Monica waved an arm and faced the bar. "Maybe I loved her too much. Maybe I was in love with her. Maybe I'm a lesbian and like women and that's why we never worked."

Darryl's heart plummeted, the weight too much to bear, and his toes tingled like his feet were asleep. He felt hot all over. "We work," he said so quietly he wondered if she would hear. "We work," he repeated, louder.

"We work in the way that two adults who are familiar with each other and don't mind banging body parts together on occasion work. We work in the way that patterns work. We're not a key and a lock. We don't open each other up. We shut each other down. We're like glue. We've gotten each other stuck in the same place for damned near two decades, Darryl. We don't *work.*"

"I disagree," Darryl whispered. He longed for something stronger than water, but that's all he could have. Damn drink. Damn diabetes. Damn life. "I love you."

"I know you do. I'm sorry." Monica pressed her palms into her eyes. "I'm so angry. It's like all the anger I've ever had is with me today."

Darryl thought of the way Monica had looked when she had first come to the Taylor Point House. He remembered the way she'd jump at any noise, jerk away from any touch. Sometimes, she'd wake up crying. Darryl had heard her. But he hadn't done anything. It wasn't his place. He'd known a man would only make it worse. So, Becky had gotten up. Becky had been the one with the arm around Monica's shoulders. Becky had been the saving grace. Darryl had been an afterthought. He didn't blame them. He envied them. He'd never be in that secret club. They were up in their treehouse, giggling and being pretty and silly for one another. No boys allowed.

"You've got a lot to be angry about," Darryl said.

Monica nodded. She sniffed. "You know, I think I hate men."

Who could blame you if you did, Darryl thought, but he didn't say it. Before Becky had died, Darryl had tried to be the example of a good man. He'd wanted Becky to be able to point at him and say to Monica, "See? They aren't all bad."

After Becky had died, Darryl had wanted to be different for Monica, in a more personal way. He wasn't Andrew's father. He wasn't, he prayed, anything like that sort of man. He'd wanted to be gentle and kind and loving to Monica, who'd been hurt by so much and had to endure for so long despite it all. Instead, he wondered if he'd just been a placeholder. A literal one; a man marking a point of rage that Monica would go back to once Andrew was grown and gone. Safe.

But Andrew was gay and that must be killing some part of Monica. It had to be. She lived to protect that boy.

"Monica, Andrew is a man, himself. He's going to be fine."

Now Monica's expression was naked pain mixed with a little girl's fear. She searched his face trying to find comfort in his insight and what he hoped to heaven was the truth. "Maybe. Probably. That's not what's bothering me."

"Then what is it?"

"You and me, it was part of the program, wasn't it? She died, and she told me to watch over you. She said things. Wanting me to be there for you, and I knew what she meant. She wanted you happy and looked after. She wanted the Taylor Point House managed. She knew what you could handle and what you couldn't. So I was there, for the accounting and the cleaning and running the place. You were a wreck. You should have been one. She was a saint. An angel. And she was gone. She'd left me there to make it work, and I did. That night when we, that first night, the first time? Of course you said her name. I didn't say anything because I knew to you, she was still all that mattered. I knew I wasn't her, but I was trying to fill in the gaps. Because that house and you people filled in so much for me. I would do anything to show you how grateful I was. I would do it all, take care of it all, be it all for each of you.

"And I wanted it, too. Don't think I didn't. I've never had purpose. I've never had goals. I was a girl who'd barely kissed a boy who ended up being attacked and knocked up and spent, just fucking spent, before I'd even figured out who I was. I've been thinking a lot about me as I was and me as I am now. If they met, what would they say? Would the younger be proud of the older? I think this shit.

"It seems like I've only been thinking of it today, but that's not true. It's been coming up for the last few weeks. Ever since that boy showed up looking for a family and reminded me of what I was like when I did the same thing. It's made me question things. Made me realize that everybody knows more about love than me. My son knows who is he and what he wants, and he knows that I don't get it. He said as much, and he's right. I've been so busy keeping myself buried alive. It's like nothing will ever change.

"That's why when I found you with the wine, I knew it was over, and you know what? I was a little relieved. We would just keep playing out the same scenes, over and over, unless I did something. It's always me. I have to make things happen. Becky knew it wouldn't be you. So did I. You're all kinds of strong, Darryl, but you've shut parts of yourself down. After Becky, after Helen, you live in denial just like I do, and I can tell you, it makes you weak. I'm so tired of being so weak."

"You're the strongest person I know," Darryl said.

Monica met his eyes. "Then believe me when I say that things have to change. We can't go on like this."

Darryl wanted to rant and rave that he didn't know what she was talking about. He wanted to tell her she was drunk and they should go home, sleep it off, and it'd be better and maybe even gone in the morning. But as soon as he opened his mouth to say that, he realized he'd be doing exactly what she said he did: denying. He'd be denying that he knew she'd been unhappy. That he'd not been happy. That he wanted to do more for her, for Helen, for himself, but couldn't figure out a way. That he knew it wasn't good to wake up about to drink the very poison that he'd worked so hard to get out of his life. He went to meetings. He'd been sober for ages. He knew it was a disease, that the want of drink never went away because it was a desire to escape into oblivion and not be responsible for choice or consequence, but he thought that at some point, it should be easier. He didn't know anybody else who dreamed like he did. Who woke up where he did. Who came as close as he did to falling off the back of that wagon without even being conscious of it.

Something was broken. It needed to be fixed. This was Monica trying to fix it. And the first step would be for him to admit there was a problem.

That first one... Fuck all, but it always sucked.

"All right. What do we do?" Darryl asked.

Monica sagged on the stool, as though his answer had shut off the electrical current keeping her bolt upright. She ran a hand through her hair. "We change."

"How?"

"I don't know. You'll think I'm stupid for saying it, all that build up and explanation all for nothing, but I've got this terrible feeling that we're too late."

Darryl's heart skipped a beat. He thought of Becky, pale and skeletal and barely breathing while machines beeped and her life slipped away from her, from him, from them. "What do you mean?"

Monica didn't answer for a while. They drank and listened to the Stones and the TV and the clack of pool balls. "I feel like our chance to change on our terms has come and gone. Fuck. I sound insane."

She did and she didn't. Darryl gulped around a lump in his throat. "Go on."

"Fine." Monica slapped the bar. "Fine. I'll say it. I'll deny it tomorrow. But I'll say it, now. I think when Jason showed up, he brought something with him. And it'll look like it's *not* him, but it is. It's connected to him, I mean. Like embodied inner demons. And it's going to unmake us."

Darryl shifted his weight, suddenly cold. "This isn't like you. It's superstitious, and that's not you."

Monica crossed herself in a nervous tic. "Maybe this is the new me. Maybe it's the old me. You don't know. I could have been superstitious. Andrew changed me. What happened to get Andrew altered me. It's not like I don't believe. I believe in God and Satan and good and evil. I even believe in Toby. All those stories Miss Teedee brings around about that kid and his skills at finding things. When she said Jason was one of those found objects, I knew, right then and there, that he'd be with us and there was nothing we could do about it. We could throw him out on the streets, and he'd hang around until we figured out he couldn't leave. It's nuts. You think I'm nuts. I think I'm fucking nuts."

Darryl shook his head. "I barely interviewed him. It didn't matter. Miss Teedee wanted him, and it was enough for me. Always has been."

"Well, she got him."

"She did," Darryl agreed. They were silent through a round of commercials. "Would it have made any difference if I'd asked you to marry me?"

Monica jerked to look at him. "What?"

"We never made it official. I could ask. Right now, I could. I need you. We all need you. I don't have a ring, but I could get one."

Darryl expected a tirade, but instead, he got damp eyes and thin lips. Finally, Monica reached over and pulled Darryl's left hand closer to her. She rubbed the wedding ring he'd never taken off as she spoke. "I want my own room back. It'll just be until I find a place for me. If Andrew wants to stay, then he can stay. But I can't. I won't, Darryl. We were done before we started."

He could see Becky's face, plain as day, in her veil and simple white dress as they stood in the front of the church. Her cheeks were pink and she was smiling as she put the ring on his finger. He promised to love her and only her, for the rest of his days. Not her days, but his.

"I'm sorry," he said to both women.

Becky had long gone silent. Monica let go of Darryl's hand and waved to Bill for another whiskey neat.

Chapter Twenty-Seven

"Psst."

Jason opened one eye in the darkness. His heart leapt into his throat and tried to strangle him.

"Psssst."

Not Judith. Not a woman's cadence hissing at him in the middle of the night. Morning? Jason wasn't sure. He was on the couch in Andrew's room. In his room. He heard the hum of the air conditioning and felt the weight of a light blanket on his bare torso.

"Jason, you awake?"

It was Andrew. Jason let out a long, silent sigh. Of course it was Andrew. He'd been dreaming of Judith. She wasn't here, looming over him with a bloody guitar string garrote in her hand. She wasn't straddling him, naked and supple and perfect, her breasts swinging as she bent forward, guiding him inside—

"Oh. Oh." Andrew heaved a great breath. "Sorry."

"No," Jason croaked. "Don't be. I'm awake. What's up?"

For a moment, Jason wasn't sure Andrew heard him. Then, finally: "I think I know for sure now that Tio likes me."

Jason couldn't help but smile. He rolled his eyes, glad Andrew couldn't see him. After Tio had left to chase after Andrew, Jason had sat next to Helen on the porch. They hadn't spoken at first. What was there to say? The heaviness of fate was suffocating. Destiny was trying to kill them. Helen had hummed softly, and it had unglued Jason's lips.

"You knew, didn't you?" he'd asked.

Helen had merely looked at him, her eyes shining. She didn't have to answer. She'd warned him in the kitchen over a batch of biscuit dough. Somehow, she'd known the past would catch up to Jason, and it would catch up to him here. She knew it'd be ugly. She'd told him only he could fix it.

If only he knew what the hell he was supposed to fix.

"Jason?" Andrew whispered.

"Yeah. Good. He likes you, huh?"

"Yeah."

"Cool."

Tio had returned home after it was full dark. Darryl had left, not even saying goodbye. Miss Teedee had vanished, likely home. The guests were quiet. The house was lit, but its rooms were empty all along the ground floor and the basement. Only Jason and Helen remained, on the porch watching the last of the season's lightning bugs wink on and off.

"Sorry, Miss Pretty," Tio had said when he'd clattered up the steps. He seemed more alive, more vivid, and his scarf was missing. He'd gathered up Helen and taken her off to the apartment over the garage. Jason thought they'd said good night, and he'd probably replied, but he had little memory of wandering down to the room he shared with Andrew.

Vaguely, Jason remembered thinking, "Oh, Andrew's in the shower," because the water was running and the sliver of light beneath the door gave Andrew away. But Jason had fallen onto the sofa and tumbled into a deep sleep full of nightmares around every corner. In them, he was hunting for something. He had fangs and no eyes, but he could see some other way. He moved slowly and he burned, burned, burned.

"Jason?"

"Mm?" He'd been dozing off again.

"I want to talk about it."

Oh God.

"It?" Jason asked.

"It. What we did. In the treehouse."

"Treehouse?"

"It's where we went. It's a place I know. It has a nice view. I go there to listen to myself."

"Andrew, you don't want to be telling me this stuff. No offense, but I just don't want to hear it."

"I know."

"You do?"

"Yeah. Because. *She's* here."

"What does that have to do with—just spit it out, already, would you?" Jason hoped the exhaustion in his tone took the edge off the impatience.

"Tio and me, we make a good team," Andrew said solemnly. "I knew we would. We climbed the rope ladder I made and keep hidden from everybody. Even Toby. Then Tio and I shut the trap door. I turned on the fake candles in the treehouse. The leaves rustled all around us, singing a song just for us. We fed each other love. I didn't know I was so hungry. I don't think he did, either. And now I feel funny because I have parts of him, and he has pieces of me. I was used to having the ones that were mine. Now I don't. And I'm scared I'll hurt what he gave me. I'm scared I'll somehow be like *her*."

"Who?" Jason started to ask, but Andrew barreled on.

"She hurt you with what you gave her. And now she's here to hurt you more. So I want to tell you how it was, with Tio, but I can't because the person you gave pieces of yourself to is bad. And here. And I should have cared more about that than myself. Even though it was good with Tio, I should have—"

"Andrew. Cut it out. It's not on you."

"But it is. You're my friend. My best friend. I couldn't run her off, but I should have tried harder. I can make Darryl listen. I could have. Even without Mama here to back me up or make people hear me. Miss Teedee didn't like her. I could tell."

Jason shivered though he was sweating and pulled his blanket higher. He could feel Judith like a sickness two floors up. "There's nothing you could have done about Judith," he repeated.

"But—"

"No."

"How do you know?" Andrew pleaded.

Jason struggled with himself. He could feel Papa Jack glaring at him from beyond the veil that divided the living and the dead, so Jason shut his eyes. "Because I stopped running. It's all I've done for two years. Town to town, over and over. I never stayed long anywhere. There was always a moment when I started looking over my shoulder. I told myself it was because I stole. I lied. I did bad things. I did them to survive, but that doesn't make them right. I told myself the feeling like I was being watched was because the cops were, actually, watching. So, I'd pull up roots and get away from their prying eyes.

"But it wasn't the police who were after me. It was her. The memories I have of her. What happened. How it didn't end right or end at all. How everything was left hanging." Jason saw Rage's toes swinging in the air. He shook his head to dislodge the image.

"I was running because I didn't know how to fight or confront her or..." He had to swallow the lump in his throat. "Fix it. I've known all along that something would happen here. I've had that feeling – the one where the hair on the back of your neck is standing up? It's been like that all the time I've been here. I had it when I was staring at the water. I had it when Toby stole from me, when I spoke to the fisherman, when Miss Teedee led me into this house... All along. It's like, whatever's happened, no matter how weird, it's just supposed to. It's normal. I've seen things. I've dreamed them. Helen makes things happen. She is..." Jason didn't know how to describe it, but luckily he didn't have to.

"Yes," Andrew agreed. "She is."

"There were a hundred times I could have run. When I had money. When I was full. When I started to understand that the people in this house – everywhere – are just as broken as me. But I didn't. I stayed. I wanted to believe it was because I was home and safe. Being here gives me hope. But I knew if I hung around, eventually she'd catch up to me. And now she's here." Jason lifted an arm and pointed at the ceiling. "Waiting."

"You're not going to leave now, are you?" Andrew asked after a moment.

"No," Jason replied, and until he said it, he hadn't known he'd intended to stay. He hadn't known he'd been weighing the options: to go or to see what happened next. A part of himself hidden from the rest had been running the odds, and apparently, it had decided to bet on the house.

"I'm really, really happy you stayed. You're partially right. Helen tries to make things happen, but usually, she's doing it from her world, which isn't all this world. But you? You've made things change around here, and it needed to happen."

"I'm not so sure."

"I know. I am."

Jason strained to catch a glimpse of the digital clock on Andrew's nightstand. He flung aside the covers. "I should get upstairs. Miss Teedee will be here soon."

"Yeah. She will." Suddenly Andrew bolted upright. "Oh. Oh! What day is it?"

"It's—"

"Nevermind! Nevermind! It's the day. Oh it's the day. I forgot about the day. You have to get upstairs now. Right now."

Andrew all but hauled Jason completely off the sofa. He ushered Jason into the bathroom and would have stripped and bathed him if Jason hadn't yelled Andrew out of the room for some privacy. Even though Jason had no idea what Andrew was so upset about, it didn't stop him from scrubbing fast and dressing while still damp.

"Hurry," Andrew said as Jason hopped into his shoes. Andrew shoved Jason out of the door. "Go find her. Now. Don't let anything stop you."

Jason was about to ask more questions, but Andrew, distraught, shut the door in his face. Jason huffed. "Figures." He wanted to dwell on the weirdness of Andrew, but knew it wouldn't do any good.

Instead, he went for the stairs with long strides. When he jogged up them, he told himself that's what he always did at the asscrack of dawn on his way to make biscuits and tarts. It had nothing to do with the rising sense of panic that Miss Teedee, to whom he owed so much, somehow might – crazily – be in need and he could help her. He grabbed the top banister post, leapt the last two stairs, and rounded his way into the central hall.

Where he came face to face with Judith, standing with her hands behind her back as though she'd been waiting for him. She was barefoot and wore another little white dress with black trim and too much black eyeliner. It struck Jason as a peculiar coincidence that she stood precisely between himself and the hallway that led to the kitchen and Miss Teedee. Judith was always exactly where Jason didn't want her.

"What are you doing up?" Jason asked.

Judith's pencil-thin eyebrows rose. "I heard that a certain someone was up with the worms. Thought I should be up, too."

"Who told you?"

"Someone." She shrugged.

"Jennifer."

Judith tipped her head to one side.

"Your new band member's girlfriend?" Jason prompted.

Judith flashed a smile. "Oh, not for long."

"What do you mean?"

"The road, Jason." She tiptoed closer. "You remember the road, how it changes everything? How it's our very own place where nothing and no one can touch us, rule us, even find us?"

"Pretty sure the whole point of the road is to show up at gigs," Jason said. "So fair bets that people absolutely can find you, eventually."

"Well, everything that is lost..." Judith trailed off and grew serious. "Jason, I want to talk. Will you come outside for a while? Take a walk with me?"

"I've really got to get to—"

"Please?"

Jason glanced in the direction of the kitchen. He knew he was early for his shift; he had time. If he got this over with now, he wouldn't have to worry about Judith invading his space for the rest of the day or week or however long she was going to stay. Maybe if he told her now that he didn't want her, didn't love her, didn't need her, she would go. It'd be quick, like cauterizing a wound.

Only problem was he didn't know if he believed that he didn't want, need, or love her; he wasn't sure he wanted the wound to close because when it did, she'd be gone for good. And so would a piece of himself. And how sick was it to want her, still? She of the glass heart, the endless narcissism, the histrionics, but here he was, diving in yet again.

With a wave of his arm, Judith whispered past him, and Jason followed her out the front door. They stepped off the porch and headed to the right, toward the side garden path. The sun was lighting the horizon, but not yet up. It was cool, if humid, and it was the breeze, of course, that blew the leaves and blooms away as Judith passed. Plants were not sentient. They were not leaning away from the poison in their midst.

"I wanted to tell you I'm sorry," Judith said. Her toenails were a weird fleshy pink with black tips, and they shone in the early morning twilight.

Jason opted not to answer, unsure if he was stunned or suspicious or both. He studied how small her feet looked on the paving stones. "Rage was buried in the same graveyard as Papa Jack," Judith said. "Did you know that? One just over the hill from the other. Since you didn't go to Rage's funeral, I wasn't sure you knew."

It'd been too much, the idea of returning to his home town for a second funeral after burying Papa Jack. Jason had worked so hard to get away from his roots and yet they kept surfacing and wrapping around his ankles and dragging him back to his start.

"I guess that makes sense," Jason replied slowly. "There's only one graveyard in town."

"You weren't there," Judith said.

"Neither were you," Jason said hotly.

Judith laughed. "Of course not. But I'm me and you're you, and you do things like go to funerals."

"You didn't seem to care at the time. About much of anything at all, except your music."

"Our music, Jason. It was ours. And it was our cure, our saving grace. With so much death and chaos and misery, wasn't it our job – our purpose – to write and share and fill the world with our pain so everyone could feel it, touch it, taste it and understand it affects us all when one of us falls?"

Such pretty, poetic, empty words. Jason sighed. "I don't know what our purpose is."

"Yes, you do. You've always known."

"Did you ever go to his grave?" Jason asked.

Judith didn't answer for a moment. "I've seen it in dreams. It's enough."

It wasn't. Jason stopped walking. "What do you want, Judith? Why are you here?"

"I don't like where we left things."

"Oh?"

"We're unfinished, you and I."

"No, I think we were pretty well done."

"'Were?' So, past tense? Not 'are?'"

Jason shook his head. "You're twisting things."

"You aren't done with me, either. I knew it. I know it."

A buzzing was growing louder in Jason's skull. He stalked

away from her, away from her peering eyes and thick lips and white teeth. "You need to leave."

Judith chased after him. "What did I do?"

"Everything. Nothing. You didn't care. You didn't give a damn."

"How do you know?"

"Because you—"

"Because I didn't act like you?" Judith grabbed Jason's arm. "I didn't cry and scream and run away? I wanted to acknowledge events and move on?"

"You weren't moving on."

"Okay, so I was running. So what? You did."

"Yeah, away from *you*, not what happened."

"Bullshit," Judith declared. "You hate me because I'm like you." Jason made a noise of outraged protest, but Judith spoke over it. "It's always been that way with us. We are two of the same entity. Pieces of each other. If I hurt, you do. If I hurt you, I hurt me. So why would I ever want to hurt you?"

"Because you're incapable of being hurt or you like pain or I don't even fucking know."

"Incapable? I'm sorry, were you with us on tour? Was that me bleeding for our fans and for the pain in my life and what's happened to me? To you? To Rage?"

"Don't say his name. You're not fucking worthy of saying his name."

Judith's eyes widened and her nostrils flared, but her voice was calm. "Name one thing I've done to disrespect him and be unworthy. Name it."

Jason's head was hurting so much, he wished it would crack. She did this, turn things around and make them so confusing he couldn't follow her. He *knew* she did it, that this was how she worked, how she won every fight in the history of fighting.

But knowing it didn't make him believe it. When they were in the middle of the anger, Jason felt insane to think that she planned her words and the outcomes of conflict. People couldn't do that, could they? It was always so real – the way she spoke and moved and what she said. There had to be real emotion, there, right?

And that emotion couldn't only be manipulation. There had to be real pain or suffering or anger. It didn't matter that Jason could recall a million instances where she'd spun the world around and made herself look good and everyone else seem to be at fault. When she was doing it, Jason couldn't remember a single example. All the conversations he had with people about her where they told him she was crazy and conniving and even that he should get away from her, those didn't seem as real as Judith, flesh and blood, screaming and accusing him of being judgmental. Arrogant. Self-centered. Overly emotional and unmanly and weak. A pussy, a coward, an idiot.

Wrong. Simply wrong.

"You can't, can you?" Judith asked. "You can't name one because there isn't one."

"The funeral," Jason croaked. He clung to his recollection of how horrible she'd been not to go, of how she'd made him feel guilty for wanting to be there, of claiming he was holding her and them back because he couldn't pick up and carry on like nothing had ever happened. She'd even said as much, hadn't she? That wasn't Jason misremembering. That wasn't him falling asleep and dreaming she was an awful human being. He had nightmares about the truth. He didn't turn the nightmares into the reality.

"You're going to punish me for that forever, aren't you? For not being able to face that circus. See those people who never understood him like I did, like we did. I was hurt, Jason. I was angry and sad and I thought of all people you would have compassion for me. You should understand. You always did, and I think you always could, but you keep projecting the anger you feel that you couldn't stop Rage from dying on me."

"What?"

"You blame me. It's okay, I under—"

"Oh my God!" Jason yelled. He wanted to scream about how she'd been a bitch for years and Rage was the icing on the cake.

He was the last straw. The last broken string. When it had snapped, the tether holding him to Judith let go.

And it was wrong of her to try to pull him back in. It was horrible that she was here tying a sweet knot around his neck. He wouldn't let her. He couldn't.

"Listen to me," Judith said. She clasped his hands, and though Jason told himself he didn't want her touch, didn't want to believe anything she said, there was piece of his heart still full of black blood that bled only for her. He didn't pull away. He stared at the places where she touched him and hated himself.

"I love you, Jason. I know—" she said in a rush before Jason could protest, "—you don't believe me or don't want to believe me. But I do love you. I do. I always have. I always will. No one knows me like you do. There are days I hate you for that. You're inside my skull, you've wormed your way into the very bottom of my being, and you're heavy and make me feel things I'm not sure are even mine to feel.

"But when you're gone, I'm not the same. I can't write. I can't hear the music. I can't sleep. I need you. Don't you see that? Doesn't that mean anything to you, anymore? Don't you want me?"

The tears in her eyes were real. The touch of her skin against his was alive and vibrant, nearly burning. Jason thought of Papa Jack when he had been tired or hung over or angry about something that had nothing to do with Jason. He remembered one time that Papa Jack had hit him, full fist to the face, and Jason had lost a molar. It'd been a baby one, but it'd hurt like the devil. Papa Jack had stood over Jason, a deep black shadow, for a long moment before kneeling. He'd examined the tooth in the middle of the puddle of blood. It'd looked so small between Papa Jack's fat fingers. "*It's nothing, boy. You should know better.*" Papa Jack had walked away, and all Jason could do was sit there and bleed and think about what he should have known. Not to exist? How to duck? Not to bleed or whine or hurt? Not to talk or ask or need something? He'd been nine for Chrissakes.

Then, later, there'd been Judith, appearing like a dark angel sent for him and only him. The only kind of heavenly body who'd ever deign to notice him. Not God, not white light, but shining, slippery, wicked blackness. And she had needed him like he had needed her. What she wanted in return didn't involve bloody baby teeth. She wanted love, too, just like Jason. It'd been on her terms, maybe, but wasn't that the way love went?

And if it wasn't, if it shouldn't be that way, did it matter? When a person wanted another, when love in whatever mask was involved, wasn't it a good thing? Wasn't that fucking magic and special and rare? How could he walk away?

Judith's need was the opposite of what he'd had growing up. It was the very fabric of Jason's universe.

"But it's torn," Jason whispered.

"What?"

"Nothing." Jason shook loose from Judith. "I have to go."

"No. Please—"

"I need—"

Judith kissed him: long, lingering, warm. "I know what you need," she whispered, and in that instant, she was right. He needed her against him. He needed his arms around her, his tongue inside her mouth, her scent in his nose. He needed her to push him backward along the path, beneath an arbor, into gray shadows. There was a bench, and he sat, and he clutched at her when she straddled him. He didn't fight her when she undressed him. He didn't marvel when he discovered she wore nothing beneath the dress. Nudity is beautiful, that's what Judith had said on their days in their hotel room when none of them wore clothes and answered the door in the buff and laughed at the averted gazes and reddened cheeks and even the anger and irritation. They didn't get it, what Rage and Judith, and Jason understood. What they knew to be true. "*Us versus them, and we always win.*"

Being inside her was reliving a memory that had once been his only reason to wake up. And as she moved and moaned and murmured at him, he stood back from himself and watched as he faded away and only Judith remained. He could see it, like someone dumped a pitcher of Jason water out and refilling it with Judith.

But instead of finding contentment in being someone else's vessel, he found a leery, exhausted, frustrated anger. He wanted to break the pitcher. He grew rougher and rougher with her, and she pretended to love it, and for the first time, Jason could tell that's exactly what she was doing – pretending. She didn't want this; she was playing the part of someone who wanted this because it was a means to an end. She thought sex was a necessary part of this bargain. She gave it because she didn't value it but knew he did, so what was the problem?

Jason wasn't sure he could answer that question, but he stopped. He let her go. He breathed and ignored her questions and touches and wanted to laugh in delight when he went soft. He slipped out of her and pushed her aside. Her voice and her entire *self* seemed so far away. He'd evicted her and she was pounding on the door wanting back inside. She didn't understand what had gone wrong or why. This worked, this always had worked, so why not now?

He realized all this, all her inner workings, in a brief shining moment that immediately went fuzzy around the edges, like the eye doctor had just changed that lens when checking a patient's vision: "*This better? Or this?*" and the second one was worse than the first.

It was okay. Jason saw enough that he zipped up and then stood up and finally left Judith hissing like a snake-woman who'd realized Adam didn't really want that fucking apple after all.

Chapter Twenty-Eight

The Horrors were everywhere. At first, as Nightmare rode astride Water's back and they slithered at high speed, he wondered why the Horrors didn't attack them. They'd likely win the fight. Water wept incessantly. Nightmare was weak, and he knew it. Ragged exhaustion weighed him down, and only the curiosity to see how this world might ultimately end carried him on.

Then Nightmare saw a massive, fleshy tendril the size of a river rip out of the ground far in the distance. Trees flew like specs of dust. A cloud of earth briefly distorted the view and then cleared as it fell. Water slowed but didn't stop. His great head turned at the sound like a crack of lightning and the echo of thunder. They observed the tendril snap and lasso around a chunk of sun. Or maybe moon. The tentacle crushed it, the sound so loud and so encompassing it wasn't a sound at all, but the sensation of being shaken and rearranged.

It was at that point Nightmare realized that the Horrors didn't attack because they didn't need to. They could destroy everything whenever they felt like it. They were toying with Nightmare and Water and Lord Nothing and Hope Star and with the very fabric of the cosmos. Why should destruction rush itself? When there was nothing left to destroy, its purpose would end.

And what would become of the other worlds touching this one? Once Via'rra and its guardians were well and truly gone, could the Horrors invade other times and spaces? Nightmare envisioned Earth full of pulsing, enormous earthworms devouring streets, buildings, and the very sky. The humans would have no chance. It would be their end.

Nightmare waited to feel a pang of loss or despair, but he was literally and metaphorically hollow. He reached into his chest and cradled the jar of salve. It survived in him, along with a few last wisps of green energy from the Feed. It would have to do.

"Mal'uud," Water said, lifting an arm packed with muscle toward an object in the distance. Nightmare focused and saw a faint red glow: sigils. It was a doorway to the Undermaze.

Without a word, Nightmare nudged Water in the direction of the portal, and Water obeyed the silent command. The ground was blasted. There were no trees, no rocks, not nothing except acres of black dust. When Water came to a halt, they wiped their faces in unison. Water's scales had dulled to a gray in the soot.

"Is this one working?" Water asked. They'd found another portal, but when Nightmare had opened it, there had been nothing but space beneath it. The Undermaze had been completely gone; only pillars of sand dropping into eternal nothing had been below the door.

Nightmare touched the doorway. It was warm. He beckoned it to open, but instead, the doorway flashed brilliantly hot and then crumbled beneath his touch. Gone. Nothing but ashen earth and sand.

He was about to bellow in pure frustration when he saw something curious: a bone jutting from the earth. He touched it, and he felt the faintest whisper of life in its marrow. The life was familiar, welcoming, and adoring.

"It cannot be." Nightmare followed the bone and soon found more of them arching out of the ground.

"What is it?" Water asked.

"Adimoas," Nightmare said, and when he spoke, the bones shuddered.

"Your lieutenant?"

Nightmare nodded. It should have been impossible. No Bone Ghost could survive Topside. And yet, here Adimoas was.

"What is he doing?" Water asked.

Together they followed the trail of bones. They grew denser and denser: a white bone web converging, eventually, at a single point. Even Nightmare couldn't have conceived of how large and broad Adimoas could stretch. The radius of the central portion of the web was huge. They stepped over larger and larger bits of bone until at last they reached what appeared to be the back of Adimoas's skull: a massive flat shape face-down in the ground, with a single bone hook erupting from the top that curved higher and taller than even Water.

In front of the skull was a delicate webbing of bone. When Nightmare approached, it skittered aside, revealing a narrow portal. There was no door; merely a drop into the Undermaze. Nightmare could see faint luminescence lighting a room. "Here," he said.

Water nodded and began to shrink so he would fit. Nightmare gestured for Water to go first. He had not traveled all this way and faced so much only to have Water flee at this juncture. Water gave no complaint. He dropped through the hole. Nightmare followed.

When Nightmare's feet touched the ground, his toes clung to an edge. With a muffled curse, he flung himself against the wall and dug his fingers for purchase around one of Adimoas's arms. Directly in front of them was the Scrying Pit. The lip around it was barely wide enough for them to stand. The dome above them had shrank until it was taken up almost completely by Adimoas's face, which flared to life slowly: darkness to pink to a conscious red.

"My... Leige..." Adimoas rumbled.

"My Wise One. My most trusted child." Nightmare kissed Adimoas's bones, and a sigh filled the chamber.

"We did as you commanded. We guarded this passageway. It is safe, but I know not for how much longer."

"We are grateful." It pained Nightmare to see Adimoas like this. It was agony to think of how many of his Ghosts were gone. And all his 'mares.

Words of comfort would be useless, and his actions would be the same if they didn't go forward with Lord Nothing's plan. "We must hurry," Nightmare said. He crouched on the edge of the Pit. He could see no bottom. There were no images, no visions or hints, or even a breeze. He wasn't sure they would survive the fall, much less what was at the bottom.

"This is where he buried the rest of me?" Water asked as he gazed into the abyss.

"Lord Nothing is incapable of lying, so yes. You are down there."

Water made no move. "What condition do you suppose my remains are in?"

"I do not know," Nightmare said, honestly. "I did not even realize there was a bottom to this Pit until we learned of its existence together. I thought it was a myth that this Pit allowed other Walkers into the Undermaze. I thought, why would they ever come here? What need would that meet? I did not consider prison. Though, I suppose, I should have."

Nightmare was stalling, and Water must have noticed his hesitation. Without warning, Water grabbed Nightmare's arm in a forceful grip, and together, they plummeted over the edge.

Falling in pure darkness is like not falling at all, Nightmare thought. He tensed, expecting to strike something solid, but as second after second flew by, and nothing happened, he began to relax. Perhaps there was no bottom. Beside him, he could hear Water panting, even scrabbling at the sides of the Pit. It was no use. They could not slow their descent. They would likely die when they landed. Or, worse, they'd be blown apart and conscious of their scattered selves.

Time bent, and when Nightmare saw something faint below them, he had no idea how long they had been falling. The glow below them grew from a round dot to a half-moon, larger and larger and larger until it was upon them. Nightmare yanked his arms up to brace himself. Water grabbed him, wrapped around him, and when they hit, Water took the brunt of the impact. Nightmare's elbow cracked against the ground and shattered. An instant later, some of Water's weight came down on the lower part of Nightmare's arm. It was crushed entirely. Nightmare had no sense of pain. His arm was simply gone beneath the elbow.

Water flattened against the floor, spreading like a giant pool. His features distorted, his body oozed apart, and the noise that filled the small chamber was akin to what it would be like if a small pond struck metal at full force. The noise rang Nightmare's ears. The impact jarred him. He rolled away from Water's center point of mass, cradling the stump of where his arm had been. That was not, however, his first concern.

The salve's container had broken. Quickly, Nightmare slathered the paste on his arm's stump. Whereas he'd felt no pain when it had been taken from him, the regrowth was sheer agony. Nightmare's face contorted in a silent scream that popped his jaw and cracked his lips. He writhed and twisted as bone reformed and sinew crackled to life. He gasped and held up his hand to watch fingers emerge. The pain ceased, but its echo left Nightmare weak. Consciousness faded from him – for seconds or hours, he did not know – and when he opened his eyes, he saw Water resting in his legged form against the wall.

Nightmare swallowed. "Thank you."

Water's eyes opened. He was bruised all over, purple marks marring his blue-toned skin. He shook his head. "How long was I out?"

"As long as I was," Nightmare said. He struggled to sit upright. His new arm looked as though it'd been burnt; the sinew was shiny and too tight. It was then he noticed there was light because he could see his flesh. He flew into a crouch, the pain forgotten.

In front of them was a pool of liquid that glowed a soft blue-white. The surface was utterly still. Cautiously, Nightmare crawled closer. He heard Water do the same.

Nightmare peered into the pool and saw small, pinkish things. He flinched, thinking of the Horrors, but then realized they weren't actually pink and certainly weren't tentacles. They shimmered with luminescence, like the pearls of Earth. They were encapsulated in little bubbles, floating without motion. He loomed closer.

The shapes inside the bubbles seemed to come in a few varieties; shards, like crystals, fetal things far along in development, as though embryos could be fully-formed humanoids, and coils of blue that reminded Nightmare of Water's tail in his natural form. Nightmare began to reach to touch one, but a sound stopped him.

Water knelt and sobbed. But these sounds didn't call to mind despair, but rather joy. "What are they?" Nightmare asked.

Water wiped his eyes. "They are potentials. The future. The eternal part of me. The part of my power that ensures I will always fight, always carry on. They are the children of Hope and Water."

The enormity of what Water said struck Nightmare with more force than the fall. If he understood, then what was before them was the way to remake Water. A memory took hold of Nightmare, as though it'd been there waiting for him to recall it. Of course Lord Nothing could not destroy Water; not exactly and not entirely. Water was the Power upon which all things in Via'rra drew upon. It fed the mundane, much as Lord Nothing fed the Lady so she could create life anew.

But Water was dual; both a being and a substance. Remaking one meant dividing the largest source of energy in Via'rra. Remaking them both would mean rebalancing an energy that would make the Hope Star's seem minor in comparison.

A world of possibility opened in Nightmare's mind. Had this always been the outcome? Had something known that Via'rra would need to be remade or even... The words failed Nightmare. Perhaps rekindle Via'rra's power? Had the Lady somehow known? Or Lord Nothing? Or possibly...

The Storyteller. If he was in all places and in all times, had he foreseen this? And is that why Nightmare was chosen to carry this quest?

It was circular in Nightmare's mind, the entire concept. It spun much like his world. If Light rose and fell and showed Nothing what he could and couldn't consume; if Nothing had to feed the Lady who then created things anew; then wouldn't the same rules apply to Water, and if so, did he always fall in love with the Star? Did they love one another, create these possibilities, and then be divided by the inevitable cycle of Light? Was this their continual and repetitive fate? How gruesome, then, the tasks of the Walkers of the Veil.

Which left Nightmare, where, exactly? What was his truth, his circle? He fingered the snapped bones of his chest and saw a shining piece of information on the edge of his awareness. It was there, right there, and if he could grasp it...

Gone. All of it. Nightmare stared at the pool and couldn't remember what he'd just realized. It was maddening.

Above them, a scream tore down the chasm. "Adimoas!" Nightmare bellowed, standing. He heard a splash. Water had dived into the pool. The surface shimmered, barely disturbed, and then the level of the pond began to lower. Water was absorbing his children, his potentials, but around them, the walls rumbled.

Nightmare was exposed and trapped. The walls shielded them from space. If they broke through them, they'd float out into nothingness until a Horror tendril snapped them up and crushed them into dust.

A faint sound like a soft hiss came from above him, and a shadow shifted. Nightmare squinted. He tried to see with all his powers of vision, but here, they failed him. He was failing. He was nothing but a target.

The sound grew louder, like water running or the disturbance of sand along a solid surface. He saw a shape, it grew closer and clearer, and a pair of eyes opened. A head, a body, all small, but a girl. No.

A Horror.

It opened its mouth, and the scream drove icepicks of pain through all of Nightmare. He staggered and fell, and spared the calmest and oddest thought to what would happen if he touched Water's children, but there was only Water, now, in the pool. He caught Nightmare, and together they hunkered in the empty pond.

Water tensed, as though ready to strike. More Horrors gathered along the rim of the pond, their screeching intolerable. They darted toward Water and Nightmare just as fins with razor-sharp edges erupted throughout the cavern. They were in the pond, along its edge, and in the walls above them. Triangular fins launched themselves through the air, striking the Horror, which flailed, spraying blood and reeling. Laughter echoed. Red dots began to glow in each fin.

"You were right, Your Majesty," Ervyn rasped. "Bone Ghosts do get to fight."

Pride and love surged in Nightmare, and then he was hurled to the side. An enormous Horror tentacle pierced the pool's bottom. The fins slashed it to ribbons, but the damage was done. There was now a hole to space.

"Come on!" Water yelled, diving for the hole.

"Are you insane?" Nightmare bellowed. He rolled as another tendril launched itself at him. That one was cut off by a flying fin, but when Nightmare came to a stop, he was face-to-face with a Horror. It opened its mouth and its tongue waggled like an electrified snake. The scream rendered Nightmare motionless.

Water grabbed Nightmare's ankle and dragged him away. Water desperately dug at the hole, widening it.

"If we go through there, we'll die!" Nightmare shouted, not even sure if Water could hear him over the noise. "There's no more of Lord Nothing's sanctuary. We will not round the world and stand beneath it. We will *fall,* Eeadian!"

Water kept digging. Nightmare wrestled with him, unsure what fate could possibly be worse: devoured here but immediately or left to float in space to be devoured at the Horror's pleasure. Seeing his fate, knowing it, but being unable to do anything but wait. It was entirely too human.

"Stop!" Nightmare screamed, and he kept screaming as fuchsia light so blinding that it singed his eyes erupted through the hole and into the cavern. Nightmare was flung against the wall, his head striking hard enough to rattle his brain. Wails, screams, dueling powers, and he saw the red lights go dim in the fins, knew Ervyn was no more.

At last, the sound narrowed into a single, high-pitched tone. The light engulfed him, and he knew what – who – it was: the Lady. He heard her cackle, mad and hungry, and always in the mood for a fight. He felt her power surge, and he knew when he was no longer solid. He was pieces of himself, particles, all floating in the Lady's light. Water was there too, and Nightmare's awareness recognized Water's, and vice versa. They clung to one another and to the Lady as they poured out the hole. They streaked through space, the Lady's power immune to its vacuum; it was her consciousness that had made this space, and thus, she could travel through it.

They zig-zagged into the darkness, past chunks of stars and planets, heading to a distant point and leaving the anguished screams of the Horrors behind.

Chapter Twenty-Nine

The lights in the kitchen were off, and in the slowly-lifting gloom, the counters and stove looked like monsters contemplating when they should move in for the kill. Jason stood listening to the swish of the swinging door behind him as it came to a halt. His heart thudded in his chest. He could smell himself – rank of sweat and half-finished sex and Judith's perfume. He looked at his hands and imagined them wrapped around her waist. It'd only been moments ago, but Jason felt out of time and its sync. He thought of Helen. He wanted to go to her, to apologize for reasons he couldn't quite fathom, and ask to use her shower. He wanted to scrub himself with iron bristles, take off a layer of flesh, and be fresh and raw and new afterward. Helen would understand.

Jason went to the sink and drank directly from the faucet. In a house full of people splitting from their loved ones, losing their minds, trying to cope, and attempting to fix what was broken, he had a shot of getting his life together. And that meant never, ever giving in to Judith again. What had he been thinking? Well, he hadn't been. Or only parts of him had. But she made him think he was a mess that only she could clean up.

He was starting to wonder if he'd ever been a mess at all and if she'd done the wrecking so she could be the savior; made him think he had a problem he never actually had, and she was the solution he didn't, in fact, need.

Jason didn't want to think of all this. He wanted to bake and get ready for the day; forget a little while and make some good food for people who lived outside of the crazy. People who didn't have long lost lovers come back from the grave of memory to chew their bones.

After turning on all the lights, Jason went to the pantry door. He swung it open and threw himself backward against the wall. Miss Teedee sat on a low stool in front of the sacks of flour, her head bowed. She was cradling her arm like she'd hurt it, and for a second, Miss Teedee was not what had been there. He'd seen something else. It'd been dark and sad and altogether *familiar.*

"Oh. Jason." Miss Teedee, now utterly a friendly human woman, wiped her eyes with a handkerchief she then shoved into a pocket on her white blouse.

"What's wrong?" Jason asked.

"You're early, dear."

"Andrew said I should come on up."

Miss Teedee smiled a sad, weak smile. "Oh, that boy. He knows things, doesn't he? Silly people, thinking he doesn't." She stood using a shelf for leverage. "But, then, well, everyone knows more than me."

"No," Jason said, firmly enough that Miss Teedee looked at him sharply. "I mean, I don't think you... You're..."

"Jason, dear, where have you been? You're a mess."

For the first time, Jason glanced down and saw dirt on his shirt and shorts. Where had it come from? The garden, obviously, but he'd been on the bench, not on the ground. He looked like he'd rolled through a pile of soil.

"Jason?" Miss Teedee was calling him as though it weren't the first time she'd said his name. "Goodness." She laughed a worried little titter. "Come here, dear. I've got a rag."

Dutifully, Jason went to Miss Teedee and held still while she swiped at him with a cloth. "Gracious, darling, but you're shaking." She peered up at him. "What's going on with you?"

"What's going on with you?" Jason retorted in a gush of breath he hadn't realized he'd been holding.

They searched one another's faces for a moment. Finally, Miss Teedee shrugged. "And here we are at the corner of Impasse Street and Stubborn Road. My Charlie used to say that when we'd fuss."

"Are we fussing?"

"Of course not, dear. We're just not telling. There's a difference."

"I'll tell if you will."

Miss Teedee stared for a moment longer, and then she tossed the rag onto a shelf. She patted his cheek. "I was just in here for flour. Be a sweetling and haul that into the kitchen, would you? We've got business to attend. Hungry mouths will be here any minute now."

It'd be an hour at least before the earliest of early birds arrived, but Jason didn't argue. He hauled flour and sugar and removed a vat of butter from the industrial fridge. He stirred and pre-heated and whipped cream. The business of the morning overtook everything, and Jason lost himself in it. He hauled pitchers of tea and lemonade and orange juice into the Solarium. He opened the doors to the dining room, set out coffee. He was so wired, he didn't want any, but his head was pounding, so he poured himself some black magic and sipped at it. At some point, he ran downstairs to change out of his dirty clothes. Andrew wasn't there, likely already out on the grounds, and when Jason came upstairs, he found Miss Teedee and Jennifer in the kitchen in a heated, low argument.

"What do you mean, 'they're lost?'" Miss Teedee asked.

The girl stammered and shut up tight when Jason walked into the room. Miss Teedee glanced at him and sighed. "Listen to me, girlie, those keys open all the doors, so you *find* them and get them back where they belong before Darryl has occasion to notice or, God save you, Monica. Go. Scoot!"

Jennifer dashed away, her face beet red. "What was that all about?" Jason asked.

"Nothing. Fool girl's all a-flutter because of her boyfriend and those band members." Miss Teedee said, "band members," as though she meant, "maggot sacks."

"You're not involved in this, are you?" Miss Teedee asked over the rim of her reading glasses.

"In what?"

"Losing things that matter? Plotting?"

Jason's pulse went wild. "What are they planning?"

"Nothing of consequence, I'm sure," Miss Teedee said. "Jennifer's just losing her mind because that boy might run off with that hell child. If you ask me, the sooner, the better. Good riddance to rubbish. If Monica was here..."

"Is she coming back? Have you heard from her?"

"Not a peep. But why would she tell me? I'm just an old woman."

It wasn't like Miss Teedee to be so down on herself or anyone, period. Jason wished Helen or Andrew were here. They'd know what to do or say. As for him, he stood tongue-tied while Miss Teedee washed her hands and went about her business. Jason trailed along, trying like hell to be useful, but eventually, he had to go on his cleaning rounds. With Monica gone, it was up to him and Jennifer and Miss Teedee. He thought about seeing if he could find Monica's cell phone number but nixed the idea. She needed her space, Darryl needed to think, and everybody else was crazy busy. He'd wanted a way to lose himself, and the house had provided.

Ms. Adlewilde and Kirkland's rooms were both open, and Jason made short work of them. Hydrangea was empty, so that was just dusting and fluffing pillows. When Jason headed for Daisy,

Judith's room, he hesitated. He skipped it and went to Iris and Lily, where Cain and Abel were bedding down. Both doors were locked. With a sigh of relief, he turned to contemplate Judith's room, and the door opened. Judith stepped out, wearing a loose, flowing black dress and lace-up sandals. In her hand, she held a ring of keys. She caught Jason staring. "Hi again, lover."

"Where did you get those?"

"These?" Judith lifted the keys. "Jennifer must have left them in my room by mistake. I was just off to return them."

"Give them to me."

"Are they yours?"

"No. They belong to Miss Teedee."

Judith seemed amused. "The keys to the kingdom go to the old lady, huh?"

"Hand them over, Judith."

"You're right. You should have them." Judith approached, and Jason stopped himself from backtracking. "I want you to have these, have everything. I thought I'd offered you everything before, but I see now that you need more, don't you?"

Jason made a swipe for the keys, but Judith snatched them away. "The fuck are you talking about?" Jason demanded.

"I'm offering you more, Jason. I thought you wanted me, but I was wrong, wasn't I? You don't want only me. You want something bigger, something greater. And you deserve it. So." Judith took a deep breath that lifted her breasts and made her seem taller. "I want you to be my new Rage."

"What?" Jason choked.

"Bass. Play bass for me. Make music for me. You'll be my equal. Front and center for all the eyes to see."

He didn't want any of this. "What about Cain? Abel?"

"They do what I tell them. It's their way. Same with Gruff. Slaves, all of them, but not you. I forgot how you are not so tempted by the physical wiles. I remembered this morning when you were inside me." Judith tucked hair behind Jason's ear. "You always were harder to reach."

Jason's head was spinning. He thought he might suffocate. He tossed his head and pulled away. "Give me the damned keys, Judith."

"You don't get it. Don't you see what I'm saying? Nobody else needs to have these." Judith jangled Miss Teedee's keyring, and even Jason understood that she didn't really mean the actual keys. "Not your precious Miss Teedee. Not anybody else in this house. I'm offering you the real keys to the world. Success, power, money... You know we'll be great. We were great. We were loved. Worshipped. With you by my side and our band behind us, we will gather up all of existence in its shattered little state and swallow the pieces. We will feel them light fires in our guts. We'll let them burn."

For a moment, Jason saw fire and smoke and bodies aflame as though viewed from a stage. He watched the sun explode and the stars fall while he played a soundtrack to the chaos. Everything he'd ever loved or wanted to love would die, leaving him with the band, the sound they could make, and then, when that was over, and there was nothing left but void, he'd be gone, too. Out like a light. One last note. Then silence.

He thought of the dinner party the first night he'd been here; of how he'd seen a world of ash as Helen had told her story. What had their names been? The Lord and Lady? Nothing and Creation? One couldn't exist without the other. One was cold, one was hot, and together, they were everything.

He thought of Helen's warnings, and it felt as though everything had led to this moment.

"Come on, Jason." Judith smiled and loomed closer. "What do you say? You with us?"

A roar like an avalanche of stone resounded in Jason's mind. He concentrated on the feel of the runner rug beneath his tennis shoes. He breathed in deeply and smelled cleaner and orange citrus air freshener. He remembered Andrew telling him not to stray from Miss Teedee, and how if he agreed with Judith, now, he'd be betraying his friend for the second time that day.

Jason snatched the keys from Judith and enjoyed the look of shock on her face. "No. I'm not with you, Judith. I never really was, and I never want to be."

Pure hatred screwed up Judith's features for a terrifying second. "We are your family," she hissed. "You belong with us."

Jason shook his head. "I wanted family, you're right. I thought I'd found it with you and Rage. But Rage died, and you... You're hollow, Judith. You're a hollow nothing. A little doll girl who likes playing with herself in the dark. I don't know why you're here, but if it's to recruit me, you lost that battle a long time ago. I'm not yours. I never will be again."

Judith stood in shock, her face draining of color. Satisfied, Jason went to the cleaning cart, the wheel squeaking again. "I'll come by later to clean your room."

Claws dug into Jason's arm, and he allowed Judith to jerk him to one side. "You don't say no to me twice," she spat.

Startled at himself, Jason laughed. "Technically, wouldn't this make three times?" Judith let go of him and recoiled as though struck.

He didn't wait for her response. He pushed the cart along. Behind him, he felt a wall of outrage and shock, and it was thoroughly satisfying. How would Mercutio put it? He'd scorned the lady thrice. He'd won, in other words.

"See you later, lover," Judith called, sweet yet strained. The door slammed. Jason parked the cart and whistled as he ran downstairs to return the master key ring to Miss Teedee. As it turned out, the skeleton key hadn't been lost after all.

Chapter Thirty

Music played nearby, and when Nightmare's eyes flew open, he registered softness and blue light and harmony. He didn't hurt. He checked to make sure he could feel his arms, hands, legs, feet. He flailed at his chest, found it cracked and snapped, and the familiar brokenness was soothing. He rolled onto his back and tried to understand his surroundings.

Nightmare was on an enormous bed covered in furs and coverlets and mounds of pillows. Silken, translucent fabric with a Shadowrock sheen was hung on the four-poster canopy and swayed gently in a breeze Nightmare didn't feel. Above the canopy was a domed glass ceiling. Through the panes, he saw stars and the distant swirl of galaxies. A fiery meteor darted past, soundless in its journey. Nightmare stared. He registered that it was very cold. To be cold enough for him to notice and be grateful for the fur blankets, it must be glacial. Despite the temperature, he was comfortable. Where was this strange, alien paradise?

He sat up. The bed was centered on a broad marble dais. Two walls of the room were covered in black vines blooming with night flowers. The vines also grew around the posters of the bed frame, made veins across the floor. Now that he sought to hear, he could distinguish the dull hum of insects and the trill of birds over the cascades of music. He stared at a tiny black and green bird that lit on a branch and sipped the flower's nectar. The smell of the blooms was rich, heady; if Nightmare took too much of it in, he feared he would sleep again.

Shaking off his daze, Nightmare studied one of the other two walls. Or, really, the lack thereof. The scene beyond the transparent barrier made no sense: it was not a painting, though at first Nightmare thought it a mural. But no, the thin wisps of clouds sliding across the full moon were in motion. Confused, Nightmare crawled to the edge of the bed, keeping a fur pulled tightly around his shoulders. The tile floor glowed faintly, as though it were crystal, not marble, and Nightmare was scared to put his foot on such pristine stone for fear he'd sink straight through and be locked in some sort of glittering ice.

He saw tiny figures moving across a hill. As he focused, suddenly the figures were larger. The scene came closer; focused. He could see they were creatures dressed – or possibly skinned – in white. They herded some kind of beast toward a circle that Nightmare suspected was a well. There were homes nearby, warmth in hearths and food taken from trees Nightmare had never seen, but found he'd like to. Women Nightmare had never imagined were cooking. Men with skin marked with hundreds of wrinkles, but not old; timeless – they were sitting and talking in a language Nightmare had never heard. It was peaceful, these words and this place. Contemplative. A space outside of time. If Nightmare wanted, all he had to do to meet these incredible people was to walk to the window and will himself there. He'd feel the cool ground beneath his feet and the temperate weather and soon would drink from cups made of...

Nightmare gasped and threw himself backward onto the bed.

He shook all over. The imagery was once again far away, the figures invisible in the distance.

But he'd been there. Wherever that was. And it'd been a bit like dying and being reborn a different thing. Had he stayed too long, he might have never come back, and he would have never been himself again.

Nightmare reached into his chest and caressed the pulse of green light within himself. It was stronger, at least rested, and he kept his eyes closed until he was certain he could open them without succumbing to more temptation.

The expansive room glowed with shimmering blue light. Behind him and the bed was a fountain situated at the northern point of the dais. It bubbled water that was clearly different colors, visible even in the gloom. To the south, beyond his feet and the edge of the bed and the steps leading down from the elevated floor was what appeared to be a glassed-in cage with an open top. Inside was a creature that flowed like ocean waves and created sounds like harp strings. It was fluid, but not made of Water. It danced more excitedly when it saw Nightmare was watching. As beautiful as it was, Nightmare suspected this musical beast had alerted the owner of the palace that he was awake. As if it understood what he had realized, the notes of music changed, grew darker, taunting, and then, discordant. The beast flashed pitch black, not blue, and it turned, allowing Nightmare a glimpse of the creature's underbelly.

It was a huge mouth lined with curved, needle-like teeth. There was no lid to the tank. Nightmare had best tread carefully. For though this was a creature of darkness, like himself, this one owed no allegiance to him.

Slowly, Nightmare climbed off the bed and forced himself to step on the floor. It defied expectations, and warmth flooded his feet and legs. The sensation was refreshing, or perhaps that was simply the relief from not falling. Quickly, he searched for doors and found two of them, camouflaged by vines and blooms. They were arched and set in opposite walls. Nightmare picked one, went to it, and opened it.

Beyond the room was a small alcove and then a gently arching bridge that lead to another alcove and another enclosed, large room. Curious, Nightmare stepped from the shelter of the stone and immediately cringed. Above him was the gaping maw of space: expansive, oppressive, invasive, incomprehensibly large and unorganized.

This was not his domain. He was a creature of tunnels and caverns and closed spaces. Lord Nothing commanded the vastness of all there was, not Nightmare.

He trembled and caught himself on the bridge's railing. Shuddering in the fur blanket, he waited for calm to find him, and he studied the mist that burbled below the bridge. It roiled and oozed, and Nightmare could hear water. He cautiously walked onto the bridge.

At first, the sights were too much to take in and to understand. This bridge was not the only one. This one led to the next square room that appeared, as the bedroom did, to be floating in the mist above the infinity of space. Another bridge arched from the leftmost wall of the next room to a bowing bridge that spanned the mist and linked to another room. And so forth around a circle roughly the shape of a star. There were five rooms in total, all linked by bridges.

Nightmare stared below one bridge. Faintly, he could see a stream. It was all colors, much as the water in the bedroom fountain had been. He followed the stream with his eyes to a central pool which stood in the middle of all the rooms. Floating above it was a gazebo, its view all of the rooms and the space around them. The bridges and gazebo and rooms were white sparkling stone, just as the floor of the bedroom had been.

What was most strange, however, at least to Nightmare, was that though he stood in the full dark of night lit only by stars, half the gazebo and two of the rooms were lit with broad daylight. The northernmost room was half in darkness, half in light. There was no sun, though there seemed there should be.

Recollection of a long-ago-told-tale tickled his mind. It was an unpleasant sensation. Nightmare turned, then, with trepidation, but he had to see. The stream below the bridge soon thereafter fell over an invisible edge with a splash and fed what appeared to be a rainbow ribbon encircling the entire structure. It seemed weak, insubstantial, barely enough to keep this place safe from the crushing vacuum of Nothingness.

And yet, as Nightmare watched, the water of the stream surged. A gush flowed beneath the bridge, making it shake slightly, and the ribbon of color beyond the floating palace grew wider.

Nightmare went down on one knee. He knew where he was. This was the Bridges Manor – the Lady's very own home. None of the Walkers but she and Lord Nothing ever came here. Somewhere in this structure was her Garden, where she grew all that lived in all the worlds that existed or could exist. Had he woken up in the bed she shared with Lord Nothing? Where they mated, however it was they did so, and thus the Lady became pregnant with ideas and creatures and the desire to manifest them?

There were dozens of stories, maybe hundreds, of the Lord and Lady. Each new 'mare came with a new one: the Lord and Lady loving one another and spawning a new world; the pair fighting and an entire universe winking out of existence; Nothing falling into despair that only the Lady could rouse him from, and she did that not with caresses and tenderness, but with her teeth and claws and spiny tail. Nothing craved sensation, and the Lady was a glutton for inspiring all things, any *thing*, every *thing*.

Nightmare turned to see the other rooms. The split night and day now made sense. Lord Nothing could only exist in Twilight or full dark. There was a legend. Millennia ago, after the Lady had brought Lord Nothing to Via'rra from wherever it was he'd been, and after the Lady had made Lord Nothing the Mountain Fortress, the Lord had become jealous of the Lady's home in the cosmos. She lit it with her power – her colors, her flame, her desire – and thus, the Lord of Nothing could not visit her there. He didn't know what she did there, though she told him she ate and created and rested. He became jealous and tried to attack the palace with his guardians.

The Lady, furious at the siege, had struck back. In that moment, it seemed they'd both forgotten that the Lady could only create if fed by Nothing who ate all that she no longer needed. Instead, they fought with the very creations they had once mated in love to make. Many had died, and much had been destroyed. The Lady, in pure rage, had cast Lord Nothing out of her Palace and turned the light of Via'rra onto every inch of ground except for Lord Nothing's Fortress. Thus imprisoning her Lord, the Lady had returned to her Manor and caroused with the gods and goddesses of hundreds of worlds for a thousand years.

When finally she began to weaken, for she had not been well and truly fed in the ways only her Lord Nothing could provide, she dismissed the merrymakers, who were by then spent and small and, at least in some part, terrified of their host, and went to the Fortress. Lord Nothing had kept himself occupied with his paintings and his servants, but when the Lady had knelt before him in divine supplication, Nothing had instantly forgiven her. Twilight once again consumed Via'rra, Lord Nothing had crossed and devoured portions of the land – had slithered through gates to other worlds, and devoured great heaps of food for the Lady's consumption. It was said that from their reunion, whole galaxies were born, including the Blue World, Earth.

The Lord and Lady had then compromised: half her Bridges Manor would be in darkness so the Lord could visit her. The other half would be in light, so her garden could grow and flourish. Lord Nothing had been more than satisfied with this, and so it was and had been since.

A noise startled Nightmare, and his sinew crawled. Laughter and then, a whisper like a lover's kiss in his ear: "Mal'uud, join me."

Nightmare hunched over and hugged himself. He didn't care if he was observed and deemed weak. He was a creature of Fear. He spoke that language, and from it, he was born and created 'mares for his realm. The Lady, however – her language was Chaos, for only in it could Creation occur. The language of Chaos could burn or caress; it carried no rules, no tithes, no constants. Before such limitless and unpredictable power, Nightmare felt small. He was a child of night somehow in the center of a supernova.

But if Nightmare was here, then so too had to be Water. And if this Manor existed, now, then it must have been recreated, and that meant the Lady must have been returned to some of her power. It followed, then, that Lord Nothing was here, or nearby, and perhaps the presence of these gods and creators in one place meant that defeating Banshee might truly be possible. He would not know, however, if he did not face the Lady.

He crossed the bridge in the direction from which the voice had come. The next floating room was a library with a dizzying two-walled display of a portion of space that was different from the one actually outside the room's walls. Nightmare didn't dare look too long, else he be sucked into a nearby black hole. Nor did he study the figures that occupied the nooks and crannies of the Lady's library. Most of them were bound in ways that had less to do with the Lady's sexual desire and more because of the creatures' innate danger. Many of them made noises behind stuffed or muzzled mouths. All of them were clearly aroused and attempting to entice him. He had no interest in such things. But the Lady thrilled in all delights, and the carnal was no different. While that did not particularly disturb Nightmare, nor did the actual sight of the bound creatures – Nightmare had done his share of binding and torture – the idea that made him uneasy was that these were the sounds and sights the Lady desired while studying the millions of tomes stuffed onto the towering shelves. She found them soothing.

Halfway across the next bridge, Nightmare stepped into daylight without the accompanying warmth. Holding fast to the fur, he held up his free hand to block the rays coming from their unseen source. He walked quickly to the next room, threw open the door, and entered. This room was a dining hall. Two walls had a view of a forest glade, so real and so near that Nightmare could hear the cries of animals and smell the murk of undergrowth.

The other two walls were solid gold and hammered into murals depicting the Lord and Lady intertwined in bliss. The domed ceiling was a swirling circle of ever-moving clouds that filtered streaming sunlight, which dappled the golden floor and fell into patches on the immense dining table. The table itself was wooden, a thousand faces carved on its legs and edges, and it was surrounded by golden chairs with red velvet backs. The table's top was covered in a disarray of jeweled plates, goblets, and platters. They were empty.

Nightmare went still. At the head of the table, lounging sideways in a gilded throne chair, was the Lady. One black boot swung idly where it dangled over the chair arm. Her legs above the boots were covered in her blood-red scale armor – said to be forged from the lives of a million beings, that armor. It covered her torso and her breasts, leaving her shoulders and arms bare. Her floor-length hair rose from her diminutive head straight up and back and then down, it's red-orange-yellow-pink hues like that of fire. Her large, pointed ears glittered with gems.

And one of her hands was entirely engulfed by her mouth, which had unhinged at the jaw, stretching obscenely. With a slurp and an undulation of throat and face, the Lady withdrew her fist and a plate. Her purple tongue snapped left-right across her lips, and she sighed in deep satisfaction before hurling the plate and laughing when it ricocheted off the walls.

"Aaaaaaall gone," the Lady sang. She held up one arm. A dozen eyes – all shapes, sizes, colors, and types – blinked at Nightmare. "Well." The Lady wiggled her fingers. She slapped the table and in blinding speed leapt onto its top. She crouched, grinning with all her teeth, ear to ear. The eyes on her face were closed, leaving hollow, black sockets. Her pure white skin stretched taut over her fine bones, her features exactly between male and female; at once one, then the other, and both. When she rose, her tail lashed between her legs, idly scratching an itch, and then she began walking toward Nightmare. She kicked aside crockery, destroyed glassware, and crunched precious metals. Her claws were extended, black as night and tipped in blood red. When she reached the end of the table, she put her hands on her hips.

Nightmare stood stricken, a confusing array of emotions washing over him. He wanted her. He longed to run. He needed to break bread and feed it into her gaping mouth. He should dive under the table and pray she wouldn't seek him out. He felt immense sympathy for his 'mares, and then a righteous swell of pride that he was even a little like this creature, this god and goddess as a terrifying *one*.

With a flash, the Lady opened her eyes. Two enormous rainbow-colored faceted gems gleamed where a moment ago, only sockets had been. Her other eyes closed into silver slits. It was a great honor. Nightmare's spine straightened.

"The Nightmare King, awake," the Lady said, her voice exactly between high and sweet and deep and resonant.

"Yes, Lady Creation."

She tipped her head. "My way of travel can be a little hard on inflexible tissues." She sucked her teeth. "Good you are intact."

"I am yet grateful," said Nightmare.

"Grateful. How dull." She cackled, leapt off the table, and was instantly in front of him. She grabbed his head, dragging him down to her level. Their lips nearly touched. She was hot; she burned. "What I want to know, Nightmare King, Mal'uud 'au Keen of the Fear, is are you ready to fight?"

The Lady's other love – war. Nightmare had forgotten. Now he remembered. "Yes, my Lady," he said, struggling to remain still in her iron grasp.

The Lady purred. Her tail wrapped around Nightmare's leg and squeezed with what he thought was affection that still scorched him and rendered his limb numb. She released him. "Good. The others await. Let us go see them. I've missed them. Oh, oh... Haven't you?"

Nightmare didn't have the chance to answer. He chased after the Lady, who walked so fast, she seemed to appear one place and then another, far ahead and always laughing, laughing.

Chapter Thirty-One

"Good night," Jason said as Kirkland and Ms. Adlewilde made their way up the stairs to their rooms. When they were out of sight, Jason sank onto the bottom step in exhaustion. The day had been insanely busy without Monica. Jason had no choice but to order Jennifer around, making her help him when the Solarium had been empty. Jennifer jumped every time he spoke to her, but she did what he asked, at least. Miss Teedee did what she could, but Darryl didn't come out of his room, and Andrew was busily hacking away at the landscaping outside. The one time he did come into the entryway, he'd nearly knocked over a lamp. Jason and Miss Teedee had sent him on his way in unison. Mercutio and Helen didn't make an appearance, even at dinner, and by the end of the day, Jason understood why Monica needed a fucking vacation.

It was exhausting, holding everything and everyone together. He was not built for this shit.

Jason didn't have enough time to finish his cleaning rounds;

he still needed to vacuum upstairs and do Judith's room. She'd been down with Cain and Abel at dinner, but they'd left during dessert. Gone off to explore or something. Jason honestly didn't care. The relief of having her out of the house was overwhelming, and he thought he'd overheard her telling her cronies that they wouldn't be there much longer, now. The idea of them packing up the next morning and leaving Jason and his new family behind carried Jason through dinner and making nice with the guests and cleaning up afterward.

Now there was nothing left but to cover the food, go handle Judith's room while she was still out, and then collapse into bed. At least he'd sleep like the dead once he got there. Wearily, Jason rose, cracked his spine, and slogged down the hall, through the pantry, and into the kitchen. The light was blinding, and he turned off the switches. The lights in the Solarium and on the back deck were lit, and Miss Teedee sat in a rocking chair on the deck facing the water. Jason froze. Miss Teedee didn't turn her head; she simply rocked; slowly, slowly, creak, creak.

Overcome with an idea that was urgent yet not quite formed, Jason crept through the kitchen. He gathered a plate and a sampling of food and desserts. A little hashbrown casserole, a dollop of peas, a generous square of apple cheesecake crumble, and a dab of blackberry cobbler – all Miss Teedee's favorites. She'd never told him as much, but he knew. He saw the way she breathed in the oven's smells when cooking the bars and cobbler, and she taste-tested the hashbrowns more often than necessary.

Jason started to pour sparkling water into a clean glass but stopped himself. Instead, he went to a half-empty bottle of sweet blush wine. He'd never seen Miss Teedee drink. But maybe today she needed it.

Loathe to disturb the peace, Jason attempted to carry plates and forks and glasses and open the screen door with as little noise as possible. It seemed to work. Miss Teedee was so lost in thought, she didn't look up until he set down the plate. "It's not exactly buying you lunch," he said, letting the offer hang in the air and seeing if it would satisfy their bargain.

"Look at you." Miss Teedee smiled, and thus accepted his terms. "If we stay this busy, sugar, it might be all we get." She forked up the cobbler and chewed with her eyes closed. "I really shouldn't indulge."

"Oh, but you should." Jason handed her the wine, and she feigned surprise. When she took a sip, however, it seemed to Jason she was stopping herself from finding the bottom of the glass in a single gulp. "Well?" Jason asked of nothing in particular.

"Well," Miss Teedee agreed. She gestured with her hand, and Jason sat in the rocker next to the table between them. "Would you look at that? The view, I tell you what..."

In truth, Jason couldn't see much of anything with the lights around them, but he heard the water, saw the tree limbs outlined against the night sky, and he saw the brightest stars and planets glowing from far, far away. "Memory gazing," Jason said.

"What was that, dear?"

Jason shrugged. "Something Judith once said. It shouldn't be called star-gazing, but memory gazing, because what we're seeing is light that happened a long time ago."

Miss Teedee made a thoughtful sound. "Maybe that's why looking up at night makes us wistful. Our memories are in better company."

"Are you remembering something?"

"Are you thinking of going off with that woman upstairs?" Miss Teedee countered.

"No," Jason said softly. "Though, I guess I am, but not in a considering it sort of way. More in a wonder-what-would-happen kind of way. And I know what would happen. It'd be more of the same."

"And the same was pretty bad, I reckon?"

"You reckon right." Jason could feel Miss Teedee studying him. She took a bite of cheesecake. There was a long silence punctuated by night insects and the serenade of frogs.

"Darling, I'm going to say this because I think you need it confirmed: that woman is a horrible little creature, and I know something about horrible."

Jason didn't answer. For some reason, it didn't feel right. Instead, he stopped rocking and tried to remain as still as possible. He waited, listening and trying to watch Miss Teedee out of the corner of his eye.

Miss Teedee drank deeply. In the light, her thin lips shone. "It's like being in a cocoon with a warming lamp on you. That's what their attention is like. They isolate you, wrap you up tight in their particular brand of affections, and they turn the brilliance of all their considerable efforts right on you. It's as though they've created a little egg, and they're waiting on you to hatch into something that will be theirs and only theirs, live for them and only them, and when that inevitably doesn't happen, well, they keep on trying, don't they? They wrap you up again, tighter this time, and it's harder to breathe, and the light almost burns. You want to hide in that cocoon, not snuggle up and sleep, and when you fail again to be exactly whatever it is that they want you to be... Well, sooner or later, that cocoon is a cord, and it's wrapped around your neck. And they're standing there, watching you dangle and gag, and they're making it out like you done wrapped that cord yourself and if only you'd done right by them, you wouldn't be hurting yourself."

"Charlie?" Jason dared to whisper.

"Oh, goodness," Miss Teedee exclaimed. Her head went back, and for a moment Jason saw the girl she'd been. "No, no. My Charlie was a pussycat. He was my darling. If anything, I worried that I was the cord around *his* neck. You spend too much time with people who like to tie you up in knots, you worry that you can't be anything other than tangled."

The truth of it hurt Jason's stomach.

"No. Charlie, well, he wasn't the first, sugar. He most certainly wasn't. There was someone before him. John." She touched her lips. "Oh dear. The wine."

"Who was he?" Jason pressed.

"I shouldn't say." And though Miss Teedee lapsed into silence, Jason held his breath, thinking that if she forgot who he was and that he was there, she might tell him everything.

"It was a very bad time, and a very long time ago." The rocking chair creaked, and the last bit of wine slid around in Miss Teedee's glass, to and fro. "I got in the family way long after anybody, including me, thought it to be possible. For the first little while, I thought it was the change of life, not, well, not a new one. Creation and breathing existence into spaces it wasn't before, that's women's work, but a woman can't do it if a man has got her cornered. And that was me. I was cornered in our little house on the outskirts of a tiny town. John didn't like me going out. He didn't think I needed friends, because he didn't need any. He went with me everywhere, even church, though he hated the word of our Lord and pastors and Christians. They had pity in their eyes, he always said to me, all of them. He was paranoid and mean, and so you see why I couldn't tell a soul about the little one I was carrying.

"I kept it to myself. I thought I could hide it forever. I always did that – tried to hide. You know how that is, don't you?" The question didn't need an answer. "But eventually, even John, dim though he could be, grew wise to my shape and condition. I thought, stupidly, that maybe he'd be happy. I was pretty sure it'd be a boy. Women can know these things sometimes, but I forgot one very important thing: no one and nothing could ever come before John. Especially a baby, who'd need everything all the time."

"What happened?" Jason whispered when Miss Teedee went quiet and the night noises rang too loudly in Jason's ears.

"Well, honey, what always happens in those sorts of situations. John only knew one way to fix any problem, and that was beat it to death. So he hit me. I don't remember much of it. I was used to it, you see, and I knew how not to be inside myself when the pain was being laid down. I watched it, floating around outside myself and wondering why in the world I didn't just leave him. When you're detached like that, you see all the answers and know you're being silly or just plain willfully stupid, but it all changes when you float back down and have to live inside your flesh again.

"When I woke up after the beating, I knew two things: I was hurt bad, and the baby was coming. I don't think men ever understand the pain women are built to bear. We're pliable creatures, and men are so solid. We bend and weave with change and wind, but men try to push against it. They want to stop it, but a woman knows how to flow with it. That's the only way we get through birth. Well," Miss Teedee clucked her tongue. "You've heard enough womanly details. I made it through, and I had a son. I remember sitting there in all that red after all that pain thinking I'd never wash it all away. But I was happy, holding him. I kissed his head and named him Addis. It's Hebrew, means 'son of Adam or the red earth.' I thought of him as born of blood."

"What did John do?"

"Oh, well, when he didn't come in to kick me for making noise, I knew he was out drinking. Blessedly so. It gave me time to meet Addis, to figure out how to walk, and... Well."

"What?"

"I shouldn't."

Jason bit his tongue on pleading. Miss Teedee picked up the fork and swirled it through the food. She didn't take a bite. "You remember that day we met, and what I said?"

Jason had memorized the conversation. It had changed his life. "Penance."

"You do remember." Miss Teedee collapsed against the chair. She rocked. "Of course you do. Well. I sat there with that baby, that fresh little life, and I thought – no, I knew, that when John came home, that baby's life would be over. One way or another, he was through. Those fingers and toes and little tummy; that sprig of hair and the teeny ears; all their perfection wouldn't save him. John would kill my boy, either right quick and there or slowly over the years. I knew it. And I knew I wouldn't have it.

"There's a strange moment when you realize you're done with something. Everything gets calm and quiet and clear. I loaded that shotgun without a worry in the world. I was dragging myself around. I was hurting, oh, honey, you just don't know, but I made up a basket. I cleaned that baby, and then I cleaned myself. I tucked that baby up tight. He had to have been hungry and cold and scared, but I guess he was more tired than anything because he barely made a peep.

"No, that baby didn't make a sound until John came home, walked into the bedroom, started to bitch about the mess, and I put a hole in his chest. Then that child screamed, and oh, my ears were ringing, but to me, it all sounded like triumph. I think Addy knew. I held him and I explained it, and he calmed down. I didn't have any way to feed him myself, not then, nothing had come in, but I gave him a little watered-down milk. I didn't know what else to do for him, and then I realized I couldn't keep him. I looked at my dead husband with a fist-sized hole blown clear through him, and I understood that the cost of doing away with one life that was trying to kill me, and us, was giving up the one that had been responsible for saving me."

"You left him?" Jason croaked. His eyes were burning and his throat was closing up. He went red, embarrassed, but Miss Teedee reached across the table. Jason took her hand.

"On the fire department's steps. I put Addy under the shelter of those big white pillars, and I explained why I had to go. It was a clear, warm night full of stars and moon; a gentle breeze. He didn't even cry. But I did, all the way to the bus station two towns over. I wept as I left the car. I cried when I used the last of my money to pay for a ticket, and I figure I'd be crying still, were it not for Darryl and Becky. It was Miss Becky who helped me find a new name and start over. She was the one who told me I was safe in this house. I thought they'd come, I waited for someone to get me, to call me out as the monster I was, but nobody ever did. The whole town had known he beat me. It was a source of his pride. And the town wasn't stupid. They had to put two and two and baby together and figure what happened. My guess is they let it all go. I was free, but I paid for it with... Oh, just everything.

"And there are times I think I should have died back then, especially today, the day that every year I recall it in detail. Living and dying color. But eventually, I conclude that it makes more sense in the balance of the universe if I live and remember what I did day after day. The toll of taking a life is grave, darling, and paying that debt takes so much more than an instant in the life taker's. Even if that instant would have been a final one." When she looked at Jason, she smiled and squeezed his hand. "With the right help, anyone – no matter what – can start over and become a new person.

"That's why I'm telling you this nasty little story, honey. You're the third person who has found a way to this house in need of safe harbor and change. This place, there's something about it. The lines of reality are drawn in sand here, not stone. You can move them around, redraw them, figure out what you want them to look like."

"What if they look the same as they always did?" Jason asked. "What if you think you're changing, but all you're doing is folding yourself into the same shape in a different way?"

Miss Teedee sighed. "I think I'm trying to tell you that you don't have to do that."

"I hear you," Jason whispered, and Miss Teedee nodded. She squeezed him one more time and then let him go. They rocked next to one another, Miss Teedee lost in her thoughts, and Jason not saying what he was thinking: that she remembered every moment of that day in her life when she changed, and none of the details had been altered. No matter how far she'd come, that pain and those choices were with her. To the mind, the past, present, and future were the same. It took more than penance and time to change anything – to atone for anything. It took a miracle. Miss Teedee's miracle was her own perseverance.

And Jason feared what his might be, or even if he had a miracle to spare.

Chapter Thirty-Two

He gave chase through a room with a view of a bustling city life, the buildings not of any sort Nightmare had ever seen. He understood rather than saw with any detail furniture in that room which was alive, sentient, and curiously savage. A lounge that could crush you. A chair that would caress you. A table that sat crouched and waiting to be fed. He was out of the room before violence became reality, and after another bridge, he followed the Lady into the northernmost room of the complex. He passed through the stone archway and paused, one hand in his chest to calm himself.

The room was mostly windows which showed exactly nothing – not the cosmos, not a place; simply a white blank. A perfectly straight line down the center of the room divided it into night and day. Also divided was a central pit of sorts, encircled by stone and filled with mud. From the soggy earth grew a slick, thick, green vine with a single, enormous, pure white bloom, not yet opened. The vine had bent entirely into the light, and the iridescent petals glittered. The fragrance of the flower was thick in the air – sweet and subtle. It was humid and warm. Nightmare wiped damp mist off his forehead.

Surrounding the mud pit were a series of rugs, and situated on them was Water in his manshape form, soaking in the sunlight. Lord Nothing lounged on a stack of pillows on another rug, and he was entirely on the darkened side of the room. Half in the light and half in the dark was a man in the prime of life, who stood when he saw Nightmare.

"Mal," said Daanske, the Storyteller. He crossed to where Nightmare stood and put his hands on Nightmare's arms. His eyes were purple skies, and his smile was benevolence. "You did well, son."

The denial of lineage died on Nightmare's tongue. Suddenly he was broken – exhausted and overwrought and too far from his caverns. He was aware of an intense pain, of something *missing*, and the flood of guilt and anguish that took him blocked the light and chilled the day's warmth.

"Easy," Storyteller said, holding Nightmare, who let himself be held until he had to pull away, else he never would.

"How are you here?" Nightmare asked.

"How dare you ask such a thing where I can hear you," the Lady said without much malice. Or maybe with all the malice. It was hard to tell with her. She gave Lord Nothing a passionate kiss before jumping into the mud pit. She went to her knees and nuzzled the blossom. She pouted. "Really, have I been gone so long everyone forgot me?"

"Never, my Lady," said Lord Nothing.

"Good, then." The Lady's eyes opened on her arms and chest. They glared at Nightmare.

"She remade me," Storyteller interpreted.

"My beloved ate well of the last salvageable parts of our world," the Lady said, still contemplating the flower. The way she stroked its veins stirred uncomfortable lust in Nightmare, and he looked away. "Enough that there is this manor, and Daanske, recovered, and soon, one Hope Star."

"You're remaking the Walkers?" Nightmare asked. "But how? I did not think such a thing was..." He trailed off, not remembering if that's the way the world had worked before the Horrors or not.

"I did it in the usual way, little Nightmare King." The Lady stood. "My beloved did not chew the Walkers, because they'd break his teeth. He gulped them whole and he carried Daanske and the Hope child around in his belly. They gnawed at him, hungry, hungry little beasties, but he's the stuff of darkness. What is pain to him?" She cackled and cut it off as though the sound offended her. "And when we came to be joined again, he sprayed their essence into me, and I planted them in the ground. There's only a little of my garden left," she sighed at the mud pit. "But once we take back the world and remake it, I will be restored. I will grow new beasts and trees and grasses and galaxies. It will be wonderful, won't it, beloved?"

"Of course, my Lady," said Lord Nothing, besotted and indulgent.

"Now that the Lady is restored, will Lord Nothing consume the Horrors?" Nightmare asked.

"Oh, he could swallow a good number of Horrors, all right, but he cannot absorb Banshee."

The name pulsed through Nightmare in a twist of pleasure and pain, and he doubled over. Storyteller rubbed his back.

"Ah, didn't remember her name, did you, little king?"

"Go easy," Storyteller said to the Lady, who waved a dismissive hand.

"Banshee's acid. That Walker is pure rot. She's made to unmake. Honestly, you are soft in the head as well as empty in the heart, Mal'uud."

"Banshee is the very idea of this world not existing," Storyteller explained. "She is dark corrosion. Ending."

"I see," said Nightmare.

"You don't," the Storyteller said calmly. "Not yet. But what matters is that even though it cost him, Lord Nothing dragged around my body and soul, and he held onto Hope's form. Her soul, though, is split seven ways, so we don't know who's going to come out of that flower."

"It will be the Hope Star," Water said.

The Lady was beside Water in an instant, and she backhanded him. Water flew across the room and crashed into a pillar. Water scrabbled away from the windows, and cold terror danced along Nightmare's spine. If Water had entered the blankness, then he would not have returned.

"Have a care, Freeja," Storyteller said.

"Oh, invoke me all you want with my name and all my history," the Lady said dismissively. "I owe that bastard more than one beating for nearly destroying my entire world. Mine. *Mine.*" She roared the repetition, and Nightmare's ears rang. "I made this land, these stars, and connected this pile of rock and ruble to the cosmic all that is, and you... You..."

Shadow's tendril snaked around the Lady's throat, and she ended her diatribe on a note of disgust. She put her back to Water, who merely nodded meekly, as though accepting this punishment as his due.

Nightmare collapsed onto one of the rugs. The room was too full of power, and the world below was too far gone. He was hopeless and near helpless. So very empty.

"Are you certain?" Lord Nothing asked, his swirling gaze on Nightmare. "I could do unto him as I did unto Daanske."

"What good would it do?" the Lady answered. She was studying Nightmare as well, all her eyes on him, blinking, scowling, assessing. "You eat him. I plant him. He grows up just as broken." She shrugged. "He'd still be missing parts. I can't remake those any more than you can digest them."

"Yes," Lord Nothing agreed, and he sounded sad.

"We'll take back what's ours, and then he lives. Or we don't, and the universe dies. Come what may. Oh, she stirs!"

The flower was moving. The Lady returned to the mud pit. The blossom was nearly as large as she was, and it was swelling bigger by the second.

"There is danger here," Storyteller said to Nightmare in a low voice. "Zee was only able to carry around Hope's body, not her soul. That has to return to the husk."

Nightmare didn't follow. "How is that a threat?"

Storyteller shrugged. "It could be dead. It could be a monster. There are things that walk these stars searching for husks to inhabit, you know. If Light doesn't grace us here, send us a piece of herself, then something else could snatch up the chance. We may or may not be strong enough to take it down. Or, of course, there's the chance nothing will happen. It'll be a stillbirth."

"Can we defeat Banshee without the Star?" Nightmare asked.

Storyteller was grave. "I doubt it, son. I highly doubt it."

"Hush, all of you," the Lady called. She caressed the petals, crooning softly. Everyone watched attentively as the Lady encouraged the flower to open at the bottom. Fluid spilled, clear and sweet-smelling. The Lady began to sing, something in an old language, maybe that of Joy, itself.

Slowly, gradually, the flower opened, and as the petals peeled back, a body tumbled out and fell into the muck. It was curled up and silver with long white hair. Definitely the Star – Nightmare could see the cracks in her skin – but no Light shined through.

The Lady, unperturbed, pulled the body into her lap. Nightmare had to force himself to watch, as though he was witness to the most private of acts and interloping upon it.

The Lady stroked the husk's hair, singing all the while, and rocking, rocking. Moments passed, and tension crackled in the air. Lord Nothing rose, as did Water, and took up stances as though ready to attack. Storyteller pulled Nightmare to a safer distance, but the Lady had no such caution or fear. She kissed her child's lips, poured breath into the lifeless silver body. She bit her own arm and used a fingertip to draw shapes in blood on the husk's form. Finally, she pried open the husk's mouth and frowned. She tipped the silver body to the side and whacked it on the back. Something fell from the husk's mouth, a chunk of malignant darkness covered in red slime, and at last, Light flickered in the cracks of the Star's skin.

The Lady crooned and sang anew, and to Nightmare, it seemed that in one instant, the Lady held the Star in her arms and in the next, Light – the Star, Hope – stood, clean and pure, her white feet on the crumbling petals of the flower from which she'd been born.

"Daanske," Hope said warmly. Her pure white eyes flashed with kindness at Storyteller. "It is good to see you here."

"It's you," Water sobbed. "My Hope."

The Lady started to rise and attack Water, but the Star put a hand on the Lady's shoulder. The Lady, grumbling, climbed out of the pit and shook off the mud and flower nectar.

"My misguided Warrior." Hope sighed. "It is I, Hope, yes, but I carry with me my Sisters' spirits as well. It took all of us to send me here, and it will take all of us to win the battle ahead.

"And we cannot win this battle with you mournful, my love." The Star beckoned to Water, who swiftly moved to kneel next to the pit. "Let me show you the power of my Sister, Forgiveness. Feel her and know her." The Star put a hand on Water's head, and the room filled with such warmth and such strength that Nightmare went to his knees. The weight of all the galaxies and the power within it pressed him, strangled him, and he feared his bones would become dust.

"There will be no more guilt, no more suffering for what was done," the Star said in a soft voice that filled every crevice of the room and its inhabitants. "Water, Eeadian, the strength of this world, I forgive you all you have done, with intent or no, causing harm or ill. Forgiveness, she is yours, as am I."

Light gleamed from the Star's skin, and Nightmare turned away, blinded. When the pressure vanished and the warmth slowly receded, he found himself at peace with Water's foolish choices. He understood them, how obsession could be love and could be worth destruction to hold onto it. He felt in the core of his being how Water had been at a loss, thinking it would not be possible to live without the Hope Star's faith and light. Nightmare saw how Water had thought he was championing Hope – stronger when had, and therefore strongest when had by the Warrior King. There had been a moment – a mere pause in time – when the balance had actually been real. Water's love had given Hope more strength than she'd ever had. But all too quickly, that balance had tipped, leaving Water scrambling to regain it.

Nightmare saw that he could have been the one susceptible. Love and need and greed and pain were all so similar. Any one of the Walkers could have been so mistaken. This was the power of Light: one was forever striving toward it.

When Hope's shine dimmed, Nightmare saw he wasn't the only one affected. The Lady lounged next to Lord Nothing, who seemed as calm and placid as ever. Storyteller sat with his legs crossed, solemn. Water stood at attention, chest expanded and scales gleaming all shades of the sea. He bowed to Hope. He lifted a hand toward her, and Hope touched her fingertips to his. Water smiled, wistful, as though clinging to one last touch, and then he stepped away.

"We need to plan our strategy," Lord Nothing said. "Time is passing."

"Yes," Hope agreed. She sat on the edge of the pit. "Water – what say you?"

Water gazed at the blank, white wall. "Can you show us the world as it is, my Lady?"

With a snort that conveyed this was a ridiculous question, the Lady rose and circled the room. A Shadow tendril followed her, curled over her shoulder. When she reached the line of darkness and light, she drew on the end of the tendril with her mouth until her cheeks bulged fat. She left the tendril in the darkness and went to the wall. She opened her mouth and blew thick, gray smoke that spread to cover the wall in lazy whorls. When the wall was entirely gray, it solidified like glass and then fell away like sand revealing the scorched, ravaged landscape of Via'rra. They all stood to gain a better view. Nightmare crossed to the wall, wary of the floor's edge.

Fires raged, and the ashes of fallen lands were crumbling into space, leaving trails of dust. Pieces of ground and Undermaze slowly spun, torn asunder from the main land. The Horrors were feasting on those, the pink worms swaying, fattened and still gorging. Long, thick ropes of Horrors linked those drifting, dwindling, divided pieces to the last chunk of continent remaining. Those ropes looked like pink, veiny vines, and they undulated with peristaltic motion – swallowing and feeding the enormous trunk of Banshee's main body. That body was rooted half in the darkness of what remained of the Undermaze and half Topside, rising like a twisted tree, snaky, unattached vines flailing doll bodies against the background of the abyss of space. The tree eclipsed all else on the land, its worms rippling, diving, cavorting like sea beasts in the crumbling ground.

The tree's trunk had a face of sorts, and its maw opened wide, as though sensing it was being watched. It screamed, then, and the shrill, deafening, enraged roar shook the Manor. In that noise was loss and pain, and next to Nightmare, the Storyteller gasped, tears streaking his cheeks.

"Banshee," Storyteller whispered. "The beginning, and so, the end."

The phrase nudged a scroll of memory in Nightmare. The furled thought rolled around, as though trying to open, but it dissolved into soot when Nightmare strained to see it.

"We must attack the core," Water said. "And not just her trunk, but her roots. There."

He pointed, and the view in front of them shifted, showing a better angle. On the underside of their world, where once the Undermaze and the Lord Nothing's secret sand garden had been, there was now a tangle of Horror limbs. Nestled in the crux of the limbs was a room, and its red walls were interspersed with pieces of Undermaze and glittering Shadowrock.

"What is that?" Nightmare gasped.

"What is left of the Heart Cavern," Lord Nothing replied. "The prison."

"Prison?" Nightmare repeated. There had been no prison in the Undermaze. Had there? No, not as such, of course not. Rooms aplenty, yes; some locked and containing creatures who had misbehaved, but all the 'mares had allies, and those allies could convince the Bone Ghosts to do their bidding; to defy the lord and release that which was contained. It was endless strife and free will in Nightmare's domain, as it was meant to be. Topside, the ideas had to conform to their creators. In the Undermaze, in the afterlife for the forgotten and fallen, paradigms could be as they willed to be. There were endless maze corridors, and the Feed room, and Nightmare's abode, and the Scrying Cavern, but not...

Pain lanced in Nightmare's skull. He saw a door – a double door made of Shadowrock. He saw pathways of Shadow – bridges, similar to the Manor – and rooms. With furniture and furs and books and...

"Mal," the Storyteller called. "Mal, let it go. You can't find it. Let it go."

Nightmare took a ragged breath from where he lay sprawled on the floor. Before he could sit up, the Lady loomed and shoved a hand into his breast. A surge of life seeped through Nightmare. She'd replenished his energy. He reached to feel the green mass in his chest, now dense and swirling and stronger. It whispered – he could almost hear what it said. It was telling him what he had to do. It was giving him instructions. He had to go to someone. He had to fill himself. He had to...

"Mal," the Storyteller said again, helping Nightmare to sit up. "Enough. Don't dwell there, or you'll never be able to save us."

Nightmare shook the voices out of his mind. He stared at the Heart Cavern, as it was so named, infested with Horrors and swollen like a blister. It did not matter if he could not remember its existence. He hadn't known the Scrying cavern had a bottom. There was much he could not remember, but he had to help his fellow Walkers win this war.

"What must we do?" Nightmare asked. "How do we defeat her?"

"We use our strengths," Water said.

"We work as one," the Storyteller added.

"And what is my strength, then?" Nightmare asked. "My Ghosts? I believe only one remains, though he is my strongest."

"He cannot go into the Heart cavern," Storyteller answered patiently. "It's pure Shadowrock walls and now, Horrors."

"Very well, then." Nightmare frowned. The other Walkers exchanged a glance that Nightmare couldn't comprehend. "Well, what is it I am to do?" he repeated.

"You will cage her," the Lady said. "Banshee."

"How?" Nightmare asked. He had so little energy.

"You'll know, son," the Storyteller said. "You'll just know."

May their faith be enough, for I have none left in myself.

Chapter Thirty-Three

He couldn't remember when Miss Teedee had left, but when Jason roused himself from his thoughts, the other rocking chair was empty. The plate of food was gone. The stars were behind clouds, and the wind blowing across Jason's bare skin rose goosebumps on his flesh.

Stiff, Jason stood slowly, feeling gravity work on each of his vertebrae. He could just go to bed, but he could clearly see Monica's disapproving mouth pulling her entire face south and pinched, and he knew he wouldn't be able to rest until the day's work was done.

The kitchen was dark. So was the hallway. A single light was on in the entryway, and the front door, always shut and locked at night, was cracked by an inch. The wind resisted him when Jason grasped the handle and pushed the door shut. The deadbolt's action was a gunshot. Jason held his breath until the ticking of Darryl's ten thousand clocks echoed in his ears and drowned out the silence.

Once, when he'd been little, Papa Jack's mother had come to visit. She was a cantankerous woman who still smacked Papa Jack with her cane hard enough to leave welts if he didn't do what she asked immediately upon her asking. Even at eight, Jason had understood he was witnessing the way time and history were a circle. Everything that was will eventually be again because only rarely does someone try to force their lives into a shape other than a wheel. Jason knew this to be true when faced with Grandmother Ruebell, just like he knew that being alone with her was dangerous in different ways than being alone with Papa Jack.

Eventually, though, it happened, and Jason was alone with Grandmother Ruebell. She wasn't a large woman physically, but her spirit crowded rooms and made it hard to breathe. Jason had woken up the third morning she had been visiting, and he had coughed as though there were water in his lungs. He'd crept out of bed and down the hall as silently as possible, but Ruebell had heard him.

"Boy, get in here."

She'd been sitting on an ottoman, not in the chair or on the sofa, as though she liked proving to everyone that comfort was not something she liked or wanted, even at ninety. Her gnarled hand clutched her cane, the swollen joints of her arthritic fingers almost more terrifying than the yellow length of her ragged nails. She wore a black dress with tiny flowers that looked like little sad faces. The lace collar around her throat seemed too tight. Her hair was silver and pulled slick against her scalp. When she turned to eye him, she looked identical to Papa Jack, and Jason froze in place: a rabbit beneath the slick teeth of a bobcat, not quite dead, but knowing it would be soon.

"Hear that boy?"

Jason didn't hear anything. He shook his head.

"The clock, boy. The *clock*."

There was a wooden clock with a brass pendulum mounted on one wall. The dials for the temperature and the air pressure looked like eyes.

"It ticks."

Jason nodded, hesitantly, because yes, clocks ticked.

"But only when you're around, boy. It's silent, and then you're here, and it's loud like the rattle of old bones. Do you know what that means?"

Jason knew he didn't need to reply; he knew being still was the best option he had.

"It doesn't trust you, boy. It doesn't like you or know you, and it doesn't trust you. Time itself is your enemy, boy, now, tell me: how is anyone else supposed to like you if time's already decided it hates you?"

Until that moment, time had been the thing keeping him away from Papa Jack's anger or drunkenness or brutal affection. It'd been the entity prolonging the school day, lengthening the time to Christmas morning when he'd usually receive one token gift that tended to be pretty nice – Papa Jack's guilt wrapped in a box with a ribbon. *Sorry I'm not better, boy. But I'm all you've got.*

It'd been a friend and a trickster, but not a bully or an enemy, and yet, Grandmother Ruebell seemed to know time much better than Jason, and surely this woman wouldn't lie to him for sport. She wouldn't tell him something so terrible if it wasn't true. Your dog was run over, your parents are dead, your best friend ratted you out, and time was your enemy: all things that were true and needed to be told fast and quick so the sting of them didn't linger.

Jason backed away from the clock and its eyes and from Ruebell and her smirk. She'd laughed, as though his fear was the most hilarious thing she'd ever seen, and he'd run back to bed and hidden beneath it. The monsters there he knew. The one in the living room, well, the clock could have her.

"I'm sorry," Jason whispered in the entryway of the Taylor Point House, and the clocks quieted. One of them chimed, cheerfully, and Jason walked up the stairs hoping that meant he and time had a truce for now.

At the top of the stairs, Jason reached for a light switch but stopped himself. There was a dull red glow coming from beneath

Judith's door. Had she come home while Jason had been outside? What time was it, anyway? The chimes were still sounding out the hours. Jason had lost count.

He walked toward the door, knowing he shouldn't. The runner rug grabbed him, almost tripped him, but he kept going. He could have sworn there was a face in the wallpaper – a gaping face, shouting in silent warning – but when Jason looked, there was only geometry, vertical lines making squares and triangles.

It could wait until tomorrow, the cleaning. He didn't have to do it tonight. After the garden and the confrontation and Miss Teedee's story, Jason could leave all this and go to bed and listen to Andrew snore.

He put his hand on the doorknob.

Stop. Don't do it. Go away.

Jason pushed his way into the room, and he saw Judith sitting with her back to him. She was bare from the waist up, and maybe also from the waist down. The covers hid some of her from him. Her tattoo was bigger and crueler than Jason's. Her tree took up all of her skin, right up her spine. The twisted limbs and the withered fruit spanned her ribs, and one, Jason remembered, slithered beneath her left breast. There were eyes in the trunk of her tree, something none of the rest of them had, and now as Jason stared, he thought he saw a little girl perched inside the tree. She moved with Judith's breathing, and Jason could smell the tree and the girl's rot. He could smell decay: Judith and all the memories Jason had of her and their time together. Jason started to speak. He took in a breath, nearly gagging.

A bang made him jump. He thought he'd been shot, but it'd only been the door. He had enough time to register that before iron arms wrapped around him, and he realized the smell wasn't metaphoric. It concentrated on a rag that was not just pressed to his mouth and nose, but shoved inside. Big fingers pushed fabric past his teeth and on top of his tongue before he even thought this shouldn't be happening. He struggled, or he thought he did, but whatever was behind him was a steel cage.

"Lover," Judith said, her voice at once a whisper and a scream into a canyon that echoed. "You always have been and always will be mine."

The room went dark.

And Jason thought, *It's time.*

Chapter Thirty-Four

When the Lady's power engulfed Nightmare for the second time, he relaxed into it. The red-orange-pink-fuchsia light beat against him. He compressed but stayed conscious. He melded with his fellow Walkers – knew their hearts, their souls, their fear, their savagery, their eternal damning and redeeming histories – and his scream joined theirs. They tore through space, its vacuum sucking up their battle cry, rendering it null. He saw, but yet didn't see; felt but not as a solitary creature; understood with finality that the Lady would pierce the walls of Banshee's lair. She dove, a comet of will and destruction and chaos, and the collision ended Nightmare for seconds that lasted lifetimes. He floated in the bliss of nonexistence and the comfort of all who had come before him and all who would come after him, and when the Lady's power released him, he sprawled on a floor hot enough to singe his sinew. He lifted himself onto his elbows. He blinked ash and dust out of his eyes. His feet couldn't find purchase, and he glanced down. He scrambled to pull himself away from the edge of eternity. Beyond the hole punctured in the rock-bone-Shadow-Banshee wall, the remnants of a field floated. The grasses were purple, unburned, but a rope of Horror was slowly slithering its way through the soil, drinking up the life of creation.

"Get up!" Storyteller bellowed, dragging Nightmare to his feet. They stood in a cavern. To their left were broken stairs that ended midair. To their right was the bottom half of a plush, stuffed chair. The floor was Shadowrock and also tile, marbled and gleaming where it wasn't streaked with mud and blood.

Around him, Water was in full armored form – his body and head enormous in the high walls of the cavern. The Lady's claws were out, her talons the length of her arm and razor-sharp. Lord Nothing's presence loomed all around them. Ahead, Hope provided their illumination. They were in a side chamber. The door to the room beyond no longer existed, but its hinges were there. Bone, just as they'd been in Nightmare's brief vision in the Bridges Manor.

"Move," the Lady said. As a unit, they crept forward, Hope in the lead, followed by Water, who shrank and grew to accommodate the room and the doorway and then the massive cave beyond it. Nightmare hunkered in what had been the threshold from antechamber into main hall.

He could see where once this had been a sort of underground palace. The space defied the eye; it was so large and so full of crevices and shadows, nooks and crannies that Hope's luminescence could not reach. Bridges arced over what had been pools of some kind—

Healing salve flowed like rivers.

—which were now writhing with the motion of hundreds of baby Horror tendrils. Their putrescence assaulted Nightmare's nose, and next to him, the Storyteller gagged. The room quaked, and the vaulted domed ceiling shook debris down upon them. It'd been covered in a mural, once; something of beauty and full of stars. Now it was punctuated by swollen Horrors. Over there, a spotless collection of furnishings: two soft chairs, pillows, blankets, tables, and a rug. Off to the other side, a bed covered in layer upon layer of ash. The floor was littered with paper, goblets, shards of glass and bone, gems, fabric, fur, wrinkled dried skins, books, feathers, chunks of broken sculpture and furniture; the debris of occupancy and life and maybe even happiness, or at the least, contentment.

"Who lived..." Nightmare's voice died. Motion in the black maw of darkness that occupied what he had assumed was the far wall of the room rendered him silent. More quakes rocked them and knocked Hope down. Fire erupted and its heat reached them, delayed by the distance. It did not matter who had once lived in this room, cut off from the rest of the Undermaze.

Banshee. Dwelled. Here. Now.

From the Manor, she had seemed enormous. In the same room, she seemed impossible. The trunk wasn't a trunk in the way wood made trees. The trunk was made of ropes of the biggest, oldest Horror tendrils. They were lashed together by younger limbs, and as a unit, they breathed. A sound so great that Nightmare's hearing hadn't registered it as distinct from the thrum of his terror beat in rhythm: Banshee's heart. Veins and lifeblood pulsed deep, deep within the Horror tendril tree. A face – a *creature* twisted and moaned and writhed. It was caught in the tendrils, terribly misshapen by their pull. This was the face they'd seen, but the face had a head, its skull malformed and cracked open and pulled in all directions. Limbs were stretched and crucified, splayed away from the main body. The creature had eyes and they wept blood amber, oozing drops rolling and building up the mounds that had formed at the trunk's base.

From all directions, Horrors erupted from the trunk and anchored themselves to the Heart Cavern. The little doll girls clung to the ceiling, some stuck with white, viscous fluid and some simply clinging by fingers and toes. Other tendrils pierced the roof, exposing it to the cosmos above. Chunks of the floor closest to Banshee were gone, crumbling around Banshee's roots. And everywhere, the pools of new Horrors squirmed in their vats beneath the bridges. And dotted here and there, like comedones on dark, dirty skin, were pink growths that violently began to shake when they sensed the Walkers were near.

Nightmare sucked a ragged breath. The stench of the place temporarily overwhelmed him. Rotten. Putrid. Death.

An enormous, solid black, glistening eye opened. Banshee looked upon them.

And she shrieked.

* * *

The bottom of the steering wheel creaked beneath Monica's grip. She was on the side of the road in front of the sign for the Taylor Point House. The light for her turn signal blinked... blinked... blinked.

After Darryl had left the bar, which he'd done in silence after a single club soda and a conversation that had ended their life together, Monica had drank until she was blurry. She liked the blurry. Or, she had, until the blurry became nauseated became her running to the ladies' room to vomit. Her whiskey had ceased to be neat.

She'd flushed and watched the water go down the hole. Her head ached, her throat was scratched by bile and liquor, but her heart thudded against her breast and her legs were restless like they wanted her to run. Not to get away, but for the simple thrill of motion. She'd stood there marveling at the sensation until the urge to throw up passed. She went back to her seat, paid her tab, and left the bar. After a brief hesitation, she had run to her car. It'd been jerky and clumsy, and it'd left her totally out of breath with a headache that could jumpstart engines through sheer force, but she'd leaned against the driver's side door and laughed until she cried.

Freedom. A bird uncaged. A ship cut away from its dock.

Gone. She could be gone by morning. She didn't need the rest of her things. They were remnants of her past. Tethers to that old foundation she'd outgrown. Fuck them. Fuck everything. She was smart, she wasn't old, but she wasn't a young idiot fool, and she could and would do this. *This* – escape and start over and find herself and rebuild. An apartment with paint she chose herself. A sofa she liked, not one guests would enjoy. Paintings that spoke to her, didn't remind her of what Becky's taste had been. A garden with chives and tomatoes and not a flower in sight. She scrambled to unlock her door and open it.

But wait.

Andrew.

Her breath caught. Held. Her future was poised on this knife's edge: the instant between inhale and exhale. Her choices fanned in front of her: go to a hotel, go to the freeway, go to the house and say goodbye.

She could call him?

No. This was her only. Her *only.*

She could go away for a while and come back?

No. She didn't want to ever return. This town was in her rearview. It was the lyrics to a song about leaving and never coming back.

It was late. She should wait until dawn, at least?

No. If she stalled even for a second, her willpower would flicker and fizzle and it'd taken decades to get that candle relit.

Monica climbed into the car. She turned the key in the ignition. She navigated the roads she could drive blindfolded, which was a good thing, because she was driving them in a kind of pain that reminded her of labor: profound and earthshattering with the promise of something new and precious on the other side.

But she couldn't make the final turn. Her foot was flat on the floorboard. It was so heavy. How could she apply it to the pedal and make herself go tell her son goodbye? How could she explain in this, the witching hour, that Andrew was right, she knew nothing of love, but she had to leave to figure it out? What words were there to convey that if she stayed, she couldn't change, but if she left, she'd shed her skin and be a babe in new light?

She could leave?

No. Andrew was in his bed, sound asleep, missing his mama, but hopeful: she had to go caress his hair one last time. She needed to tuck it behind his ear and lean over and whisper that she loved him. She had loved him more than herself for so long, she'd forgotten she was even worth loving. He had Darryl. He had... lovers. Men. He had to find himself without her there being jealous in the twisted, worst kind of way. She had to take his courage, his overpowering sense of self, and let it inspire her into transformation. Otherwise, she'd be to her only son what cancer had been to Becky: mercilessly negating.

She turned off the signal. She lifted her foot. She turned the wheel. And the next thing she knew, her foot was hitting the driveway, and she was out of the car, breathing in the night air again, but this time, and for the last time, the Taylor Point House loomed in the night like an oversized dollhouse. There were more cars parked in the lot, and that was good. Guests would come and go. They didn't depend on her being there. They'd come even though she'd left.

The world would just keep right on spinning without her meddling with it. Wasn't that a kick in the head?

Silently, she made her way to the basement side door. Determined to wake no one until she reached her son, she selected the right key and fit it into the lock with barely even a jingle. She turned and pushed and for a moment, thought that somehow she'd gotten it wrong. Was there another key that fit this lock?

No. She didn't think so. She pushed again. The door didn't budge.

"What the hell?" Monica muttered. She knelt and examined the knob and the lock. All seemed to be in order. Was this some sort of cosmic sign to run away now, before it was too late?

For a second, she leaned toward the car, the way she'd come and also the way that would take her onward to her new life.

But no, the damn door didn't work, and how could she leave with that kind of simple thing broken? Something was wrong.

She felt along the jam and noted, strangely, that the door didn't meet the frame snugly. There was a slight space where there should have been a seam. She pushed her fingers into it, letting them creep, and frowned.

Coins. There was a stack of dimes shoved so that the door was forced away from the frame. There were two stacks of them, actually: one about a foot above and one about a foot below the lock. They were preventing the door's mechanism from working – forcing the door to strain against its confines and not give enough room for bolts and pins to maneuver their way to opening.

Dumbfounded, she yanked out the dimes. They came unmoored with only the faintest scratching and seemed so innocent in her palm. Still studying them, she turned the key and the door opened without issue.

Why would someone shove dimes into the doorjamb? Maybe Andrew was worried about intruders again. He'd been afraid of the "stealers" when he'd been a boy; thieves and robbers coming beneath the cover of night to take away what he valued the most. But he'd outgrown that fear. Or so she'd thought.

No, the dimes were on the outside. Though she'd tried to get in and not get out, she had no doubt that the dimes stopped the door from working from both sides.

Was this a prank? It had to be. And she had to tell Darryl. Some idiot was playing games that could be potentially dangerous. If something happened, some sort of emergency, then nobody could use the basement door from inside the house. They'd have to be let out. And if there was nobody to let them out, then...

Monica got moving. She jogged toward Darryl's, and formerly her, room. She'd think of what to say about her return later. She could offer excuses, and no, her leaving wouldn't be as clean and tidy as she'd wanted, but the urge to tell, to explain, to *warn* everyone was upon her, and she couldn't shut it up. She raced through the hallways in near darkness, her knowledge of the path honed by years and years of practice.

In front of the bedroom, she reached for the doorknob, and paused.

Dimes. In the door.

There were dimes in the door of Darryl's bedroom. If he was in there, he was locked in by a cruel prank.

Someone had locked Darryl into this room and then, presumably, barred the way to getting outside.

If there were two doors locked, were there others?

Were there dimes in the doorway of Andrew's room?

And was that... Did she smell smoke?

"No," Monica whispered.

* * *

Hope began to glow. The cracks of her skin blazed with pure, white energy. She took a step toward Banshee, despite the blood beginning to ooze from her ears that matched the trails running down all their cheeks.

Nightmare went to one knee next to a pool of Horror worms. Beneath Banshee's wail, he could hear their higher-pitched screams. They sang it, their Horror song; the vibrations rattled him, their pitch rocking him on different wavelengths than Banshee's scream. They twisted, danced, and one of them shot sideways to the side of the waterless pond. Another crept over the side. Another leapt over the edge of the pond and landed on the path in front of Nightmare.

Dawning realization struck Nightmare just as the Storyteller shouted, "Hope!"

A Horror tendril sprung up from a pool beyond Hope and shot toward her. She dodged.

And then a full grown Horror tendril ripped through the air.

* * *

Monica spun to run for Andrew and hit something solid and unforgiving. It had on leather. She could feel it where she clutched the thing with both hands. It smelled of bad cologne and stale breath and sweat.

"Sorry," it said. Its teeth gleamed in the dull light. It backed away.

It left a knife with a four-inch handle embedded deeply in Monica's belly.

She knew no pain, but her vision went white.

* * *

With a resonant cry, the Storyteller leapt forward. He blurred out of focus and became not one person, but many. Some were young – boys – and some were men in their prime, but they all moved with speed that defied the eyes' ability to track it. The main version of Daanske pulled a knife from his belt, and then all versions had the same knife. He hacked the tendril that pierced Hope until it snapped away, spewing foul blood. Hope collapsed, and the Lady went to her.

To Nightmare's right, a pustule broke open. A creature half Horror doll and half worm slithered out. It had fangs as long as Nightmare's fingers. It coiled and sprung, attacking one of Storyteller's forms.

Around the room, the other quaking pustules split open, and the Horror doll worms started to fly. They were so fast, only Daanske had any hope of keeping up.

"Take cover!" Water yelled to Nightmare, who rolled and upended a table. He crouched behind it, struck mad with terror at the sight of seven dozen versions of Storyteller fighting a wave of doll worms.

And on and on, Banshee screamed.

* * *

Helen bolted upright. She was soaked in sweat and her head throbbed.

Something was wrong. Horribly, terribly wrong.

She smacked her lips and put a hand to her throat. She'd been dreaming of a dark place full of screams. Had the yelling stayed in her mind or had the sound made it to this world? And if she had yelled, then where was—

"Helen!" Tio burst into the bedroom, bare of chest and foot. The buttons on his pajama top were undone, and the shirt flapped at his sides.

Tio never called her Helen.

She was out of bed and in her house shoes in a single leap. She ran for the window, Tio at her side. The curtains brushed her arm. Her breath fogged the glass panes. She was here, she was alive and real, but her senses were slipping, sliding, as though a brick wall was tearing apart to reveal a reality beneath consensus reality.

Beyond the second story of the garage, on the other side of the cheerful yellow railing and sprawling across the gravel driveway and the well-kempt grass, an infestation of bloody worms had taken over the garden. An oak tree covered in Spanish Moss just that morning was now a demonic banyan tree, full of eyes and teeth and the monsters who wielded them. A koi pond was full of crawling, screeching, baby monsters. Furniture littered the yard – massive chairs, a table once covered in china made of actual bone – as though her father had suddenly decided to clean out the attic by tossing everything out the highest windows of the house.

And the house was smoking. It seemed to breathe – to cough, with it.

Helen's bladder was too full. Her stomach heaved. She hit her head against the glass, and it hurt, so it was there. "What do you see?" she whispered.

"Nothin' good." Tio held up his cell phone. He hit buttons with a ferocious intensity. "Shit."

"Not working," Helen commented, and that slice of reality clicked into place, as though it had been waiting for her to find its home. The doom was here; the end she'd foreseen and knew only Jason could stop.

The yard was on fire. Helen didn't know if that was *here* or if it was happening *there.* Which might also mean the fire would be here any moment.

"We have to go." Tio grabbed her arm and pulled her to the front door. He turned the knob. The door didn't budge.

Tio didn't hesitate. He let Helen go and threw aside the curtains on the living room window. He jerked and screamed. The window broke. The barrel of a shotgun stabbed into the room. Helen's feet and arms and torso moved forward while her soul and mind remained stationary and confused. She shoved the barrel of the gun as the blast went off. Mercutio rolled on the floor. Gone was a picture of them that had hung on the wall, and now she could see into the kitchen. She yanked the gun, and it came free. Helen twirled with her own force. She stumbled, and Mercutio caught her. His lip was cut, and in his eyes, she saw smoke and fire and endless darkness.

"No!" Mercutio cried, his mouth forming the sound in slow motion. Helen knew, because she could see it through Tio's eyes, somehow – as though she was both here in his arms and also on the far side of the room and also on the ceiling and even outside on the porch – that the man who had the shotgun also had a handgun.

A ferocious lance of heat struck Helen's shoulder. The right side of her went too hot and then numb.

And in Tio's eyes, she saw stars and black holes and then nothing, because this world was pain and she was falling, falling into Tio.

* * *

"He's weakening!" the Lady yelled, pouring her energy into healing Hope's wound. Shadow tendrils spun around her, grabbing the Horror doll worms that tried to attack her. Shadow engulfed the worms and then they were gone, but Nightmare could see them within Lord Nothing; the Lord of Shadows was a python that had swallowed acid rats. Pieces of Shadow were beginning to smoke and hiss.

Water, enormous and with armored tail lashing, knocked the doll worms aside and spun to wrestle a Horror tendril away from the Storyteller, who had been overtaken by the doll worms. The doll worms chewed and smacked and moaned, partaking of their pound of flesh, and when the Storyteller fell, all versions of him fell. The doll worms seemed to realize which one was the central one, and they raced toward him.

Roaring, Water grew and flung himself onto the ground. The quake knocked Nightmare to one side, and he rolled over broken pustules and almost into a pit of writhing tendrils. Water had crushed enough of the doll worms to send them into a retreat, and Lord Nothing's Shadow went to work tearing the worms from the Storyteller's body.

Enraged, Water lunged toward Banshee. He snapped fully grown tendrils left and right, still charging. Dolls rushed him, and he shattered their skulls with his fists. He changed forms at speed, leaping in his manshape over the broken ground and landing again with his battle tail intact. He reached the tree and plunged his hands into it, striving for the heart. He tore and yanked. Shadow was there, helping, but the more they tore, the more they released Banshee from the prison. And Nightmare saw what would happen an instant too late.

Banshee's arm broke free and slammed into Water. He flew and struck the side of the cavern. Banshee's neck and head shook loose of the tendrils and lolled forward, misshapen and hideous and furious. She flicked a hand and dozens of tendrils rose and shot through the air. As they traveled, they peeled themselves, as though the air were razors, and when they reached Water, their tips were spears that pierced Water's chest and pinned him to the wall. Blood gushed from between Water's lips and his form morphed – Warrior, Nāga, man – and convulsed.

* * *

Darryl woke up coughing. He wheezed, trying to catch his breath. Thrashing, he fell half out of bed, hitting the rug with a concussive shock that brought him to full consciousness and sent waves of agony down his spine and into his joints. He kicked at the covers and crawled until he was fully on the ground. He panicked, thinking heart attack or stroke or both. His vision was hazy, and he was having difficulty breathing. He felt along his arms and chest, patting for the pain he expected to be experiencing.

He breathed in, trying to remember everything he could about what to do if you were dying. Stay calm. Call for help. He tried to yell, coughed, and remembered his phone.

Fumbling, he snatched his cell off the nightstand. It was on and charged, but when he tried to use it, the screen informed him there was no signal, which made zero sense. He spent way too much money with one of those massive cell phone companies with the commercials that came on every five seconds during primetime TV to ensure that he would have service on the damned moon, and now it wasn't working in his own home?

He tried and tried to dial, but there was nothing. The more he tried, the more he gasped and lunged for air, and finally, he registered the smell of camp fire. Rich and thick, like when he'd taken Helen and Becky to the Smoky Mountains for a vacation. Helen had been tiny, and everything had been an adventure. Becky had been such a good sport, though mosquitoes had eaten her alive and she'd thrown her back out trying to haul the cooler out of the car.

But at night, they'd made a fire in a pit surrounded by stones, and they'd sung songs Helen was learning in preschool, and it was perfect. He'd never forget the smell of burning wood. It meant Becky in his arms, and Helen asleep on an air mattress with a smile on her face.

Was this his life flashing before his eyes? People remembered in smells and sensations. He could still recall the feel of whiskey burning his throat.

Darryl gagged. He fumbled for the bedside lamp, turned it over, but also turned it on. The haze in the room was still there. Some of it was because his eyes were watering. The rest was smoke. There really was a fire somewhere. Which was ridiculous. Who would build a fire in this hellish weather? Especially indoors. That would burn the place—

A fresh batch of adrenaline dumped into Darryl's veins. His mind woke up, time slowed down, and he understood fear and proximity to death with cold, calculated singularity.

"Oh, God." Darryl scrambled across the rug and to the door. It wasn't hot, but it wasn't cold. That was good. The knob would turn, also good. But the door wouldn't budge.

Bad.

"No, no, no, no..." Darryl wrestled with the door and his panic wrestled with his mind. There was no fire. There couldn't be a fire. And if there was, then there were fire extinguishers. Their hotel was small and old and also similar to a private home, so they weren't required by state law to have external fire escapes. There were extinguishers on every floor with instructions. There were signs indicating safe passage out of the building in case of an emergency. There were posted notices clearly indicating that there was no sprinkler system required nor installed in this establishment. Darryl always meant to fix that. He'd started to put one in years ago, but Becky had argued with him. They had antiques and books and water would destroy them. So would fire, Darryl had argued, but Becky thought a fire escape on the outside would be better. They'd asked for estimates. They'd sworn they would put it into the budget.

Then Becky got sick, the money was gone, and until this moment, Darryl hadn't thought of the fire escape or sprinklers again.

Calm. He just needed to calm down. Darryl quit struggling with the door and tucked his face inside his shirt. He took a breath, smelled his deodorant. There wasn't a fire. There couldn't be. If there was a fire, then the alarms would be sounding. They had been deafening in the tests. They were wretched when their batteries needed replacing.

Also, they had a security system. It'd send a signal over the magical airwaves that powered cell phones and satellite TV and alert the fire department. If this was a fire, then the firefighters would already be here, breaking in windows and rolling out ladders.

So this wasn't fire. This wasn't the end. This was smoke. Just smoke. A lot of smoke. Choking and eye-watering levels of smoke. Like when he'd been a kid and his buddy, Mike, had put the smoke bomb in the boys' bathroom. They'd been evacuated. Both the principal and Mike's parents had skinned Mike's backside until there was nothing left but one huge welt.

Okay, so no fire, only smoke, but still, it was suffocating. And Darryl needed to get out and evacuate everyone. Darryl snarled at the door. Why wouldn't it move? His eyes burned, and tears splashed down his cheeks. God, it was too much. He had to get out of here. He grabbed the knob, threw his weight backward. The knob came off in his hands, the door stayed shut, and he thumped to the ground, knocking the precious wind out of him. He rolled and spat phlegm. He dry-heaved and an image of a woman – *that woman* – overtook his mind. Judith. That bitch. That fucking *bitch*. She had done this. She was the only one among them wicked enough to do this. And she'd locked him in here, somehow. She'd set off a smoke bomb. She was trying to kill him.

No, not him – all of them. Oh God, the guests. Mary and George. Two floors up, what would the smoke be like? Had they escaped outside? Or were their doors stuck and their phones not working? They didn't have landlines anymore. It'd seemed like an expense they could cut. Because of the ridiculous internet bill.

So if they were stuck, and there was smoke...

God, it was hot. And say – just say – it wasn't only a smoke bomb. And that the detectors had failed. It'd be easy to shut them off. They were on a breaker in the furnace room. Darryl could see how he'd do it: get Monica's keys, including the little one that locked the desk in the entryway. Inside the desk was a list of the security codes, passwords, everything you weren't supposed to write down. Go to the basement, enter the code to turn off the security system, flip the breaker on the smoke detectors, somehow lock people in their rooms. Set off the smoke bombs.

Or maybe... start the...

Fire. Were they on fire?

Impossible. Nobody would do that. If they'd started a fire, they'd get everybody out. Why would anyone want to burn down the house and kill half a dozen innocent people? Even psychopaths were afraid of fire. Judith would go and get help. Or her goons would. Someone would. Jason's van had been in the parking lot when Darryl had come home.

Oh, God. Jason. Was he here? And was he with Andrew? Oh, God, oh fuck, oh mercy, *Andrew.* Monica's boy. His own son, if not by blood, then by time and so many kissed bruises and long hugs and help with math homework. His boy. One of his children. One of them.

Darryl's heart stopped. "Helen."

His little girl. Oh, God, his baby girl. Helen in that purple dress she'd loved when she was six. The smell of her first thing in the morning, musky from sleep and hot to the touch.

He couldn't breathe. He couldn't think. He had to run, to go, to get away, to stop this before it destroyed them all.

Sobbing, Darryl went back to the door. He slammed the knob back onto its rod, trying to get it to work again. The world flipped upside down, and he saw not the door and the wall, but stone, like a cave. And he heard something. A screech, like metal twisting when a car hit a guardrail. Like the single tone of a flatline.

"Goddamn it!" A coughing fit took him, and the door and the wall were familiar again. He had to get help. What if Helen was trapped, too? What if he was locked in here so somebody could get to Helen? To hurt her? What if they were doing horrible, unspeakable things to Helen and Tio? And Andrew?

What was happening to Andrew? What would happen to Monica if anything happened to Andrew?

To any of them?

The knob wouldn't stay on. Darryl tried to shove his fingers between the door and the frame. The skin around his nails shredded. He bled. He didn't even feel it. The universe shrank to panic and heat and suffocation and flashes of his babies burning up in fiery cradles.

"Help!" Darryl screamed as he wrestled with the door. "Help us!"

* * *

Shadow engulfed the cavern. It swarmed over the walls, raced along crevices in the floor, put up a solid wall in front of Water. The wall stopped more honed tendrils; stopped them and absorbed them.

"*Lay down your swords*," Lord Nothing's voice intoned. "*You must cease this endless suffering*."

The Lady and Hope rose to their feet. Hope held one hand over her wound, but she began once again to glow. The Lady slashed tendrils with her claws and tossed them into the depths of Lord Nothing. Shadow swallowed everything to Banshee's base. Lord Nothing lashed through the air to eat the last of the doll worms. He covered the pools of budding tendrils and dipped into them, devouring.

Banshee's constant scream hitched. She snarled and freed her other arm. Loose from the tendrils, her head and upper body were beginning to remake themselves. Her brittle hair thickened, grew dark and glossy and began to grow. Her gaunt face began to fill. Her skin grew paler and paler.

But her eyes remained hollow and her mouth, a gaping slash with rows upon rows of teeth, remained wide.

* * *

"Hey, hey, pretty lady," Mercutio crooned. Such a sweet sound. Helen wanted to sleep to it.

"No, now, stay with me and stay still," Mercutio said. "I've got pressure on you, and you're gonna be just fine, but you don't need to get up and go dancing, okay?"

Every single one of Helen's thoughts was muted by pain. Her body felt violated and separate from her, more so than she'd ever experienced before, and for the first time, she realized she wanted her body and these organs and her own skin. She was very fond of her physical form, she realized. She was certainly not ready to vacate it, yet, even if being inside it was the white-hot-singe of a bare finger to a hot iron.

"The shotgun," Helen gasped. "The man, the pistol?"

"Oh, he'll be all right, too, honeydew." Mercutio's voice wavered, too high and too quick. He was struggling for calm as much as Helen was struggling against the tide of agony and the waves of nausea. "He's got a new hole in his leg, but I bound it up with my belt, good and tight, and he's out on the porch thinking about what he's done." Mercutio's laugh was brittle. "They took out our cell phones. They've got some sort of jammer. There's a whole operation going on, here: Operation Catastrophe."

"I know," Helen said. She turned her head, opened her eyes, and the living room, the exterior wall, the porch, and the wounded would-be killer, fell away. She saw Water pinned and dying. She saw Madeline – no, the Star – wounded but trying, standing with the Lady, and while not all hope was lost, all was not going well. Helen knew in the way children can speak other languages, and mathematicians can see patterns that if the Taylor Point House fell, so too would Via'rra. If Via'rra fell, then everything – Earth and all other worlds beyond it – would crumble. The Taylor Point House was not the only place where a battle was raging that could help or harm Via'rra's cause. But Helen was only human, and she could only see her world and that of the King of Nightmare, the Lord of Nothing, the Lady of Creation, and all the rest. Here, in her small, historic little Southern town, and in a dozen other spots all over the globe, the lines were blurry and the division between worlds so thin, that what they did could reshape the essence of existence. If they could win their battle against the tree girl's pain, it could affect the battle for the rest of the universe.

"Tio," Helen said. She coughed. "You have to go."

"Going nowhere, lady love."

"I'm not your love." Helen grabbed Mercutio's wrist. She dragged him down to speak in his ear. "You love Andrew. And he needs you."

Mercutio whimpered, cleared his throat, and tried to be firm, though his body leaned toward the house. "No. If your daddy found out I left—"

"He won't live through this without you."

"Honey—"

"You have to save Andrew and Darryl, and most of all, Jason. He's what will stop everything. He has to fix this. Only he can. But we are here to help him. *You* have to help him."

"You're not making—"

"I'm here in this body for a while, Tio." Helen sat up even though Mercutio protested almost as much as the rest of her. "But that won't matter if you don't get to our family." Helen spied the pistol on the floor. She picked it up, her fingers not quite wanting to work, but she encouraged them gently into folding and gripping. "Tio, you are the spaces in between all of us that bind us together. You are the fuel for one of the strongest among us. Go. Please, go. If you love me, if you love him, then—"

A tear streaked down Mercutio's cheek, and he silenced her with a finger. "You stay *right* here. If you go anywhere – shining lights or blackness, one – I just won't ever forgive you."

Helen smiled. He understood. He would think it was all about the healing – about being a nurse when there were wounded people – and it was, in a way. But there was a bigger picture, here, and Helen's heart soared when Mercutio climbed out of the broken window and vanished into the smoky night.

* * *

As Shadow crept into Banshee's roots, she lunged forward, the snapping of tendrils like a forest of wet trees breaking. Her fingers elongated, faster than the Horror tendrils, and faster than Shadow. Four fingers the width of table legs slammed into Hope and pierced her. The Lady screamed, Water cried out, but Hope's only sound was a damp grunt.

Banshee lifted Hope high into the air. Her other hand grew, and more fingers dug into Hope's body. They twisted her, as though she were the shell of an egg, and they tore her first in half and then into pieces. Water's anguished cry competed with Banshee's wail of triumph. Twin fists crushed Hope into shimmering dust and pale blood, and all of it gleamed with blinding brilliance. Before Nightmare had to turn away, he saw a mass of tendrils snatch pieces of Hope's body and fling them wide. The cavern was filled with the illumination of a hundred suns.

Lord Nothing did not scream. He did not curse or cry. He could only retreat through the holes in the ceiling and the floor, escaping to the safety of his cosmos. Horror tendrils started to chase him, but they were sliced by magenta bursts of energy; cauterized to smoking stumps.

The Lady burst into magenta fire. Her body's eyes sealed themselves. Her scale armor gleamed with heat. Her real eyes opened, and her mouth cracked her face in half in a sinister smile. "Oh. Oh. My turn."

* * *

The bad dream wouldn't leave him. He was in the bathtub, and the water was melting his skin. He held up an arm, which was now only bone, and he tried to explain to the wicked woman standing over him that he needed his flesh, but she kept twisting the tub's knob hotter and hotter.

"Oh!" Andrew broke out of sleep like a prisoner from a cell. "Oh?" It didn't feel like he was awake. The room was as hot as the bath had been, and he heard screaming. The screamer's voice belonged to Darryl. Andrew told his body to move, but it wouldn't listen. It still thought it was stuck in the bathtub with the shark-snake lady.

"It's okay," Andrew told his body. He managed to lift a hand and pet his torso. The body was paying more attention now. "It's going to be okay. But I need to get up."

The body was still wishy-washy, but it allowed Andrew to make the final call in the argument. He rolled out of bed, landed on all fours, and understood several things all at once.

The house was on fire.

Darryl and the guests were trapped. Or Darryl was worried the others were. He definitely was.

If they were all trapped, then the door to Andrew's room was likely not going to work. Nor would it listen to Andrew's arguments. The wood would be very stubborn about it.

The air was hot and acrid and quickly turning into pure poison.

Andrew needed to save himself so he could make arrangements with doors and walls and big puffs of fire that would mean his family kept their lives.

Well, that seemed simple enough. Andrew crab-crawled and stood to scoop random items off a shelf. He stuffed them into his pajama pants pockets. He didn't know what he'd need to use to bargain with fire. He'd never tried to reason with it before. Best to be prepared.

Next, he went to the bathroom. The tile was cool, and he put his face on it for a second. It gave him a chance to think. He'd need more clothing. He yanked a shirt off the towel rack and pulled it on. He grabbed some boots, which turned out to be

Jason's, so they were a little small, but they'd work for a little while. He picked up a wrench he kept next to the toilet because that's where it lived. The wrench came in handy when he had to turn the water off to the commode when it didn't want to cooperate. He almost paused to consider why he thought he'd need such a heavy item but quickly stood so he wouldn't get distracted.

There was a window above the tub. It was longer than it was tall, and it wasn't very tall at all. The hinges were rusty. Andrew had a quick chat with his body, and his mind went to sleep for a little while. He watched as a passenger as his body used the wrench and strength to yank the window off its hinges and away from the wall. Now there was a hole. He had to pull himself up and squeeze through it. He put one boot on the tub's faucet, and he heard it creak. "Sorry, sorry," he whispered, and then he could do nothing but think very small, slick thoughts: moles, bunnies, slithery little snake babies. Drops of water, a splatter of olive oil in a pan, a persistent creek weaving through leaves and rocks and dirt.

Halfway out the window, Andrew's mind and body rejoined to work together. There was gravel just beyond the window, and retaining rock to keep the soil at bay. The stones were sleepy, but they woke up when they heard Andrew coming. They moved out of the way to reduce the scrapes and scratches on Andrew's skin. Thankfully, his shirt was long-sleeved. It tore before he did. He bunched himself up in the indentation outside the window that let in light into the bathroom, and he didn't panic when he caught a foot in the window. His mind told his body to turn it sideways, and when the body obeyed, the foot came free.

He was out, and the air was sweeter and cooler. Still, there was smoke, and Andrew needed to get a move on. Thanking the gravel and the window and everybody else, because in his haste he was sure to forget someone, Andrew climbed over the retaining wall and looked around. He heard scuffling before he saw the men fighting, and his body moved him before his brain agreed with the plan. There was an internal tussle – the mind wanted more information, the body claimed to have enough – and Andrew let them fuss. He focused on the two people throwing punches at the base of the steps that led up to Helen's apartment. One was Tio – Andrew would know that body's outline anywhere – and the other was unfamiliar. Bulky, dark, aggressive. Lopsided and favoring one leg, but still going for Tio's throat.

That settled things nicely in both the brain and body's world. Andrew asked the grasses to help him be silent, and he raced up behind the fighting duo. For a second, Tio was struggling with an oversized worm, and that was confusing, as worms were usually pretty friendly, but this one wasn't, and so Andrew bashed it over the head with the wrench. The worm-man fell, and Andrew flew to Tio and began checking him over.

"Stop, I'm fine, I'm fine," Mercutio said, pushing Andrew away. "I shot him!"

"Who?"

"Him. He's..." Mercutio laughed, but it didn't sound like he thought anything was funny. "How was he even walking?"

"Drugs," Andrew said calmly.

Mercutio didn't seem to hear him. "He's going to have one hell of a bad day when he wakes up. If he wakes up."

"He was trying to hurt you."

"Yes." Mercutio nodded. He groaned as he struggled to stand. "He... And... Helen. She's... Christ, I know him. That's one of the guys with Judith - Abel."

Andrew looked down at the worm man. Oh. Oh! Yes, it was one of the twins that traveled with that bad woman who was after Jason's soul. Abel was now bleeding from the head and, Andrew noted, the leg, and he simply couldn't feel too sorry about that. Still, he willed the dirt to take pity and staunch the wounds, please and thank you.

"I've got to get Helen." Mercutio turned and raced up the stairs. Andrew's body wanted to run away, but his mind overruled, and he followed Mercutio. At the doorway, they stopped, and Mercutio struggled with the door. Andrew, seeing the problem gleaming, plucked the dimes out of the doorjamb.

"Fuckers," Mercutio spat, and Andrew agreed enough that he didn't reprimand the language. "It's a frat boy trick. Been played on me. Should have known."

"You were in a frat?"

"Not the time, baby."

He was still Mercutio's. That was so nice. But when they made it inside, and Andrew saw all the blood and Helen's pale face, not to mention the gun she pointed at them, he understood the situation was bad, bad, bad.

"It's us, lady love," Mercutio said. She dropped the weapon. Mercutio picked up Helen, and she started to cry. Sob and sob like a little girl who'd lost her kitten. Andrew's heart broke into tiny pieces, and through the cracks, rage slipped into his bloodstream. He didn't like anger. It made him think of what he imagined his real father had been like. But Helen was hurt, bad hurt, and Abel had hit his lover.

The rage sizzled, flowed hotter. It boiled and burned, and Andrew tightened his grip on his wrench.

"I'm going to destroy these assholes," Andrew said. His mind was startled. That voice barely sounded like him. It sounded mean. Like it belonged to that shark-snake woman in his nightmare.

Mercutio held Helen and kissed Andrew. "Go get 'em, honey-Drew."

* * *

The Lady dissolved into streaks of razor-sharp, magenta energy. Pieces of Banshee and chunks of Horrors sprayed the walls of the cavern with pink and cream blood. Nightmare was struck in the face by a piece of scorched flesh, and he clawed at his sinew, squirming away and hiding from the Lady's chaos. He considered changing forms and joining her fight, but when he began the transformation, he knew he'd be too weak to do anything other than change shape.

Frustrated, he crouched behind a table, waiting for it to be time to cage this creature.

* * *

Jason opened his eyes and saw Judith sitting naked on the edge of the bed. Her guitar was across her lap, and she strummed chords, singing.

> *"We're the flakes of ash, fallen cities, ended lives*
> *in my forever destructive night*
> *But all our deaths will be undone*
> *We'll rise, a family of phoenix, feathers-fire*
> *And we'll race toward the blackened sun."*

Jason moaned. His skull throbbed like two dozen power drills were sunk into his brain. His mouth was dry, and his lips caked with stale spit. His shoulders burned, his arms were numb, and his hands must be bound behind him because though he couldn't feel his fingers, his wrists chaffed against sharp edges that cut deep. He lifted his head enough to see his knees and ankles were also bound, but a wave of dizziness overtook him. The room spun, and his vision went gray at the edges.

"It seems he's finally awake, my loves."

Judith turned. She had been speaking to a camera set up to have a wide shot of the bed and room. Its ready light was glowing. Judith wore nothing but her tattoos and a host of fresh razor cuts, all bleeding freely. A long one across her white belly had matted her pubic hair. Circles around each of her nipples stained her breasts arterial red. Two on each cheek painted her skin with shiny blush.

"Just in time, too." Judith slinked around the foot of the bed. She curved a hand around Jason's ankle. "I was worried you'd miss this."

"What?" Jason winced. His throat was completely raw. He didn't remember screaming.

Candles burned everywhere. Their smoke made his eyes water. "Blow them out," he begged. "Can't see..."

Judith laughed. She caressed his leg, and now he discovered that he, too, was nude. He squirmed, but Judith grabbed his penis in a cruel grip. Jason whimpered. Judith smiled, squeezing and stroking.

"Tell them, my love," Judith sang.

Jason flung himself to one side, but Judith straddled him, forcing him onto his back. "Tell who, what?" Jason gasped.

Judith turned both their heads toward the camera. "Tell all our fans how we have to die because you stopped loving me."

Jason coughed. "What are you talking about?" He didn't see the smack coming, but it ignited his cheekbone. Judith squirmed in his lap, and God help him, but he was getting hard.

"Do you want to fuck me again? One last time? We can dance in the fire." She reached for him, and that – this, everything – was enough.

Jason bucked, and Judith fell aside. She cackled when Jason managed to squirm his way to the edge of the bed. He craned his neck, searching for a phone, a knife, a way out, and saw, instead, that the floor was smoking.

"Judith..." The whole room was filled with smoke, actually. So much that breathing was a real struggle. Condensation dripped down the panes of the floor-to-ceiling window, the curtains pulled back to show the night was glowing, faintly; flickering with flame.

"What did you do?" Jason croaked.

"Pennies from heaven, dimes from hell." Judith danced around the room, her breasts bouncing and her hair swaying. "I told them that coming here was the end for me, for them, for everyone. One denied, and one believed."

Judith sang half her words, and Jason spied the bloodied razor blade on the bed's quilt. He also saw the bottles of pills with their lids off that littered the dresser. She was high. Gone, and high, and out of her mind.

"And then I said, 'If Jason joins me, I can be saved. We can all be saved.' And so they came with me, my devil twins. They met you, they understood, and when I said you'd hurt me, you'd broken and ripped and taken me, they decided... Well. Killing you was really best, isn't it?"

"But I didn't..."

"Didn't you?" Judith yelled. She smacked her chest, her face, and her leg hard enough to leave reddened marks that would work their way into bruises.

Jason, unbidden and to his utter humiliation, began to cry. Tears of pure frustration streaked down his face.

"Oh, lover." Judith sighed. She swayed her hips and caressed herself for the camera. "Don't you know? If I can't have you, then no one will."

"Then take me! But don't do..." Jason's chest hitched. The floor... smoke... heat...

Judith had always loved to play with matches.

"Oh, baby," Judith cooed. "It's already done."

* * *

Down the steps, across the lawn, and Andrew paused in the driveway. Far to his right, the water lapped at the dock: fish, ducks, forest, all safe for now. To his left, he saw his mother's car.

Pure fury engulfed both Andrew's mind and body. He ran to the basement door. It was open. Inside, it was too hot. Andrew retreated. He spied the outdoor spigot and the automatic system that turned on the sprinklers. Water and fire didn't play well together. Good. This was good.

Andrew pulled off his shirt. He knelt, turned on the faucet with one hand and hit buttons on the electronic keypad with his other. The sound of nozzles emerging from the grasses all over the Taylor Point House grounds was musical. Water began to spray everywhere, and Andrew soaked his shirt under the spigot. He wrung it out, tied it around his face, and picked up a shovel on his way back into the house. He stalked through the smoky hallways. He passed his door, barricaded by pocket change. No one in there to help. He rounded a corner and...

"Mama."

While Andrew's brain wailed in anguish, his body dropped his wrench and his shovel. He raced to Monica, gently lifted her, and swiftly carried her outside. He wanted to take out that death knife, but his hands could do nothing more than flutter over the handle. Monica's face was pure white. Her clothes were soaked with blood. She was sticky-tacky. She was almost...

The wind rustled the rose bushes, and the garden told him they'd watch over her. There was more to be done inside, only he could do it, and Mama might be beyond... She might not...

"I love you," Andrew sobbed. And he might be too late for her, but he couldn't be late for everyone. "Oh, oh. I love you, Mommy." He brushed back her hair. And then stood and went once again into the house.

* * *

Though it pained him, Nightmare's eyes were open in the glare of fragmented Light that dispelled Lord Nothing. He saw when Banshee freed herself from her tree. Ropes of vein-like roots connected her to the husk, but she stood on sturdy feet and sent wave after wave of doll worms after the Lady's power.

At first, it was of no consequence. The scent of burning flesh filled the cavern. The Lady annihilated Banshee and the Horrors down to the main tree and Banshee's form. For a brief moment, Nightmare knew what it meant to win this battle. He could see victory.

But the Lady needed to be fed. She was not a creature of infinite stores. All too soon, she fell to the cavern floor, gasping. She was smaller, half the size she'd been when they'd entered. Her skin sagged, the bones beneath the aging flesh were sharp. Her body's eyes drooped. Only the ones in her face still glowed.

Streaks of magenta lightning crackled. The Lady was on her knees, growing smaller and smaller. Banshee began to laugh.

* * *

Andrew put his mind to sleep, letting his body take control. He went to Darryl's room, yanked out the locking change, and found Darryl unconscious but with a pulse. Andrew knew how to check for pulses. He knew CPR. He could help his dad – the man who should have been his father – to safety.

Lifting Darryl into a fireman's carry, Andrew raced down the hallways and outside. He put Darryl on the grass, near the gently rising flower bed where the *phlox paniculata* lived. They were a highly organized breed, the phlox, so Andrew felt safe leaving Darryl in their care. Dad was breathing, so Andrew could breathe easier, too. He sat for just a moment, a few brief seconds, trying to let his body figure out what to do next. He stroked the flowers and kept two fingers on Darryl's pulse, trying not to think of his Mama, and wondering how he could get to Ms. Adlewilde and Mr. Kirkland.

"Andrew!"

He blinked at the flowers. Were they yelling at him? No, these phlox were little girls. That was definitely a little boy's—

"Oh, my Lord."

And that was a powerful woman's cry of concern. "Miss Teedee!"

Andrew spun and ran up the gravel driveway to where Toby stood, holding Miss Teedee's hand. Miss Teedee had her other hand over her mouth, and her eyes were wide, wide, wide. Andrew put himself between Miss Teedee and his Mama's body. His knees went weak, but he knew he had to stay standing. He was strong. He could do this.

"What in..."

"I brought her," Toby said to Andrew. His eyes were glassy, like marbles. He was half somewhere else. "This is where she needs to go." He held Miss Teedee's hand out to Andrew, who took it. In Toby's other hand was a tire iron.

"What's that?" Andrew asked.

"Something for someone else," Toby replied. Andrew didn't question further. Toby was doing his job: taking things and bringing them to those who needed them.

"I just... I was... Oh, God, I knew something horrible was happening. I did, Lord save me." Miss Teedee wore tennis shoes, silk pajamas, a robe covered with daisies, and a scarf over her hair. "I woke up. I was having the most horrible dream. And then Toby was knocking on my window, and I started to fuss, but he said I had to come here, and so I did, and what in heaven's name is happening, Andrew?"

He told her what he could. There was a fire. Tio and Helen. Darryl. He couldn't quite speak of his mother, but before he could figure out how to talk about her without using words that would make him cry, Miss Teedee turned and marched away.

"Follow her," Toby said,

"I was gonna!" Andrew replied, annoyed both with the kid for being so obvious and also with himself for being so short-tempered. "Sorry," he whispered, but Toby was gone.

Miss Teedee opened her car's door and dug around for something. When she stood up, she had a little handgun. "It's my lady's .38. Not much damage, but I've got delicate wrists. Can you tell me why my cell phone isn't working?" She held it out, and Toby rushed up to her, out of nowhere, and snatched the phone. He raced off toward the road.

"Well, I'll be..." Miss Teedee began.

"I'm real sorry, ma'am, but I have to go save more people."

Miss Teedee scowled at Andrew. "What do you mean *you* have to?" Miss Teedee flipped open the wheel chamber of her pistol, squinted at the loaded rounds with one eye shut, and then snapped it closed. "Let's go, now. That fire's getting bigger every second." She stomped up the front porch, tying the scarf around her face, and Andrew followed.

* * *

"Judith." Jason kicked at the bed until he was upright and leaning against the headboard. He fought the urge to vomit. His head really fucking hurt. "Please."

"Talk to the camera," Judith said, waving at the lens. "I'm recording all this for my blog."

"Help!" Jason screamed. "Call 911! Our address is—"

"It's not live, silly!" Judith yelled over him. "The jammer we're using kills cell signal, Wi-Fi, security, the works."

"Jammer?" Jason glanced at the useless cell phone on the bedside table.

"Mmhmm. All the lines are cut, and the systems are down. We're floating, love. We're an island, adrift. A landslide."

Despair weighed down his limbs. He wanted to curl up and sleep. "You have to stop this," he said.

"Don't worry." Judith held her hand over a candle's flame, coyly eyeing the camera. "It'll be over soon."

"You're going to die."

"Of course I am."

"We're *all* going to die. Where are the twins?"

"Cain's right outside. Abel and Gruff are out there, everywhere, jamming doors and setting fires."

"Where's Jennifer?" Jason persisted.

Judith picked up the razor blade and pricked her fingertips, one by one. Blood welled. "Last I saw her, she was in the library with her mouth stuffed and taped. Gruff was fucking her in every other hole." She laughed. "Oh, Gruff. High maintenance boy, that one."

Jason swallowed bile. "And the guests?"

Judith glanced at him, frowning. "Hmm?"

"The other guests. On this floor?"

"Oh. Dead, I guess." She shrugged.

Jason went cold. "How can you—"

"How can I?" Judith threw the razor at Jason. He dodged, and it bounced away. "How can I, what? Kill this new adorable little family you made for yourself? That you replaced me with? That you thought you could choose them over me? They don't love you. They don't need you. They don't know how to make you come, make you cry, make you breathe in life and... God!" Judith streaked blood through her hair. She reached for one of the candles as if to throw it.

"You're right!" Jason screeched. "You're right. Oh, God, you're right." He sobbed, and it was okay this time because it made him seem more legit. "I didn't want to see it. I didn't want to admit it. You know how I am."

"Fucking stupid," Judith muttered, but she set the candle down. "Fucking stubborn."

"Yeah. All that. You know me. I know you know me. I'm not good enough for you."

Judith flew to his side and cupped his face in her hands. He had to make himself stay still and not yank away from the squelch of blood and the scent of her – sweat and copper.

"You're not. But I can make you good enough. We'll die and be transformed and never apart again. Ever. I promise." She squeezed his skull so hard he thought it might break his jaw.

"Let me..." Jason panted. "Untie me, baby. Let me hold you."

"Hold me?" Judith didn't hide her disgust.

"Fuck you." Jason swallowed. "I want to die in you with my arms around you."

Judith cocked an eyebrow. "You accept you're going to end here?"

"I do. I can smell it, baby."

"So there's no use fighting?" Judith raked her nails through his hair, scraping his scalp.

"No," Jason babbled. "You're right... It's... it's done. Everybody I lo—Everybody I thought I loved is probably dead. You're it.

You're the real deal. The one, the only, and I just want you to... I want to—"

"Shhh..." Judith picked up the razor. Jason's heart stopped in his chest, but she bent to start working on the zip tie keeping his ankles bound. "I'm here," she crooned. "I'm right here."

* * *

Crouched behind a pile of shattered bone, crumbling rock, and a fractured table, Nightmare thought of all the times he knew humans to pray. He'd visited their churches, he'd watched in the woods as they baptized believers in running water, and he'd marveled at that kind of faith; in something greater and more powerful that could choose to crush them or protect them. Now, as he watched the Lady battle Banshee, he understood the frenetic desperation that made the fragile call out to the immortal. If the Lady fell, it'd be up to him, and he was not strong enough. He was not powerful. Not anymore. Possibly not ever.

Something tickled his hand, and he saw a Shadow tendril pooling in the safety of the pile of rubble. Nightmare glanced at the Lady, at the tendril, and resolve washed through him.

"Into me," he said to Lord Nothing. Nightmare flattened to the ground, inviting the Shadow into his chest. It darted behind Nightmare's broken ribs, burrowing deep into his sinew. He went icy cold and sluggish, but he crawled out from behind his refuge. He slunk to where the Lady stood her ground, though now she would barely reach Nightmare's knees if he was standing.

"Feed her," Nightmare said to Lord Nothing. "Take of me and feed her. Anything, just... help her."

Nightmare reached to touch the Lady's ankle, creating a conduit and providing a darkened space for Shadow to travel. He felt his life force ebb and flow, and he shut his eyes.

* * *

The first one he and Miss Teedee found was Jennifer. She was hurt really, really bad – purple and blue and green with bruises and there was blood in places Andrew refused to let himself look. He took her outside. She was alive, but her pulse was thready. That was Miss Teedee's word. He would have said it was trying to be more.

The fire was doing funny things to Andrew. The air was wavy, and he was used to it being straight lines with patches of light and shadow. The heat was big, like when you opened the oven and the blast hit you in the face, except this was all over and blast after blast. The soles of his shoes were getting sticky, and his clothing had black smudges and tears. His armor was failing.

And it was loud. Andrew had never thought of fire as loud. It sucked all the sound up and replaced it with a whoosh, as though he was underwater. He barely heard Miss Teedee yell for them to head up the stairs, but she pointed, and he went where she directed. The floor felt like it was springy, spongy, not quite sturdy.

The actual flames weren't in the main part of downstairs. They were in the dining room, Darryl's office, and the library drapes and one rug. Miss Teedee had slammed doors shut, cutting off the fire's path temporarily.

Upstairs, the guest rooms were burning. Mr. Kirkland's door was swinging open, blackened, and there was nothing but fire inside. Andrew let himself cry, but he ran for Ms. Adlewilde's room. Her door was still shut with the dimes. Andrew burned himself on the metal when he yanked them free, and inside he found Ms. Adlewilde under the bed. She was limp when Andrew dragged her out. He didn't check her pulse. He scooped her up and ran for the stairs. He passed Miss Teedee, who was struggling with a fire extinguisher. On the front porch, he nearly ran into Mercutio, who took one look at Ms. Adlewilde and closed his eyes. Andrew was crying so hard, he missed a step and nearly dropped the nice lady. He put her gently on the lawn near some roses who already grieved, and charged back into the house.

Mercutio had found another extinguisher, and he and Miss

Teedee were spraying everything. Andrew zipped by them, avoiding the spray, and a sickening crack halted his steps.

Above them, a line had formed in the ceiling plaster. The house was splitting apart.

"Jason!" Miss Teedee screamed. "Get Jason!"

Andrew knew he had to get his best friend. He couldn't let the house fall on Jason. The problem was, he didn't know which room Jason would be in. His home was with Andrew in the basement, but Jason hadn't been there. His other home was the kitchen, with Miss Teedee, maybe—

Force struck Andrew in the middle of his back, and he went to the ground. His knee did something it shouldn't do, and pain zinged up his thigh and down into his foot. He struggled, anyway, and came face-to-face with a man with burning eyes and bleeding gums. His hair was singed. He had blood smeared on his face like war paint.

Cain. The other twin.

* * *

It wasn't enough, what Nightmare could give to Nothing to feed The Lady. In a last barrage, the Lady shot magenta flames in every direction. Banshee squealed and retreated, her worm doll pools depleted, her Horrors maimed and torn and lying in reeking, dead piles. But her trunk still stood. Her cocoon still beat with a frantic pulse. The cords tying her to it had not all severed.

And so when the Lady shrank into her tiny seed self, it was with but a flick of a far-reaching finger that Banshee sent the Lady skittering across the floor and down a hole into space.

* * *

Cain had a gun, and he was pointing it in Andrew's face. Andrew thought of Tio and shut his eyes. The gunshot scared Andrew, but he didn't feel pain. He also didn't feel dead. Would he *feel* death? He thought he would. He'd felt it when life left trees as they were cut and weeds as they were pulled, so surely, he'd feel his own dying.

"Andrew, are you hurt?" Miss Teedee asked, kneeling next to him. Her eyes were red from the smoke. Next to them, Cain was writhing left and right, his mouth open in silent agony. He was bleeding from his side where Miss Teedee's bullet had struck him.

Andrew felt himself all over. His back hurt where Cain had struck him. His knee was an odd sort of super cold and achy. It wouldn't work when he asked it to. "My knee. It's not working like a knee, right now."

"Oh, Lord." Miss Teedee started to touch it, and they both heard a crash from a bedroom down the hall.

"Go," Andrew said. "Go, go, go! Jason. He's in that room. With the horror girl!"

Miss Teedee struggled to get up. She was tired, Andrew could see. Her face was gaunt, the bones under the thin skin pronounced. But she was also determined. Her forehead knitted in concentration. She picked up Cain's gun. Weapon in each hand, she headed down the hallway.

* * *

Everything in the cavern went still: Water, pinned to the wall with his head bowed, dead or defeated or both; Lord Nothing, banished from all crevices in the pure white light of a million shining Light shards; the Lady retreated and lost; Storyteller eaten by doll worms, now destroyed and splattered in viscera spray on every surface.

And the Horrors were reforming, slither-squelching into whole bodies as they were fed by Banshee, who crooned at them. Horror dolls half as tall as Nightmare formed regimented lines, their bodies bent forward, their arms hanging heavy, and their empty eye sockets fixed on Nightmare. They didn't attack. Nightmare waited.

And waited.

But still, they didn't move.

Nightmare took a step closer to Banshee. She stood, both feet free, arms wide and at the ready, twisted features unreadable. The pulse of her cocoon slowed, thrummed, and shook the Light shards on the ground.

Another step was one too far. The Horror dolls were in front of him, and then they were behind him. They leapt onto Nightmare's back. They weighed less than he thought, though combined, they wore him down to a crawl. On all fours, he struggled forward, waiting for pain, anticipating the end.

They did not chew or rip or even scream.

They pressed. They squeezed. They clung.

Hard to keep going, impossible to think he could, but Nightmare did. One hand, one knee, one pace at a time.

Going... going... He had to keep going.

* * *

Monica sat on the edge of the Taylor Point House roof and stared down at herself. From here, she was dark hair fanning out from a pale, round head. She was one shoe on and one shoe off. She was damp blue jeans on her shins. She was entirely red and black in the middle.

When she wasn't looking at herself, she was staring at the rip in the air above the dock. It was the length of all the water she could see. It was bright over there, whereas here it was nighttime. She kept getting stuck on that bit of reality: the light versus the non-light.

She had no urge to go toward the rip, and she didn't think she should. It wasn't exactly supposed to be here, just like she wasn't exactly supposed to be hovering around the roof. She was scared of heights, or she used to be, but now she wasn't. Looking down at herself, she was pretty sure she was dead, and of course the dead would have no fear of heights or falling or pain.

But she did fear what was going on through that rip. She understood that this world and that world were linked like two bicycle wheels and a chain. The wheels happened to be lined up just *so*, and they'd be synced for a while longer. While they were, what happened here affected there, and what was happening there was not going well.

Not that what was happening here was much better.

She was dead, after all.

Monica wanted to be next to her body, and so she was. She stood over herself, thankful her eyes were mostly closed. There was blood on her lips. She reached down to wipe it away but stopped herself just before she touched her former skin.

Toby had appeared. He'd been in the shadows made by the chimney stack, and he clearly could see her. He moved his mouth, as though he spoke, but she couldn't hear him. She knew if she wanted to understand his words, she needed to touch the blood and her body and slip back into that damaged skin for a while longer.

That would hurt.

That would hurt *a lot.*

Monica considered. She glanced at the rip.

Madeline.

Was that...?

No. All Monica saw was a shimmer that was shaped like a woman. The view through the rip had changed. Now Monica saw stars. They weren't her stars – this world's stars – because she was looking not up but straight ahead, so the sky through the rip was perpendicular to the ground.

Seven stars twinkled at her. Her choice affected what they did next, but she had no idea what that would be. Something that would help, though.

But she'd have to pay this price. Monica thought of her Andrew boy. She wasn't afraid for him, exactly; she didn't feel much at all. But she reasoned that if this would help those stars, which would, in turn, help them out here, which meant it'd affect her baby boy, then ultimately, she did this for him.

As she did all things.

So that was okay.

Monica knelt and touched the blood at her lip.

* * *

He wasn't going to make it to Banshee. The Horrors were too heavy, and he was too afraid of being responsible for unmaking the world. The dolls formed a solid wall before him, and he hallucinated, seeing not a mass of sightless dolls but a door with a burning knob. The heat wouldn't hurt him. His sinew was made for pressure and temperature. He reached for it, instinctively, and the cavern trembled.

The dolls evaporated. The light was so bright. Nightmare covered his head with his arms.

"Al'issaemeth," a chorus of voices said. Women. Seven of them. He couldn't see, but yet he could see: they stood in a line, hands linking them. All the Light shards in the room were now remade into a conclave of female-shaped stars.

Before him stood all the goodness in the universe: Love, Gratitude, Understanding, Curiosity, Forgiveness, Kindness, and Hope. Nightmare bowed his head.

"Banshee," Light sang. "Walker. Be calm. We are here. You can stop this."

* * *

The instant Jason was free, he put his hands around Judith's throat. He shoved her onto the mattress. A gun materialized in her hand. It'd been hidden beneath a pillow. She'd known, all along, what he would do.

Barrel in his face, Jason let go and put his hands up. He inched backward, off the bed. Judith slinked forward, following. "Jason, muse, mine. You disappoint me."

"I'm-I-I'll-"

"Just like Rage." Judith shook her head.

"What?"

Judith huffed an impatient little sound. "You will take this razor and slit your wrists." She spoke slowly. "You will do this because you love me. Also, because if you don't, you will burn to death. I've made my peace with the fire. I welcome its agony. You, it will consume in a great flood of excruciating pain, my love, so you will kill yourself."

"Why don't you just shoot me?"

"That's what he asked, too," she said thoughtfully.

"Rage?"

"Mm."

"You killed Rage?"

"No," Judith denied, affronted. "He killed himself. It took so many drugs for him to understand that his sacrifice would prove his love for me, and that he had to do it, and even then, I had to help him along. Like I'm helping you."

Jason saw Rage and the guitar string and the severed arteries and all the red, pooling death beneath his feet. "You made him hang himself. You held him at gunpoint until he..."

Judith laughed. "Of course I did. He was always so angry, so sad, and he was clearly coming between us, and I couldn't have him interfere."

"But he did, anyway. I left."

"No," Judith said with carefully crafted rage. "Papa Jack's death drove you over some edge. Now I'm back, baby. I'll fix you and your destiny. The world will end, just as it was meant to."

"The world isn't going to end if we die."

"Of course it will," Judith fumed. "We'll take it down with us."

"That's crazy. We're not gods, Judith."

Judith cocked the pistol. "Aren't we?"

The door swung open to Jason's left. No creak, no drama, just a slow swing. Judith pivoted, and Jason shoved her. The gun went off, but the bullet embedded itself in the door's frame, and not in Miss Teedee, who raised a gun of her own. She was pale and drawn, clearly in pain, but she stood steady. Behind her was a gushing sound. White mist poured around her ankles. Jason heard familiar voices shouting warnings. A shape loomed behind Miss Teedee in the fog: Gruff, Jennifer's boyfriend.

* * *

Pain would work with you if you were willing to give it room to exist. At first, Monica struggled and fought against pain, but Toby had been there. He bent, whispering.

"Don't fight it. Fight *them.*" He'd pressed a tire iron into her hand. It was warm and heavy and solid. She'd fixated on the heft of the weapon, and second by second, inch by inch, she'd negotiated with her pain until she had stood and walked and climbed.

Her insides were broken beyond repair. She could feel them sloshing against the walls of her skin, swelling and failing. Her soul knew this body was finished. Her soul also knew the body had one last task, and it was important enough to bargain with pain and death for a few more minutes. Just a few more ticks of the clock.

Darryl. I'll miss you.

One stair at a time. The back stairs, the servant's stairs.

Mercutio, love my boy. Jason, take care. Miss Teedee, look out for all of them. Andrew...

When Monica stumbled, somebody sneaked under her arm. Blinking in surprise, Monica smiled at Becky, who looked nineteen and shining with health.

"What are you doing here?"

"Helping you do one more crazy thing," Becky teased. "Come on. Just a little more."

"I really don't think I can."

"Andrew's at the top of the stairs, Monica."

And just like that, Monica could move again. Becky hadn't lied, exactly, but Andrew wasn't the only person at the top of the stairs. "Not yet," Becky said when Monica tried to bend to her baby boy. Monica's vision was blurred: she was half in and half out of the body, shambling down the hall, leaving a trail of blood. The knife was keeping most of it in, but it was now the opposite of life. The blood was poison.

"Monica," Becky whispered, though she wasn't there anymore. "Focus."

Miss Teedee stood just inside the Lily room. Behind her was a man Monica had never seen before, but he clearly meant to do Miss Teedee harm.

"We'll do it together," Becky whispered.

Becky helped Monica quicken her pace, helped her raise one arm, helped her bring the tire iron up and in, and when it made contact with the man's skull, there was a *crack-crunch*. He went down.

"Good job, girl," Becky said. "I'll see you in just a sec."

Monica didn't understand at first, but then she saw Andrew. He was lying on the floor rubbing at his shin, and Mercutio was spraying flames with an extinguisher. Through the mist, Andrew's eyes met hers.

"Mommy," he said. "I love you."

"I love you, too."

Her body fell, but Monica didn't. The house faded away, and all that was left was pure white and Becky, smiling.

* * *

When Light retreated, only the floor of the cavern remained. The cosmos spun around them. Ahead of Nightmare, Banshee was curled on her side, softly crying.

She was no longer a tree, but a child with bark-like hide and black holes for eyes. She had no nose and no lips, but lots of teeth. Her hair writhed, the pink Horror worms constantly in motion. In one arm, she clutched a battered doll. In the other, she held a red and black heart. It beat with a steady pulse, the bulk of it red with rippling black veins pumping, pumping.

Nightmare knew that heart. He knew that girl.

"Al'issaemeth?" Nightmare asked, but he knew it was she. He went to her and crouched. She shied away from him, trying to hide her heart.

No, not hers.

Nightmare looked at his cracked ribs. He reached for the heart and for the girl.

When he touched them, he remembered.

* * *

Judith was going to fire the gun again, and this time she wasn't going to miss. Jason tackled her while she was off her guard. The seconds slowed to hours. He saw his choices, and he knew what he had to do.

It'd be like that Halloween funhouse, all those years ago, before Judith had let her imbalance sway entirely to chaos. They'd just performed at some tiny club, and they'd seen the sign – FINAL NIGHT SPOOK FEST. They'd been drunk, but so had everyone, and they'd stumbled along on the tour of a big house rigged to be haunted. The guy with the chainsaw, he'd hidden in a closet and on cue, he'd chased them. The other guests had scattered, and he was only supposed to follow so far, but he recognized Judith's Hell. He thought it would be funny to corner them, take off his mask, and ask for an autograph. When they'd jumped through the window, he'd followed. The chainsaw had died as they all lay on the grass outside, panting and laughing. It'd been break-away glass. It'd been the first floor. The mummy was supposed to crash through the window later, but the mummy had been smoking a cigarette nearby, bored. The glass window broke into predictable pieces so as not to hurt the mummy or his costume, and when put together, it looked like a patterned window. So pretty. Judith said she wanted to build a house and have every window look like that one. She'd drawn the little house next to their names when they'd signed the autograph for the chainsaw guy. It had looked like a Victorian dollhouse.

Like this house.

Everything made so much sense. Jason burst into laughter, loud and manic, as he dragged Judith toward the Lily room window. She squirmed, but he was stronger. His skin was burning, the room so very, very hot. Miss Teedee was screaming. Judith was wailing. Jason caught a glimpse of Andrew and Tio and even Monica, who had her arm around a woman he knew was Becky without having to ask.

The glass in the Lily Room was not break-away, but it was superheated. It shattered when Jason hurled his and Judith's combined weight against it. This was not the first floor, but the third, so there was a long way to fall. The breeze was wonderful, so soothing. The shards of glass gleamed in the air around them, floating as though frozen in time and space. The ground below was so green and alive. Judith screamed. Jason kissed her.

Everything went black.

* * *

Banshee, true name Al'issaemeth, seventh Walker who was born of Infinity and the King of Nightmare, Mal'uud 'au Keen, wiped her nose with her arm and gazed at her father-brother-lover-son with fathomless black pits for eyes. "Are you the one who wants me?" she asked.

"I am," Nightmare answered.

She considered this. "Is it safe, now?"

"I'm here. You are safe," Nightmare said.

"Are the worlds all gone?"

"No. Not entirely."

Her lower lip trembled. "Did I do bad?"

"No." Nightmare smoothed the girl's hair. It hugged his hand. "You did as you were meant to do. I was just not here with you to stop you when it was done."

"Are you mad?" she whispered.

"No. I could never be mad at you for being who and what you are."

She leaned against him. "I'm so sleepy."

Nightmare gathered the girl in his arms. "Then let me tell you a story."

"Yes, please."

Chapter Thirty-Five

When she woke up, it was as though she'd been asleep for twenty years, and finally, she could see the light of day. It streamed through a bank of windows along one side of the private hospital room. Helen took a deep breath, sensed all was right in all the worlds, and knew they had done it.

Balance had been restored. She would be her old self, renewed, and everyone could grow and change and carry on.

"Is she—?"

"Hey there, honeydew."

Miss Teedee sat in a new robe covered in hydrangeas. There was a hospital bracelet around her wrist and a standard gown peeping through the V of her neckline. Andrew sat on the other side of the bed in a wheelchair with a footrest extended. One leg was in a cast and propped up. Mercutio sat next to him, holding his hand, and he wore dark glasses. Darryl was next to Miss Teedee, wearing his own clothes, but with oxygen cannulas in his nostrils.

"Tell me," Helen said, sitting up with her father's help.

Mercutio knew what she meant. "Well, let's see. My eyeballs took a beating. They got burned, if you can believe it. But there's this awful salve stuff they make me use that's supposed to fix them up. Cuts, bruises, and one sprained wrist, but I made out better than Drew-baby, whose knee is now full of pins—"

"I'm metal and flesh," Andrew said with a secret smile.

"—and rods and whatnot," Mercutio continued. He raised eyebrows at Darryl.

"I've got burned lungs," Darryl said, his voice raspier. "And they've got me hooked to this damned tank—"

"It's to help you breathe, dear," Miss Teedee chided. "That hardly makes it damned."

"And this old gal, here, her ticker quit on her."

"Just for the briefest of whiles," Miss Teedee amended. "Mild heart attack, one stint. But I did have a time with the smoke. Put me in that hyperbolic chamber thingy."

"You mean hyperbaric, darling dear," Mercutio said.

Miss Teedee waved a hand at him. "Yes, well, I'm out now. They tell me rest and oxygen will cure anything else that ails me."

"And where's your tank, woman?" Darryl asked.

"In my room. We respect each other's space."

Darryl wheezed a laugh. Helen relaxed in the bed. She hesitated, letting the unasked questions hover all around them.

"Ms. Adlewilde and Mr. Kirkland are no longer with us," Darryl said softly. "And..."

"Mama didn't make it," Andrew said softly. "But she got to say goodbye, and she's with Becky. They're drinking Mai Tais in heaven and dancing to the Stones."

"And I hope they're tap-dancing on the bones of the man who did it," Miss Teedee said. "She got him, Monica did, in the end. Clubbed Bill to death, did the world a favor."

"Miss Teedee," Andrew said, pleading.

"I know, dear, but sometimes one person's nightmares are another person's dreams come true." She sniffed daintily. "The twins lived, but every charge we can muster will be pressed. The police have come and gone more times than I can name."

"Mmhm, and that one gentleman more than the other."

Miss Teedee blushed. "Oh, stop it, Tio. He's just doing his job."

Mercutio leaned to Helen's ear. "He's a silver fox with the hots for Miss Thing, here."

"Well, the uniform isn't unpleasant," Miss Teedee conceded.

"What about—" Helen began.

"And you, darling," Tio interrupted. "Are going to be spic and span in no time. They fixed up your shoulder, but I have to say, you kept us waiting an awful long time."

"I know," Helen said.

Darryl, Mercutio, and Miss Teedee exchanged looks. "You've been in a coma for two weeks, my love," Mercutio said.

"Longer than that," Helen said. "But I'm better now. I'm sorry it took so long to find my balance." She laughed. "Had to save the world, first."

"Indeed," Mercutio said, hesitating, as though waiting for the shoe to fall. Helen couldn't tell him that she wouldn't need him anymore, not as a nurse, anyway. Time would have to do that for her.

"I'm glad you're all okay, and I'm so sorry, Andrew, about your mama." Helen took a breath, feeling the loss and letting the ache rest in her bones.

"We all are," Darryl added.

"Tell me what happened to Jason?" Helen asked, breaking the silence that flooded in the spaces between their grief.

No one said a thing for too long, and Helen began to sweat. "Is he—?"

"No," Darryl said softly. "Not exactly."

"He's in a coma, himself," Mercutio said. "They don't think he'll wake up."

"Tio," Miss Teedee admonished.

"No, I need to hear it," Helen said. She shifted her weight, testing her pain and her ability to move. Her shoulder was muffled by medication, and her arm was trapped to her body in a sling. She hadn't gotten out of bed in days, but with help, she would manage. She would have to.

"What are you—" Miss Teedee began.

"Honey, don't," Darryl said.

Helen paused, the love these people had for her filling her up and bringing tears to her eyes. She wiped them away. "I know," she said. "I shouldn't. But he won't wake up unless we're all there. Especially you," she said to Miss Teedee.

Such a prophetic expression had them all thinking she was her old self – her unbalanced self. "He killed her, didn't he, Judith?" Helen asked. "It's the least we can do. I want to see him. And I need all of you to help me."

"Okay," Andrew said, first. He rolled backward. He glanced at everyone. "It's time for my daily visit, anyway," he said.

"We've all seen him," Darryl said. "He's not been alone."

"It's optimistic, dear," Miss Teedee said, her voice low. "To think he will..."

"Come on," Helen said.

Mercutio helped Helen into a wheelchair. Slowly, painfully, they crept as a group to the fourth floor, Green Wing, room 4115. Colors were brighter and scents were sharper than Helen ever remembered. She was distracted by so many small things; the pattern on her hospital gown, the weight of her body, the carefully sculpted eyebrows of a female nurse walking with a patient. Life, it was everywhere and in her and them. Her heart fluttered in her breast as they pushed open the wide door to Jason's room. Monitors beeped, and a ventilator whispered. There was a sign saying only two visitors at a time were allowed, but they all ignored it.

"Hi, buddy," Andrew said softly. There was a small collection of action figures on a table next to Jason's bed. There was also a stuffed animal next to Jason's limp wrist. Andrew had definitely been there.

"Pretty lady says you need to see us," whispered Tio.

The machines whirred. People strolled in the hallway beyond the door. Helen bit her lip, waiting. Jason didn't stir. He was nearly too tall for the bed. He'd wasted away somewhat, thinner than he should be, with dark circles under his eyes. His hair was paler, as though going gray from the trauma.

"He only broke his toe," Miss Teedee said. Her voice was wet. "Can you believe it? All that way down, and... Well." She removed a tissue and dabbed her eyes. "Thank heavens Toby ran off with my phone and called 911. The paramedics were on him almost as soon as he landed."

"And the fire department came," Darryl added. "They put out the rest of the fire, but the house won't ever be the same."

"Maybe that's not a bad thing," Helen said. "We can rebuild it better."

Bleakly, Darryl nodded.

"Daddy, it's okay," Helen said. She stopped herself from adding that they saved all the worlds and rid this one of a great evil. It was true, but it would only upset him knowing that what they had done, the cost they had paid, had been so important. It was hard enough to fathom losing Monica, and he was trying to stay so strong. They all were.

"I'm sorry," Darryl said. "I have to... I'm sorry." He started to leave.

"Wait, Daddy," Helen said, grabbing his wrist. Tears spilled down her father's cheeks. "Just a little longer."

Darryl nodded, unable as always to refuse her anything, Helen knew. They regrouped and hovered around Jason, who remained indifferent. Helen could feel the weight of guilt and pain in everyone. It swayed her in the chair.

"They don't know what's wrong," Miss Teedee said. "They think it was the shock. The impact, the fall, just all of it."

"There's very little brain activity," Mercutio said. "No apparent physical damage, other than smoke inhalation and abrasions. He cut and bruised himself badly, but like Miss Teedee said, only one broken toe. No fractures to the skull. No swelling of the brain. He's just asleep."

It was exhausting, being the one who had to destroy in order to reset the balance in all the worlds. Helen bit her lip. She touched Jason's shoulder. Miss Teedee, as though inspired or maybe in support, took Jason's hand.

No one had any more words. What had happened was unspeakable. It had scarred them. It had ended them. It would reshape those who still lived.

"Jason," Helen said softly. "Please."

The clock on the wall had been ticking loudly, but suddenly Helen couldn't really hear it. Blinds covered the windows, but one slat was bent, and as the sun began to set, magenta light pierced the room and struck Jason square in the chest.

The Lady owed them one, and she always repaid her debts.

It took mere seconds for Jason's eyelashes to flutter, and his body begin to struggle with the ventilator. Everyone leapt into action. Darryl yelled for someone to help. Miss Teedee hit the call nurse button. Mercutio ushered them all away, giving the team space to work when they entered the room.

Helen sat in her chair, off to one side, watching the orchestrated dance of hope play out in front of her. She saw it in snapshots when the bodies cleared: Jason, rising as the tube came out of his throat. Jason again, with a sponge in his mouth, greedily sucking water. A nurse, taking measurements, a doctor, checking pupil response, and the rest of them standing back, waiting, waiting.

"Mom?" Jason rasped, his first clear word echoing in the room. "Where's Mom?"

Helen felt the glances fly around the room. Miss Teedee stepped forward. "Honey, your—"

"Mom," Jason said in pure relief. He reached for her. Miss Teedee took his hand, bewilderment in her eyes. "What happened? Where am I?"

"Ah, Jason, my friend, that's—" Mercutio started.

"Your mama," Andrew finished firmly.

Miss Teedee glanced at them all and stared at Jason with tears running down her cheeks. She cleared her throat. "Well, honey, um, you had a bit of a fall. But it's all going to be all right." She patted his hand. "Yes. All right, now. Everything."

Slowly, the survivors who lived in the Taylor Point House crept forward, forming a circle of family; remaking themselves, whole and anew.

Chapter Thirty-Six

"A long, long time ago," Mal'uud 'au Keen, the King of Nightmare, began, "the boundless expanse of Infinity organized itself and thought of existence, with boundaries and purpose and creatures.

"But the same moment, it occurred to Infinity that all could be undone. And in that moment, we were created, my child. For I was the idea of existence then balanced by you, the idea that the Universes, that Infinity itself, could not exist. Infinity knew that our balance must be kept in order for all else to spin. In truth, we were the spindle of the axis, the start of Via'rra, that spawned all else. Infinity made of itself the Lady Creation, Freeja, who embodied the ability to form life. Freeja, who knew she would need to remember so much, but had so many things to do, asked for the Storyteller, Daanske, who was made to be in all places and all times at once, so she would never forget a single bloom or fingernail of any she made. Freeja also knew her creations would be vulnerable as they grew, so she asked and was granted Water,

Eeadian, the Warrior of All Worlds. He was Might and Power and the very spirit of continued existence, built ever to strive toward it and defend it at all costs. The Lady toiled endlessly for millennia, and eventually became lonely and hungry and tired, for her power was finite. She sought out the opposite of herself – for if she was the beginning, she sought the ability to unmake what she no longer needed. She had me, the King of Nightmare, who tended all the Intangibles – all her ideas that did not work, all the tales that Storyteller scribbled over, those were given unto me and also unto you, my twin, my daughter, my heart. I had no effect on the Tangible, and so the Lady found her Lord of Nothing, the Eater of Worlds, the Ruler of Shadows, once a mighty mage in a timeless world. He had existed outside of Infinity, was, perhaps, Infinity's balance – the Finite; the ending.

"So great was his loneliness that when the Lady found him, he would do anything and everything to stay in her favor. When he saw me and understood my Kingdom was in disarray, he begged his Lady to create a home for me and you and mine and ours. Thus the Undermaze was made. As ideas and thoughts and fears and hopes and dreams are the very fabric of what keeps all worlds aloft, the Undermaze became the pinions upon which all of Via'rra and thus, all worlds, was built upon. Lord Nothing gave us the Feed, a physical embodiment of the mechanism he used to feed his Lady. And so the Intangible were made physical were unmade to bones and ghosts to keep me and you and our home thriving and in balance.

"All was well, my child, for eons. You lived here, inside my breast, in charge of my heart as I was in charge of your mind.

"Then one day, one of the Lady's creations rebelled against her. The creature was pure energy and knew Lord Nothing's weakness to light. It was faster than Shadow and more vicious than even the Lady. It could weave between time and worlds quicker than Storyteller. The Lady cried out to Infinity, as she had so many times, and it, in turn, tapped into your power.

"You woke me, and I let you out of my chest. My heart – our heart – stayed within me, and so I knew all you did and all you thought. Your power was pure destruction. Permanent ending. You did not give what you destroyed unto something else, as Lord Nothing did. You unmade without any of the guilt or sadness that Infinity would face should it choose to end pieces of its very fabric; its very self. You attacked as a child would defend its loved ones from a menace, and you eradicated the Lady's rogue creature.

"But once you'd tasted the blood of destruction, of chaos, you wanted more. You discovered a hunger insatiable and started unmaking more of the Lady's garden. I knew your mind, as I had your heart.

"So I came to you then, as I come to you now. I told you it was done and over and that I cannot exist without you. I would be undone should you choose to end everything, and your love for me – for yourself, for the heart and soul we share – triumphed over your thirst. You came back to me, and I caged you in my chest."

Al'issaemeth had shrunk to the size of Mal'uud's hand. Her eyelids drooped, and their hearts beat slow, slow, slow. Gently, he placed her within the ruin of his broken ribs. From the corner of his eye, he saw a baby appear – a small boy. The child crawled, blurred into walking, blurred into standing, and the blue of his eyes knew Mal'uud. This was Daanske, resurrected and starting again.

"But I knew something then that I could not unknow," Mal'uud continued. "I knew you would eventually be unhappy, confined for all eternity in me. You were not only a child. You are a Walker; you are power and chaos; and you would need room to roam, even if that room was warded to ensure you would not unmake yourself in the name of using your power.

"I begged of the Lady and of Lord Nothing, and to repay the favor you had bestowed upon her by answering her cry for help, she built us the Heart Cavern. Lord Nothing sealed it with the most powerful substance in all the worlds – Shadowrock. Within that cavern's confines, I could let you out. You could be young or old or something in between. We could sit together, talk, read, and share thoughts and what we'd learned. I would Walk the worlds and return to you, tell you all I'd seen.

"Observing us in our happiness and curiosity and joy and compassion gave Infinity the last piece of what was missing in all of its creation. And so it was that the Light Constellation and her endless cycle of balance and harmony was born. A piece of her would fall to Via'rra so her power would radiate out to all worlds. They fell in a cycle dictated by the rhythm of Infinity. The balance of all things was now achieved, and Infinity receded into every molecule across every plane of existence. Its children took up the call, and for eons more, all was well."

Nearby, a Shadow tendril crept out of a hole in the cavern floor. It carefully deposited the Lady in seed form on the ground and began feeding her, slowly. The seed split, and she began to grow.

"Then what happened?" Al'issaemeth asked, almost asleep, now.

"Something unforeseen," Mal'uud answered. "The Walkers betrayed themselves, and the cry went up for some way to undo what had been done. The anguish was so great, you ripped out of me, taking our heart with you, and thus, my ability to remember you. Unchecked, you unleashed the full brunt of your power, and I was lost, powerless to stop you.

"But now, my child, I remember. I know how to cage you, which isn't to cage you at all. It's to know your darkness and respect it, not change it. It's to encourage you to focus on the good and the bright and the balanced. It is, dear one, to love you. It's the only cage which leads to ultimate freedom."

Blinding white light interrupted Mal'uud, and before all their eyes, Kindness – the new piece of Light – fell. She was plump and wide and curved. She glowed pale pink and green and lavender from between the cracks in her silvery skin. She dusted a space in the floor, and Shadowrock retreated. Beneath it, a familiar skull began to emerge. Adimoas was smaller, but he yet endured.

With a contented nod, Kindness then went to Water and knelt next to him. "A gift, dear Warrior, for all you have done and will do." Kindness kissed Water's head, and his wounds healed. Gone were the Horror spears that pinned him. He rose, great and mighty, and stretched to his full width and height. He blocked out stars and seemed to reach the very heavens.

Al'issaemeth, Banshee, fell fast asleep. The Lady, now fully re-formed, healed Mal'uud. His ribs and sternum regrew, his sinew became shinier, and his whole being became infused with green, pulsing energy.

He was whole.

And as the Walkers of the Veil stood guard, the King of Nightmare's heart – his and Banshee's – began once again to beat to Infinity's rhythm. Balance was restored. Their world, all worlds, though diminished, still spun.

"Let us begin," Lady Creation said, and she cackled and flew, streaking magenta power across the sky.

THE END

Dear Reader,

One night while I was in the middle of trying to survive heartbreak, a creature wandered in through the back door of my consciousness and ambled over to sit in an oversized, wooden chair. He appeared to be covered in shiny black shoe leather, had red, glowing eyes and pointed teeth, and though he looked like something that would gladly eat my liver without a second thought, he introduced himself politely: *I am Mal'uud 'au Keen. In the language of Fear, my name means, 'He who walks.' I am one of the last Walkers of the Veil. I would like to tell you my story.*

Gobsmacked, I scrambled for pen and paper and what you hold in your hands or have captured on your screen is the result of those long chats. And somewhere in the process of trying to do his story justice, I discovered I was also piecing myself back together. I'm not sure I've ever been whole, but after finishing this story, I think I'm more whole than I've ever been. Sometimes stories expand your view of reality; sometimes they give you the tools to learn more about yourself. And sometimes, if you're very lucky, they do both.

Like all good recreations of self, however, this process began with a self-destruction. The hardest thing we can do in our lives is rebreak ourselves along our fault lines and reset ourselves to allow healing to happen at long last. If this story reaches you in the particularly dark hours of such a time, then I hope it somehow provided some comfort or distraction. May your own Hope Star guide you. Remember: if you find yourself in hell – keep going.

Thank you for reading my weird book. It means the world to me that you're here, eyes on these pages. Well met, fellow traveler. I've been so happy to have you along for this ride.

Light, love, and laughter – with a smidgeon of chaos and shenanigans for spice,

A.

Acknowledgements

All my love, thanks, and the baked goods of your choice to the people who had to listen to the story of this story for the days, weeks, months, and years I worked on it. Ben, thank you for loving me and my words and for bringing me tea all those times and reminding me to eat. Oh, and thank you for showing me that ventriloquist documentary and helping me to remember who I am, even when I wanted to forget. You are now and will always be my Bliss.

Mom, thank you for listening and encouraging, even when you wondered how in the world your daughter came up with this crazy shit (her words, not mine!). And special thanks to you for helping me name the world when the first iterations were entirely too literal and for your hyper-critical editing and continuity eye – Universe bless your love for murder mysteries and details.

Enormous, pointy, vicious thanks to Henley, whose chain-and-fire pom-poms were waving the entire time, even when we were very, very tired. Thank you for hearing this story, for encouraging it, for begging for one more chapter, and for telling me it was good, even when it needed a ton of work. You get a whole paragraph of thanks all to yourself! I know you don't play well with others – but I thank God you play well with *me*.

Thank you, Heather and Liz, for listening, reading, supporting, and all else. Extra thanks to Heather for all those hours when we were kids playing The Game, helping me to sow these seeds and learn how to navigate all the worlds on the leyline. And extra thanks to Liz, who kept my body together when I overextended it with thousands and thousands of words and who helped feed my soul by cheering and crying with me when I learned the Lady was a Seed.

Thank you to Flu for the beta listening, the read-through, and the art direction idea for the cover. Oh, and also for the amazing fanart, which will be on my walls forever and possibly buried with me. It will always be incredible, no matter how many times you Level Up the Skillz! Thank you, Corinne, who read this story without hearing about it for years on end and provided me such glowing and startlingly positive feedback that I was convinced I could actually keep going, page by page, chapter by chapter. Last minute thanks to Hoopi for the author photo and for the proofreading eye that caught some sincerely hilarious typos. You are a wonder, and I'm so happy we're wandering the pages again together.

Huge shout-out to my Patrons who read this story one chapter at a time, one month at a time – your patience and support are precious. Thank you Fesbra for the amazing art. And thank you to the industry professional who told me the only way this book would ever get published is if I ripped the fantasy out of it and left the humans flailing, story threads akimbo. I didn't do that, and never would, but you helped me see the path to get this story into the world, and for that, I am grateful.

Thank you to whatever mystical forces conspired to let Mal'uud wander into my head that night – may I do you justice and may I always honor the Story. And thank you to the countless people who have left me comments, sent me emails, hit up my DMs, and generally sent love notes over the years about the words and what they meant. I keep them like treasures, close to my heart and right next to the door I open to hear what's on the other side. They remind me why I keep going, and I am eternally humbled and grateful.

Extra Special Thanks

The King of Nightmare was first sent to my Patrons over on Demented Tours Patreon. While some have joined to my delight and left with my gratitude, there are a few who helped get me rolling and most of them continue to keep me sane.

Thank you to the official Patreon Start Up Team and to my Blazing Comet Patrons:

AF Henley
Bengeance
Cheryl V.
Flu
Jamie H.
Jennifer C.
Kagamimi
Kourin
Liz T.
Lucy O.
Passiflora182
Phil H.
Rachel H.
Rebecca M.
Tandy Hard
Teresa R.
Wendo

It's an ever-evolving creative journey over on the Demented Tours Patreon. Come join us at patreon.com/DementedTours.

About the Author

A. Rogers lives halfway between this world and the multitudes, and keeps the company of monsters, aliens, spirits, the Fae, and similar ilk. She is most at home at twilight in winter buried in soft blankets, sitting next to a fire with a stack of good books to read and with her family and friends close by. She'd like you to know that everyone and everything matters, and we're all connected. She'd also like a (gluten free) cookie and a nap.

You can find her on Twitter @ARogersAuthor1
and online at **www.arogersauthor.com.**

CPSIA information can be obtained
at www.ICGtesting.com
Printed in the USA
BVHW041923030521
606359BV00013B/279/J